BONOBO!

TRACY DUVALL

This is a work of fiction. Names, characters, businesses, places, events, and incidents are either the products of the author's imagination or used in a fictitious manner.

ISBN-13: 978-0-9975476-0-3
ISBN-10: 0-9975476-0-X

CONTENTS

ABSTRACT

I want
fuck love and
make love and
know you love and
be yourself love and
puppy-dog eyes love and
found interesting love and
you need help love and
do it together love and
everyone is beautiful love and
trust you love and
self love and
there, there love and
let's play love and
Merry Christmas love and
love the one you're with love and
you can do great things love and
hang out love and
proud of you love and
forgive you love and
Golden Rule love and
so many other loves.

Don't you?

Let me tell you a True story—or really two stories (Dale's and mine) that, in their own way, come together. Then I'd love to hear yours.

TRACY DUVALL

INTRODUCTION

Gainesville, Florida – 1998

My academic adviser, Doris, invited me to her modest bunga-low for a small celebration. I had just received a minor grant that would help fund my year-long ethnographic fieldwork on drug trafficking and Mexican popular culture: songs, movies, baseball caps, key chains, and more. The award was her pretext for inviting me over for dinner. Other reasons might have been to thank me for serving as her teaching assistant, to wish me well in my fieldwork, or to relieve her loneliness as a single, young faculty member in a college town.

I had just sold my car, so I went by bicycle. I could have borrowed a friend's car, but, I thought, this is how I am, the real me. To offset the too-real me, I wore my loosest jeans and an untucked guayabera to maximize ventilation, and I pedaled slowly, to avoid perspiring. As sweat inevitably started to trick-le across my skin, I began to focus on it, willing it to stop. It was a familiar routine, as it seemed that my concern about the sweat only added another reason for its production. By the time I reached Doris' address and walked the bike up to the front door, my only hope was that this was the cleansing per-spiration of a Native American sweat lodge. What could I do? The show must go on. I rang the bell.

Those were the days of the little black dress, and, when my adviser opened the door, it seemed mildly provocative that she was wearing one. A Miracle Bra optimized her decent breasts, and her gams—always impressively taut—looked a little better in red heels. Her face didn't ruin the package, especially given her frequent expressions of enthusiasm. I estimated that she was maybe 33 or 34, which seemed significantly older to me then, especially since she was my boss and teacher and could converse collegially with senior faculty members. I was just 27.

"Hi, Nat, how was the ride?" Doris was smiling.

"It feels like it rained inside my shirt."

"*Always* wear a raincoat." She swiped a finger along my glistening forearm and briefly tasted the sweat she had gathered. "Maybe not! If rain tasted like this, I'd build a tank out back to catch it." *That* wasn't mildly provocative. All of a sudden, my pants didn't fit so loosely. Did she mean to turn me on? It seemed so casual.

"Uh, I'm sorry, but is there a place I can put my bike? I've already had two stolen."

She opened her garage so that I could park safely within. Then we walked around and entered her bungalow through the front door. I had stopped by a few times before to drop off or pick up papers, but this was my first time over the threshold.

She showed me around. It had the usual anthropological knickknacks on the walls—exotic-looking masks, exotic-looking wall-hangings, framed photos of exotic-looking locales and of my adviser standing with exotic-looking people. Bookcases were everywhere and filled with important-looking tomes; she must have hidden her *Chicken Soup*s and *For Dummies* in a closet. The table that served as a desk in her little office looked out a large, square window onto a flower garden and, around that, the usual grass and trees. The walls on either side of the desk held some personal photos. To the right it looked like family, friends, and childhood memories (bad hair). To the left: surrounded by photos of friends apparently taken at grad-school parties, a couple of chimps appeared to enjoy rubbing their swollen, pink vulvae together.

I leaned in closer; was this taken from a textbook? I felt her put a hand on my shoulder. I could smell her shampoo, or maybe deodorant. My dick got hard again. "Bonobos," she said.

"Oh, right. It's hard to tell them apart from chimps."

"Unless they're doing that!"

"Friends of yours from grad school?" I turned to look at her as she perused the photo. Her face was pretty like that.

"You could say so." She smiled. "I used to be one." Doris turned to me. "All of these pictures are from Bonobo parties."

"Oh, wow." I felt horny, embarrassed, out of my element, yet oddly secure. I turned back to the photos. "Uh, I've read a couple of articles about Bonobo. Is that ... what's his name—the leader?"

"'Leader, but not ruler': that's Dale, there, with Ron, who pretty much organized things. I was there when Dale had the idea, so I'm basically a charter member. In fact, Dale and I were the guinea pigs for the first 'Bonobo handshake'—or 'ritualized greeting,' as I had suggested. Have you ever done it?"

"Well," I smiled knowingly, "not like you mean."

"Then let's give it a go. Okay?"

She wanted to make the experience as real as possible, to give a sense of how the greeting would work in a mundane context. We went out into the backyard. Shaded by oaks in the gloaming, we stood at opposite ends and walked toward each other as if we were going in different directions across campus. The skirt of her dress flounced as she strode toward me. The movement of my legs forced my erection to rub uncomfortably against the hems of my underwear.

As we approached, our eyes met. "Oh, hi, Nat. How's it going?" We now stood face-to-face, and she, without any vixenish expression, reached out and pleasantly rubbed my dick through my pants. I shuddered and felt some pre-cum against my skin.

"It's going all right." I pretended to be nonchalant. But I felt tremendous anticipation. I reached out my hand to rub her pussy, but then, as I touched the black, silky fabric of her dress I hesitated—how do I do it? Do I force the dress between her thighs? Do I move my hand under her dress, to her underwear? Is she wearing underwear? What if she were wearing a long dress? Or a tight leather skirt?

"I know. It's tricky with women, isn't it? In this situation, I recommend that you go for a boob."

So I did. I wondered how much she could feel beneath the considerable padding—I certainly felt more bra than breast—but perhaps it's the thought that counts. We exchanged pleasantries and then continued on our respective ways.

Sold! That was a world I wanted to live in. But I'd need to get used to it happening over and over each day, because my balls were already beginning to ache.

We had dinner inside. Doris served up the usual green salad, some pasta-and-shrimp dish, and wine.

She didn't talk like she usually did. Instead of a teacher and boss, she reminded me more of graduate students who had returned from their fieldwork—senior by experience, but not structurally superior. Amid stories of her research and graduate studies and our comments about grocery stores, films, and other quotidian topics, she mentioned the obvious: since the field site for my research, Playatlán, was where ¡Bonobo! was located, it might be handy for me to know Ron and Dale. Fieldwork didn't need to be undertaken by a lone, heroic ethnographer in the wilds among the natives—and it rarely had been in the past, anyway. Plus, if I met with her old friends, it would be like sending them a human postcard from her.

I thanked her for the introduction. Privately, I wondered whether I could get easy sex at ¡Bonobo! by befriending them and visiting the resort.

She also asked whether I had a girlfriend.

"No, not anymore," I said, which was true. A week before, I did have one. But, like in *Apocalypse Now*, I had adopted a scorched-earth policy to my attachments. I didn't want to be celibate, faithful, and alone for long stretches in Mexico, and I didn't want to lie to my girlfriend in Gainesville and whomever I approached in Playatlán. So I left her like I left the car—to facilitate my fieldwork.

After dinner, Doris smiled devilishly. I started to notice attractive little features that I hadn't seen before, like the smoothness of the skin just under her ears. She said she looked for excuses to give herself treats, which meant gooey brownies for dessert. If I desired, I could add vanilla ice cream and chocolate syrup.

I desired—very much so.

As we slurped and savored, she told me more about Bonobo's early days. A couple of times, she had me take a mouthful at the same time as her, while we gazed into each other's eyes. It looked like she must be oozing. Then she got up to take away the dishes and mentioned that her friends had given her a special send-off just before she left for her fieldwork. She had been the first Bonobo to leave the troop like that. As she moved around to get my bowl, she noticed a smudge of chocolate by the edge of my mouth. "Let me get that for you." She dipped her index finger into her mouth, rubbed its moist tip on my cheek, and slid it inside my lips. I sucked it and played my tongue over it. She put her other arm around me and leaned her torso, her breast, against me, and I put my arm around her hip and looked up into her eyes.

"You're my first," she said, clearly meaning her first advisee, "and I want to send you into the world properly. Would you like that?"

I had often pictured similar scenes with Madonna, so I was prepared to say yes.

Notes from sex with Doris:

- I came twice. Each time, I felt a burst of warm ooze inside my chest and, despite having my eyes open (see below), literally saw fireworks in my mind's eye.

- She owned a large collection of condoms, in many varieties, which she kept in an exotic-looking bag. When she asked what my favorite brand was, I trotted out my joke that liking condoms was the same as the Stockholm Syndrome. She giggled, but I had to choose. "Always wear a raincoat."

- She looked into my eyes a lot, especially during her orgasms, and panted, "Look at me," several times, especially during mine. She explained between the two episodes that, for her, great sex—like sharing brownies, but more so— created a lasting, intersubjective bond, because now we'd seen and accepted each other intimately. We'd penetrated each other's balloon of categorical difference. Really looking into each other's eyes, our soul windows, sealed the deal. The experience couldn't be forgotten and thus didn't need to be repeated daily. Now we knew each other in a qualitatively different way, perhaps Biblically.

- Nonetheless, knowing she could have sex routinely brought a kind of calmness to her life, like meditation was supposed to do, although meditation actually made her horny. "Finding fuck friends, Nat—it's the Bonobo Way." (I could tell she didn't mean me.) With the addition of the profound, existentially bonding sex such as we had just shared, her approach became "Bonobo Plus."

- Of course, I considered the ethics, legality, and creepiness of the encounter in little spurts as the night wore on. What can I say? Context is everything. I consented over and over, and I never feared that she might punish me otherwise. Anyway, I no longer worked for her or took classes, and a more senior professor was my official adviser. Above all, knowing that Doris was initiating me into the Bonobo movement lent some legitimacy to the lewdness.

When the copulating was complete, we lay sprawled across her yoga mat, semi-entwined, panting lightly and sweating on each other. We faced the ceiling of her small exercise room. Eye contact now might have given the wrong impression—or an impermissible one. We had never made it to her bed, and I sensed that that this was because I wouldn't be sleeping over. "I guess I should be moseying along."

"Good luck finding all your clothes. I'll help."

I twisted around to pick up the squishy, used condom lying nearby. I rolled over to the trash can and dropped it in. Then I stood up and hunted for my belongings.

It wasn't so difficult. My sandals and shirt—smelling of sweat—were by the dining table. My jeans were on one side of the couch and my underwear—still drying—on the other. The first condom, cold and moist, was on the coffee table, and I gallantly threw it away under her sink. I took a peek at what she had there. An interesting-looking matchbook caught my eye. I started to open it—maybe it would reveal Doris' private rounds—but I heard her rummaging nearby, so I slid it into my pocket.

She had found her dress by the sofa and slipped it on. Without bra and panties, she walked me through her house to the garage. "Your bike's still here, safe and sound." She put her hand on my back; it felt supportive.

Do we kiss goodbye? I was unsure. We had mixed tongues passionately just minutes ago.

"Probably it's better to say goodbye in here." She faced me, grabbed my genitals again through my pants, and fondled them. I reached out with my right hand to caress the breast over her heart. She smiled at me sweetly. "I'm so glad we had the chance to share this. Let me know if you need a letter of introduction to anyone besides Ron and Dale. And good luck with your preparations. I'll see you on campus before you go." She slid her hands to my back and embraced me briefly. "Make me proud. You're my first!"

What could I say? I looked her in the eye. "Thanks for everything. Dinner was delicious. I'll come by your office for the letter."

She opened the garage door. I walked my bike past her, out to the driveway, and hopped on.

"No helmet?"

"I didn't want my hair to be sweaty."

"How'd that work out for you?"

"Bye." I lifted a hand to wave.

"See you on campus." She closed the garage door between us, and I pedaled into the still, moist night air. I looked back briefly and saw that she had turned off the garage light. Show's over.

Well, this circus was about to leave town, anyway. As I eased toward my apartment, the active emptiness of my mind matched the chattering insects. I felt good and right, and I needed nothing.

But the next day, like every day for the past fifteen years, I craved sex again. I wanted fuck love, and now, thanks to Doris, I wanted know-you love, too.

PART I

BONOBO – A HISTORY

IF WE WERE BONOBOS

1991

"We should open a theme park, right here in Tucson. That way we can trick people into learning about anthropology." Dale was in a bar by campus, bantering with friends. "Think of how many people believe that New Orleans is like that chunk of Disneyland."

"I wish! New Orleans with convenient bathrooms would've saved me some trouble—finding the right car to pee on ain't as glamorous as it sounds."

Dale appreciated Ron's humor, but this was his topic. "Instead of a Jungle Cruise, there could be 'Trobriand Island: Where All is Not Cricket.'"

The group, made up of graduate students in anthropology, laughed at this nerdy, members-only joke. Ron piled on with, "At the Petting Zoo (which Disneyland doesn't even have), visitors could be treated to a Balinese Cock Fight."

Others suggested additions of declining quality, which Dale found embarrassing. After a while, the staleness of the topic reduced his appetite to validate others' efforts. But it was his idea, after all; he could tell that he was getting credit for the exchange because of the way that people addressed their suggestions to him in particular. So he smiled as the others laughed. Judging by her goading of others to continue the interminable string, Doris, in contrast, seemed to find increasing riches in the repetition.

Dale started to look for a gracious way out, and he remembered the bathroom. As he was waiting for the right moment to excuse himself, his One Great Idea hit him, and he didn't realize it, and he couldn't stop himself from impressing others with it. Had he foreseen how this throwaway line would grow into a ball of lint that enveloped his life, and ultimately mine (years later), he might at least have peed first. His heart would have raced, just like when he was about to call a woman for a date, knowing that she and anyone in whom she confided would see his heart exposed. Instead—

He raised a finger to make a proclamation. "I would want to operate the ride in ... Bonoboland." And that inane remark started the whole notorious affair.

The others laughed, a few feigning scandal. Rudy bravely asked, "Aren't bonobos like chimps? I pretty much don't know that stuff."

"How can you call yourself an anthropologist?" Ron teased him.

Dale explained, trying to not sound didactic—or idiotic, since he was hardly an expert, either: "Bonobos are the 'hippie chimps,' although they're not really chimps—they're another species. They're peaceful, have sex all the time with anyone—I mean their own kids, enemies, old farts, male-male and female-female. And—perhaps there's a relationship here—women dominate."

Doris added, "And they're humans' closest relatives. Go, sisters!"

"Tied with chimps, I believe, for the dishonor of Humanity's Closest Relative. If you're a Republican, you might prefer to identify with the chimps, since they're male-dominated, much more violent, and have sex less often and with fewer partners." Dale paused. "Of course, I'm referring to the chimps."

Lars threw in, "Maybe chimps are more closely related to married people, and bonobos are closer to Scandinavians." That guy had drunk just the right amount of beer.

The bantering wits might have directed this topic down the same drain as before. But Dale, beginning to fathom his idea's greatness, diverted its course. "Aha! What someone could do—and, in the interests of science, I'll risk it personally—to test the Bonobo Effect (trademark!) is to perform a little pre/post comparison on the effects of lots of sex. Are we really like bonobos? I guess that means we need at least two people to have sex all the time. Then, as controls, we can find celibate people—you know, priests, convicts, married people, soldiers—and see whether they're male-dominated and aggressive. Perfect study!" Goofiness was de rigueur, but Dale had a serious thought. "But, seriously, who knows whether bonobos' hippitude is genetic or cultural? Maybe chimps, or even humans, could become contented lovers-not-fighters if they just tried a little tenderness. Okay, tried a lotta tenderness."

Lars said, "Yeah, and bonobos apparently avoid fights by having sex when they're upset. Can you imagine what great therapy that could be, if we really are so similar? 'Sure, honey, we can watch *Oprah* instead of basketball.'"

"That's a great idea—we should do it! We could start a movement." Ron sounded like he was answering a statement that no one else had heard. And he was. "Oops! That was the Monologue Formerly Known as Internal. But I think we should try it once—be bonobos."

Ordinary people don't say things like that. ~~We're~~ They're content to let daring possibilities remain intriguing, even when they can predict that years of longing and regret will result. They find a reason to not take that bus trip across Asia, to not run for office, to not attend the organizational meeting. But

Ron, while seemingly the prototype of normality, was a first child swaddled permanently in a psychic security blanket—an enactor, a catalyst. He was the sort of person who starts high-school newspapers, band contests, and orgies governed by by-laws. Not especially creative, but constantly creating, he either was ignorant of others' inertia or ignored it because he enjoyed and depended on their involvement.

"How different would this scene be, if we were bonobos?" Dale rejoined. "Instead of wondering who'll dance with you and whether you'll get some from your girlfriend or boy-friend—*if* you have one—you'd know that you'd be bathed in physical affection sometime soon, and you'd have gotten some recently, to boot. We'd feel free to be ourselves, because we'd all know—really *know*—that we'd constantly be giving and re-ceiving."

Karen spoke up: "Except that the women, if they were bonobos, would be trying to dominate the others. How relax-ing is that—for anyone?"

"That's definitely a danger." Dale felt quick. "Maybe, though, our brains are just a little more prehensile than bono-bos', and we could actually use our one percent of genetic dif-ference to improve on our bonoban masters."

"We'll show those bonobos who's who," Ron agreed.

"And who's us!" Dale couldn't help himself.

He had already grown to like Ron, through group interac-tions at parties and conversations between classes. Ron seemed ego-less. It was hard to tell how smart he was, but it was clear that everyone liked him. When other students gave presenta-tions, they looked at Ron. He set them at ease. So it came as a shock that Ron wanted to organize an orgy, which seemed un-settling; plus, this proposal smelled like a threat to Dale's pro-prietorship of the idea.

Thus Dale co-opted Ron's co-optation of his suggestion. "Here's how we should do it." He thrilled to think so clearly under pressure; it just popped out. "We invite a select group to a Bonobo Party, establish clear guidelines, get it on, protect everyone's privacy, and discuss the results within the group afterward. Oh, and collect the Nobel Prize for Anthropology twelve years later."

Ron apparently had no intention of competing with Dale. He asked more questions to tease ideas out of Dale, others in the group made occasional suggestions while referring to the experiment as "your party," and Dale served as the main inspiration and arbiter of the developing plan for the first Bonoban gathering.

Later that night, in bed alone, Dale relived his triumph, congratulating himself on his genius and wit. Who knows? Maybe this could revolutionize humanity. Could this be how innovations happened? Maybe someone came up with pottery or agriculture while bantering at a happy hour. Still, a Bonobo Party seemed like the sort of thing that people like to plan at first but then pretend to forget about later. Maybe it would be like all those group projects in high school, when 'let's make a movie' would turn into writing a report.

But what if bonobos really did have a better way of living? Wouldn't that be more valuable than anything else he and his friends were likely to achieve as anthropologists? Could individual meekness foil human salvation? He started picturing Bonoboland and masturbated.

THE NEXT DAY

Hey, Dale,

Did you ever start drinking, have a great idea, probably involving sex, and then wake up the next day thinking that beer makes you stupid?

Well, I hope that didn't happen to you just now, because we have a party to plan. The future of humanity awaits!

My number is at the bottom. What's yours?

Ron

Ron's email sealed it. Dale felt that reality was becoming the slightest bit dreamlike. He sent Ron his number and a few more ideas, and, filled with anticipation and dread, he walked home from the computer lab.

THE FIRST PARTY

Actual bonobos gradually evolved their way of relating over hundreds of millennia, probably without consciously considering the changes. Such was not the way of these New Bonobos. First, Dale, Ron, Doris, and a few others carefully selected the participants. This made the process a bit clubbish, but it also allowed them to ensure a balance among men and women. It must be said, too, that each invitee found the other participants physically attractive or at least not repugnant—young, vivacious, plausibly fit, and ostensibly hygienic.

They tried to engineer intellectual compatibility as well, by limiting the group to graduate students in anthropology. Unlike sociologists, their training focused on humans as highly flexible and creative apes. They searched for constraints on this behavioral openness, if there were any, by surveying the amazing—and liberating—variety in human social relations. Even when studying the (post)modern United States, anthropologists highlighted examples of diversity, rather than dismissing unusual arrangements as oddities, statistical outliers. And, given anthropology's signature method of *participant* observation, these students had learned to experience different situations firsthand as an analytical tool. So friends from other fields might have seen a bonobo-themed party as a lark—in fact, as not much different from a lark-themed party. But these bantering-but-earnest anthropologists-in-training saw it as a playful-but-serious exploration of human possibilities. Or so they told themselves.

To draw up rules, the participants met informally on campus, called each other at home, and availed themselves of email. Someone (possibly Kim) pointed out that the party would devolve into an orgy, or a vacuum, if they didn't establish another purpose for being there. Thus, with a sense of irony—of which they were always conscious—they declared that each participant would have to briefly present knowledge—a 'Semenar.'

Also, everyone had to sign the following consent form (my exegesis is in brackets):

I the undersigned do hereby agree to the following rules:

- Unless I obtain the written consent of every other participant, I will not reveal any aspect of the Bonobo gathering taking place on the date of this document, whether in private conversation, as part of research, or in any other format, with the exceptions of 1) private conversations with other participants and 2) programmatic discussions with future participants.
- I will not make any recording of the events, including but not limited to drawings, photographs, video recordings, or audio recordings.

Avoiding the Tragedy of the Commons, aka No One Rides for Free

- Upon arrival, I will greet each other person at the party with a significant erotic rub lasting at least thirteen seconds [the average length of bonobo copulation]. This shall be known hereinafter as the Bonobo Handshake.

- If I am a woman, I will wear one of the provided ribbons to indicate whether I prefer that my breasts (blue), genitals (green), or either (pink) be rubbed. If I am a man, I will abide by each woman's preference, as signaled thus.
- Except for solitary trips to the bathroom, I will remain in the same general space as the other participants. [No hiding!]
- I will touch other people—erotically or otherwise—whenever feasible.
- I recognize that sexual acts are permitted as part of the event and that neither I nor anyone else can object to them, unless I am one of the persons engaged in the aforementioned act, in which case I can desist at any time.
- Excepting Bonobo Handshakes, participating in a sexual act with another person requires his or her explicit agreement.
- I will not engage in sexual contact in a fashion that will interfere with group activities, for example presentations of knowledge.
- I will not allow any penis to penetrate any of my orifices unless a condom covers it. If I am a man, I will not attempt to penetrate any orifice with my penis, nor allow any orifice to encompass it, unless a condom covers said penis.
- I will employ a Bonobo Handshake whenever I wish to express congratulations or gratitude

[such as for fetching a beer] or to conclude any dis-
agreement, regardless of its character or
intensity.
- I recognize that any three people at the
event can vote to expel me for violating the
letter or spirit of these rules [for example by
picking an argument simply to cop a feel] and further
ostracization may continue for an indefinite
period after the event.

No one should accuse the organizers of impulsiveness.

Ron was the most active organizer, as even Dale had to recognize. It was Ron who arranged to use Rudy's detached garage,
recently remodeled to include a bathroom. And he aided Karen, who worked on a project to understand homeless teens'
sexual practices, to expropriate scores of condoms. Nonetheless, Ron acted eager to include Dale in any planning. And he
described the genesis of the party with terms such as "Dale's
revelation."

Dale involved himself less in the logistics but did insist on
providing the ribbons with which women would signal their
preferences. Secretly, he didn't trust anyone else to bring this
essential safeguard and to have it ready from the start; otherwise, women might leave prematurely. Perhaps he also wanted
to be the gallant man credited with their protection.

He daydreamed that particular women would invite him to
affix their ribbons along titillating turns in their topographies
as they ground against him or jerked him through his pants. He
would notice the smooth, taut, creamy skin of, say, Karen's
neck and kiss it with his open mouth, and she softly gasped as
he moved his hands inside the top of her dress and cupped and
squeezed her fulsome breasts. She bent over, leaned her hands

against the back of the couch, and allowed him to raise the bottom of her short, black dress, past the top of her smoky garters, and enter her from behind, his cock sliding into her tight, wet sleeve, as they merged ...

It's unlikely that anyone wasted this opportunity to dream up such stereotyped encounters and, at the same time, fear that they might come to pass. Indeed, these first Bonobans entered a state of modified expectations, in which they found such scenes possible.

But (as I found out years later), if people have 'spontaneous' sex because they expect to, they undermine the affective character of their fantasy, because they feel the desire to follow a sort of script, however inchoate, rather than experiencing the spontaneous passion that they have rehearsed. In short, the only naïve and artless beginning of Bonoban society occurred in participants' minds as they masturbated before the actual party.

The big night arrived about a week later. It was a quiet, antiseptic Sunday—a slight, warm breeze blew a quiet energy around the desert; the moonlight radiated down from the magnificent celestial vault to illuminate the revelers' path from their cars, across the gravel yard and driveway, to the stuccoed cube that held their fates as founders of the future.

For most, trepidation found its mask in 'Tucson time'— that is, arriving fashionably late. Nonetheless, Dale and Ron had to arrive early to prepare. Karen was there, too, along with Rudy, the host. Inside the spare, remodeled garage, they busily moved furniture, set up refreshments, and positioned pens, papers, signs, ribbons, and condoms. Each pretended to ignore the impending deadline with destiny, yet each followed the wall clock's progress with apprehension. Who would go first?

Finally the clock hit 9:00—show time. His heart pattering, yet moving in a dream-like ether, Dale looked up at Ron and raised an eyebrow. Ron shrugged, and they walked over to the doorway, where a table held the sheets of rules and the 'ladies' choice' ribbons. The others stopped their busywork to watch. "Make sure you read that contract carefully," Rudy called helpfully. "You don't want to get screwed."

Dale and Ron pretended to chuckle. Dale's hand trembled slightly as he signed the sheet and placed it in the proper bin. Ron did the same, and then they stood up facing each other but looking past.

"Watch the clock, guys," Ron said.

"Say when," Karen answered.

"Okay," Dale found himself saying, quietly. He stepped forward and reached out to rub the crotch of Ron's shorts, and Ron reciprocated. Both were soft with terror. With a quavering voice, Dale intoned, "This is one trip to second base for a human, but one home run for humanity."

Ron started to tremble and then, unable to control himself, to laugh hysterically. "God, did you practice that?" he gasped. "It's horrible."

Dale suddenly felt himself doubling over, too, giggling uncontrollably, and they struggled to maintain contact for the remaining seconds until Karen yelled, "Time."

Then they removed their hands and let go, unable to stop guffawing, supporting themselves on the furniture as their eyes turned red and their breathing labored. They started to regain control, glanced into each other's eyes as Dale said, "Sorry," and went into hysterics again, until their stomach muscles ached.

Eventually those hardy pioneers gathered themselves, and the various dyads present exchanged Bonobo Handshakes, learning just how long thirteen seconds can be. Technically, these were not the first Bonobo Handshakes: as part of the group's planning, Dale and Doris had experimented a few days earlier in an empty classroom. Nonetheless, the repeated, public exchanges, especially among same-sex partners, provoked an emotional breakthrough for everyone involved that night and beyond, for they had to repeatedly confront their insecurities regarding size, technique, and signs of arousal. They constantly faced exposure, and, with no chance of escape, most participants found the result liberating, even thrilling.

Starting that night, these new Bonobans began to enter a weird world, where some spent ever-longer periods. They increasingly regarded Bonobo to be natural and ~~our~~ your ways to be odd. Still, many changes were in store for that strange realm.

As Dale, Ron, Karen, and Rudy discussed the initial results, other participants began to arrive. Anxious but excited, Doris entered next. As she chose her ribbon (blue for breasts because of her period) and signed the rules agreement, the first four lurked nearby, joking in a loose fashion. "You guys look more relaxed than I feel," she said.

"We're experiencing communitas," Dale joked accurately, demonstrating the practicality of their education.

"Well, I want some of that," Doris said. She took a breath and crossed the threshold too.

Eventually twelve people arrived, rubbed and got rubbed, and then ... not much happened.

Actually, that's not true: plenty happened. They ate chips and drank beer, gave brief presentations of differing levels of seriousness, chatted, flirted, joked, peed in the bathroom, groped each other as specified in the rules (sometimes dicks and nipples became hard), and discussed how it felt. They also endured pauses when they sensed that something should happen to push them into an orgy, but nothing did; they remained clothed, and silent about this.

Still, when the party wrapped up, Dale, among others, thought that they had taken a bold step by creating a novel and beneficial experience. Their pride and contentment at committing such a transgressive act far outweighed their varying levels of disappointment at failing to have sex. Plus, a couple paired off and went home to screw anyway, and two of the women drove to a popular club downtown to find partners for a one-nighter. Dale, and probably the rest, went home to masturbate.

REVISE AND RESUBMIT

The next morning, Dale sent this email to the participants:

Hey, guys,

I hope everyone had an interesting time last
night. *Insert* pun here. Actually, my favorite
presentation was Karen's, mostly because she
somehow worked 'insertion,' 'ins and outs,'
'penetration,' and of course 'dating' into a
talk on processualism.

Anyway, it occurred to me tonight that the genius of bonobo society—the actual bonobos—is
that they all get sexual release as a matter of
course. It's never been long since their last
orgasm, and they don't have to wonder whether
it'll be a long time until they get some again.

At our party, on the other hand, everyone got
excited (at least I batted my eyelashes all I
could), but getting satisfaction was a different story. We weren't bonobos so much as anti-
bonobos, maybe 'no-nobos.'

I didn't say anything about this during the
party because I didn't want it to seem like I
was trying to pressure everybody into sex. But
what do you guys think?

Dale wondered with ambivalence whether the slightly antiseptic course of the party would end Bonoban activity. His
message didn't imply that they should hold another party. The
single transgression that they already had committed would
give them a story and sense of savoir-faire to savor for a long
time. A few years down the road, when they would hold jobs
as faculty members, each would project a mysterious, knowing
look as the topic of bonobos rolled around in class. That probably was enough, wasn't it? On the other hand, weren't they
anthropologists engaged in *participant* observation? Weren't
they supposed to analyze their own experience to more clearly
and comprehensively understand all human experience and all
human possibilities? Plus, everyone might attribute the relative
failure of the party to the flawed nature of his Great Idea,
when in fact a little elaboration on the original concept might
reveal its brilliance.

In any case, Ron interpreted Dale's message as a call to "re-
vise and resubmit." So further parties ensued. Bonobo's organizing logic eventually started from the premises that 1) most
humans want frequent sex with varied partners but societal
rules interfere and 2) most humans fear ostracization more
than frustration. So the group made rules that, depending on
the situation, enabled or required sex (not just frottage)—a sex-
based society that ostracized the abstemious.

To get it right, the group, with occasional shifts in membership, held all sorts of test parties over the course of that first
year. An early one required that everyone have an orgasm just
before going to the event. (One wit unfortunately asked everyone he greeted, "Are you here with someone, or did you come

alone?") They dubbed the obligatory groping 'aftplay.' The mood was relaxed, the jokes were easy, the cheeks were flush, the hair was wavy—in Arizona!—and a light eroticism suffused the air, even when participants weren't groping each other. It was a great way to organize a get-together.

But it was no way to create an all-day Bonoban society. Dale kept his eye on a prize much larger than soirées. As he wrote in his de rigueur post-party email:

It's too lazy. We displaced responsibility for each person's sexual satisfaction to his or her partner(s) or self. But it takes a village, no man is an island, and I am my brother's keeper. Our Bonoban society falsely abjured its respon- sibility, manufacturing a beneficial externali- ty for itself in classic neo-colonial fashion.

Still, as a party qua party ... ¡Qué partay!

Other Bonobans noticed that the tone of Dale's messages had become more authoritative, although not strictly authori- tarian. They wouldn't deny that he continued to have the pre- ponderance of insights about their experiment. Maybe he thought about it more than they did. And he appropriately lis- tened to and cited others' contributions. Nonetheless, he seemed to have arrogated the right to speak last, and he talked and wrote as if he assumed that his opinion counted more than that of others. It didn't help that sometimes he acted as if he regarded this responsibility as a burden.

Anyway, Ron's opinion might have had more heft. This was partly because the others (including Dale) liked him more, even if they respected him less; he seemed to recognize that he was their peer. But Ron's real power was that he got things done:

arranged venues, stored supplies, reminded people about meetings, circulated germane articles.

These differences came out in the way they talked. Regarding the next party, Dale unspooled thus: "Bonobos are really familiar with each other's genitals, and they constantly see each other having sex and beating off. We need to develop the same sort of familiarity. One way to do that is by jacking off in front of each other, so that's the plan the group came up with for the next gathering." Ron, in contrast, said, "This time we're all going to sit in a circle and masturbate."

That Bo-Knows-Bo party represented a breakthrough, as this was the first time for most of the Bonobans that anyone, much less friends of the same gender, had seen them beating off. In fact, few of them had stated outright to anyone, ever, that they pleasured themselves. After the requisite academic presentation, the Bonobans sat facing each other, naked, in a big circle inside the same refurbished garage. Some couldn't maintain an erection, some faked their orgasms, some seemed more interested in watching others than in diddling themselves, one person brought toys that others found unsettling, and a few were too loud or messy for their comrades' taste. But, as a group, they did it. With each step, the participants felt more self-conscious and more liberated—as is generally true among new Bonobans today. The standard Bonoban fondling afterward, as the party continued, was much more familiar than it ever had been.

Frank, though, was unimpressed. He was a rarity in that crowd—a Tucson native—and perhaps the years of explaining cactus and monsoons to newbies had swollen his self-assurance. It was unclear to what extent he was a student, or what his age and sexual preference might be, but he somehow ended up at a lot of parties, bars, and cafés with graduate students in anthropology. So, seemingly by osmosis, he had become part of Bonobo's expanding roster, starting on the night of the Bo-Knows-Bo event.

Far from grateful, he acted as though he had a missionary position within the group. During the circle jerk, he followed the rules and easily blew his sperm onto his stomach and chest, yet his facial expressions alternated between "*This* is how you do it," and "What is wrong with you people?" Afterward, as the revelers clumped in conversational groups and casually groped each other, Frank let loose. "This is, like, Montessori-school-level bullshit. That was like washing hands or something. Sex is dirty! Where's the dirt?"

In reply, Dorinne clarified that Bonobo wasn't exactly an orgy; it was more like sex to get beyond sex. Doris helpfully elucidated the analogy with bonobos, while Lars gave a brief history of the group, which by then had been meeting for a couple of months. Eventually Frank, regarding them as if they were explaining addition in a calculus class, blurted out, "I've been listening to you guys talk about this for weeks now. I get it! But you need to put more *sex* in the sex. I'm sure bonobos would agree."

He then informed them that he had participated in a Jack-and-Jill Off—a real one—which had just as many rules and safeguards as the Bonobans had. But it was hot and dirty. ("Like the landfill in summer?" Ron sought clarification.) And, while not everyone touched everyone else, everyone came— and more than once, and ... it was just hard to describe how awesome the whole thing felt. It was "a fucking totality."

Frank's eloquence didn't match his exuberance, and the others tired of his attitude more quickly than they wearied of his idea. Plus, none of the long-timers wanted to cede authority to this newcomer, whose intellectual commitment was suspect. So, in subsequent days, Dale, Doris, Ron, Karen, and others searched for information about Jack-and-Jill Offs. They scrounged around their apartments and the library for back issues of alternative newspapers to look through sex-advice columns, and they called or emailed friends.

One bright afternoon Dale accompanied Doris to an adult bookstore, where they searched the covers of books, magazines, and videotapes for references to Jack-and/or-Jill-Offs. Dale felt mortified. What if he saw a professor enter the store, or a friend? Doris, in contrast, acted as if an audience were following every highly liberated movement and comment she made. For research purposes, and kicks, she ended up purchasing a couple of regional swingers' magazines. Dale played it cool but harbored illicit hopes that she would emulate the products on the shelves.

Finally, Bonobans quizzed their openly gay and lesbian classmates in the most abstract fashion possible. For example, Dale sidled up to Novak and greeted him as they were walking across campus. Had he heard of Jack-and-Jill Offs?

Novak hesitated, as if searching his memory, then smiled inscrutably. "Yeah, I have."

"Oh, cool. Do you know what they're like? I mean, I've heard the term, but I still don't quite get it." Based on other snippets that the group had gathered, Dale suggested, "I heard that people touch each other but don't have sex—I mean, not all the way."

Without indicating whether he had ever participated in such a thing, Novak replied, "Well, sometimes it's like that. But sometimes not."

Dale couldn't bring himself to press for details.

Eventually, what their collective inquiry produced was this: done right, a Jack-and-Jill Off was an orgy without penetration. Participants stroked themselves, but they also masturbated or otherwise manipulated anyone else present, regardless of gender or relationship status, as long as both expressly acceded. The rules allowed oral sex only if a condom was properly in place for male recipients or if cellophane or another barrier were used on women. Penetrating an ass or pussy with a penis was expressly disallowed, and participants vocally policed this and other rules. Nonetheless, in practice, people who wanted to screw simply moved to other parts of the premises.

Within this framework, participants in Jack-and-Jill Offs ended up trying all sorts of new experiences. Men touched other men for the first time; women touched women; gay men sucked women's breasts; lesbians received pearl necklaces; skinny people groped fat people; fat people exposed their bodies. Many found it addictively liberating. On the surface, it looked a lot like Bonobo.

But it wasn't Bonobo; it was simply an orgy with extra limitations. Thinking about the differences sharpened Dale's ideas about their experiment. First, the Jack-and-Jill Offs featured sex almost exclusively, whereas Bonoban parties added an activity from an otherwise non-erotic domain. Second, all contact at an Off was voluntary, whereas Bonobans committed—in writing!—to fondling everyone else, and they faced other requirements that integrated erotic contact into ordinary sociability. Third, the Jacks and Jills might have no relationship with each other away from the orgy; indeed, some might feel mortified to encounter an orgy mate elsewhere. In contrast, the very essence of Bonobo was that sex would become part of everyday relations, even antagonistic ones, much as it was among bonobos. So Bonobo depended on interactions among its participants occurring away from the parties.

Dale saw that an Offing would constitute a logical and enticing escalation, but was it too much? In discussions, he came to represent the puritanical side of Bonobo: having sex to get beyond sex. If more often than not he advocated making sex mundane, it was because he felt that others wouldn't speak up—or at least not as eloquently as he. Plus, this was the original point of what they were doing, and he would hate to give up on this potentially superior basis of social interaction. And, yes, maybe he did so because he owned the original idea, while Frank seemed to have the local franchise rights on a Jack-and-Jill Off.

Yet, at the same time, Dale found Frank's call for automatic, dirty sex to be seductive. Dale thought "long and hard," as too many jokes stated, about how to meld the two approaches. At least once he ended his contemplations in the stall of a bathroom in the Anthropology Building, spurting his spunk to images of his friends jerking or sucking him off as he stroked, licked, or blew them.

His capitulation was inevitable.

Thus, the group held a Bonoban Jack-and-Jill Off. And here the roller coaster veered unexpectedly, because, it turns out, most of the participants thoroughly enjoyed touching and being touched on their bare skin. They liked it so much that some of the men had two orgasms and, since everyone was moving around and facing in different directions, no one could know whether any particular person didn't have at least one. It was dirty; it was nasty; it was messy. Guys saw other guys' cum up close for the first time; some even touched it or got hit by it; women learned how their pussies were different inside, how their breasts felt different. Some people got scratched, and others were caressed without inhibition in ways that felt new and liberating and, all of a sudden, necessary. This was a keeper.

And it was still Bonobo. After everyone had put their clothes back on, three more people gave presentations related to their studies. As the audience members listened, they massaged a neighbor's neck, gently goosed a friend, leaned against someone who riffled their hair absently, and, of course, rubbed each other's breasts and genitals. They asked quietly about scars that they had encountered earlier, and they appreciatively teased a friend about, say, the shrubbery growing on his lower back. They had agreed that no one could retreat to another area to go at it, and it was strictly forbidden, on pain of ostracization, to fuck and run. So they all stayed to the end of the presentations when, as individuals or couples took their leave, many felt obliged to state the obvious: "This was good."

Some of the Bonobans went off to fuck again, some went to a diner to hang out in a smaller clique, and some who suspected this felt a little jealous and a little rejected, but these feelings were manageable. That night, during the party, all had been accepted, and all had been accepting.

Dale had to admit it: Frank was partially right. And, actually, the fucker had surprised him by following not just the letter but the spirit of the whole occasion. Sure, a couple of times during the Offing he had exclaimed, "*This* is what I'm talking about!" but he hadn't acted like the instructor of a master class. Moreover, during the presentations he was indistinguishable in attitude from the mass of graduate students. ~~Maybe he wasn't a threat, after all.~~ Maybe his ideas wouldn't threaten the ongoing social experiment.

A couple of days later, Dale blandly mentioned to Ron, "Hey, that Frank guy was all right the other night."

Tellingly, Ron replied, "Yeah, that was a relief."

Enough had been said.

TROUBLE IN UTOPIA

You've probably spotted it, and those early Bonobans definitely noticed it: Why were a couple of men leading a group modeled on bonobos? Bonobos' appeal, after all, was tripartite: they were promiscuous, relatively nonviolent, and matriarchal. But somehow a man had come up with the idea of Bonoban humans, and he and another man led the organizing of their activities. How could this be?

No one involved would have suggested that humans were inevitably more like the patriarchal, warlike, and sexually abstemious chimps than bonobos. Aside from a general faith among anthropologists that humans have great flexibility in gender relations, they knew of influential female anthropologists starting with Margaret Mead. Outside of academia, they saw examples from Margaret Thatcher to Madonna. Indeed, female graduate students were thinking up and organizing all sorts of activities, including a student journal.

So had Dale and Ron become the leaders of Bonobo because of lingering sexism? Because of accidents of their individual psychologies? Or had they actually earned it?

Whether it was cause or effect (or both), Dale and Ron were clearly the Bonobans who sustained the highest level of interest in the experiment. Ultimately it killed—possibly euthanized—their academic careers. In contrast, others entered the group with great enthusiasm but soon moved on to other passions, some simply wanted an orgy and quickly felt disgruntled, but most assumed that it was a radical path that marked them as 'cool' and that would end as soon as they traveled away to do their field research or found a job at some far-off university. Then they would trade in the condoms and KY for tweed jackets and photocopier codes.

When the topic of matriarchy came up, thinly draped in humor, no one could actually pinpoint any moment at which Dale and Ron had denied leadership to women or, for that matter, arrogated it to themselves. It happened incrementally. For example, when Doris suggested at an early planning meeting that the parties should include wine in addition to beer, she looked around the circle of collaborators but ultimately rested her gaze on Dale. He didn't say, "Okay, we can do that." He said, "I agree. What does everyone else think?" But somehow the others saw that as his decree. Afterward, Ron was the one who canvassed the others about the best kind of wine and ensured that vino was provided at each party.

Of course, others did sometimes confront Ron and especially Dale about the irony of their leadership. Ron noted wryly that a woman had organized the intramural football team. Dale, perhaps a bit too sincerely, argued that no one, actually, was in charge. They were more like a hunter-gatherer band, maybe Apaches. No one was forcing anyone else; anyone could withdraw, as it were, or form her own group; and anyone, actually, could try to persuade the rest of the group to enact her suggestions—all without fearing that he would pull rank, which he didn't have anyway, although it might be true that some deferred to him because it was his idea originally. Maybe this was a case in which the humans were showing the bonobos who's who—if anthropologists in 1991 couldn't judge each other by the content of their character rather than that of their underwear, then who could?

Privately, though, Dale questioned his position. (Actually, he questioned his 'positionality,' but you haven't signed up for that.) Regardless of the basis of his leadership—personality, appearance, dumb luck, precedence, pheromones—the complaints demonstrated that his gender was salient to others, and Ron's more obtrusive masculinity compounded the problem. But he feared that he would endanger the experiment's continuity and its ongoing improvement if he withdrew from prominence, even preeminence. That is—not that he could ever express this out loud—maybe others recognized an exceptional individual and acquiesced to him to the benefit of all.

Then there was the other niggling feeling. A little part of his mind thought that women who focused on gender issues—even the ones who fucked a lot—were inherently prone to turn any situation into an opportunity to seek vengeance in the name of all women throughout all time against all men throughout all time, not coincidentally in a way that disenfranchised even sympathetic men while improving their own résumés. As a result, might it be that, purely for historical reasons that could change in coming years, white men were the only people in America equipped to be, insofar as anyone can be, impartial? When other men raised this idea away from women, Dale ridiculed it. But he semi-believed it at the same time, and hated himself for it.

His self-loathing matched that of the female participants. Doris asked herself similar questions, but with more acid. Who had failed? History, Ron and Dale, the women themselves?

This was hardly the only point of contention. For example, there was homophobia.

In 1991, quite a few people who felt sexually attracted to others of the same gender hid these feelings to avoid discrimination. Others kept their preferences unclear—even to close friends who thought they might be dating them. So, from the start, Bonobo included homosexuals and bisexuals. But the group didn't include any *openly* gay people, even as the parties grew in size and as some early participants withdrew and needed to be replaced.

Kim seemed to enjoy stirring up difficult situations—for other people—in a way that jibed with her politics. So she raised the question of including homosexuals with ever-increasing vigor at parties and organizational meetings. Maybe she thought that this was her Little Rock school system, her lunch counter to integrate. Pointedly not addressing Dale or Ron except as part of a larger ensemble, she advocated including Yelena, a self-described lesbian, and Novak, an openly gay man.

By the time Kim's suggestion gained traction, the Bonoban events had reached full maturation, including all sorts of penetration. This probably increased the seriousness—really, the fear—with which many group members considered the question. Along with brandishing terms such as 'heteronormative,' Kim asked, "How can people willing to have sex with almost anyone be homophobic?"

Her insistent campaign generated open debate. None of the Bonobans took exception to Yelena and Novak per se. On what basis could they object to such well-liked classmates? Privately, though, many voiced concerns: they 'knew better' but still feared AIDS, or they felt an unwilling repulsion toward homosexuals.

In his journal, Dale tried to work out defensible reasons for his own opposition. He thought that, because of a history that denied public forms of sociability to gays qua gays, they ended up sexualizing everything, which was against the core spirit of Bonobo—getting beyond sex. He also wondered, Don't gays already get sex whenever they want it, at discos and bathhouses or whatever? (Please note that, if Dale were right about this, he and the group could simply have studied gay people to determine the effect of guaranteed erotic contact on social groups.)

He also feared that gays would eventually dominate Bonobo, thereby making the movement less appealing to straights, regardless of their commitment to its purpose. And, yes, he suspected that, being straight, he would face difficulty maintaining the de facto leadership of the group—just as he would in a mostly female Bonobo. After all, he himself reflexively supported female or gay candidates for political office as a personal form of affirmative action.

Thus, Dale wanted to steer the debate, and he knew that they couldn't put off a decision for long. Kim was pressing the issue during all of their gatherings, and the group's unspoken consensus to "Stonewall" her (as Ron punned) was eroding. So he scheduled a ~~showdown~~ meeting.

The group reserved a study room on the fourth floor of the library, which usually was deserted except for older perverts waiting to masturbate in front of the occasional student searching for a book. Luckily, not everyone showed up, but about ten Bonobans crowded into the small room, either sitting around the wooden table or, like Dale, leaning against the surrounding wall. That was a good spot because he could see everyone without claiming centrality. Ron sat at the table, and Dale hoped that this would indicate to others that they weren't a team, which they weren't, officially. And of course Kim was there, also at the table, along with a smattering of guys and women, in fortuitously equal numbers.

The early arrivals talked about the usual school topics until the room was full. For fear of getting arrested, they didn't greet each other in the Bonoban fashion. Eventually, Ron asked, "Are we ready?"

After scattered comments of "sure" and "thought you'd never ask," Dale stated, "Uh, I just wanted to suggest at the outset that, no matter what anyone's opinion about inviting Yelena and Novak is ... I mean, we're all in class together: no one here is a homophobe. Shit, we've all at least fondled each other. So I hope that everyone can feel comfortable speaking openly without fearing that anyone else will call them names. What do you guys think?"

Kim was notably silent, staring at the opposite wall, but others nodded, muttered, "hear, hear," or otherwise signaled assent.

After a pregnant moment, Kim said, looking straight at Dale, "Then, since we're all such enlightened *liberals*, how could we possibly exclude gays? On what basis? Does anyone have a problem with Yelena or Novak?"

After everyone again made clear that the question was categorical, unrelated to any individuals, the debate ensued as if most of them hadn't already discussed it. And, truly, they hadn't reached a prior agreement or formulated any plan. Most, like Dale, probably felt an inchoate dirtiness about the whole thing, but they had an intuition that they wanted to honor. So there they were, uttering phrases like, "It's still a fragile experiment, and it's just not ready yet," "The current mix is working, and once it's changed we can never go back, so why chance it now?" and "Are there gay bonobos?" Ron echoed Kim to reverse her meaning, "How can people willing to have sex with almost anyone be homophobic?"

At first, Dale only suggested points as if he were a devil's advocate, reported comments by unnamed "someone elses" who might or might not be in attendance, and asked questions. Others made similar moves, perhaps to demonstrate their open-mindedness. Still, nobody except Kim argued outright to include Yelena and Novak—not even a closeted lesbian who was there. Kim increasingly struggled to maintain her composure as she countered her opponents' slippery arguments.

Finally, Dale sensed that it was time to suggest a magnanimous deal—without, of course, ceding the main victory. "Kim, how about this? I think we all want to be as inclusive as possible while making sure that the whole thing continues successfully." He looked around for confirmation, and enough people nodded. "Can we just table the question for the time being?"

He saw her contemptuous, disgusted expression. "But wait—here's the rest of my suggestion. We'll set a definite date for discussing it again, just as seriously. What do you think?" And he looked around at the others, "It's just a suggestion off the top of my head. But it gives us a chance to think about it more concretely, now that we know it's on some future—specified—agenda. What does *everybody* think?"

Kim sighed and shook her head. For a moment, no one responded, and then Karen asked how long they would delay a final decision. Dale didn't much care, as long as they kicked the can down the road. So he pointed out that the only permanent decision would be to admit openly gay people. To not admit was only to say "not yet."

Then he restated the question. "Does anyone have a suggestion regarding the timing?"

Kim grumbled, "The sooner the better. Tomorrow. I doubt we'll know anything next month that we don't know now."

Karen—Dale felt ecstatic that it was a woman—spoke up again, "Well, we can't keep talking about this every week. It'll kill the buzz; it already kind of has. How about two months? It's not tomorrow, and it's not next year."

"I second it," said Ron.

Done.

As everyone started to file out uncomfortably, Kim stared into the distance.

Then Doris made matters a little worse. She noted, as if it were an abstract issue of pan-primate jurisprudence, that real bonobos used sex to re-establish social bonds after disputes. So, if they were serious about the whole thing …

Kim rolled her eyes, said, "No, thank you," and got up to leave. The end of her career with Bonobo was not far off.

During the rest of that first year, whenever new members raised the issue of openly gay members, they received only a vague comment along the lines of, "Yeah, I think there was a meeting about that, and we decided to keep it simple until we had some stability." Perhaps no one felt satisfied with the state of affairs, but no one disliked it enough to press the issue again. To this day, Ron and Dale's version of Bonobo continues to say 'not yet' to gays, the elderly, obese people, and others.

On a happier note: Doris' proposal to copy bonobos' method of reconciliation was golden. (As you'll see, it worked out well for me.) Dale felt quite happy that a woman had suggested it. He encouraged Doris to send an email explaining her recommendation to the group, and he gave his support to it in an unprepossessing way that somehow still reminded others of his preeminence.

Thus, from that point forward Bonobans had to finish any significantly antagonistic interaction by bringing each other to orgasm—'fucking it out'—much as bonobos humped each other after a spat.

MORE THAN A FEELING

Standing in Rudy's converted garage, Ron read from a scrap of paper to the promiscuous primates seated around him: "'We've come a long way, baby—and a lot of times, too.'" Giggles, gentle groans, and a bit of disdain greeted this proposed summation of a bizarre year. "Okay, maybe that's not your favorite so far, but keep it in mind. It might grow on—Hey, they wrote another version on the back: 'I came a long way, baby—help me wipe it off my chin.' Now that's nasty!"

Apparently, Ron wasn't the only one who thought so, as others enjoyed their disgust.

Sitting in back, Dale appreciated the humor but couldn't help feeling a bit officious. What if *that* won the contest?

"Next one: They put in parentheses, '(Instead of bonobos aping humans) ... Humans aping bonobos.' I get it—because humans are apes, too. Very an-thro-po-lo-gi-cal. Next we have, 'Year 1, Bonobo Era, or B.E. 1' Maybe you have to see it on the paper, but 'B.E.' looks like the verb, 'be,' which seems to *be* profound, may*be*. Or it could just be that the B.E.E.R. is doing my thinking for me."

Dale disliked it less than the others because it was bland and descriptive. The basic task was not to make everyone laugh momentarily; it was to name the final Bonobo party of the year, the capstone of all that they had experienced and developed together. So, yes, he was feeling a little officious. Was there some way to sway the others without it showing?

Argh. Could he stop himself from trying to control every-thing? Even though entries were anonymous, he had refrained from participating in the contest to ensure that someone else would name the final party. He also had made sure that some-one else read the entries—Ron was doing a bang-up job, but any other Bonoban would have been better politically. And he had commanded himself to not even comment on the con-tenders. He put "Let It Be" on the mental jukebox and acted disengaged.

Eventually, after a discussion and vote, Ron announced, "Tune your air guitars. The winner—in a tight one, as it were—is 'More Than a Feeling'."

A good one after all. Not as awesome as "We come in peace," but Dale felt a touch of pride. He really was just the first among equals, and he knew when it was important to use his special powers and when to let others shine. Not counting a few ragged edges, he felt complete. He had come twice that night, and he had his coursework in hand, a plan for the sum-mer, and a bevy of friends who respected him. Postmodernists might write endlessly about the 'fragmented subject,' but his parts fit nicely.

Ron plopped next to him on the couch to talk about the house that they would share over the summer with Layla. His parents somehow had connections with the landlord, who was a linguistics professor, another trust-fund baby, and thus of course a residual hippie—an 'emissary from the past,' as the Mexicans say. Anyway, the Hippie Professor had a friend who usually lived on a houseboat in Marin County but who was going to travel around the Old World for a year, undoubtedly staying at Buddhist monasteries and Moroccan vineyards. So the Hippie Professor was taking an unpaid sabbatical to live on the houseboat, and Dale, Ron, and Layla got to house-sit for him as long as they paid the bills, kept up the upkeep, and didn't piss off the neighbors. Dale sardonically and Ron appreciatively suspected that their landlord would leave them a bag of weed as a housewarming gift, an expression of the gracious countercultural etiquette.

Dale asked whether he knew that they might, in return, leave him indelible semen stains on his adobe walls.

"Probably," Ron said, "but he seemed to think it was cool when I told him what we're doing," meaning Bonobo. "He said he 'grokked' it. ... I didn't ask."

Dale couldn't fathom why Ron would endanger their awesome deal by telling even the Hippie Professor about Bonobo.

"No, he's cool. And it's better to be upfront about things, especially since my folks told me to call him. Anyway, as far as the cum stains go, we might need to watch out for his."

Dale wanted to ask whether Ron's folks knew about Bonobo, but, if they did, the consequences were out of his control, and at that moment he preferred to let it go. Dale's parents certainly didn't know much about his life, and, as far as he was concerned, they never would. His mother and father seemed uninterested even in basic issues like whether he had friends or a hobby—anything besides grades, girlfriends, and money. If they had been different, he might have told them more. But Bonobo? Could Ron really talk with his parents about things like that? Dale envied people who were friends with their parents, but he wasn't sure how that worked in practice; probably he would find out over the summer. Maybe Ron's parents would half-adopt him, like his old roommate's big sister had, but this time with money. Would they invite him on a family vacation? He basked in a wave of unearned warmth.

The remainders of the party recaptured a wistful Dale's attention. A dwindling group by the keg was riffing on the entries in the party-naming contest: "Friends come in handy," "Give piece a chance," "Sir Cool Jerk," "Bedtime for Bonobo," "Bone-oboe" ... A downward spiral, diminishing returns—why don't people know when to quit?

Maybe all those orgasms would never make him completely content, after all. Still, he felt a flow of tranquil energy that helped him deal with all the other bullshit. He wished that pacifying current would continue flowing into him each night in bed, as he struggled to sleep. These days, the past, present, and future confronted him as if they were open questions demanding answers. It would be nice if the parties never ended, like in that Talking Heads song.

He walked over to the remaining few revelers to embrace them and say goodnight.

INERTIA

Doris felt Lars' dick thrusting inside her, and she squeezed it rhythmically while she gyrated her hips. Dorinne was sucking and tongue-tickling one of Doris' nipples, and Rudy had a big, sweaty hand cupping and massaging her other breast while his tongue was rimming her ear. She felt her own hands rubbing their hair and backs. She knew that she was panting and dripping and screeching. She felt so animal. And then the intensity increased. She locked onto Lars' eyes. More, more, more, more—she bucked, writhed, screamed, surrendered, pressed, expired. She exhaled what little was left.

Whew, she shook again. "I'm going to miss this. What a year."

Lars was still moving in and out, keeping his dick hard inside the condom. Apparently he hadn't come yet. Amazing—what would it take? He smiled to her, "I told you not to pass your exams. Maybe you should do your fieldwork in Tucson."

"Yeah, if only I'd known about this back when I chose my topic. Ha!"

Doris was the star of the night. She would soon fly to Indonesia for a year to do fieldwork for her dissertation. Her reward was special attention during the orgy, plus the assignment to describe her impending research during the mundane phase of the party. To think that some students merely received a report card to end the semester!

For many Americans, going off to live in a remote, foreign village for a year simply to do research on an academic topic was as outlandish as participating in an orgy. But most of the Bonobans had chosen anthropology because they dreamed of this crucible experience. They spent several years preparing for it and another year or more, afterward, writing their dissertations about it. They had heard returning students' stories and saw how experienced they looked compared to mere classgoers. Doris was about to walk into the unknown, from which somehow she would return knowing.

Dale and Ron expected to do the same a couple of years later. But Dale was still searching for that One Great Idea that would embody his intellectual greatness and ensure his successful career as a professor. Alone at home, especially late at night in bed, he tried to squeeze out a chunk of genius, as if his brain were constipated. Usually, before much time had passed, his thoughts would stray to more-immediate topics, such as classes, Bonobo, or the rent. Sometimes they devolved into jealous complaints about the quality of other students' ideas or even those of the gurus whose ranks he longed to join.

Dale's adviser, Dr. Collins, hardly deserved the title. The two had been matched arbitrarily upon Dale's arrival a few years earlier. The expectation was that he eventually would bond with some other faculty member, under whom he would apprentice. Ideally, they would form a relationship of deep affection and respect, occasionally sharing dinners or research work. Dale would increasingly appear to be a semi-autonomous extension of his adviser's professional persona, and, without coddling his protégé, his adviser would shepherd him through each hurdle: Master's report, preliminary exams, dissertation research, and job hunt. After that, when they saw each other at conferences, they would grab a coffee together and talk about deep theoretical questions and momentous career issues. Eventually, Dale would develop his own cadre of apprentices, and he and his former adviser would quietly share pride in a successful and growing lineage of anthropologists. Many years later, as his adviser officially retired, Dale would organize a festschrift in his or her honor, and it would generally be accepted that Dale had been the adviser's greatest protégé. Perhaps then Dale would return to Arizona, to fittingly take his mentor's position.

None of that happened. It doesn't happen for many students and advisers, in the same way that few people find full-fledged, lasting love. (As you'll see, my experience was considerably closer to the ideal.) But Dale's case fit within a particular genre of failure, since both he and Collins acted as though no problem existed.

When Collins—lanky, blond, in his 50s—met with Dale, he would ask what ideas the student had for his dissertation. This choice would shape the topics that Dale would have to cover in his preliminary exams, which he had to pass before he could do his fieldwork. Collins had cut his teeth on the symbolic regulation of agricultural cycles among a small set of hamlets in Papua New Guinea. But he wasn't pushing that issue on Dale. In fact, he wasn't pushing any topic, nor was he actually pushing Dale to make a decision or even to make another appointment to discuss any issue whatsoever.

Dale, for his part, was afraid to admit that he couldn't generate any idea that he found exciting. To do so might expose him as a fraud unworthy of any professor's active support—which he still expected that Collins would produce once Dale reached some unspecified stage of accomplishment. He joked with his friends about finding that One Great Idea as the key to a career as a guru. But he didn't admit to anyone his paralyzing fear of choosing a mediocre topic, especially when he sensed that the Great Idea would eventually pop up and relentlessly taunt him if he started down some other path.

Dale could have switched advisers, as most other students had done. When he joked about Collins' distraction, his classmates would suggest possible replacements. But, even though Dale had developed good relations with professors during seminars and found their ideas interesting, he could see their flaws—one was gone too often, one was a little too intense, another channeled her students into her own projects, and so on. Collins wasn't much of anything, including a disaster.

Nonetheless, Dale recognized that he suffered from considerable inertia. Maybe, once he found his idea, he would shape his collaboration with Collins—or a new adviser—much as he was shaping Bonobo. He gave himself a firm deadline of summer's end to develop a research topic.

In the meantime, he continued to beset Dr. Collins with sporadic, anonymous pranks.

His crimes were relatively benign. For example, after working late in the computer lab one weekend, he climbed the stairs to the third floor of the Anthropology Building; walked to the hallway-off-a-hallway on which Collins had been archived; removed the yellowing, dryly leftist cartoons (mostly Doonesburys) from around his office door; and taped up replacements from Nancy, Garfield, and the Family Circus. Another time, he studded wads of chewed gum with dried boogers and placed them on the underside of the doorknob to Collins' office and then on his car's door handle, out in the faculty parking lot. Then he typed lust letters to Collins from an anonymous undergraduate admirer, sending one via campus mail; he later put another under his windshield wiper, then slid a third under his office door, and finally, late at night, stuck one in his mailbox at home. Dale sweated out the consequences of this last act, since it could have endangered Collins' marriage. As far as he could tell, it didn't, and he moved on to a new series of shenanigans.

He did all this so secretly that no one else knew he was the culprit. For his part, Collins didn't make a big deal of the pranks—for example, he simply removed the cartoons and left the area outside his office unadorned—so only a few people knew of each individual attack, and nobody else knew that a series had occurred.

Dale wasn't consciously trying to achieve any specific reaction, even from himself. It was just something in which he had indulged since grade school. The standard progression was this: He would commit little, anonymous affronts against an authority figure, then he would simultaneously: a) enjoy a secret thrill, b) fear being caught and having to explain his pointless behavior, and c) worry about whether he was a bad person. After his excitement died down, for a long time he would resist the urge's return, while planning how to submit to it. Finally, he would give in and commit a different offense against the same person.

I like to think that with each successful prank Dale felt a little fireworks in his soul—be it a party popper, a Roman candle, an M-80, or, sometimes, a dud.

A DREADED CALL

Fall semester, 1992

The phone rang, which happened too often those days. Dale was lounging on the leatherine couch in the living room of a big, heavily shaded house not far from campus. He let someone else—or the machine, for all he cared—answer it. He had just started reading another article on the 'psychology/ies of the fractured subject(s)' for his exams.

Ron picked up the phone. "Bonobo House. This is Ron. ... Oh, hi, Dale's Mom. ... Hi, Dale's Dad." Dale looked up to see him smiling as if this were a routine call from his own parents, rather than the inevitable disaster that Dale had been dreading. Now they had to know.

The alternative weekly in Tucson had caught wind of the Bonobo House within weeks of its establishment, just before the fall semester. The subsequent article publicly exposed the Bonobans, including to the bemused faculty in anthropology. The notoriety made it extremely unlikely that he or Ron would find regular girlfriends anytime soon, should they decide to try. But such consequences struck him as inevitable and even as a sign of intellectual commitment. Anyway, the problems would be local, like the story. As students they weren't planning to stay in Tucson forever, and no letter 'B' had been branded into their foreheads.

But, hey, what responsible alternative weekly wouldn't like to edify its readers with a hard-hitting, sober feature exploring an different social vision ... involving orgies? The Tucson paper sold the story from coast to coast, and Bonobo exploded across the map. Even I read about it—many times, while beating off—as an undergraduate in far-off Rocky Top, Tennessee. Good times, those.

It thrilled Dale to become famous-ish. Most people, even in Tucson, didn't know who he was by name, much less by appearance, but at least *he* knew that people across the country had read about his idea and actions—along with those of the other Bonobans, of course. He felt unsure about how to express this to the others as news reached them regarding the article's spread, so he defaulted to a pleased yet unsurprised look. Ron, for his part, yelled, "Hoo, yeah! *LA Weekly*, baby!" with the rest.

Yet Dale felt foreboding, too. While he knew that his parents would never find this article on their own, he sensed that the perverseness of fate meant that some meddler would inform them. He just didn't know when it would happen or how they would deal with him. He had no reason to fear their reaction except that they were his parents. It pained him to feel their disappointment, and it would thrill him to impress them one day. At least he didn't rely on them financially, thanks to his salary as a research assistant and ever-mounting student loans, so the only leverage they could wield was emotional. Well, okay, they could refuse to fly him home for Christmas and give him fewer gifts, but he wouldn't change his life for that.

Ron's parents might actually have given their son *more* presents because the article came out. Ex-hippie philanthropists, they acted supportive and intrigued. "They think it's cool," Ron told him. "They just want everyone to wear condoms."

Dale sensed something patronizing in Ron's parents' detachment, as if Bonobo were a lemonade stand. He had egged their car and soaped it with fake gang tags during their summer visit, but of course it was "just a rental," and their credit card's built-in insurance already covered it. Apparently they didn't even feel anger or great frustration—just bemusement. Ron's father cheerfully noted that he and his friends had done much worse as kids. Dale listened blankly. He imagined firehosing manure all over Ron's parents' well-adjusted faces, their elegantly casual clothes, and their inconsequential rental car. Support that.

Anyway, he felt relieved that Ron had answered the phone when his parents called. This gave him time to prepare emotionally for the upcoming ordeal. But as he listened he realized that they weren't discussing Bonobo after all. Instead they were quizzing Ron about preliminary exams. Veteran torturers, they had found Dale's other sore spot. Prelims were the main intellectual hurdle in graduate school, the one place where anyone flunked out. After that, the dissertation was just a question of perseverance. Most students dedicated an entire semester to taking the exams. Then they would proceed to exotic locales for a year or more to complete fieldwork, return to write their dissertations, and apply for jobs.

Ron and Dale had entered graduate school at the same time, and, by chance, each planned to take his prelims in Fall 1993, one year away. But first Dale desperately needed a dissertation topic. While his near-panic might seem premature, these exams required a huge amount of preparatory reading and consultation with a faculty committee. Adding to the pressure, the choice of topic was extremely consequential: through the prelims and dissertation, he would declare his specialization to future employers, and the university that hired him would expect him to adhere to that specialization for years to come.

Unfortunately, as far as Dale knew, he still hadn't produced his One Great Idea.

Of course it had occurred to him that Bonobo could be this genius stroke, but turning it into an academic research project was problematic. He could never get informed consent from all of the participants, a Human Subjects Committee probably wouldn't approve it, and then it would be difficult to get a job as an orgy-ologist. Nonetheless, he fantasized that the feature article making the rounds would prompt Collins or maybe some other faculty member to suggest the topic to him and explain a route through those obstacles. So far, nothing of the sort had happened, but, just in case, he secretly had started taking more-comprehensive notes in his journal.

Now adding to his distress, somehow his parents knew about prelims. Had he told them? And they were asking Ron how his own preparations were going—probably to have a point of comparison in hectoring Dale. Of course, they were going how they were supposed to; that was Ron. But Dale couldn't resent him because Ron gently defended his comrade. "Dale's adviser isn't as proactive as some, but I'm sure he's got a handle on it. Dude's really smart." Feeling that he should express his thanks, Dale looked up from the article he was trying to read, but Ron was leaning against a counter, facing away. Then he turned around, smiling like an insurance agent who had just sold a policy. "Anyway, I'm sure Dale's eager to talk with you guys, so I'll let you go. Here he is."

As he handed over the phone, he and Dale used their other hands to briefly rub each other's crotch through their shorts. It was almost rote, now that others' eyes were omnipresent. Foucault's panopticon, thought Dale, though maybe it was different. He should look that up.

Deep breath. "Hi, Mom and Dad." He moved to the front porch, as far from inquisitive ears as the phone's signal reliably reached.

"Hi, Dale." And so it began. "What were you doing? I'm glad we caught you at home. Your mother thought you might be at the library."

"I was just sitting on the couch, reading an article." That could lead in the wrong direction. "For school."

"For your prelims?"

"Yeah, I guess so. But it might come in handy for other things. It's pretty interesting. It's about psychology."

"So, Dale, Ron says that your adviser—what's his name? Collins?—isn't very proactive. Is that right?"

"Yeah, Dad. Collins is a bit laidback. But it's okay. I'll make sure that everything gets scheduled."

"Laidback, huh? I guess that means lazy. I just want you to be sure you get your degree on time."

"Somehow in the past 28 years, I hope I've learned to manage my life."

"Well, Son, it did take you a little longer to get out of college."

"Dad, almost everyone takes five years these days. And no one here thinks I'm taking a ridiculous amount of time. So how're things with you guys?"

Of course, nothing was different—not in their lives, not in their attitudes. The seasons just rotated. Actually, Dale could tell from the additional stiltedness that *something* had changed for his parents, but each of them felt too uncomfortable to talk about Bonobo. His folks apparently feared even to reference the same semantic domain, so for once they didn't put him on the spot about a girlfriend. By the time Dale finally said good-bye and hung up, it was unimaginable that he and his parents would ever discuss his famous creation. And this was a relief.

He returned the phone to its charger. Then he crossed the 'loving room,' where he saw Garrett productively reading and taking notes in the Barcalounger and Jennifer dozing on the couch with her short skirt riding up her toned thighs, revealing the whitish panties covering her crotch—safe and secure, because of him. He'd like to slide in and out of her tonight. He started to get hard at the thought.

He walked up to his room, found his backpack, and threw in his notebooks and journal. He needed to spend some time in isolation at the library to plan out his future, without distractions. His parents had left him with a vague dissatisfaction about being diverted from his dream, his sole plan, of becoming a professor. He skittered down the stairway.

The bulletin board by the front door listed upcoming events and the ever-changing rules. Above it, a banner that was laser-printed across several sheets of paper read: "Welcome to Bonobo House: Home of the Golden Rule." Some jester had scrawled underneath, "But not Golden Showers." He reflexively shook his head before catching himself. Some people had no intuition about the ephemeral and the indelible.

As he strode out of the house and across the dusty yard toward campus, Dale's mind shifted to finding a topic for his research and creating a timeline for his exams. He had several hours before he would need to return for that night's Pile. At 7 pm, the doors would be closed, the blinds lowered, and the sentry posted.

A FISHY OFFER

Fall Semester, 1993

John "Johnny" Fish was a friend of Ron's parents from back in the 1960s, when they all had sincerely committed themselves to countercultural ideals in ways that wouldn't jeopardize their trust funds. Much more recently, Fish had read the reprinted article about Bonobo in the Taos alternative weekly, and, seeing Ron's name, wondered whether this was the little boy he had tolerated at read-ins and marches. The tyke's ability to fill a diaper had inspired Johnny to dub him "Doo Doo Ron Ron."

Fish had attained moderate fame as an idiosyncratic venture capitalist with a penchant for supporting utopian projects: off-the-grid co-housing in the desert, for example. He found Ron's parents through mutual friends and gave them a call. Was their son one of the leaders of this Bonobo movement? They were proud to tell one of their old friends, who shared an understanding of what really mattered, that indeed it was their Ron. Johnny told them that he would like to talk with Ron and his friend about what they were doing, so they gave him the number of the Bonobo House. Ron's father immediately telephoned his son to let him know that Fish might call; instead he got Dale, whom he regaled with the tale of Johnny's relations with Doo Doo Ron Ron. As far as Dale could tell, Fish was simply an old family friend who had emerged from the woodwork, like so many other curious people, once Bonobo became known nationwide.

But Johnny Fish was different: he had a plan. When Ron called him back—and after reminiscing about interactions that Ron couldn't remember—Johnny asked him, "What's next?"

Ron and Dale had asked themselves (but not each other) the same question and had even joked lightly with each other about it, mostly riffing on the idea of opening franchises, establishing their own country, or inhabiting bonobo exhibits in zoos. It was an uncomfortable topic because, to Dale at least, there was no reason to end Bonobo, or his involvement with it, once he left graduate school, except that it just seemed like the sort of thing that ended that way. In fact, he could start another chapter wherever he found a job, although doing so might hurt his chances of getting tenure. On the other hand, his need to do a year of dissertation fieldwork posed a more immediate challenge to Bonobo's continuance. At the same time, an overt discussion with Ron about Bonobo's future could lead to a concrete plan that he might regret and to an admission of what was now obvious to all: he and Ron were in charge. So they avoided confronting the future while enjoying the present.

"The same, but better," Ron answered Fish's query.

Johnny Fish didn't care about Dale and Ron's future; he wanted to shape The Future. Now he saw the opportunity that he had hoped for. He said that he would like to fly to Tucson to talk with them about a business proposal—just Ron and his partner from the article. "Don't worry—I'm not trying to get laid."

So Dale and Ron spent a couple of hours in the library, searching for clues to help them predict Johnny's mysterious plan. Would he want them to endorse a brand of condoms? How would they split the profits?

When Fish arrived, he drove his rental car to the house, arriving twenty minutes early, and honked. Once Dale and Ron were in the car, away from the other Bonobans, Johnny introduced himself. They shook hands like squares. The friendly exchanges continued during the short drive to a Mexican restaurant that Johnny already had chosen. Between ordering and eating, he got up to greet the manager in his office, along with a couple of his family members who were working the cash register and supervising the waiters. When Fish returned to the table, he smiled, "They call me Juan Pez. Some go so far as to call me El Pez-idente." He leaned forward a little. "I think they mean it as a compliment."

After lunch, exuding a strange intensity, Fish unveiled his plan. He thought the "boys" had a great idea that deserved to be pursued, for the lessons it might teach humanity. He liked to support such experiments as part of his legacy. These projects were his children. Like a parent, he wanted to ensure that they could develop to fully express their own potential, and he also wanted them to be able to support themselves within this fucked-up world.

He had concerns about the boys' ability to sustain the Bonobo movement. The problem wasn't Dale and Ron, who had done an impressive job of nurturing Bonobo—much longer than most communes had lasted back in the 1960s. The problem was that, for understandable reasons meant to protect their health, there was no mechanism to spread the experience. Moreover, their committed cadres, being students for the most part and mobile in any case, were likely to disperse and, once away from the group, normalize. Bonobo's viability in the long run as an inescapable organizing principle of society was thus impossible to evaluate. And what would happen when Ron and Dale graduated and wanted to live like full adults, with incomes that reflected their education and achievements? This project held too much promise to leave it in such a precarious position.

Now, he knew that the magazine article had sparked nationwide interest in "nerdy orgies." And he imagined that Bonobo Clubs or some other distortion of their idea had sprung up, with little likelihood of longevity or of transforming society. Most of them probably just wanted to get their rocks off in a transgressive fashion. But he appreciated that Dale and Ron understood that Bonobo had to be an all-day, every-day commitment and that the goal, again, was to transform people's lives and the very structure of society.

Wow, thought Dale, he really gets it. This was Dale's first real, direct discussion of Bonobo with an authority figure. He felt flattered—and vindicated—that such an imaginative, successful, and well-known person validated his idea and their efforts. But what was Fish's offer?

The plan Johnny announced—not exactly an offer yet—was to use his capital, connections, and expertise to establish what we now know as ¡Bonobo!®. He put it smoothly, even gently, but he made it clear that he could do this without Dale, Ron, or both. Of course, that's not what he wanted. In fact, he wanted only to help them get started, and he would be happy if they quickly became "effectively autonomous." The "truly exciting part of this opportunity"—a phrase that Dale failed to recognize as a mask for 'the part you might find the most questionable'—"is that we've found the perfect location." It was an island off the coast of Playatlán, Mexico.

What? Why? That's bizarre-bitrary, thought Dale.

"You boys have heard of Playatlán, I assume."

"Yeah, you can't miss the posters around campus for Spring Break trips," Ron said. "But I've never had the pleasure."

Dale shook his head. "Same here."

Johnny continued. The island was owned—"more or less; it's complicated"—by none other than the Mexican patriarch of the family who owned the restaurant in which they were sitting. (I learned later that this esteemed gentleman was widely rumored to launder drug money.) Having an island to themselves would help Bonobo to control "comings" (his tone suggested no pun) "and goings," which was vital for protecting everyone's health. It also would allow them some privacy from prying eyes; great autonomy from local society, including protests by "nationalists or religious zealots"; and thus an excellent opportunity to develop and study Bonoban relations away from the contamination of "normal, fucked up society." Finally, what set this tropical island apart from, say, an isolated compound in the middle of the Nevada desert, was that tourists—"or pilgrims, if you prefer"—would actually want to visit, thus allowing the resort "to sustain itself financially while transforming dick-brained dilettantes into committed cadres" of the Bonoban revolution.

To Dale this proposal was overwhelming. Here was someone, out of the blue, flattering him and offering to hand him his future on a silver platter. But it was threatening to think that Fish was willing to commandeer—and commercialize—the movement. The idealistic graduate student in Dale recoiled at the compromises built into the plan, and it irked him that Fish presented it as a fait accompli, rather than as a first draft that they could refashion in collaboration. How could someone who had never even participated in Bonobo take such liberties? Still, the proposal had beguiling aspects ...

Fish gave the boys exactly two weeks to decide, but, he twinkled, "I'd understand if you wanted less time." He flew home.

The offer provoked Dale and Ron into talking with each other more directly than ever before. Previously, Dale hadn't known whether Ron was brashly honest or simply blustering as a façade. Now his comrade revealed more of his calculations. In short, Ron was all in: Fish's plan and all. Bonobo worked for him, at least for now. He was happy; he faced challenges with equanimity; he enjoyed the sex and friendships; maybe it really could help others. Plus, he found he enjoyed managing things, which is what they, or at least he, would be doing. That would look good on a résumé, if he ever changed directions. An uncertain academic career "blew" in comparison. He had applied to graduate school because he didn't know what else to do; now he did.

Dale thought, Really? Is that it? Can Ron's life be that straightforward? Should mine be? He still dreamed of becoming a professor. He liked thinking about big issues and impressing others while helping them to understand. He trusted that an arrow of influence led from academic publications and the college classroom to significant changes throughout society. Most of all, when he daydreamed about the future he saw himself leading an academic life. His parents did, too.

But he wasn't blind. The lives of only a few professors matched his daydreams. Further, only a couple of the program's recent graduates had obtained prestigious positions, and who knew whether they'd get tenure? Many others were teaching for a pittance without job security or time to conduct research. They looked haggard.

Like Ron, he enjoyed the automatic sex and friendships of Bonobo. And, although he sometimes felt wistful about romancing girls, it was easy to remind himself how painful and even humiliating his many attempts and few relationships had been. Bonobo seemed to work for him, too. But was he missing something valuable? Shouldn't he strive more? Yet both he and Ron were progressing in a top-tier graduate program. Perhaps Bonobo really did offer an easier way to achieve—the opposite of Victorians who thought successful people had to divert their sexual energies into building railroads. Wasn't this worth demonstrating to the world? Maybe he could find a way to report his research on Bonobo once it was relocated to Mexico. Maybe he would win a MacArthur Genius Grant.

But what if ~~he~~ they failed? Could he get back on the academic train? According to the college catalog, he could take leave for up to a year. He knew of cases in which this had been extended by a couple of years, but that was iffy.

He was pretty sure that, if he accepted Fish's offer, his friends and professors would lose all respect for him—not because of the sex, but because the revamped project would incorporate insidious aspects of the dominant paradigm: hierarchy (he and Ron would be managers; other Bonobans would be workers), commercialization within capitalism, colonialism (setting up in Mexico), phallocracy, and probably more. His parents might finally disavow him completely.

On the other hand, what would all those people think if he gave up a chance to run a fascinating and important model community—if he gave up control over his own movement? How would they weigh his heroic humility and self-actualization versus this colossal failure to seize an opportunity—especially if he didn't even get a professorship? Would he end up a sad footnote, like the guys who rejected IBM's offer to develop DOS? It was *Dale's* idea and *Dale's* movement (okay, his and Ron's).

He didn't confess all of these considerations to Ron—far from it. Instead, he emphasized his abstract commitment to the promise of better social relations. Beyond that, he clearly implied that he and Ron should retain something like their current roles (theory and praxis, respectively, as Ron joked). He expressed concern that, even though Johnny Fish's track record supporting alternative social relations was impressive, he might get tempted into maximizing profits at the expense of the movement's core principles.

Ron agreed. Certainly he felt no special relationship to Johnny.

Finally, they made a pact to discuss every issue together in private in order to present a united front to Fish or to any other friend or foe.

These deliberations took several days, with "the boys" meeting in cafés away from Bonobo to avoid making their conspiracy obvious to the other Bonobans.

Ultimately, while Dale and Ron have left their mark on the design and operation of ¡Bonobo!, Johnny Fish set many of the basic parameters within which they acted. Over the next few years, whenever Dale wanted to claim credit or had to confront a problem, this simple fact nibbled away at his contentment.

PASSING THE TEST

Dale and Ron did finish their preliminary exams. Ron expressed the common anxieties about his work and resentments toward faculty members as he labored for three weeks over the take-home essay portion. The exam committee gave no hints afterward about the quality of his performance. When he met with them for the oral exam, he sweated, stumbled verbally, and distracted himself by imagining how he would announce this failure to his family and friends. But after he passed he saw the humor of it all and felt a filial bond to the committee members, who joined him for a congratulatory beer at a bar down the street from the Anthropology Building. The process wasn't like having sex together (for example, most of it was excruciating), but the aftermath shared some features.

That took place during Fall semester, 1993, not long after Dale and Ron had accepted Fish's offer. Dale's exams took another semester to orchestrate. Before the advent of Johnny Fish, Dale had finally decided to focus his dissertation on sexual relations and modernity among young Brazilians in Fortaleza, a city favored by study-abroad programs. Apparently, a fairly stable group of local young men had sex with the ever-changing horde of visitors. In layman's terms, Dale wanted to know why they did this, how it fit with and affected their perception of their place in the world, how other locals perceived and treated them, what they got from the visiting students besides sex, and how this experience altered the long-term course of their lives.

At least, that's what he claimed, and, in one part of his mind, he sincerely prepared to do it. But, while the scene in Fortaleza certainly wasn't Bonobo, getting ready for this research helped him to study it, too. For Dale had written notes in his journal on all Bonobo gatherings since their inception. Some parts read like diary entries: "Cold hands again—not cool!" But he composed the great majority like ethnographic observations: who did what with whom and in what context. He also ventured hypotheses, preliminary analyses, and questions to ponder regarding the course of Bonobo, often with reference to his readings in sexuality. Of course, this research violated a rule that he had helped to formulate and enforce, so he was careful to keep it secret.

One of his best ideas from this period—maybe his Second Great Idea—was porn versus drama. Not surprisingly, he usually equated Bonobo with porn, but not because of their shared association with sex. Indeed, for people like me, any experience with Bonobo would have been more 'dramatic' than 'pornographic.' Here's the difference: he realized that pornographic films held no real suspense or surprise for the viewer. In 99 percent of the cases, the guy in a porno would have great sex and then ejaculate. The same comforting predictability was true of other entertainment that Dale labeled porn, such as a *Better Homes & Gardens* photo spread, a favorite film that someone watched multiple times, the retelling of a fairy tale, a hit song on the radio, a cooking show, or friends reminiscing about a shared experience. Such productions were bereft of surprise and suspense, but they greatly satisfied a lot of people. (I would add that porn in this sense was the most popular form of entertainment worldwide.)

Drama had an unknown ending and thus tension, suspense. This was the model of entertainment almost anyone in Dale's circles would claim to favor; it had such prestige that, for many people, it was unquestionably desirable.

The difference between drama and porn wasn't in the production but in the experience of it. *Star Wars* thrilled many viewers the first time they saw it, but some kids just kept watching it, to the point that they could recite the lines. For these recidivists (including yours truly) the film had gone from thrilling drama to comforting, predictable porn. Conversely, Andy Warhol's film of a sleeping man had no plot, tension, or suspense; this contrast with ordinary films made it thrilling (dramatic) for many to watch, at least for a while. In general, drama possessed the potential to deliver more-intense pleasure than porn, but deeper disappointment was possible, too. So porn was a safer bet.

Dale saw that these categories of experience were ideal types—rarely if ever present in pure form but perhaps useful for organizing thoughts. Most aesthetic experiences would fall somewhere between the two, or possibly not fit very neatly anywhere on the scale. For example, many viewers found *Star Wars* on its first release to be *mostly* dramatic and a special-effects wonder, but in many ways the film deployed hackneyed devices that made it comforting (white = good; black = evil) and predictable (the happy ending): that is, pornographic.

Finally, Dale extended these ideas to characterize other domains of experience. Thus, his routine with Bonobo had become highly pornographic because it was formulaic and provided daily satisfactions. Overall, it was clear that Dale grew to desire a balance of porn and drama that included more drama. Yet Bonobo, and the prestige of leading it, worked well enough that he couldn't leave its comforts for the uncertainty of academia.

While Dale developed this contrast in his journal, he had no appropriate vehicle for expressing it publicly. Because of the group's no-research rule, he couldn't write an article about its application to Bonobo. If he were to describe the concept in conversation, someone else might appropriate it, or it could spread locally like a slang term, robbing him of credit for his intellectual property. So he speculated in his journal how the porn/drama concept might apply in Fortaleza, in case he actually did that fieldwork someday. Could that be his ticket to guruhood?

Anyway, two obstacles seemed to doom Dale's desire to even take his prelims. First was Collins' lethargy, which retarded the scheduling by months. Second, it became general knowledge among the faculty, after Ron's exams, that he and Dale were planning to open the ¡Bonobo! resort. Some professors thought, Why go through the hassle of orchestrating Dale's exams, if he plans to abandon the program? Dale asked himself the same question many times. Then he thought of the pressure from his parents, who still didn't know about the resort. And he considered that he might want to return to his studies, if ¡Bonobo! didn't pan out financially or emotionally. Plus, he felt a lot of inertia toward this academic goal, and he wanted a capstone to his years of studies. Finally, without admitting it to himself, perhaps he hated the prospect of achieving less than Ron, whom he considered to be his junior partner.

Then Dr. Helen Rodasky adopted him. Rodasky presented herself as a free-thinking rebel even compared to other anthropologists. Legends of her sexual exploits with graduate students and other faculty members over the years had led Dale and others to masturbate to her (mentally airbrushed) image: the tight black turtleneck, exotic jewelry, and intense eyes. Dale had taken a course from her two years before but doubted that she remembered his name.

One day, to his utter surprise, Rodasky accosted him in the hallway of the Anthropology Building and invited him into her office. Where others might have posted a diploma, a Papuan penis sheath hung on the wall. She asked about his plans (Dale's answer focused on the official, academic program) and then about his progress toward taking his prelims. Sensing the truth behind his vague response, she told him that Collins was a "lazy bastard" and offered to serve on Dale's committee, to ensure that he had a chance to take his exams. Dale accepted.

"Have you considered studying your Bonobo group, instead?" Rodasky asked. Dale was taken aback; this, oddly, was the first time that a professor had spoken to him substantively about Bonobo. "Your proposed work in Brazil does seem interesting—and possibly you can make it innovative—but what you're doing here is intrinsically fascinating. It would be a real challenge to anthropology as we know it."

Dale didn't want to alienate his new benefactor by seeming analytically timid, but, as he told her, he could hardly expect to get permission from a Human Subjects Committee.

She suggested that at least he could study himself, as part of the self-reflexive turn in anthropology. But he recoiled before he could even think consciously about the suggestion. Plus, he reminded himself that he would never complete any dissertation; he had another fish to fry. He told Rodasky that it was a flattering suggestion but politely demurred.

She nodded in imagined comprehension. Then she picked up the phone on her desk and, looking Dale in the eye, called Collins and told him that Dale had asked to add her to his committee. "Let's schedule his written exam as soon as possible. ... I don't think we need to waste time arranging a meeting"—she rolled her eyes for Dale's benefit—"I'm sure we can do this through email. I'll send a message to everyone once we hang up. If anyone doesn't answer by tomorrow at noon, I'll call them. ... All right. I look forward to getting your reply."

A grateful Dale already was thinking of how to vandalize her office.

Ultimately, it wasn't so quick or easy as Rodasky had made it seem, but, months after Ron's success, Dale completed his exams. The committee members shook his hand and wished him luck, without referring to Bonobo and hardly mentioning his false dissertation project. Dr. Randall, a Brazilianist, did say that the project had merit, should he have the opportunity to pursue it. As the other faculty members drifted back to their offices, their duty done, Rodasky invited him back to hers. She told him that Collins should have arranged a post-exam drink, if not a party. Then she said, "I do think your dissertation proposal is interesting, but you have a more consequential project to pursue. I still hope you let the world know what happens. There must be a way." For her, "the world" consisted primarily of academics who would, presumably, transmit the message to the rest of humanity.

Missing the fanfare and celebration that usually marked such a momentous achievement, he again felt the warmth of gratitude rush over him. With great sincerity he thanked her and promised to keep in touch.

Then Rodasky, too, needed to return to work.

Wandering down the hallway of the Anthropology Building, taking a longer route in the hope of running into someone who might congratulate him, Dale felt precarious. After so many years, his academic career was over. Rodasky's words continued to strike him deeply, and he wondered yet again whether he had chosen the correct path. Had he even *chosen* his path? Maybe he should have bucked inertia and asked Rodasky to be his adviser, so he could become a courageous and creative academic like her. But he knew it was too late; the die was cast. Holding his backpack to fish out his sunglasses, he pushed open the exit and strode into a bright, cloudless afternoon—so routine that he hardly noticed. As he walked home, his mind swirled. He felt elated yet alone, as if he had just won a secret Olympics.

Arriving at the Bonobo House, he saw balloons on the door. Above it, a shiny banner read, "CONGRATULA-TIONS," and next to that someone had tacked a sheet of office paper laser-printed with ", Dale!" Inside, his housemates—his true friends, he felt unreservedly for the first time—embraced him happily. They had seen how he had worked for this achievement. He shared the cake they had baked, he shared the beer they had bought, and, that night, he merged his body and what felt like his soul with them. This was right.

THE ONE IN FRONT

Playatlán, Mexico – 1995

"I won't embarrass you by insisting on the Bonobo hand-shake—or 'glandshake,' as some unfortunately call it," Dale told Susana, the latest reporter. She was cute, while gray roots in her reddish-brown hair and tiny trenches radiating from her eyes hinted that she had experience. Writing for a local news-paper, she presented a refreshingly professional demeanor compared to many journalists who had traveled to Playatlán to cover the grand opening of ¡Bonobo! She even wore typical office wear: white nylon slacks through which the unremark-able outline of her panties could be discerned; heels, despite the terrain; and a sheer, shiny blouse that didn't completely ob-scure her bra. He found her instantly appealing, a forbidden fruit for him but probably humdrum for most middle-class Mexicans.

"Actually, it's our policy for journalists," Ron added, "alt-hough, if you're curious, you might be able to find someone here who'll do it anyway."

Was Susana disappointed? Relieved? Maybe she felt con-temptuous. Or maybe she didn't quite understand everything, given the linguistic difference.

"An oral greeting will be good enough."

Cheeky! They all smiled. For a long time now, such comments had struck Dale as irritatingly trite, but coming from unexpected sources freshened them up. He liked her a little more.

Susana expressed curiosity about the changes they had made to the island. When she was in her twenties, she and a few friends would hire a boat to take them there, where they would tramp around, swim, and eat a picnic. "Maybe some people came here to fool around, maybe tourists." She smiled lightly. "Now I guess that this has finished. I can say goodbye to our island and tell our readers what it has become."

For those of you who have awoken recently from a lengthy coma, what this small island off the coast of Playatlán had become was the site of ¡Bonobo!®, a small resort. This privatized playground got its labor from an adjacent utopian community named Real Bonobo (also with an ®), which the resort supported financially. Dale and Ron didn't—and legally couldn't—own the land, but they oversaw the community and resort.

"Do you know the name of this island?"

Of course they did, but, after all, Bonobo is about the Golden Rule, so they let her tell them. As an extra little gift, Dale increased Susana's satisfaction by saying, "I believe the name is La Isla de San Lorenzo."

"That's what it says on the map, but no one calls it that way. Playatlecos call it something different. We call it 'La de Enfrente'—'the One in Front'—because it's in front of that beach." Dale looked east across the glittering water at the broad arc of sand facing them; he could barely discern individual people moving about. Behind them, tiny-looking cars and buses motored along the seaside road, in front of moderately sized, modestly decorated hotels that had seen better days. Susana turned toward the north and pointed at the next island. "That one is 'La de En Medio'—the One In-Between—since it's between this one and the next one. And then there's 'the One Behind.'

She named a few more. Dale appreciated her didactic and animated manner and thought how odd it was that the locals replaced saints' names with sexual positions. But he and Ron had agreed that it was politic to present their neighbors with a relatively sterile, corporate image, so he kept this observation to himself. Eventually, Susana completed that unit of 'morally, this place belongs to me and not you.' She seemed to be entering another lesson when, to get things back on track, Ron said, "You must have quite a few questions and a deadline."

Turning reportorial, Susana confirmed that Dale and Ron were anthropologists. "We have a joke here," she said. "Instead of calling them 'antropólogos,' we call them 'antropófogos.' Do you know what that means? It means cannibals." (A few years later, she told me that joke, too.)

Then she asked Dale and Ron how they had ended up there.

Ron said, jovially, "We went fishing and ended up getting caught." Not only was this an inside joke; it wasn't entirely accurate as an analogy.

Susana cast her own line. "They say that really you are a front for Johnny Fish, or maybe the Coronado family. Is this true?"

"A front? Wouldn't that make us 'los de enfrente'? No wonder we ended up here." Dale's strained, evasionary pun elicited a weak smile, but Susana insisted. Finances—and especially rich benefactors—were Ron's territory, so Dale let him answer.

The resulting article, which I read years later, focused on the process by which a local oligarch—Susana chose to ignore the rumors of money-laundering—had assumed control and apparently ownership of the island, despite the widespread belief that the Mexican constitution made all islands property of the nation. The fact that this tycoon then gave use of the island to a sex resort built and run by Americans was icing on the cake.

Susana was just one of many reporters who visited Bonobo during its inauguration. Apparently, news organizations had an appetite for stories about utopian orgy islands. As a result, Dale was riding high. Millions more people would learn of his experiment; maybe they would start their own Bonoban communities. In interviews he encouraged the curious to spend time at the resort, to experience and discuss in depth the operating principles that they had developed through trial and error. Privately, he thrilled to receive so much attention, especially for something so positive. The compromises inherent in Fish's plan nagged at him, but this was just the beginning. If experience showed that changes were needed, he and Ron could make them as they gained increasing control over the operations.

The articles in U.S. publications invariably mentioned those compromises and the contradictions between the organization of the resort and that of actual bonobos. Most reporters adopted a wry, detached posture toward the entire enterprise, guarding against seeming uncool while avoiding enthusiasm for what was probably a flash-in-the-pan oddity. It was through this distanced, cynical, and quizzical filter that most readers regarded Bonobo. Rock and roll got much the same treatment at its inception.

I read a couple of those early features about the resort. At the time, I had just completed my MA in anthropology at a university in Florida, and, as Dale had feared, I considered him and Ron to be sellouts of both anthropology and utopian ideals. Because I studied Mexico, I enjoyed the occasional opportunity to opine authoritatively on this topic in cafés and at parties. ¡Bonobo!, I said, comforted the jaded by providing "yet another example of the inevitable hegemony of the dominant paradigm, thus naturalizing neoliberal ethics." Further, I noted that the articles left unclear whether it was the journalists or the Bonobans who failed to understand basic anthropological information. For example, was it Dale or was it *Time*'s correspondent who referred to humans as non-apes and to bonobos as "a kind of hippie chimp"?

Despite these concerns, I masturbated many times to fantasies of ¡Bonobo! It was one of my favorite scenarios. If I remember correctly, I pictured awesome, cathartic, and automatic sex—rather than the utopian social relations accruing therefrom.

HARD OPENING

The sweat encasing Dale's naked body reflected the coppery light flickering from the fake tiki torches. He knelt, intense and erect, amid the writhing Pile, waiting for inspiration. To his left, a few couplings over, he saw a visitor—Jake?—thrusting with Susie like sweaty, panting beasts; he sensed catharsis building between them. Crawling over unopened condom packets and then lying on his side, he took Susie's nipple in his mouth and Jake's balls in his hand while he ground his erect dick against their thighs. Jake soon pushed faster, jerked, and moaned. He fell to one side with a whole-body expression of spent contentment ("cumspentment?" Dale wondered). Susie had come too, but only twice.

She rolled onto her back and, her eyelids drooping like a viper, smiled at Dale. "Let's do it bonobo-style. Da-le," she added in Spanish. His dick felt more engorged than he could remember; he was so ready to screw. He picked up and opened a nearby condom package, unrolled the rubber across the bulging veins and ridges on his cock, and pushed inside her. On his knees, he propped his knuckles on the mat next to her petite hips, pinning her in place. His dick felt massive, his body strong and virile. Susie could barely keep her eyes open as she writhed and bucked, played with his nipple and her own, and rubbed her clit, while he churned back and forth, in and out, over and over, until finally his vision turned to starburst, the dam broke, his semen spewed forth into the condom's reservoir tip, and he dropped down to hold Susie in his arms, their sweat bonding them as they felt their chests heave together.

After several moments, they disentangled. "Oh, man, this is the best job ever," Susie said. She playfully shoved his shoulder. "Best boss, too."

Dale needed that release. The grand opening (the "hard opening," as Ron insisted on calling it) had finally ended. After two weeks of interviews, little emergencies, and simply living a new role with new people, Dale had felt frazzled. Now the reporters were gone. Johnny Fish was gone. The first batch of visitors had turned over, and all of the new Bonobans had begun settling into their new lives. With one fantastic, explosive fuck, he'd let it all go.

He and Ron walked together from the open-air Pile pavilion to the office. The cleaning crew was placing the cushions into a rollable bin for decontamination and arranging new ones across the floor. It was 1 AM and felt even later. The crew conversed in muted tones, as did a few pairs of guests who lay in divans around the grounds, looking up at the moon and listening to a quiet lecture on astronomy as the surf crashed against the island.

Everyone was new. Ron was the only fixture in Dale's social universe. All of the original Bonobans back in Tucson had chosen to pursue their own paths. Some expressed anger about Ron and Dale's sellout/power move; some didn't mind or care about it very much; and some from each category kept the original Bonobo House in operation, independent of Ron and Dale's influence. (Over the next few years, it slowly slid from a social experiment to a principled party house.) The newbies at the resort did inappropriate things like call him "boss" after fucking him.

Add to that the anticipated estrangement from Dale's parents—who certainly wouldn't come down and whom he couldn't visit very easily—and his life had changed almost completely. He was far from isolated, but he lacked a comfort zone, situations in which he could go on auto-pilot—it was almost all drama and no porn. It increasingly struck him that this, ¡Bonobo!, constituted his only, really-real life.

As they walked, Dale could hear the chugging of a few small fishing boats crossing from Playatlán to the more productive waters on the other side of the islands, along with the thin thump of distant discos. He looked over the wall to the mainland and saw the lights of far-off hotels, nightclubs, and cars moving along the coastal road.

Undoubtedly, people sat along Playatlán's shore or danced in its beachfront discos and gazed out at ¡Bonobo! Probably they envy me, Dale thought. Maybe they'll try to copy us. Hmm. Would it be because of globalization, or maybe out of the universal need we're addressing? It'd be interesting to study.

He and Ron chatted about mundane tidbits, ensuring that no Executive Decisions had to be reached before the next day. They entered the boxy administrative building, which sat on the border between the resort and the workers' quarters (aka Real Bonobo). Across the spacious workroom, Ron's office door was on the right and Dale's on the left. Arched between them hung a wooden banner that read, "Thanks for the Fish." This misquote (and misinterpretation) reminded them to appreciate their luck yet stay true to their ideals.

Dale's rule was to return to his office each night and close the door, exiting perhaps an hour later. Ron never asked why. He took his leave, rubbing his hand briefly on the crotch of Dale's shorts. "Well, that's all done."

Dale returned the frottage. "Yeah, what now?"

"More of the same—only better." Ron grinned.

Loose with fatigue, Dale slapped the banner with his right hand as he unlocked the office with his left. "Good night," he yawned.

"Good morning," Ron corrected him. "It's already tomorrow."

PART II

BONOBO – A MEMOIR

SMILING WHITE GUYS

1998

Lightning might strike you out of the blue sky, even if you're standing under a shelter; then again, you might walk across an open field carrying a metal rod in a thunderstorm, screaming, "Here I am, Lord," and not get fried. So it was that my adviser, of all people, laid me without warning, whereas Ron and Dale kept me from ¡Bonobo! for almost a year.

When I first met them, in late summer, I had been living in Playatlán for about two months. Doris had expected me to contact them as soon as I arrived, but, as much as I fantasized about ¡Bonobo!, I wanted to find my own way in local society. This perverse predilection was only bolstered by my concern that associating with Dale and Ron would somehow taint me in locals' eyes. (It did.) Ultimately, I doubt that they could have helped me much anyway, given their isolation.

It took some time to find an apartment and equip it, to introduce myself to local intellectuals and hint that I would like to find work, preferably at a university, and to plan and begin my routine of research. Simply meeting with Playatlecos was incredibly time-consuming: finding their actual telephone numbers, reaching them (answering machines made no sense to most people, since anyone who really wanted to contact them would keep calling), arranging a time to meet, and waiting for the other person to actually arrive, either late or never. Including the time it took to recuperate from eating the wrong taco at a sidewalk stand, I passed a month simply moving in.

Contacting Dale and Ron was even harder than making an appointment with a potential landlord. Cellphone service certainly didn't extend out there, and I didn't have a marine radio, which was one way to reach them. They had a website—one of the first for a business in Playatlán—but I, like almost everyone else in town, didn't have regular access to the Internet for email. Plus, I wanted them to read the letter from Doris, which I thought would persuade them to meet with me. I saw two options: either identify which boats serviced Playatlán and hand the letter to a crew member, hoping that s/he would actually deliver it to the right person, or, crazily, send the letter to the postal address in town that was listed on their website. I tried the latter, and, amazingly, it worked. Ron wrote me back, suggesting that we meet at Café Océano on the Plazuela Manchado downtown. If I couldn't make it, I should leave a message with one of the café's workers, and Ron would call me to set up another time. He and Dale occasionally came to town for business, so we would have plenty of opportunities to connect. They were eager to hear more about Doris, and they had a mysterious request of me.

Up to that point, I hadn't had many straightforward communications in Playatlán, so Ron's clarity was refreshing.

Playatlán is a city of about 300,000 people on the Pacific coast of Mexico, in the state of Conaloa. Actually, no one knew the population, thanks to widespread rumors, even among census-takers, that the latest count had been manipulated to favor the state capital, Culichitlán. Playatlán lay one smidgen inside the tropics and 750 miles south of the U.S. border. I had chosen it as a field site because it was a center of drug trafficking, like the rest of Conaloa, and because it was home to various bands and even to a couple of genres of popular music that had become associated with drug traffickers, or narcotraficantes. For Americans west of the Mississippi—especially for underage drinkers during Spring Break—Playatlán was an inexpensive beach resort. At the junction of the Sea of Cortés and the Pacific, it also hosted a large fishing fleet and a decaying cargo port. And, in addition to the usual government bureaus, universities, and other offices and shops found in cities of its size, it was the home of popular brands of beer and coffee.

Café Océano sat downtown. This area had seen much better days, as many of its opulent old buildings from the nineteenth century now lay abandoned in different states of ruin or were occupied but on their way to ruin. Many of the newer structures were grungy concrete cubes. It was refreshing to see any older building reanimated by a recent coat of paint, and many of these were clustered around the Plazuela Manchado. Most of this small, rectangular park was paved, but trees and other greenery grew within designated spaces behind low, white fences. Visitors sat on the benches scattered around the paved area.

Ron and Dale might have liked the Café Océano per se, but they also might have wanted to signal to me that they were bona fide locals. Or maybe they gazed at Playatlán from their island and daydreamed of more-ethnographic surroundings. My bona fides as a local-like foreigner went far beyond visiting a tourist-friendly restaurant-bar (that is, I subsisted on a tight budget and lived in a dump), so I would have been happy to meet at a resort, especially if they were buying.

Speaking of which—here, free of charge, is a tip for improving the chances that others will foot the bill: show up after them. If I had arrived before Dale and Ron, I would have had to pick a table and order a drink, preempting the possibility that they might explicitly offer to buy my drinks as I sat down.

On my budget, such mundane machinations determined the quality and quantity of food, drink, sex, or anything else I might purchase. Arriving first, I would order the vilest beer available and nurse that one glass until the check came; arriving last, I *might* be granted the opportunity to indulge myself. This strategy had roots in Biblical exegesis, what with the last being first and whatnot. Anyway, conditions in Playatlán afforded so many plausible excuses for tardiness that arriving fifteen minutes late might make me the early bird, the responsible one. However, these gringos might have different expectations, so I kept it to ten minutes.

Thus, after exiting the bus at the market several blocks away, I strode directly to the plaza. It was mid-afternoon—siesta time—and blazingly hot. I quickly confirmed that no one was sitting at the outside tables. Turning to enter the doorway, I saw ... blackness. After a few seconds, my pupils had dilated enough to make out the long wooden bar, the alcoholic Vietnam vet on a stool, the dormant projection TV, the impassive bartender, and last, at a small, round table in the darkest recess, two tanned, attentive, relaxed, and smiling white guys.

Blecch.

I walked over to them. "I'm going to make a wild guess: are you Ron and Dale?"

"Very good, Grasshopper. But which is which?" After all the publicity they had generated, and seeing Doris' photos, this wasn't such a challenge. Ron was the one who seemed a little shorter, was more direct in his bearing, and didn't put me on the spot by asking this question. He also wore khakis, a polo shirt, and loafers, apparently by choice. Sunglasses were propped on his forehead. Dale wore blue jeans, huaraches, a leather belt, and a short-sleeved button-down with his sunglasses in the pocket. This was the vanguard of the revolution.

It wasn't clear whether Dale's question was rhetorical. "I'll take another wild guess and say that you're ... Dale."

"Amazing! You may sit." I did. "I spared you a joke about Chip and Dale, and another about Chippendales, so you owe me. Nonetheless—what are you having?"

Score!

At first, we had an easy-going conversation about the beer; about Doris (I didn't mention doing her); about how coming ashore, even for business, was like a vacation for them; and other chit-chat. Although I knew that they hadn't quite reached as far in their academic careers as I had and that they had been out of the game for a few years, they seemed like senior colleagues to me. Maybe it was because they were coeval with my adviser—though they were only about five years older than me—or because of their positions and notoriety, or the fact that they were paying, but I caught myself deferring to them and even desiring to please them.

So, when they asked about my research, I wanted to impress. But which side of them—the former academics or the utopian entrepreneurs? I told them that my fieldwork focused on how drug trafficking and popular culture had mutually constituted each other in counterhegemonic discourses vis-à-vis the state's attempts to impose and simultaneously create consensus around a sanitizing discourse in line with a cosmopolitan imaginary of modernity that existed nowhere in practice, yet both the state's imaginary and this opposition permeated each other in ways that went beyond vulgar dialectics. "For example, I'm studying songs about drug trafficking and comparing them to popular music that gets on TV." I threw in a few sentences like that to reassure them that I wasn't lost in a fog of theory.

Ron and Dale expressed as much interest and support as I could reasonably expect. To my hidden irritation, they saw "Doris' fingerprints" all over the theoretical approach. Speaking seriously, Ron urged me to be careful: "You don't want anyone to wonder whether you're a DEA agent."

"Study the songs, but don't become a lyric," Dale added.

They wondered about my living arrangements. I had walked around Playatlán and talked with contacts in search of a neighborhood in which I a) observed a lot of the things I planned to study, b) could afford to live, and c) felt less likely to be murdered. Colonia No Reelección fit the bill, from the drug distributors on the corner and brass bands practicing in buildings, to the moderate-sized market selling, among other things, baseball caps and belt buckles with marijuana and AK-47 symbols. This neighborhood bordered the oceanfront boulevard, and adventurous foreign tourists occasionally ended up in its restaurants. The same could not be said of some other areas that locals had warned me against.

My landlord was the gruff proprietor of a metalworking shop, which unfortunately occupied the part of his house that abutted mine. When he had work, it was noisy. Nonetheless, I couldn't see any way that his job might directly involve him with drug trafficking, which was reassuring. The downside was that his semi-precarious financial position led him to give me the 'amigo price' on the rent; that is, as I learned later, he overcharged me. The amigo price hurt me more than most Mexicans could imagine. They assumed that all white Americans had money to burn, whereas actually I was financing my research with a few small grants. Once those funds ran out, I would resort to credit cards or student loans.

I didn't lay out the entire sob story to the guys, but I did communicate that I was living locally and that my limited finances dictated this situation almost as much as my research topic did. A couple of times, as I yammered on about my plans to interview a cross-section of society and to observe a cross-section of entertainment and consumption, Dale and Ron looked at each other meaningfully. Were they ready to leave? Did they think I was a genius? Had I resolved a doubt about the pronunciation of Culichitlán? It was disquieting.

As I discussed my situation, Lázaro, an acquaintance who worked at the nearby historical museum, entered the bar, apparently just to greet the bartender. I already had learned that, in such a situation, I should drop everything and go to greet my acquaintance, so I did. Otherwise, he might think I was snubbing him. Moreover, I wanted to ingratiate myself with him, in case he could help me obtain work at the museum or the state university, where he sometimes taught courses. We exchanged greetings, and he asked what had brought me there. He clearly wanted an introduction to Ron and Dale, but I was enjoying Gringo Time, and I thought that the guys hadn't signed up for the lengthy commitment (in broken English, I feared) that inviting Lázaro to drink entailed. To excuse myself in the face of Lázaro's unspoken expectation, I told him that we were involved in a business meeting; maybe when we were done, if Lázaro were still around, we could all hang out and drink together. Lázaro knew as well as any Mexican that a drink deferred is a drink denied, that mañana never comes. Of course, he accepted my excuse with outward equanimity. But it was entirely possible that he would interpret this unspoken rebuff to his unspoken desire as a direct affront. In that case, he might describe me to mutual friends as presumptuous and otherwise work to ruin me.

If so, I still made the right call. When I returned to the table, Ron and Dale were not, to my surprise, preparing to leave. Instead, they got down to business. As when Dale had his One Great Idea, they had little inkling of how profoundly their proposal would change our lives. "Nat," Ron said, "we find you appropriate, and we'd like to offer you paid work. You could help us solve a problem, and we can help you cover your expenses."

"Mutual aid—it's the Bonobo Way," Dale added. "Don't worry; it won't stop you from pursuing your research, which sounds interesting. We know you didn't come here to study ¡Bonobo!"

"In fact, we wouldn't need you if you lived on the island with us. We need eyes and ears here in Playatlán."

I nodded and tried to appear engaged and curious rather than desperate and confused.

Ron looked at Dale. "Maybe we should say what the job is."

"That does seem appropriate. But maybe we should have described the job earlier, several sentences ago. We might have missed the chance."

"Then I see two options: either we try it now and determine whether we have the resilience to succeed in the face of such adversity, or we start the conversation again and describe the job at its optimal moment." Apparently this was Tantric conversational foreplay for them.

"Ron, I concur. And, at the risk of seeming precipitous, I will suggest without further ado that we pursue the former course of action, pending your agreement."

"I do agree. Nat, do you wish to share your perspective?"

By now, I was leaning back my chair, with my arms folded and a bemused expression on my face. "I don't have a curfew. Maybe we should just start again at the beginning, just to show our commitment to excellence."

"He's called our bluff, Dale. And we do have a curfew."

So they told me that they would like me to perform a little investigative work for them. Someone had been vandalizing their resort at night. Thus far it was infrequent and inconsequential—splatters of paint, tiny explosions, condoms containing possibly symbolic objects thrown into the compound, a dead fish left on the dock with "El Pezidente" etched into it—but they would hate for it to escalate. They had another investigator working different angles, but I had a unique position. Plus, even if I didn't find out who was attacking ¡Bonobo!, I could help them understand how the local community viewed them, which undoubtedly would prove useful in the long run. In exchange for, say, quarter-time work, they would pay the rent at my current abode.

My initial reaction was, Money! But, I also wondered, does this mean no orgies at all? Or maybe just when I needed to visit? (Would I need to visit?) And, yes, I quickly considered how the excitement and novelty of conducting an investigation might distract me from my fieldwork.

As these thoughtlets flashed through my consciousness, I knew that I wanted to say yes. Money, possible free sex, a good story to tell my classmates later, and more purpose in my life—it seemed like a no-brainer. And then a brain intervened. But it wasn't mine.

In the brief pause as I, dumbfounded, considered their of-fer, Dale reassured me that they understood that I couldn't ethically mix my investigation with observations for my disser-tation. (My research subjects had to give "informed consent" for me to study them, and, unlike psychologists, anthropolo-gists don't trick people first and explain things later; we had to be open from the start. In my case, my life literally depended on my neighbors trusting that I wasn't a DEA agent.) I should just do the best I could under the circumstances.

I openly appreciated this attitude. And I secretly felt a little embarrassed that the potential ethical conflict hadn't occurred to me immediately.

Ron added that, if at any point I felt compromised, I could withdraw from the investigation. Likewise, they reserved the right to end our deal if I appeared to neglect my duties or if, for whatever reason, they decided to end the investigation. "But," he winked, "I don't see us pulling the rug out from un-der you. We want to help. Doris will know we did right by her."

MAN OF THE PEOPLE

"Don't jump!" I stood on a stone wall that separated the wide sidewalk from a broad beach of soft sand five feet below. Turning from the sea, I saw my friend Raúl—a glib, creative, and unproductive sociologist at the university. Equal parts animation and slack, he was a bit like Baloo, albeit less sentimental. He approached along the walkway. "Please contact the manufacturer for details. No warranty is implied."

"Dios mío—you saved my life! And interrupted my chain of thought. What a great friend." I hopped to the sidewalk and sat on the wall to chat.

"What are you up to, Little Fly?"

"Thinking about my research, and trying to watch a boat pass around that island."

"That island? It's probably some drunkards trying to catch a bonobo fish."

We bantered a while in that vein. Having heard (like so many others) that I'd met with Dale and Ron, he suggested that I must be a reverse primatologist, studying humans in their habitat—which, in a way, I was. It was a quiet evening. The crashing surf, the light breeze, and the scattered clouds in the moonlight calmed my restless heart and instilled it with quiet energy. After maybe thirty minutes, Raúl suggested that we get something to drink nearby.

This was a rare opportunity for me to enter a cantina. Anglo-American tourists think that any Mexican bar is a cantina, but chances are slim that they would recognize a real one as they whizzed past in a taxi. They were rough places. I felt I needed an escort to deter some drunkard from picking a fight with me, and many of my friends—even boogie-board vendors—considered cantinas to be low-class dumps beneath their lofty social standing. Plus, the only women allowed inside were working, so mixed groups never considered entering one.

Raúl, though, was a man of the people, and we headed inland about four blocks to Cantina La Reforma. I had walked past it many times on lonely nights, tempted to join in the sociable din that leaked out of the nondescript, concrete box. I imagined, though, that my entry would spark a scene straight out of a bad Western: everyone would stop talking and watch with hostility as I ambled to the bar and ordered a sarsaparilla. From there to a hanging rope, or more likely a stab wound, would be as short and certain as a walk off the plank.

As we approached the cantina—a sort of men's house—I saw the usual notice painted by the entrance, denying admission to women, minors, and uniformed personnel. We walked through the swinging saloon doors and around the blind that prevented members of the aforementioned groups from observing the bar's patrons as they spent their meager finances on alcohol. Inside, long, weak fluorescent lights cheesed down on about twenty working-class men sitting in plastic chairs around plastic tables or at the bar. The walls and ceiling were painted a washed-out aquamarine and sported a mysterious brown smudge-line at about hip-height. A jukebox playing "Hotel California" competed gamely with conversations among a few men, although about half communed with their own thoughts and their well-nursed beers. Amiable, worn-looking women in miniskirts served drinks, and a trio of middle-aged musicians stood against the wall near the entrance, hoping that customers would pay them instead of the jukebox for a song. It was, in my limited experience, typical.

Raúl spotted a friend who was standing at the bar and gestured for him to join us at the only empty table, a little off from the center of the room. The first sign of trouble was that the friend didn't come when called.

I didn't see his reaction to Raúl's invitation, because I was surveying the room as circumspectly as I could manage. Of course, my interest was ethnographic, but also I didn't want to get killed. Every few days the newspapers carried a story about someone who had last been seen at a cantina but later washed up around the docks with stab wounds. All I saw were men—some darker, some lighter; some with mustaches, some without; some dressed like ranchers, a few like accountants, most like proletarians; some were in their twenties, others in their fifties; all of them looked Mexican—and none of them appeared to be watching me. Reassuringly, no one wore the stiff-looking jeans and silk shirts that I associated with drug-traffickers out on the town.

Raúl told me to wait a second and sauntered over to the bar to greet his buddy more directly. I felt a little exposed as I sat alone at the table, without even a beer to legitimize my presence. Usually I couldn't go anywhere dominated by locals without some stranger addressing me, most often in a friendly fashion. Now I was surrounded by tough-looking, inebriated men who were actively ignoring me. Maybe no one wanted to be the first to sell out to the gringo in their midst, lest he be ridiculed as a traitor; maybe they collectively wanted to signal that this place was for locals only, that the management should add "gringos" to the blacklist by the door; or maybe these men went to cantinas to escape from all the reminders of the daily humiliations they faced, only to see me, a shining example of the most encompassing affront. In the U.S. I was insignificant, but in Playatlán I signified like a motherfucker: I repeatedly learned of the pleasures, hopes, humiliations, and anger that my mere presence provoked.

So there I sat, occasionally looking over at Raúl as he discussed what seemed to be a serious matter with his friend at the bar and gesturing vaguely toward 'our' table. The friend never looked my way, but eventually Raúl led him to the table and sat down. The friend remained standing, hesitant.

"C'mon, man, have a seat. We're among friends. Right, Nat?"

I thought so, at that point. Why wouldn't we be? Was the friend shy? Did he want to go home? Was he waiting for another acquaintance to arrive?

With signs of great reluctance, he sat down, placed his bottle on the table, and nodded a greeting to me. Something about him shouted, 'no handshake.'

"Benito, Nat. Nat, Benito. Benito works at the university, in Social Sciences." I mistakenly assumed that this meant that he was a faculty member or, more likely, on the administrative staff. Later I found out that he operated a hot-dog stand and helped maintain the buildings. A sturdy but slightly flabby man about forty years old, he wore a cream-colored, short-sleeved button-down, which was tucked into his belted black slacks. He apparently had slicked back his remaining hair with some type of tonic. His brown, unfocused eyes were tinged with red. "Benito's a nationalist, Nat, but I explained to him that you're different. You're living here respectfully, learning about our culture."

I tried to acknowledge this description, or maybe praise, without appearing to effect a sales job on Benito.

As Raúl hailed a waitress to take our orders, Benito gazed at the bottle of beer that he had brought to the table. I ordered Océano, mostly because it was brewed in Playatlán. That way, I could support the local economy and local pride, ingratiating myself to anyone present who worked at the brewery. Raúl ordered a Tecate. Then he went to the toilet, leaving me to commune with Benito and his half-empty bottle.

A pregnant pause ensued. Many locals—although certainly not Raúl—could sit comfortably for an hour or more with a bottle and their thoughts, and it appeared that some of the tables around us harbored clusters of such meditative Mexicans. But most described their default state as boredom, so perhaps Benito would welcome a little variety, perhaps a conversation on a novel topic with an American.

For me, a cantina would be a new, valuable place to ask people about my research on drug-trafficking and popular culture, especially since the music being played on the jukebox didn't include popular songs about gangland shootings. Why not? And no likeness of Jesús Malverde, reputedly the patron 'saint' of narcotraficantes, could be seen, even though this neighborhood, where I lived, hosted occasional shootings and home invasions.

But discretion was the better part of research, and I decided to earn some of my pay from Ron and Dale. Could nationalists' anger at ¡Bonobo!'s usufruct of an illegally owned island have provoked them into vandalizing the resort?

I started with a gentle patrol around the topic's perimeter. "Hey, Benito, before Raúl interrupted me, I was watching a boat go around La de Enfrente. Do you know whether they go fishing over there at night?"

Impassive, Benito took a swig and then resumed regarding his nearly empty bottle.

"I mean, it looked like a little fishing boat from the beach over here—not some Party Yacht or whatever. But it just seemed like there would be more than one if it were a good time for fishing. Of course," and here I added a little reminder of Raúl's avowal that I was respectful, "I'm not from here, so I don't really know."

Benito hesitated. Then, looking somewhere between his bottle and me, he said quietly but firmly, "I don't give a fuck for your orgies or your whorish women. Others might bow down to your racist, imperialist country, but why don't you go fuck yourselves with your damned dollars?"

I sensed that he was drunk, but it seemed as though he didn't understand even the basics of my question—perhaps because of the noise? "Look, I've never been to ¡Bonobo!, and I certainly don't approve of the United States' history here in Mexico. I just was wondering about something I saw over there, by the island."

Raúl returned with a couple of beers and looked at Benito. He seemed to guess how the conversation had turned. "C'mon, man. Nat isn't the entire United States."

Benito looked me in the eye and unloaded: "I shit on your country. I shit on your democracy." He banged his bottle on the tabletop and practically shouted, "I shit on your CIA coming here and asking questions. Fuck yourselves." He folded his arms.

Oh, shit—he was one step away from calling me a DEA agent, which was one step from calling me a DEAd man, working for the DOA. Alarmed, I stood up, told Raúl as calmly as possible that I was going home, and, rushing, left some money for the beer I never drank. Without looking at anyone, but sure that everyone was watching me now, I strode out the door and into the night, listening for signs that someone had followed me.

FIREWORKS

I turned right and hurried down the sidewalk toward the ocean and, before that, the road on which I lived. The street around the cantina was dark and quiet, and I wanted to find refuge as quickly as possible. I had gone merely a half block when I heard someone striding fast to catch up with me. Not stopping, I turned my head and saw a short, thin man in jeans and a work shirt. On other nights, with even less provocation, small groups of young men had followed me and made jokes about raping me. Other times, individual guys like the one behind me had trailed me for more than a mile, crossing the street when I did, waiting outside businesses into which I had ducked for protection, always staring at me with menace.

I walked faster. My heart pounded. I feared stopping at my doorway for my keys, so I resolved to continue to the well-lit seaside avenue, where other people's presence might protect me.

I turned my head again. My stalker raised his hand a little, calling in a friendly voice, "Don't worry. I'm a friend."

I kept going. The seaside walkway wasn't far now. "You're not even an acquaintance. Why are you following me?" I called.

"Sorry. I know who *you* are. I just wanted to talk."

"Oh yeah? About what?"

"I was in the cantina just now. That was crazy."

"I'm not a CIA agent. And I'm not gay. And I'm not carrying any more money. And, excuse me, but it's just a little weird for someone to want to talk to me like this." I sounded a little frantic.

Eventually I reached the seaside walkway. Because a group of Mexican teens was hanging out by the Monument to the Women of Playatlán, I stopped near them and agreed to talk to my pursuer. Ultimately, I had no safer option.

He claimed that his name was Carlos. He frequented the same hair salon as I and had heard me describing the basics of my research to the stylist.

I apologized for not recognizing him. In fact, I didn't even recognize him from the cantina.

"Does that happen to you a lot—getting yelled at in cantinas?" He smiled.

"It's not my usual evening activity. It seemed dangerous."

"I bet your heart started beating like fireworks—or maybe bombs."

In fact, my heart was still pounding, although it had begun returning to normal.

Carlos explained to me that he lived for such moments. He called himself an "explosion addict" and argued that everyone else was, too—only they didn't recognize it. We sat on the steps of the monument, and he explained his philosophy. In short, he classified all experience along a continuum from fireworks to quiescence (not his word). People "naturally" sought to maximize internal fireworks; examples might include giving birth, winning the World Cup, having sex with a particular woman for the first time, or simply falling in love. But repetition decreased the intensity of these internal explosions—another kid, another session of the old in-out, and so forth—until the thrill might even disappear. Then people would seek new experiences to restore the booming inside them, just like Michael Jordan had switched to baseball.

Nonetheless, most people most of the time simply endured, existing in a latent phase, flatlining until something exciting happened to them or they saw a chance to make their own fireworks. They called this "boredom," but it was the default state. Most often, the best relief available was to generate a few transitory puffs by doing something vicarious: watching television, gossiping, leering at tourist women on the beach, or maybe catching a confrontation in a cantina. "I have to thank you for that."

"Don't mention it."

"And here we are, chatting, instead of feeling bored at home with almost no signs of life."

"I guess, then, that I should thank *you*."

He used my adventure in the cantina to illustrate that sometimes the internal explosions were more like bombs than fireworks. In such cases, the excitement wasn't an unadorned good, but it wasn't wholly negative, either. "I have a sister who serves drinks at a disco—you know Pago Pago? I thought so. Well, when she got the job, she thought it was so exciting: foreign tourists dancing on tables, the music ... She bragged about it all the time. Now a couple of years have passed, and she fantasizes about robbing banks." He suggested that other Mexicans ended up dreaming about drug trafficking in the same way—it was a plausible avenue to maximum excitement along an otherwise humdrum highway of existence. And, if they died, "it wouldn't be from boredom."

How fascinating! I really didn't know how to react. Who was this guy? "That's interesting. So ... are you at the university?"

"Me? No, not anymore." It turns out that he sold fresh dairy products at a stand in the market in my neighborhood. He had seen me there, too. For a couple of years he had attended the state university, which "cost less than a lunch at McDonald's." But his father suddenly stopped working one day, with no explanation and no attempt to find another job, so Carlos had to quit school and work for his uncle full-time to contribute to the family's finances.

"Wait—so your father just sits at home all day?"

"Yeah, but he goes out each evening to drink beer. Then he comes back."

"Doesn't that go against your theory of explosions?"

"I think he just got so frustrated that he gave up. He's not the only one. Now he's one of the undead—you know, like a zombie in the movies."

By now, my synapses were lighting up like Liberace's Christmas tree. Carlos had given me a valuable gift, which might enrich my research. I requested permission to reference his ideas in my dissertation. This was clearly his intent from the start, and his subsequent comments gave me the strong impression that he hoped to be mentioned prominently in a book. In fact, he urged me to take his picture "for the book," but I didn't have my camera with me. That was a dud.

Eventually, well after midnight, I felt that it was time to walk back home and write some notes about these adventures. Carlos lived in a similar neighborhood a little farther up the coast and inland, so we took leave of each other along the shore. I thanked him for not killing me and told him sincerely that he had given me a lot to think about.

I sauntered to an all-night hot-dog stand and downed two along with a bottle of water. Then I walked the few blocks inland to my home, savoring the stillness, which only my footsteps breached.

It was my habit to write research notes just before going to bed. On busy days—and especially after busy nights—I often wrote mere reminders of the day's events ("Cantina with Raúl—Benito, CIA—Carlos, explosion addict: vicarious thrills

= reason for liking narco corridos"), knowing that I would have to dedicate a large part of the next day to filling out the details. After typing a few lines on my portable computer, I brushed my teeth and lay in bed.

And lay in bed.

And lay in bed.

A gecko on the ceiling, near a corner, twitched. It skittered a short distance. It lay still, like me.

But my mind was in happy, constant motion. In school I had learned to expect moments like my chat with Carlos, when a key informant would suddenly appear and give insight into local experience in a way that, for unknown reasons, most people couldn't. Our encounter left me with a swirling array of questions and topics for exploration.

With my hands behind my head and my eyes aimed at the gecko, I tried to work through them.

Was Carlos right? And, if so, was he right about all humanity or only about other Playatlecos? How could I determine this? At first blush, he had me convinced. Eventually, though, I remembered from school that such metaphors—especially a mixed one like this—inevitably failed to account for all human experience. Indeed, many of them distorted the phenomena that they focused on describing: "pissed off" came to mind. But we inevitably form some sort of model of how things work, so the question ultimately becomes how the model shapes people's lives. Thus there were two main questions to answer: Did other Playatlecos think in the same terms as Carlos? And how did this affect their experience?

That was Academic Nat. Investigative Nat felt excitement (fireworks?), too. I had no indication whether Benito even knew about the vandalism, but his hostility made it clear that nationalists might feel enough righteous anger to attack ¡Bonobo! On the other hand, the extremity of his emotion led me to intuit that nationalists would protest in ways that were more serious, public, and openly symbolic than petty damages known only to the Bonobans. They could get a bigger "bang" if they chose to picket, say, the wet T-shirt contests that were restricted to U.S. spring breakers, yet they didn't do that, either. Nonetheless, whoever was performing the vandalism probably was seeking a thrill. I resolved to put that in my report to Dale and Ron.

Human Nat took longer to work through the implications of Carlos' explosive theory of motivation. As I finally turned onto my side and sought to sleep, I began to consider how well his model described me. Was I addicted to novelty? Hmm, here I was in a new country, seeking out new people and experiences at every turn, after having dumped my girlfriend … Bingo. I wondered whether my life might be better if I adopted Carlos' philosophy, even knowing its analytical weaknesses. People have to make choices somehow.

Over the subsequent months, I occasionally dipped into the local market-building, hoping to take Carlos' picture. In that setting, he looked like an unexceptional, albeit cheerful, variant of 'market vendor,' which meant nearly flatlining. Perhaps looks deceived, or perhaps he wasn't so unique after all.

Anyway, despairing of capturing his philosophy and image together in a photograph, and even more dubious of publishing it, I took a few snapshots just in case and returned a couple of weeks later to show him the developed prints. His eyes sparkled as held up the prints to a neighboring butcher.

TRUE BONOBO

I had two reasons for visiting True Bonobo: solve the crime and get the girl.

Holly was the ~~girl~~ woman. She had established her movement's encampment pretty close to nowhere, but, ironically, not so far from ¡Bonobo! itself. Maybe hatred loves company.

My only company on the way to find her was a taxi driver who was bemused by my destination and stone-faced while negotiating an exorbitant fare. It cost my brothel budget for the week to get dropped off at an unmarked spot on the coastal highway north of town. From there I descended along a dirt footpath through a mix of tropical and desert scrub until I reached a narrow and shallow inland waterway, streaked with a rainbow of industrial effluent. On the other side was a low, thin island that followed the coast. I saw litter marking a path across from me, through acres of coconut palms. I looked to the right and left, hoping to find someone who might verify that I was on the right track, but I was utterly alone. The buzz of insects in the scrub was the only other sign of life under the still blaze of midday. I propped my backpack on my head and waded across.

Once I had trudged up the sandy bank, a vision of paradise confronted me, straight out of a beer commercial. Through the rows and rows of palms, I could see foamy surf crashing into a wide, white beach; the blue-green sea; and tiny, vertical islands of rock jutting out among the far-off waves, stained white with bird shit. As I approached this beach through the coconut palms, I noticed a few tents and lean-tos loitering here and there inside the line of trees.

When I reached the camp and looked around, I detected a fit-looking young man and woman sitting under a tarp and facing the ocean. He was lying back, propped up on his elbows, while she sat cross-legged, reading a worn paperback that I later identified as *Even Cowgirls Get the Blues*. She wore a monotone, light-green bikini, and he sported colorful nylon swimming trunks that extended to his knees.

They looked toward me but apparently found me unremarkable. So I trudged across the hot, shifty sand toward their perch. I noticed that their positioning of the tarp was ill-advised. Half of it served as a roof, and the other half as a back wall. But this back wall faced east, a direction already shaded by the coconut plantation and then the hills and mountains. Its only real effect was to block breezes.

Once I got near enough to them, I said, "Hey."

They each said, "Hey," back. Now we all knew that we all were cool.

"Are you Holly?"

"Yeah. Who are you?"

"I'm Nat."

"Hey, Nat. Cool name—good on your parents. If you're here to visit True Bonobo, I guess we ought to stand up and say hi like true bonobos."

So she and the guy stood up. My heart started pounding light and fast, as I realized that I had committed myself. She put her right hand on my crotch, which had just gotten hard, and with her left hand she guided my right one onto her breast. She moved both for a few seconds as she looked into my eyes, smiling genuinely, and said, "Hi, Nat. This is Toledo."

She stepped aside without releasing my hand. Toledo stepped forward, put his hand on my crotch and gently moved it around, smiled, and told me, "Hola, Nat."

While this was going on, Holly moved my hand onto Toledo's crotch, which was soft, and I briefly mimicked his grip on mine as Holly moved my wrist. I said, "Hola, Toledo," and then he smoothly retracted his hand. Holly did the same with mine, clasping it into her own.

It was over in just a few seconds, but I felt I had broken through.

Holly was still smiling—not in a sexy way, but welcoming. Maybe she always smiled, like the Joker or Vanna White. "I only help virgins. From here on out, you know what to do."

"Cool."

We all sat down, and she asked, "So what's your story, Nat?"

I told her the truth. I was a graduate student in anthropology, doing ethnographic fieldwork for my Ph.D. dissertation in Playatlán. My focus was on the narco culture and not getting killed. I had heard a lot about ¡Bonobo! of course, and then I found out about True Bonobo, so I thought I'd check it out. I didn't know whether she was familiar with anthropology, but we take a holistic approach, and you never know when something that seems tangential at first might be intimately linked, if you will, to your main topic.

She and Toledo took a moment to digest this while together we appreciated the pounding of the surf.

I silently congratulated myself for telling the truth without revealing the Truth. The Truth was that 1) I expected to have a sexual adventure, hopefully without incurring a medical one, and 2) I had come to investigate whether her rag-tag colony of purists had vandalized the well-appointed colony of quasi-idealists at ¡Bonobo!

This suspicion seemed plausible because Holly had established her camp as a remonstrance against the compromises that "Dale Carnegie" and, much better, "Ronald McDonald" had instituted to achieve a modicum of respectability in the eyes of the sick society to which they purportedly represented an alternative. That is, rather than subverting the dominant paradigm, they had found a way to fit within it; they had domesticated themselves, turned themselves into a zoological curiosity or an ethnotouristic adventure. They seemed satisfied to feel the love without spreading it.

"That's cool," she said. "Aren't those sell-outs over at ¡Bonobo! anthropologists?"

"Yeah. They got their Master's degrees—"

"So did you go there? Do you know them?"

"Yeah, we've met. Do you know them?" I hoped that neither of them heard an edge to my voice.

"I haven't had the pleasure. But Toledo met them when they were setting up their amusement park over there."

"Oh, that's cool. How did that happen?" I turned to him, trying to divert the conversation away from myself. I did this all the time in my research.

"So tell me, Nat—how did you meet them?" She was persistent.

"Oh, well, it's a kind of a long story, but basically my adviser at Florida was part of the original Bonobo group back in Tucson, so she kind of introduced us."

"Huh. So what did you *guys* talk about?"

I think Holly illicitly hoped that the leaders of ¡Bonobo! had spoken with fear about her purist challenge to their halfway house. Actually, they had mentioned True Bonobo only briefly in a lengthy and colorful list of possible attackers. She didn't ask about that directly, so, seeing a path, I spoke the little-t truth. "Well, we talked about my adviser, graduate school, my research—that sort of thing. It was weird to think that I had gone farther than them in school." She was still smiling but looked a little impatient. "Obviously, we talked about ¡Bonobo!, too." I kept it cool and made my gambit. "I didn't know that someone was vandalizing them. That was weird. I mean, maybe you'd expect horny guys to try to sneak in—"

"Do they think I—*we* have been attacking *them*?"

"As far as I could tell, they don't know who it was." This was the Truth.

"Well, I think I know who sent a lawyer here, along with some gorillas with guns in their pants, telling us to stop using the word 'bonobo' in our name. Maybe Kentucky Fried Chicken is suing Popeye's for using 'chicken' in their name. And, anyway, *they're* the ones trying to turn a profit from a fake revolution. We're not exactly into marketing." Her mouth was still smiling, but not her eyes. The Joker.

Later, I wondered whether she greeted the lawyer and goons with the Bonobo handshake. At that moment, though, I hoped that silent contemplation might pass for sympathetic consolation, so I just sat there.

It didn't work. Holly said, "Did they send you here, too, Nat?"

Caught. "Well, yeah, they did ask me to check it out, just in case."

The Truth really angered her—not, she said, because they suspected her. People like that, who built a fortress for love, had their heads up their asses anyway. And her colony had nothing to hide. Just look at it. No, what really pissed her off was that *I* had lied to them. In this Garden, the forbidden fruit was secrecy and deceit.

Throughout all of this exchange, Toledo mostly continued to gaze out to sea, sometimes briefly turning to watch me or Holly.

Holly took a deep breath, exhaled, and said, "You either need to leave and never, ever bring your lying ass back, or we have to fuck this out."

What? I looked at her for a moment, trying to calculate a response.

"That's how we do it here, Nat—like bonobos. Thus the name. When there's hostility, we fuck it out. So either drop trou or ship out."

Toledo kept looking out to sea. Was he going to join in? The thought terrified and intrigued me. I unbuttoned the top of my shorts and pulled down the zipper. She unfurled a towel that had been lying rolled up nearby and laid it across the sand in the nicely shaded rear of the lean-to. She took a condom from a small bag.

We fucked like beasts. Screwed, sucked, licked, heaved, grasped, clutched, thrust, wrestled, and enacted quite a few other verbs until, at her urging, I filled that condom. I pulled out and collapsed on top of her as our sweat bound us.

Toledo still sat there. After a few minutes of lying under me, our lungs pulsing in synchrony, Holly asked him to get us all something to drink, and he complied. She rolled out from under me and said, "Man, I feel so much better." She sat up and started to put her bikini on again. "So what's your plan, Nat?"

I hadn't arrived with much of one, and I had already addressed my two goals (the crime, the girl), so I felt free to tell the truth: "I don't really have one."

"What's all that in your backpack?"

It looked bloated. I had brought money, sugar-free chewing gum, deodorant, shorts, underwear, a T-shirt, condoms, a frisbee, and some food, just in case I ended up staying the night. But, if I did, I needed to return to town early the next morning.

"Oh yeah? You have to report back to your faux-nobo masters?"

I told the truth: "Oh, no. I don't see them very often. I actually don't know when I'll meet with them again." I lied: "I just have an interview set up for my dissertation research." And I explained honestly a little more about how I had moved to Playatlán to understand the local development of narco-culture in popular music and other mass media.

Here Toledo finally entered the conversation. He wanted to know in which part of town I lived, whether I had heard this band or that song, and what my ideas were. As always, I refused to divulge who my sources were, which made it easier to maintain the lie about my appointment the next day. I asked him about his family and how his experiences related to my topic. Although Toledo spoke English passably, we had switched into Spanish, and now Holly sat watching the ocean placidly. Apparently my research didn't anger Toledo, because we kept our pants on.

We got out some of my food and some of theirs. They complimented me on the quality of the tamales I had brought, which I had purchased from a neighbor who sold food from her house. I offered to reimburse them for any of their food that I ate. I secretly hoped that Mexicans' highly developed generosity would make this gesture merely symbolic. Holly, a good American, dispelled that hope directly. "You might not have to pull your own pecker, Nat, but everyone has to pull their own weight."

As the afternoon deepened, others arrived. I employed the Bonobo handshake with increasing confidence, fondling breasts and crotches—no forms to sign or ribbons here—while exchanging banal pleasantries. Unlike at ¡Bonobo!, anyone was welcome: a party of delinquent stoners, a few tough "transvestites" (transsexuals) selling food on the side, a couple of chunky female tourists from the U.S. sporting ¡Bonobo! t-shirts with the zestful naïveté common to the species, adventurous couples on a lark … Fat aside, they ranged from the froggish to the downright sexy. A few were new, like me, but most weren't. Some lived at True Bonobo, but most didn't.

Eventually, we numbered perhaps twenty. Holly told me that she had chosen that location because it was too difficult and expensive to visit just for free sex. In fact, after a bad experience closer to town, she had compared the going rates for prostitutes and taxis before settling at this distance. A few adventurers might show up once or twice, but most participants—and especially the residents—felt committed to the cause.

I spent the afternoon contemplating the sea and the people around me—a little circumspectly when they were doing each other—and started to imagine that there was no difference. I waded into the ocean and chatted with my potential mates, played soccer and tossed frisbee on the beach, and downed a beer or two while others smoked cigarettes or pot.

That night, we lounged around a scraggly campfire built mostly from debris that had fallen from the coconut palms, along with some food wrappers. The surf rolled continuously a few yards away, and occasionally a little salty spray blew onto my face.

After a while, Holly addressed us all. She laid out the basic rules of any Bonobo gathering anywhere: everyone must either participate or leave, consent must be given explicitly, and no penetration without a condom, regardless of the recipient's preference. She added with sermonic conviction that "the True Bonobo Way is to follow the Golden Rule: do others as you would have them do you. Lay yourself open to be known, cherish everyone around you, and you will create liberation. It starts with sex, so let's have an orgy." Her smile widened.

What the monolingual Mexicans took away from this oration was unclear. But, as we began laying out sheets, blankets, and towels in an overlapping pattern to create a mostly sand-free space, I found myself thinking very concretely about touching these unfiltered companions—caressing the sturdy, mannish torso of that transvestite, or feeling that obese woman's fat, sweaty thighs and pendulous belly rub against me as she ground on me from on top. I recognized that certain African groups stuffed their daughters silly to develop such loads of inviting flesh, but that didn't happen where I grew up. This would be quite different from my fantasies or my cathartic encounter with Holly. Could I fake my way through it? I certainly couldn't "lay open" my narrow range of attraction "to be known" by the others; that would be both impolitic and cruel.

I reminded myself that the essence of anthropological research was participant-observation. In this spirit, I resolved to cherish those around me, favoring the sexy ones as much as I could simply as a survival strategy. Undoubtedly I would learn something from the experience. Plus, at that hour I had no safe way of leaving.

So we had an orgy—my first. I had already ejaculated once that day, which meant that I was good for perhaps two more orgasms, given sufficient inspiration. As we finalized the preparations, I began by drifting toward Holly, hoping that she might reach out to me again. I pretended some sheets near her needed a little adjustment, but she chose that moment to walk out among the palms to pee. Given a second chance, and disgusted by my dependency, I stood up straight, took a deep breath, and walked toward a young woman from Playatlán. I had forgotten her name since meeting her earlier, when she had arrived with a small group of drunkards and stoners. Chubby, with frizzy reddish hair, freckles, and laughing eyes, she had just finished strewing condom packages across the bedding. As she saw me approaching, her reception made it clear that she had experience. A bonobo handshake quickly led to a long French kiss. Her wet, beer-soaked tongue forcefully rolled around my mouth as her free hand pressed my head to hers. By the time she had started unzipping my shorts, I felt other shoulders and hands brushing against me. Her friends and their partners had moved next to us, and they helpfully addressed my partner as Líssy.

In fact, they talked a lot. When Líssy took off her shirt, her friends cheered. She smiled to them. When I unsnapped her bra, grabbed a hunk of flab on her back to anchor myself, and fitted my mouth onto her fleshy boob, they cheered for me. Later, while I was screwing one of Líssy's friends doggy-style, the guy next to me, doing the same thing with a transvestite, put his hand on my shoulder and remarked how beautiful it was to do it on the beach at night, among friends. I tried my best to fit in, although I mostly responded to others' comments or joined in group cheers and songs. The American tourist women yelled, "Wooo," a lot.

I entered an altered state, in which the wonder of the setting and people's relations dominated all other perception. Fat, ugly, masculine—I still noticed these things, but they didn't matter in the same way. Some of it even turned me on. Seeing their pleasure excited me. Our mingled sweat and saliva and cries bound us in splendor, and this kept me aroused. I did, in fact, have my two orgasms. Then I lay with the others on the bedding, Líssy's head resting on my leg. I looked up at the stars and the sliver of moon through the clouds. The musky smell of sex mingled with the salty, fishy scent of the ocean. We chatted in low tones about extraterrestrials, sex, music, the pinche government, and the beauty of the night. I drifted into a sweet sleep.

I awoke with the aurora. I had a hard-on, but it was to pee. I slid out from among the other bodies and stood. In the gray light, I could see a couple of people sitting up and looking sleepily out to sea. One of the obese American women—Sherry—was wading out beyond the waves, occasionally submerging her head. Picking my way over the bodies, I walked out to add my part to the ocean. I treaded water while urinating and then paddled over by Sherry. Her makeup was gone; her hair now lay flat against her head. She looked plain but healthy, with a sweet aura of communicable bliss.

"Isn't it amazing?" she asked. "I'd love to just live here." She arched an eyebrow and looked me up and down. I wasn't sure I could do it again, and I already felt some chafing, but she might misread my hesitance as rejection. So I nodded. With a sly, seductive smile she reached down to rub my dick. I caressed her bare back with one hand and a gelatinous boob with the other.

"Usually I go for a bigger man." Was she serious? I knew I wasn't fit to be a porn star, but no one had ever implied … Then she lightly squeezed my bicep, such as it was, and drew her hand across my unimposing chest to pinch my waist. "But variety is fun."

A lesson learned. "It's not how big it is; it's what you do with it," I assured her. We grinned at our wit.

"So why not go to ¡Bonobo!?" I asked disingenuously.

"I wish. I applied, but I'm stuck on the waiting list. Anyway, this seems more … organic. Know what I mean?" She took my hand from her breast and put it on her clit. I could feel her fluid mixing with the sea.

Without condoms, we had to improvise. After some mutual masturbation, I went down on Sherry as she floated on her back and I supported her with my arms. "Take me under when I come!" she gasped. So, once she started convulsing I dropped her hips and my mouth below the surface and she arched her head back. When she was done, she popped back up to exclaim, "That was awesome!" Her eyes were wide. "Do you want it like that?"

The idea of complete immersion just didn't appeal to me. It was too mechanical, and how could I breathe? So I stood while she indulgently rubbed me with her buttocks, her breasts, her vulva (and came again), and then her hands. Maybe the pressure to perform prolonged the festivities. Feeling guilty, I wanted to tell her that it was okay to stop, but she seemed to enjoy feeling sexy and generous. And, actually, I had started to find her more alluring as a result. When my sperm finally trickled into the Pacific, I witnessed the sun of a new day rising over the hills, and I remembered that I had an appointment in town.

Soon I bid farewell to Holly and the others still on the beach. By now, the bonobo handshakes had become almost routine. Would I return someday? I sincerely assured them I would. It had been beautiful.

In passing Holly's lean-to, I saw that she had left some handwritten pages under her paperback. I dropped my backpack nearby and pretended to rearrange the load, as a pretext to get a closer look. I discerned the edges of what appeared to be diagrams—of what, I couldn't tell. The pages called to me, but perhaps Holly hadn't overcome her initial distrust. Probably she was watching me. Not seeing a way to sneak a better peek, I left them.

As the temperature shifted from cool to scorching, I hiked back through the palm plantation, waded across the channel, scrambled up the hill, and started trudging back toward Playatlán. I felt that I should analyze my experience in light of post-structuralist approaches to gender and sexuality—surely I could turn it into a conference presentation—but an unmovable psychic peace quelled the impulse. It was too early.

Plus, I faced a more pressing concern: how to reach Playatlán in time. For the Truth was that my gorgeous, virginal girlfriend was expecting me at her sister's birthday party. Today I—an American!—would be on display for family and friends, so I had to be there.

Passing cars honked as I plodded along, waiting for a random taxi to pass. After a few minutes, a rise along the ocean side of the road obscured my view of True Bonobo. Then a beat-up sedan stopped a few yards ahead of me. Could it be bandits? My heart started to race. But a smiling face leaned out the window: the car held Ricardo and Tomás, a couple of guys I knew who taught at the local university. They were driving to work.

I clambered into the back seat. As we followed the highway to Playatlán, my friends enjoyed guessing where I had been. Finally I gave them a truth that they hadn't sought: I had visited True Bonobo and engaged in a transformative ritual, characterized by liminality and communitas.

Usually, a solid academic analysis abstracts the life out of anything. But these guys took my response as a challenge. They tried to tease a game summary or at least a box score out of me, but, for reasons I couldn't admit to myself, I found their prurience offensive. Perhaps in some other situation, on my own terms, I could explain what had happened. "A ride isn't enough—this tale will cost you at least a beer," I joked, and feared that they would remember.

To shift onto solid ground, I diverted them with a preview of my upcoming appointment. Ricardo told me to beware: he recently had watched a TV show about a flower that attracted insects, only to devour them. His buddy said, "I saw the same thing—at my wedding." They were teasing, but they were right. Camping on the beach and having open orgies probably wasn't sustainable, but a marriage founded on artifice, inertia, and temptation shouldn't be.

"Maybe I'm the flower," I joked.

"You certainly don't smell like one."

Ricardo was right again. The Truth was, Holly might or might not have vandalized ¡Bonobo!—who knew?—but she had tagged my psyche.

THE FIRST BEAD

I originally met my girlfriend, Blanca, after a beauty contest
that she had lost. But she had won others, so her disappointment was bearable.

An extraordinary array of organizations sponsored pageants
in Playatlán, and, with such a glut, only the winners of a couple
of high-profile competitions received much celebrity and def-
erence. Blanca wasn't one of those.

But she had her crowns, which were important to her for
personal pride and to her mother as certificates of merit that
could attract men from "better"—that is, richer—families. In
addition, they both enjoyed beating other girls at the most
prominent female sport in town. Only in exceptional cases,
when the winner had a distinguished résumé and came from a
family of long-time economic prominence, did Blanca and her
mother accept defeat without hinting that the victor had bribed
judges.

I happened upon this particular pageant by accident. Walking along different paths through the city, making notes about
the music I heard in different contexts, I got to the seaside
walkway by the historic center and heard English-language
dance-music blaring into the open air. Following my ears led
me to a plaza on the seashore, where a stage had been erected.
A small crowd of maybe two hundred people had gathered in
front, and the contestants, in light but formal dresses, were in

the midst of declaiming on the topic of Playatlán's future development.

Wow, I thought, how many people get to do that? And they've asked beauty contestants instead of social scientists. The eventual winner gave a top-notch speech, substantive and self-assured. During another contestant's talk the sound mysteriously cut off, which prompted folks near me to grumble openly about corruption. Blanca's disquisition was stilted and filled with generalizations that led men around me to comment to each other and smirk, but ~~they~~ we didn't turn away, because she exuded a public sensuality, an exuberant and captivating eroticism. Plus, she had big breasts.

Of course, stating such a thing makes me seem shallow and sexist. A New Man would never notice or appreciate such a thing, just as feminist women never noticed Michael Hutchence's hair. I haven't said yet that our relationship depended on those breasts. I'm just giving you some Truth: despite my sincere and sophisticated critique of events like beauty pageants, I found it pleasurable and enticing to watch her, along with several of the other contestants. By the way, you might assume that they all wore ostentatious gobs of makeup to match their sparkling dresses and tiaras, but they had perfected a style of preparation that bespoke moderation.

As the contest continued, I wrote notes about the musical aspects, shot a little video with my miniature camcorder, and racked my brain for a plausible question to ask one of the contestants after the event, in order to start a conversation. It was far-fetched to get them to opine on narcocorridos (although, if they got to hold forth on the city's future, why not that?), and asking directions or commenting on the weather seemed ludicrous.

Eventually, I saw my chance and took it. Or, rather, it saw and took me. After the winner was crowned, the contestants filed offstage and went to greet, thank, and gossip with their cheering sections. I drifted between the pods of people and, to legitimize my presence, wrote some extra notes about the day's observations. My main focus, though, was on making flirtatious eye-contact with any of the contestants who had attracted me. Indeed, I enjoyed an orgy of eye-contact with several contestants and their sisters and friends, but, for practical purposes, the conversational pods were self-contained, impervious to any witticism or suave remark that I hadn't come up with anyway. Chatting wide-eyed among their friends, the contestants stood like champion roses in a garden of winners.

Then my patience was rewarded. As I happened to be shuffling nearby, a middle-aged woman started to peel away from Blanca's group to check on something. She saw me and asked, "Young man, what are you writing in that book?" This turned out to be Blanca's mother, Flor. Now that they wouldn't seem like brazen hussies for paying attention to me, Blanca and her entourage turned to hear my response. A couple of the others were as pretty as Blanca, but something about having been onstage lent her a lingering sheen.

"I'm composing the future history of Playatlán. I'm just writing the last details I heard from—excuse me, your daughter?—while they're fresh in my memory." Blanca's eyes lit with delight at the witty flattery, and the whole bouquet of flowers around her looked ready to pick.

"You're not from here? Where are you from?" Her mother seemed just as happy to meet me. I felt startled that they had thought that I might be local. But brown hair and long pants were enough to appear presumptively Mexican in Playatlán; shorts, in contrast, would have stamped me, "Made in USA."

I explained that really I was there to study popular music for my PhD and that ordinarily I lived in Florida.

"Florida!" Blanca exclaimed. "It's my dream to go to Orlando and see Disney."

Assuming (wrongly) that she would find my snobbery a turn-off, I chose to avoid the topic. I stilled the temptation to joke about people from Orlando wanting to visit ¡Bonobo! Instead, I complimented Blanca on her performance in the beauty pageant.

Wrong move.

"It's not a beauty contest. I don't know why people call it that."

"Really? That's what we call it in the United States. What do you call it?"

"It's just a contest for a crown. Do you really think it's about beauty?" She pouted and looked a bit spoiled. I think she wanted the contest to be more substantial—and also feared that losing meant that she wasn't as pretty as the winner.

"Well, I know that you do things like give speeches, but the rest of the time they judged you in a swimsuit and different kinds of clothes."

"Mom?"

"The young man has a point, mi hija." The mother glanced at me, still smiling. Blanca playfully harrumphed.

Having learned from Casanova that listening was the key to a woman's heart, I was about to ask Blanca and, really, any of the other pretty girls whether they went to college. Undoubtedly, my next resort would have been to inquire as to their majors. But this urbane exchange would have to wait for another day, as a different contestant came up with some friends and suggested that they all go to a restaurant. The girls started talking about it as though I weren't part of the plan, which Blanca's mother clarified by turning to me and wishing me luck in my research. I understood this polite brush-off and felt a little thankful for it, as I wasn't completely sure that I was lonely or desperate enough to devote so much time to beauty contestants.

Nonetheless, during my quiet walk home, I practically convinced myself that Blanca—or any of her friends, or the other contestants, or their friends—was filled with anticipation at the possibility that I might ask her out. Once in bed, I beat off to the thought of sex with her—the first bead in a long rosary.

THE BROTHEL

Encounters like that happened to me quite frequently in Playatlán. I was able to handle them with more aplomb than in the United States because, applying a lesson from Bonobo, I had sex regularly. Each week I frequented a brothel.

Why not? It was legal (or at least it would have been had I gone to the official red-light district), the prostitutes weren't trafficked but instead had chosen this path over other economic opportunities, and I treated them with an affable respect, which included wearing condoms without protest. Moreover, everyone works with some combination of body parts, and the privileging of work that depends mostly on the brain, or the hands for that matter, is just another manifestation of the Western mind-body dualism that withers at the slightest deconstruction. Just like at most other businesses I frequented, I paid the brothel to make me feel good.

On the other hand, the problem with female prostitution as practiced in Mexico was twofold. The unfair lack of widespread male prostitution for female clients reinforced, however indirectly, all sorts of sexist attitudes and practices. Perhaps more importantly, no career path existed for most women within the industry as they aged. Nonetheless, other professions had comparable injustices, I felt sure.

This is not to say that I announced at parties that I had just come from screwing with a prostitute. In fact, it might be fairly stated that I skulked into and out of the compound where I did my diddling. I felt no guilt, but I realized that friends and acquaintances might judge me harshly and gossip about it—or might even shame me directly at some gathering, as an entertaining way of testing my reaction.

At the brothel, I played no favorites. I desired variety and feared ending up with a mistress. Quite a few times my partner would act coquettish after I, and possibly she, had come. But on this point I was obdurate—no regular partner. Plus, my desire for secrecy led me to fornicate during the workday, when I was least likely to cross paths with men I knew. This schedule meant that relatively few of the sex workers were available, and I simply caught as catch could.

Going for sex just after siesta had the additional advantage that my partner and her room would be fresher and sunnier than at night. On many a visit I shared relaxed conversation and—call me naïve—mutually pleasing love-making with a young or not-so-young woman. I was much happier to give my money to her than to a seaside disco whose business depended on the mere possibility of sexual encounters with tourists.

While regular visits to prostitutes might seem utterly hedonistic, weekly sex was considerably less frequent than I had enjoyed with any girlfriend in college. I actually felt a bit deprived, rather than depraved.

The whole endeavor proved quite useful to my research. Those women knew an amazing amount about select aspects of society, and they had a lot of 'down' time to think and chat about my ethnographic inquiries. These were little puffs of interest to punctuate their hours flatlining between, and perhaps under, clients. But nobody rode for free, and they waited until I paid them again for sex before they gave me more information. They could identify the kind of music different types of men wanted to hear while trying to maintain an erection, the kind of clothes they wore, and the sorts of role playing that turned them on. Apparently, even some narcos fantasized about being narcos, at least as they were depicted in song. This, especially, called for analysis (maybe psychoanalysis) since the corridos' protagonists often died in massive gunfights. You can slog through my other dissertation for that.

THE BABY JESUS

One Friday afternoon, I saw Blanca again. Having surveyed murals and graffiti in an upscale subdivision, an area reputedly populated by drug lords and their money-laundering cousins, I was ambling along a sidewalk and she was on the other side of the street, coming from the opposite direction. I was on my way to bed a prostitute; Blanca was en route to caress the Baby Jesus. Obviously we were a match made in purgatory.

She looked so different that at first I wasn't sure she was the same object of my fantasy that night after the pageant. She wore less makeup, and her clothes were quite casual: crisp blue jeans and a breezy red top that merely hinted at the magnificence of her breasts; plus, she was neither on a stage nor surrounded by supporters. All of this transformed her from an erotic goddess to an attractive mortal. In fact, had I not deciphered that this was Blanca, I wouldn't have paid her much attention.

Would she remember me? She very obviously did. Before I could tentatively call her name from across the quiet street, she smiled to me and began to cross to my side, saying, "Ay, Nat, here you are. What a surprise."

A lot of people knew my name without my knowing theirs, simply because asking each other about strangers alleviated their chronic boredom. But Blanca said that her mother had asked whether she had seen me again, a sure sign that I had made an impression. I took it as flattery.

Blanca moved so close to me, smiled so brightly, and looked up into my eyes with such attention that I briefly forgot my destination. Maybe my brain was too distracted by trying to keep my erection down. She looked me over and, noting the backpack, asked where I was going.

I regarded her with stupefaction and then, having remembered, with panic. "I was doing some research for my doctorate, recording graffiti and murals in the neighborhood."

While not answering Blanca's question, that seemed good enough for her. Maybe Playatlecos avoided pressing each other for details regarding their wanderings as a sort of professional courtesy among prevaricators.

"So where are you going? Do you live around here?" I asked. It was a sincere question, showing that I was clueless.

"Ay, Nat—I wish!" And then she didn't fully answer *my* question. "I'm going to the House of the Baby Jesus. Do you want to go?"

"The what?" It sounded a little like a Protestant church, but maybe I had misheard.

"The Baby Jesus. Haven't you been there? Whenever I need to feel peace, I go there, and He always makes me feel so calm."

I never asked, or knew, what disturbed her. "I think I've never heard of it."

"Then you should go with me," she said, cute and resolute. "Do you have time?"

Fateful moments of decision! On the one hand, predictably pleasant sex with a prostitute; on the other, exploring the romantic and spiritual unknown with a vivacious beauty queen— Dale's pornography versus drama, respectively. And, for better or worse, I chose drama. Blanca did, too, I suppose.

We walked briskly through the neighborhood, her body tantrically close to mine, her perfume battling, like sperm, through the still, humid air to my avid nostrils.

She asked about my research and then expressed unadorned admiration for my tentative analyses. For the first of
many times, she asked me my opinions of Mexico, Playatlán,
Mexican food, and "the Mexican family." I had been down this
road with others, so I gave her the most popular answers that
weren't false. Her enthusiasm for my replies embarrassed me.

Then, still in the subdivision, we rounded a corner, and she
said, "There it is. Oh, isn't it lovely?"

She looked at me for an answer, but I wasn't certain that I
saw what she was indicating. Ahead lay three ranch houses on
the right side of a dead-end road. A broad, grassy shoulder and
a high wall bordered the left side.

I vaguely indicated that it was nice.

She acted a little puzzled at me as she sped up to reach the
final house. This was our destination: a modest-sized Crafts-
man bungalow, with a fresh yellow coat of paint, white trim-
ming, and a thoroughly manicured lawn. Spanish Colonial being the architecture of choice (copying modern California—not
colonial Mexico), this was a little unexpected but hardly worthy
of an exclamation. I grew a bit more curious as I saw that, past
the porch, the front door was wide open. A couple was exiting
as a trickle of people moved toward it.

Then I noticed the toys. Hundreds of simple toys, still
wrapped in plastic from the store, lined the lawn. They had
been arranged topically—soldiers here, cars there—and positioned with precision. A young couple set down a new package
among them.

Blanca and I surveyed the rows. "Who are these for?" I
asked, bewildered.

"For the Baby Jesus." Her smile deepened at the thought.

"So they don't go to regular children?"

"No, don't you see? People want to make the Baby happy;
it makes *them* feel happy."

Hmm, I thought, it might make the proprietors feel happy once they resold them. But I said nothing. Blanca looked sweetly delirious.

We walked inside, exchanging peaceful greetings to the strangers leaving. That was miracle enough. But, as we sat in the family room, which had been converted into a spare but home-style anteroom, I read framed newspaper articles posted on the wall.

The Baby Jesus was, to the uninitiated, a generic, life-sized plastic doll that a Mexican family had bought in the 1950s. The articles were vague on the details, but, not long after being purchased, the doll performed various miracles and began to be adored as the Baby Jesus. Prominent Roman Catholic figures and celebrities were reported to have blessed Him or sought His favor, respectively. Possibly the original doll disappeared—doubters pointed to differences in the Baby's appearance over the years—but the proprietors disproved such allegations by pointing to continuing miracles. Now people came to ask for the Baby's help with all sorts of problems but especially with pregnancies and children's afflictions.

A nondescript woman came into the waiting area and had a brief, subdued conversation with Blanca. They seemed to know and like each other. Blanca put money in a locked box attached to the wall and came back to my side. Her eyes flashed wide as she told me that we were about to see the Baby.

Soon a small, polite man about forty years old ushered us into an adjacent room, decorated as a nursery. He smiled to me gently. In the crib was the plastic doll. Blanca, in front of me, cradled it in her arms and slowly rocked it back and forth, looking at its unyielding face. Such pure happiness. She turned and offered the doll to me. I demurred, but the man smiled again and nodded for me to hold it. Pressured, I took the doll in my arms and rocked it mechanically for a couple of seconds, concealing my resentment. I looked up to see Blanca expect-antly searching my expression for the anticipated transfor-mation.

She had no idea who I was, so I forgave her.

I handed back the doll, which she set in the crib and ca-ressed briefly. As we exited, she turned to me with shiny eyes and an upward sweep of joy on her face. "Did you feel it, Nat?"

"What?"

"Oh, didn't you sense it? I always feel so peaceful, whenev-er I hold Him."

I hesitated. She exuded an air so sweet and pure and ardent. The women at the brothel never looked so enticing yet unat-tainable. And I desired her, in a way. What good would it do to express my derision? Should I wittily remark that the Trinity was a minor theological conundrum compared to having a ba-by Jesus and an adult one at the same time? Instead I said, "I'm sorry. I wish I'd felt the same thing. It looks like it was won-derful for you."

By now we were crossing the lawn, past the toys that needy children would never enjoy. Poor people who lived on the out-skirts of Playatlán were so desperate for money that they sold bent keys, rusty nails, and used paper clips at flea markets just to eat. Their children could only dream of playing with the crappiest of the toys reserved for Jesus.

We walked a while together in silence. Then she looked up into my face again.

"Nat, do you believe in God?" Unbeknownst to me, this sincere but formulaic question implied that she was interested in a serious romantic relationship with me.

Blanca took "no" (softened with hints of equivocation) for an answer and never tried to proselytize me. She and her mother subsequently dedicated themselves to converting me into a husband instead. They noted—out loud, in my presence—that Blanca had snared me with her eyes and heart, rather than her boobs, a sure sign of "a good man."

I sometimes took this flattery to mean 'an easy mark.' Surely, they must have thought, adding a bit of cleavage and some tongue would seal the deal.

DANGLING THE BAIT

Looking back on our courtship, I recognize that the party for Blanca's sister took place only about two months after we visited the Baby Jesus. Still, our relationship moved so quickly, despite considerable stretches apart, that we were like astronauts bounding across the moon. But to where?

When Blanca and I got together, we talked. Maybe we would go dancing, lie under an awning along the beach, sit in MacDonald's, or, worst of all, pass time in what she called "my mother's house" (even though her father lived there, too). Sometimes we attended a book presentation or movie or sat in some friend's house to celebrate his or her birthday. But, wherever it was, we mostly talked.

Isn't this obvious? It wouldn't be from watching other couples: the longer they had known each other, the longer they sat without speaking. Occasionally, the woman—or girl—would ask her partner, "How do you see it?" and he, flatlining, might not reply, or he might come up with an observation that would prompt a flurry of exchanges lasting, if they spoke slowly, as long as thirty seconds.

Sometimes our conversations weren't much better. Quite frequently, apropos of nothing, Blanca would ask, "How do you see it?" Occasionally I would punish her by discussing theoretical aspects of my research. A few times, exasperated, I asked in return, "I don't see anything. How do *you* see it?" At my craftiest, I would preempt her and ask first. Ha!

This might be why many husbands and wives spent little time together at home. Typically, men would be elsewhere, with their friends, mistresses, or thoughts. In fact, it surprised me whenever I found Blanca's father at home; to witness his interactions with her mother was fascinating simply for its rarity. He had a job waiting tables at an upscale, beach-side restaurant that appealed mostly to Mexican clients. I had seen him a couple of times as I walked past along the sand and could hardly reconcile his confident and jovial manner with the domestic ghost I otherwise knew.

This, I thought, could be my future with Blanca. But was it so bad? Maybe men had more in common with other men and women with other women. After all, they had grown up separately and worked separately. Why would I expect spouses to become best friends forever?

Anyway, Blanca and I never reached the point where flatlining was the default and conversation a rare treat. I grew to suspect that occasional dead spaces arose mostly because she feared that being too forceful and opinionated, like her mother, could derail the runaway marriage-train that she supposed we were on. It was better to feed my ego by encouraging me to talk without reciprocation. Oddly, life had prepared her to give speeches during beauty pageants but not to speak her mind to her presumed soul-mate.

Notwithstanding all that, we actually talked quite a bit, and rarely about the reasons that I couldn't luxuriate inside and all over her. So, in bits, I learned a lot about her and her family.

Like many people in Playatlán, Blanca's mother Flor was in denial that her biological ancestors could have included mulattoes—such as the first Spanish-speakers to settle the area—or any significant number of Indians, Aztec or not. (In most cases, not.) In a big-hearted way, she was willing to admit two kinds of Europeans as ancestors: Spaniards, for obvious reasons, and good-looking French rapists, as the result of their invasion of Mexico in the 1860s. So Flor named her first child Blanca, or "White," as part of her ongoing attempts to mold reality. The couple's second child, one year younger, was also a daughter: Nieves, or "Snows." In combination, the daughters formed Blancanieves, the Spanish equivalent of Snow White.

Neighbor women who saw Blanca as an infant remarked that, though she wasn't pale, she wasn't "ugly"—that is, dark—either. Her mother, like most others, ensured that her girls didn't get any darker; for example, when they went to the beach on Sunday afternoons they sat under an umbrella or tarp.

The other great favor she did for Blanca was to protect her reputation for chastity—no mean feat given that her daughter was such a "statue" or "hide," as some of my male friends called her. Flor's sister had been forced to marry as a teenager simply because she had returned home late from a dance—her first unchaperoned date. Her parents wouldn't let her back in the house for fear that her shame would infect the entire family. They saved themselves and Flor from contagion by insisting that the sister marry her date.

"So what did the boyfriend say?" I asked Blanca's mother.

"'Okay.'"

Subsequently, the sister—forced by her parents into marriage, and thus her first sexual relationship, with a boy she barely knew—regained acceptance within her family. The marriage was a disaster.

By those standards, to which some families still adhered, Flor was a moderate. She personally would not leave the house without a family member or another woman, not even to cross the street to visit a neighbor. Her husband and daughters urged her to venture out on her own (if only to avoid escorting her everywhere), and she acknowledged that probably she could, but ...

In contrast, she let Blanca go almost anywhere on her own during the day ("I trust my daughters, Nat") as long as she never, ever went behind any closed door with a boy or man, singular or plural—cousins, teachers, and priests included. Once darkness fell, Blanca had to be with an approved chaperone or with her friends at all times. And her mother had developed an ever-expanding list of areas that were off-limits at night, such as any beach, a well-known make-out area along the oceanfront boulevard, a long list of notorious discos, most places downtown, and many more. Given her goal of protecting Blanca's reputation, she probably was right.

As far as Flor was concerned, the best place for Blanca and me, day or night, was in her house. Like almost all the others in the area, it was made of concrete block. Flor's husband, aided by friends and relatives, had built it wall-by-wall over many years after the young couple had joined the land invasion that created their neighborhood. The structure was painted tan inside and out, although cobwebs, knickknacks, and built-up grime gave each section its own character. In back, the paved, walled-in courtyard held the toilet, shower, clothesline, and a couple of plastic chairs.

Flor wanted us there partly because she desired company—more like an audience—in her open cage. In earlier years she had felt lonelier, but, when the Mexican economy crashed in 1994, she contributed to the family's finances by opening a small store in a part of the house that opened onto the street. Kids, men, and adventuresome women could come to buy cheap packaged sweets and gossip with or spy on her family. Other women had done the same throughout the neighborhood, so no one grew rich, but lots of them stopped flatlining for hours on end. Thus, Flor and the rest continued to manage their stores under the pretext of necessity even after their husbands' and children's incomes made the proceeds the icing rather than the cake.

Surprisingly, the other main reason that Flor wanted Blanca and me in her house wasn't precisely to keep an eye on us. In fact, over time it became clear that this was the only reliable location where we could make out. Flor, perhaps in collusion with her daughters, provided this space to keep me lured until I bit the hook. It reminded me of a clown I liked to watch operate along the seaside esplanade; he had to keep each onlooker invested until the payoff at the end.

How did they dangle the bait before me? Flor might suggest, "Why don't you show Nat your photo album?"

"Ay, mamá!" Blanca would feign embarrassment.

I would politely express interest, and Blanca and I would retire to the small, messy room she shared with Nieves. We would sit side-by-side on the edge of the thin mattress of her single bed, our shoulders touching. Almost without fail she wore a shirt that highlighted her magnificent cleavage, upon which I could look down with aching desire. As my erection strained for freedom within the compacted crotch of my jeans, she would dutifully flip through some photos or notebook. We would comment on the prop—Blanca looking up directly into my eyes as I complimented her achievements. Then I would lean over and we would work our tongues around.

My hands? Typically, one propped me up and the other cupped her smooth, caked face or stroked her slightly sticky brown hair. She thwarted any movement toward her chest or thighs by demurely withdrawing her tongue and moving my hand off her body, lowering her head to look up at me bashfully, and shaking it. She might even return to discussing the photo album. In short, while kissing, I could feel pre-ejaculate tippling out of my penis, I could feel my balls ache, but I could not feel those breasts.

The more I thought about it, the odder this seemed, because I did, in fact, touch them at other times—but only with my arms. Really, they touched me, as Blanca would be 'forced' to rub her melons against me on a crowded dance-floor or while grabbing my arm for stability when a wave crashed on us. In many ways, sensing their volume and firmness only made me want to touch them more—to say nothing of thrusting inside her pussy while doing so. It added the spice of specificity to my masturbation.

But I also started to resent her breasts. By what arbitrary principle was my upper arm 'safe' but not my hands? Or my mouth? Or penis? It made no sense unless her goal—coached by her mother—was to deny pleasure to both of us as a sort of extortion against me. Blanca embodied the opposite of True Bonobo: I could get a free lunch, but no free milk. Did they think that a lifetime commitment was a fair trade for getting to handle her gazongas? What if the years of chastity had made her unlikely to fully enjoy sex, or at least sexual experimentation? I couldn't even figure out how they had turned my autochthonous fixation on penetrating women's orifices into a breast-manipulation fetish. Amid my fantasies, I began to have involuntary visions of popping them like balloons, or simply bopping them back and forth.

When dark moods struck me, our mutual focus on sex and especially on access to Blanca's jugs weighed heavily. I had lost sight of the person who had appealed to me so purely at the Baby Jesus' bungalow. And this was mostly because she had reverted into her mother's creature, a goal-oriented marriage-monster rather than the goodhearted and vivacious girlfriend I had envisioned. Amid all the cold showers—the only kind available at my apartment, anyway—I felt like a firework climbing higher and higher into the sky without ever exploding.

The positive side of this manufactured frustration and of Blanca's desire to otherwise grease the rails of our relationship was that she didn't ask potentially embarrassing questions. If I said something stupid regarding my research, she said, "That's right." And, if I said that I wanted to spend Friday afternoon on my own, she didn't ask why. Undoubtedly she assumed that I went to prostitutes or took advantage of my relationship with Ron and Dale to visit ¡Bonobo! Most Playatlecos—men and women—asserted that men had needs that women didn't share. Instead of grilling me, she asked when we could see each other again. If she heard from friends that I had danced with a tourist at a bawdy disco, she didn't ask whether I had had sex with her; in fact, she didn't even mention it. It was 'don't ask, don't tell.' And potentially it was a sad rehearsal for a marriage.

What made me a desirable husband? Sometimes it seemed that all three women (who knows what the father thought?) found the prospect of going to Florida, because it contained Disney World, more enticing than admitting me into their family.

Nonetheless, to their eyes I did have some other attractive attributes. I would like to tell you that, even back in Florida, I had to fight off swarms of women because I looked like Eddie Vedder. But I didn't. Maybe I had a certain pastiness in my favor, but in Playatlán, and especially in Blanca's neighborhood, to marry a white American—even a swarthy one if you had to—was automatically an achievement. That was my main selling point. Indeed, another reason that Flor wanted me to visit her house was so that the neighbors would see me going in. I wasn't a very good white American, given my lack of family. But most Mexicans had little respect for American families anyway, making an orphan only slightly worse than the rest.

Plus, I had more education than some men being called "doctor" at the university, so they thought I must have prospects. I found this at once bemusing, disturbing, and flattering and tried to explain the contingent future of a PhD-holder in anthropology. "Nat, don't be so modest," Flor once teased me.

"Blanca might run away with the guy who sells cassettes door-to-door if you don't watch out." Blanca then assured her mother that she found this exotic modesty, unknown among most Mexican men who talked to her, quite charming.

Add it all up, and I was better than the alternatives. Leaving aside the married men, my competition to get inside Blanca's pants or shirt consisted of guys who sometimes looked better but who held tenuous, or simply crappy, jobs. Maybe the cassette vendor didn't bother trying, but she was beset by waiters, beach vendors, office lackeys, sailors, fishermen, brewery drudges, and, worst of all, fellow students who didn't even have steady jobs yet. Flor and Blanca's frame of reference started from their family's working-class straits, spread out through their neighborhood—in which the people who lived on paved streets acted like gentry—and barely reached the fringes of the "middle class," whose lower rungs lived with fewer amenities than most undergraduates in the United States. From that perspective, Blanca had found a lottery ticket to the First World, if she could redeem me. Maybe, I thought, they should create a new lotería figure: El Gringo.

For her part, Blanca had more than looks and feels going for her. I eventually admitted to myself that I had patronized her at first, due to my stereotypes regarding beauty queens and believers in magic dolls. If I had only our conversations to go by, I would never have changed that opinion, as she steadfastly affirmed almost anything consequential that I said and turned childish in her mother's presence.

But Blanca was a Communications major at the Autonomous University of Conaloa. One day she left me alone in her room while she went to discuss a pageant issue with Flor. A demurely shut folder, leaning neatly against the wall, batted its eyes at me. Listening for Blanca's steps, I bent down to retrieve it. It was from her English class, and I quickly scanned it. To my surprise—which I guess was insulting—her work was very good. For example, although her spoken English was closer to 'her broken English,' her essays showed not only linguistic mastery but intellectual depth and what appeared to be emotional honesty. As I heard Blanca's voice getting nearer, I replaced the folder.

Once she had come back and we'd swapped some spit, I nonchalantly asked her, "What's in there?" and pointed to it. She acted mortified to show me, but now I sensed that she had placed it so conspicuously with this hope in mind. We went through her work and discussed it for quite a while. I took part of that time to verify (again, insultingly) that she had written it without help; she took my inquiries in good humor, joking about her difficulties speaking English yet interpreting my disbelief as a compliment to the quality of her written work. Someday, I thought, she might feel comfortable enough with me to hold forth in top-notch conversations.

But when would that be? And would she simply sound like an educated version of her mother? Like with sex or buying a car, I wanted to do thorough testing before making a long-term commitment.

The truth is, I could never see marrying Blanca.

ALCHEMY

Thus, after returning from True Bonobo, I headed to Nieves' birthday party feeling determined to finally end this relationship that was based on false pretenses and sustained by suspended desire. I didn't need Blanca, and I refused to allow her mother or anyone else to drag me along in their current.

I arrived punctually at the Mar-a-villa restaurant where the party would take place, so of course only family members were there. I savored the moment, because, while my affection for Bianca was ambivalent, I certainly loved being in the midst of her clan. I greeted her uncles, aunts, cousins, parents, and sister, all of whom were still affixing red and white balloons and streamers, arranging food, and setting out table decorations. A 'mobile disco,' or sound system transported in a van, blasted dance tunes in local and cosmopolitan styles. This marked the affair as middling. A poor family would have hired a group of mariachis or one of the trios who plied cantinas; a rich family, if willing to declare its wealth openly, would have hired a band that recorded albums and played concerts. Likewise middling, the Mar-a-villa was neither a taco stand nor a place to brag about frequenting. Clean, with a varied menu and hired staff, it opened onto a wide, commercial street in a mostly working-class area. A large, white tarp shaded maybe twenty white plastic tables, at which no one sat yet.

I would have wondered how Blanca's parents could afford to rent such a sound system and restaurant, but I already knew that they couldn't. The restaurant belonged to Flor's brother—and thus Blanca's uncle—Chuy. Early in our relationship, while walking along the shoreline, Blanca had told me that Chuy was a narco—but "not the type you see walking downtown with a pistol in his pants." Those guys (whose presence scared the crap out of me) apparently were of an inferior class. I quickly asked her to stop telling me about him, because I wanted to send the clearest signal possible that I wasn't worth killing. Still, it became clear that he used the restaurant for laundering money and for employing people he wanted to help or obligate. That explained how the Mar-a-villa, like so many other eateries in Playatlán, had almost no customers, ever. It also helped to explain how Blanca and Nieves' parents could afford the beauty pageants: Chuy (and ultimately American consumers) underwrote their social climbing. "He does what he does for his family," Blanca once told me, apparently convinced.

Depleted from my escapades with Holly and the others, I drifted into a corner, away from responsible action. Blanca, truly radiant in a white sundress, approached with a bottle of beer and an expectant smile. If I hadn't just come from True Bonobo, I might have proposed to her right there, just to reserve that vision in perpetuity. Why couldn't we at least enjoy a Bonobo handshake? She turned to stand by my side, letting her bare arm rub against mine. We scanned the scene.

"Nieves is a lucky girl," Blanca observed.

Nothing that I knew about her little sister had prepared me for that remark. At this moment, she was setting out plastic plates at her own, poorly attended birthday party. "To have such a wonderful sister?" I ventured. Blanca routinely performed alchemy on my empty compliments, turning them into golden tributes. She took my hand and squeezed it.

"Aside from *that*, she's especially lucky because this year she gets two birthday parties." I sensed that, despite her matter-of-fact tone, Blanca was being catty.

I could do catty, but at that point I felt fatigued and imbued with the last embers of the True Bonobo afterglow. "Really?" was all I could muster. "Is this one of them?"

"Obviously. And you missed the other one, which was yesterday." We went on like that—Blanca manifestly wanted to tell me something sordid, but, because of her great decency, she forced me to force it out of her. First she made me notice who hadn't come to the party. By that point, a female friend or two had just arrived, but, from my perspective, the list of laggards was long.

"What about Arturo?" Blanca asked.

"Oh, right, what about Arturo? Did he throw her another party?" This was Nieves' boyfriend, a recent college graduate who lazed around as a lackey at the municipal library. He struck me as a bit nondescript, earnest but likable. We had conversed pleasantly about graduate school and, of course, music. He claimed to like Nirvana and Maná, but who didn't? When I saw them together, Nieves looked at Arturo with adoration, another mystery of the heart.

So, yes, he did throw her a separate party, which only a few of his friends attended. Flor had convinced Chuy that Nieves (or they) could find a better match. So, at their instruction, Nieves never mentioned today's party to her boyfriend. "Don't worry," Blanca preemptively reassured me, "you'll be the guest of honor at my party." One part of me did feel reassured, but the other remembered my vow to free us both before then.

About an hour later, Flor's full strategy became apparent as the true guest of honor arrived. He was a young man, dressed in khakis and a short-sleeved button-down shirt, but with unkempt, unwashed hair. His special feature was that he carried a camera bag and press credential. In short, Chuy and Flor had bribed a newspaper to send this photographer to take pictures of the party for the society pages. Flor explained: "Young men from good families will see that she's pretty and available." The photographs would serve as a visual pheromone.

"We think she can do much better than that lazy kid she dates," Chuy chimed in. "Maybe even get a good gringo, like Blanca." He gave me a self-satisfied look that passed as an avuncular smile.

How refreshing, I thought, to hear snobbery from a drug trafficker. And he approves of me because I'm American. I might have had a few beers by then and perhaps had entered the testy phase of tipsiness. "You know," I wanted to say, "I don't like to boast, but I even linked up with Blanca when she had her cleavage covered. I probably deserve to have a street named after me."

The photographer saved the day (and my life?) by putting down his twice-emptied plastic plate and cajoling different groups of us into poses of great conviviality. In order to suggest that Nieves merited a similarly high-quality beau, Flor made sure that I graced most of the shots, but she also kept Blanca between me and Nieves, lest anyone mistakenly think that the younger one had a boyfriend. (I had trouble imagining eligible bachelors shopping for brides in the newspaper, but an enormous variety of Playatlecos did report seeing my picture.)

The photographer must have noticed that Nieves was pretty and available, or maybe he simply wanted to boost her self-esteem. In either case, he hung around the party after taking the photos and chatted animatedly with her. I was sitting at a table, idly hanging out with Blanca when I saw Flor walk over to say something to Chuy, who walked over to say something to the photographer, who immediately prepared to leave.

Blanca watched the same scene with moderate interest.

"What does Nieves think about this campaign to replace Arturo, but not with the photographer?" I asked.

"Ay, Nat," Blanca sighed and turned to me. "She says she doesn't like it. Imagine—doing that to your boyfriend. But, look, she goes along with it. Our mother knows what's best for us."

Us? I once heard a professor talk about calculating the "rate of human stupidity," based on how long it took ancient people to adopt the use of pottery. The rate was slow; ergo, people were stupid. Coincidentally, I was a person, and for the first time I wondered: Could Blanca have left her own Arturo for me? Was pressure from her mother what kept us together?

I sat there stewing as the party wound down. Oblivious, Blanca got up to hug departing guests and to help clear away some items that her family would take home. More than ever, I wanted out. This was worse than prostitution, which at least was an honest, finite transaction. I thought of how prostitutes—never having trained as pageant princesses—betrayed their feelings with minimal smiles or with full ones, with bucking orgasms that draped cum all over my condom or with perfunctory cooing, with relaxed conversation after doing the deed or with a quick collection of the rubber and a light embrace to hasten my departure. And then I thought, How low have I sunk? Is paying prostitutes the standard by which to judge my relationship with Blanca? What about True Bonobo? Or my girlfriends in the U.S.? Or my adoptive parents' marriage? But the ugly truth was that, structurally, our relationship failed even when compared to frequenting a brothel.

At the same time, and really for the entire party, I felt more at ease with Blanca than ever before. In chatting alone with her and while we interacted with others, I felt as though we had become a settled couple. It was nice, in a bourgeois way, and complemented the gush of attraction that overwhelmed me as I viewed her dazzling figure in the glory of the late-afternoon light. Was that love? Perhaps, instead, it was a premonition of later regrets.

I steeled myself to end our affair and walk away forever—there and then. I began to consider the most appropriate moment to have a word with her in private, near an exit, and then to walk quickly around the corner and out of sight. A rough draft of the words I should use scrolled into my mind, and I edited them to near-poetry, perhaps a telegraphed haiku—brief and evocative but ending in "STOP."

From across the restaurant, Blanca turned to check on me and saw that I was considering her. Her smooth, bare shoulders dropped a little, her head tilted a bit to the right, her delicious lips curled into a smile and pursed, and her eyes flashed slightly with warmth, possibly love.

She was good.

"How do you see it?" she called. In lieu of any other truth, I raised a nearly empty bottle in salute. She laughed at me and, shaking her head, turned back to the guests.

It took an eternity for the remaining guests to clear out. Saying goodbye among Mexicans might last longer than the visit itself. Some even came back after a few minutes, just to say one more thing to Nieves or to change their plans to go dancing with her later. Finally, it appeared that only Chuy's and Flor's immediate families remained, in addition to the restaurant employees tasked with cleaning up the mess. The mobile sound system had driven away. Dusk was turning to night, as a wind coursed through the tent.

The time had arrived. I liked to travel light—and maybe I was drunk and nervous—so I stepped into the restroom to urinate. I slapped my face a couple of times to wake myself up. Upon emerging, I saw them all standing together, chatting and chuckling near the opening in the fence that served as an exit. It was now or never.

I walked over and congratulated Chuy and Flor for hosting a wonderful party and thanked them for inviting me. I turned to Blanca and asked whether we might speak privately for a minute. Of course she agreed, but the family had taken the spot near the exit that I had envisioned using. We had to move to the middle of the dining area, farther under the tarp. Once Blanca started crying, I would have to stride quickly and resolutely past Chuy, onto the sidewalk, and around the corner to the right.

We stopped in the midst of the plastic tables. A waiter lugged a trash bag past us, knocking chairs out of the way. I knew that Blanca's family must be watching us and commenting.

Blanca looked up into my eyes, a wry yet simple smile on her face. "So, my love, you want to say something?"

My love! She had never called me that before. Ah!

But this provided yet more reason to not let the charade go further. I launched into a stuttering version of the preamble that I had rehearsed: "Well, I just wanted to say that you look—that you've been so beautiful today. I want to always think of you like this." This was True. "And it's been great getting to know you over the last couple of months. I can't believe how fast our relationship has developed."

Her eyebrows rose in expectation. Suddenly it occurred to me: Did she think I was about to propose? Her voice thick, she said, "I know—and only because I went to the Baby Jesus that day." Happy, joyful tears glistened in her eyes. "Ay, Nat, that day I made a prayer ..."

And when I think of Blanca now—when I miss her—I see her on that day. If it weren't for her mother, her desire for children, fucking Disney and the international border, who knows? I could have had Blanca, her relatives, unlimited time with my friends, sex with prostitutes (if Blanca were uninterested), and these memories, unsullied by regret. Maybe staying was the best thing I could have done.

But it's not what I did.

And, okay, sometimes I do beat off to the thought of sex on our honeymoon.

SAGE ADVICE

"I looked into her eyes, and I thought of her family standing between me and freedom, and … I just couldn't do it. I just couldn't. In fact, I think I made things worse. She'll be expecting a ring soon." I confided in Raúl as we each nursed a beer and slowly worked through the complimentary popcorn at the cheapest restaurant in the main tourist zone. It was late afternoon, and we were the only customers on the deck. A waiter lounged nearby, to ensure that we didn't stiff him. "So I come to you, as a treasured font of information on the ways of the authentic traditional Mexican, to ask: how does the typical Playatleco end a relationship?"

The sage paused to contemplate before speaking with great authority. "The first thing, Little Fly, is that you can't mix compliments with a rejection. Maybe you're trying to be nice about it, but it just confuses things."

"Okay, no 'I like you as a friend.'"

Raúl looked puzzled, in a judgmental way, so I explained the American formula to him.

"No—that's just fucked. It has to be ugly, so don't try to put makeup on it."

What about confessing to Blanca that I had sex with a tourist, with prostitutes, and at True Bonobo, so she'd hate me? That would be ugly.

"Nat, men and women are different. She doesn't care about the sex; she cares about the relationship." In fact, Blanca and other young virgins had told me several times that sex wasn't important to them the way it was for guys. "Plus, she probably already thinks you're doing those things. She might have doubts about you if you weren't. I mean, everyone knows you're friends with those guys from ¡Bonobo!" The wise one took a drag from his cigarette. "What she couldn't accept is if you had another girlfriend here in Playatlán."

"Awesome—I could have the same problem with another girl! Two months later, it's on to another. Eventually, I'd be facing a cartel of ex-girlfriends."

"It can be simpler, man: I saw in the newspaper that a pretty young woman named Nieves is looking for a boyfriend …"

I folded my arms and fixed him in my gaze.

He leaned forward and jabbed the air with his cigarette as he spoke. "No, Nat, you have to be a man. And a man simply announces that it's over. You can do it either by being seen publicly with another girlfriend—one from here—or by sending a note. You don't win any cosmic points by making it nice or by doing it in person. She'll hate you forever in any case." He leaned back and blew out some smoke. "Personally, I'd try one last time to grab her tits before ending it. She's a statue."

"Okay, I hear you. Thank you for sharing your sagacity. Have more popcorn, please. Just one more tiny issue: if she were hypothetically to have a close relative who's a narco, will he kill me?"

"Maybe not—not unless he's crazy. I've never heard of it happening, but who knows? It's a good question."

Ultimately, I sent the note, without further attempts on Mount Blanca.

CARNIVAL PARADES

Imagine my happiness upon discovering that Playatlán hosts one of the world's largest Carnival celebrations. With its own long history and plentiful idiosyncrasies, it was no mere copy of Mardi Gras in New Orleans, Rio de Janeiro, or Venice. The municipal government sponsored concerts, parades, food fairs, fireworks, a poetry contest, block parties, and, of course, beauty pageants. It punctured the monotony of almost everyone's life.

I especially enjoyed the violence. During parades in New Orleans, the people on the floats threw beads, cups, doubloons, toys, and gilded coconuts to the masses of grabby onlookers. Conversely, in Playatlán members of the crowd along the coastal boulevard turned anarchist and threw confetti-filled eggs—cascarones—at each other and at the people riding the floats. The Carnival Queen, a real pro, smiled and waved through an almost continuous pelting; sometimes she affected a naughty smile and launched eggs back at her attackers. From down on the sidewalk, I got into little wars with people on different hotel balconies: a couple of boys, a mischievous middle-aged man, and a coquettish married woman. Eventually, after exchanging a few volleys, a group of beer-drinking strangers waved for me to join them on their deck. A couple of families from a nearby city were sharing the suite, whence we viewed and assaulted all sorts of targets. Fighting was an excellent, if temporary, bonding mechanism.

Perhaps we all got carried away, though, when we pelted a police truck. It stopped abruptly and eight of Conaloa's finest poured out and flooded up into the hotel, apparently looking for our suite. This panicked my new friends, and we all ran to other rooms. The cops found only angelic bystanders and left quite slowly. That basically ended the orgy of egg-throwing, and I soon took my leave.

There was a downside to the free-for-all. Re-used eggshells from cascarones represented the greatest danger, as cheapsters, drunkards, and mean people would fill them with sand or small rocks and then hurl them at anyone on a float or just marching along. Others simply took raw eggs and hurled them. To civilize the masses, the organizers encouraged the riders on the floats to throw things to the throng, as in New Orleans. So, as part of the new, 'healthy' Carnival, the Boots Girls threw packs of Boots cigarettes indiscriminately into the crowd.

When the Boots Girls rode past, I felt relieved that Blanca wasn't among them. Undoubtedly such assignments would cheapen the image that she and Flor had cultivated.

I had moved along the seaside walkway to a spot with only a thin line of spectators. I needed a break from so much noise and novelty—basically, to reset.

The parade suffered from long lapses between floats, whether due to mechanical problems or tardy riders. One such lull had hit this stretch of the route. So, turning from the street to gaze across the bay past ¡Bonobo!, I watched the sun become a lush red as it set into the humid haze above the sea. I lost myself in the sound of the waves crashing against the beach and then receding.

After a few minutes, I could hear another set of floats approaching, blaring the song of the moment—a comic tale of cuckoldry—and the awakened chatter of the families around me. I turned for a moment and saw a well-made float in the guise of a fire engine approaching. The men on it were using stylized hoses to douse fake flames.

The sun was almost down; I watched the last, scarlet sliver descend and meld into the crimson layer of haze just above the horizon. Satisfied that it was gone, I turned around and found myself looking directly at Blanca, who was wearing a glittery, silver dress and waving from the near edge of the bright red float. My heart leapt. What should I do?

Her eyes swept over me like a swell trundling far above the deep ocean bottom. I saw her not-see me with total clarity. She looked happy.

I not-focused on her as the float chugged exuberantly down the boulevard.

I'd had enough of the parade. So I crossed the road and walked home via interior streets. I wanted to rest, in anticipation of that night's festivities.

Raúl and some other friends who taught at the university told me that during the block party I could find them in front of the Vaso de Agua, or 'Glass of Water.' The problem was that I could find almost anyone there. It was a faded restaurant-bar that usually was as lonesome as the rest of downtown. But during Carnival hordes thronged the street, jostling to reach a meeting point, pushing in chains through the crowd, dancing in place to a band on a nearby stage, or simply hanging out and drinking. My friends professed an exclusive interest in the latter, which had its own verb, 'pistear.'

There are two poles of pisteaje, between which any particular episode falls. The no-fireworks version occurred every day in almost every corner of Playatlán. In the afternoons, in the blazing heat and sweltering humidity, even little old ladies might escape the discomfort of their houses, which had no air conditioning, by sitting in front, nursing a beer, and cherishing any slight breeze or novelty that might blow their way. Conversation was minimal, formulaic, repetitive, and mundane. Men resorted to similar delights in low-rent cantinas, and others could be seen here and there along the beach and on municipal benches. (To an untrained eye, this was what so many heavy-drinking, sunbathing tourists were doing too, although they claimed it was blissful.)

Carnival provided opportunities to experience the other pole of pisteaje, as Playatlecos enjoyed continuous pops of pleasure (mostly) while they hung out and drank. It's a feeling that I wanted to prolong in perpetuity. This form of pisteaje could be found among carousing buddies at a cantina, adult siblings out for a special dinner, and verbose friends along the beach. For those adept at conversation, it was the default, but the majority needed a boost of external stimulation, which Carnival provided in spades.

So there I was, swimming against the current of humanity just to dart around the shoals of the Vaso de Agua in quest of Raúl and company, who promised to be hanging out and drinking "like fuck," when I ran into Líssy and her pals from True Bonobo. I felt surprise at how glad I was to encounter them again.

The entire block party stretched for about a mile, with ten or so stages placed about two hundred yards apart. They featured bands playing basically the same list of songs, all in the same regional style. Líssy's group had formed a train of about seven people, this time for locomotion, who were chugging along through the crowd to get to a favored dance spot a couple of buildings away.

I greeted Líssy and the rest with hugs but no Bonobo handshake. Still, an intimacy had been rekindled. I was about to join them in their expedition, when I glimpsed Raúl and Ricardo a few yards and many people away. Quickly figuring that it would be better to warm up with the talkers and then end up with the dancers, I told Lissy that I would find them later.

Bottles were forbidden at the block party because they might serve as weapons, so, once among friends, I held my beer in a plastic cup as the masses jostled past. I stayed mellow, letting the party come to me. I felt like each encounter was a living, two-way Rorschach test. I gauged others' reactions as they passed or stopped to talk with someone in our group.

Most people, of course, just pushed on without taking much notice. Sometimes a teenager or young adult would smash a cascarón into my open mouth or my hair or would squirt foam aggressively in my face. At one point I was facing the Vaso de Agua and thus had my back turned to the main stream of revelers. I felt a hard knock on the back of my noggin and quickly turned to see a thirty-year-old man wearing a white stetson. He waded away through the crowd, draping his arm around his girlfriend's shoulder. He stared back at me with a hard expression for several seconds as they moved northward into the distance.

In the midst of all this hustle and bustle, one of the first people to stop and talk was a middle-aged man in shabby business attire—slacks, a short-sleeved button-down, and worn black shoes. By that point, Ricardo had finally bought me a beer and was pressing me for juicy details regarding my night at True Bonobo. I once again tried to keep the discussion abstract by comparing True Bonobo's ritual features to those of Carnival. I scanned the surroundings as we bantered, and registered that this newcomer soberly greeted Raúl, a few people down from me. He looked vaguely familiar. As they chatted, Raúl glanced my way a few times. Then he slid next to me with a cheerfully efficacious demeanor, and suddenly I saw that the other guy was Benito, the nationalist from the cantina who had verbally defecated all over the U.S. Oh, shit, I thought, I don't need an altercation in the middle of 200,000 Mexicans in the world center of drug-trafficking. Perhaps it was time to find Lissy.

I must have flinched, because Raúl said, "Stay calm, Nat, Benito's here to apologize. He's not drunk now, and he feels bad. Will you shake his hand?"

"Sure, I'll shake his hand. I'm not the one who attacked him."

"Relax, Little Fly, I told you—he's sorry."

We forced our way back to Benito, who didn't actually apologize. But we did shake hands, and then Raúl and Ricardo chanted, "Hug!" a couple of times. So Benito and I sheepishly exchanged a light embrace. Raúl, acting as justice of the peace, then pronounced us all friends.

Relieved that it was over and not wanting to spoil my new friendship by actually conversing, I moved back to the other side of Ricardo. Raúl and my new friend chatted for a couple of minutes, and then Benito headed north.

"Have you been on the north side?" Ricardo asked.

"Not yet, but I'm curious. Is it different?"

"The music's the same, but you shouldn't go there."

Why can't people just say it straight? Maybe this is how they fill hours of nothing. "Why not?"

"That's the working-class area. It's too dangerous."

"Dangerous?"

"Drunkards who pick fights. Myself, I'm a drunkard who avoids them. I wouldn't go there late at night."

I thought we already were in the working-class area, but I kept that to myself. Now I was even more curious about the other side.

As the night flowed on, I flirted with my friends' former students, chatted about poetry with an Uruguayan professor, entertained historical speculations by a journalist, discussed my research with a young neighbor who had never acknowledged me on the street, enjoyed theories regarding the chupacabras and other extraterrestrials, prompted a pretty, leftist dentist to opine about the vandalism at ¡Bonobo!, and met the scion of a drug-trafficking family.

Around midnight, though, I suspected that Líssy's crowd might interest me a different way. For example, I might get laid. So I took my leave of the pisteadores. As parting advice, Raúl warned me to not stray too far north. "It's dangerous."

XÓCHITL

I had to push through only a half-block to find Líssy and the gang. Located in a stretch free of stages, it was the only section where rock was played, in this case by a mobile disco rather than bands. Here teenagers dominated, with occasional clumps of people in their twenties. They clearly had set themselves off from the rest of the crowd—even the other teenagers—by the way they dressed: a large percentage looked intentionally ragged, like rockers in the U.S. Of course, some of these young slobs must have come from straitened circumstances, but so did the people listening to regional music at the other stages, and they had the decency to wear collared shirts.

Most Playatlecos associated the slovenly style common among these young toughs with gang membership, and sometimes they were right. But there also were lazy-dressing druggies, rockers, beach vendors, and run-of-the-mill slobs who had nothing to do with gangs. One of the surprises was that, whereas the gang members probably did drugs and got drunk and maybe did some small-scale dealing around town on an ad hoc basis, the full-on drug traffickers—the ones cutting off their rivals' heads and leaving them by the highway—were the respectable-looking people. Maybe some narcos dressed too flashily, but they always tucked in their silk shirts.

It was easy to spot Líssy's pod not just because they dressed a smidgen more respectably but because the seven of them were standing, drinking, and dancing on the low, concrete wall that separated the block party from the beach. They saw me and yelled my name—even the ones I hadn't met—and waved for me to join them. One of the guys, Arturo, unnecessarily reached down to help me mount the wall, and Líssy likewise put a hand lightly on my back to steady me. Once the greetings and introductions were complete, we joked and made observations about the people with whom we'd talked or not talked and about the awesomeness of the night.

At one point, while dopily making a circular dance move, I noticed that, off to the right across the bay, I could barely discern the muted lights of the south end of ¡Bonobo! Usually it was Playatlecos (and I) who gazed with curiosity and longing at ¡Bonobo! But the rules of the resort kept the guests and workers quarantined there. Could the shoe now be on the other foot? Were the Bonobans, their genitalia spent and drying, gathered on the parapets, wishing they could experience the fireworks, the drama, of Carnival?

Eventually most of us clambered down from the wall to talk with friends passing by or to find a surer platform on which to sway drunkenly. I pretended to have a similar pursuit in stepping down, but the Truth is that I wanted to maintain contact with Líssy's friend, Xóchitl. Diminutive and athletic, she seemed several years younger. Her voluble voice reminded me more of a mountain brook than of the waves crashing a few meters away. Her wavy brown hair reached her shoulders, and her brown eyes sparkled even as the corners started to droop from the weight of inebriation. Maybe because of her height, she stood erect, but she made constant adjustments while interacting with the rest of us, which lent her an air of convivial elegance—an impression accentuated by the sleeveless, coppery top she wore over white jeans.

In sum, I wanted to fuck her—and more than I wanted to fuck Líssy or anyone else at whom I had a shot. However, none of them—not Xóchitl or Líssy or Anaís or anyone else—

clearly wanted to fuck me. We were a ball of friends, at least some of whom participated in orgies. Still, I felt my chances took a great leap forward when Xóchitl revealed that her boyfriend would not be coming. His parents had chosen to flee the depravity of Carnival with their children for the quiet of his mother's ancestral village. Apparently, experience had taught them to not leave behind any adult children with keys to the house. The friends laughed while reminiscing about the fun they had had there.

Suddenly the entire crowd, packed and colliding like molecules under pressure, magically expanded, pushing those of us on the periphery every which way. I turned to see an ever-widening, impromptu arena, and, in the center, two teenage boys facing off with wide eyes and short blades in their hands. One wore a blue bandanna; the other red. The young people around the area chattered as they focused their excited eyes on the duelists, who now had no choice but to fight. One lunged at the other, and a joyfully fearful exclamation arose from the onlookers.

As those in the front row pushed backward to avoid getting slashed and latecomers tried to jostle closer to the action, our pod of friends was rent apart. I had to make a fateful choice, a decision of destiny. Thus I got myself jostled in Xóchitl's direction, where we—alas!—found ourselves isolated from the others. My right side was next to her and my left side behind her. As the color-coded combatants circled and lunged and jumped back, and the crowd oohed and aahed and sagged back even more, Xóchitl hopped on her tiptoes to get a better view.

Then she looked up, smiling. "How do you see it?"

"The crowd moved back really fast. Does this happen every year?"

"Yes, Nat, now you see how we are. It happens every night during Carnival, right here. Maybe there will be more."

Anyway, the fighters continued to semi-attack and mostly defend, and one possibly received a cut shirt or a bloody scrape—it was hard to tell. Xóchitl and I got ourselves pushed together a lot, and we smiled at each other during the major jolts. A few times, to brace her, I put my hand on the back of her shirt or on the bare, smooth skin of her neck or shoulder. And she once tucked into my chest, which felt oddly massive just then, to shelter herself. My dick felt massive, too, and a little pre-ejaculate lubricated its path against my skin.

After an absurdly long time, a couple of cops strode through the crowd, which parted as for Moses—because everyone feared the police as much as the gang-banging idiots. When the cops were about to penetrate the circle on the red fighter's side, he turned to face them, and the blue one honorably took that moment to slash at his opponent's forearm. He then sprinted away through an instant passage in the crowd and the red one gave chase at full speed. The two cops ran after both.

The crowd collapsed back into the hole, and people returned to chatting and dancing. Humanity still clogged the few yards between Xóchitl and me and the nearest remnants of Líssy's crew.

"How do you see it?" she asked me, with eager eyes.

"Well, that was interesting. That's the first gang fight I've ever seen in person. What about you?"

"Ay, I don't know. That's Carnival." She hesitated. "Nat, where do you live?"

I told her and asked, "Do you know where that is?"

"Of course, do you want to go?"

Thank you, idiot cholos! May the Virgen de Guadalupe rain down a million blessings on you.

I expressed willingness to accompany Xóchitl to my homestead. We fought through a few people so that she could inform her closest friend, Anaís, who smiled slyly and glanced at me occasionally. I stayed out of the conversation and watched as a couple of medics pushed quickly through the crowd in the direction of the cops and cholos. At that point, after waging their own seesaw battle, my balls needed care, too, or at least anesthetic; all my hopes were on Xóchitl. As we took our leave, Anaís sternly looked us in the eye and warned both of us to take care of her friend. Then she brightened and exclaimed, "Have fun!"

Off we went, despite the many warnings I'd received, to the north. We really had no acceptable alternative: given the location of the gates and the closed-off streets and the other events, it might take hours to get to my apartment by any other route. Anyway, I was a little drunk and quite curious—maybe what I saw would be useful for my research. Plus, Xóchitl simply started walking that way, and I was in the mood to accede to her desires.

We worked our way, holding hands, past stage after stage presenting the same bands playing the same songs as on the south side. Beer stands sold the same drinks.

The people, though, were a little different. I noticed more cowboy hats and wider belts, and men were more likely to mutter something about gringos as I passed, and to bump shoulders with me. For a long stretch an extremely drunk and apparently resentful young man walked a little to our right, staring at us with laser-like enmity. We lost him only when Xóchitl stopped to greet a couple she knew. When the way seemed clear, we set out again.

For me, filled with apprehension and anticipation, the walk seemed endless. The gate loomed in my mind like a light at the end of the tunnel of death. From there, my apartment was only a few blocks, most of them well-lit and familiar to me.

All of a sudden, Xóchitl wanted to prolong the party and boogie. This I knew—if the woman one wants to screw wants to dance first, then dance one must, even if one is surrounded by men who might want to hurt one. The band was playing a well-worn standard about a red demon. I wrapped my right arm around her firm back, stuck my right leg between hers up to the crotch so that we were intertwined, and pulled her back and forth like a hobby horse. She rested her arms around my neck. We regarded each other with amusement and desire.

"You like 'El Caballito,' Nat?" Coy. She must have felt my hard-on.

I wanted to say something about her enjoying El Caballo but thought better of it. I just smiled—suavely, I hoped.

After a couple of songs and no altercations, we finally exited the street party. It must have been about 2 AM. People who couldn't afford tickets milled about or sat along the seawall, drinking beer and talking genially within earshot of the bands. Some villagers from the hinterland had set up tents along the beach or slept en masse in the back of rented semis. Music from a few quiet radios leaked low across the ether, riding just above the sound of the surf to our left. We stopped at a hotdog stand for me and, a couple of blocks later, a pancake stand for her. We exchanged mundane comments about the sweet, tranquil night with other customers.

Finally, we reached my street, which glowed empty and silent under a yellowish streetlight. The night air was warm and still away from the beach. Xóchitl held my hand and we rubbed shoulders as we walked the half-block to my thick, wooden door. As I inserted and turned the key, I told her, "Here we are. Mi casa es tu casa."

She grabbed my arm and, on her tiptoes, pulled close, whispering with warm, beery breath, "And mine is yours." Her moist lips kissed my cheek.

We entered the front room and, with my back holding the door closed, we explored each other's torso with our hands and slid our tongues together. After necking for a couple of minutes, practicalities demanded attention. It had been hours since either of us had peed, the front door needed locking and the curtains closing, and apologies for various messes seemed politic. I went out to the patio to use the bathroom first, in part to ensure that the seat was clean. Then, while Xóchitl was on the toilet, which I and any wakeful neighbors could hear, I rummaged through her jeans, wondering what I might find. Not much—just a wad of bills, a few coins, and a mysterious phone number on a small, torn-off slip of paper. As soon as I heard her trying to get the toilet to flush—it might take an hour for the tank to fill—I replaced everything and called to her to not worry about it.

Then, with a fresh, more deliberate approach, we resumed our embraces. First, she stood before me, with her back to the side of the bed. I reached down to pull her top over her head, kissing her exposed neck along the way, and then unbuttoned her jeans, which, with a few tugs, fell to the floor. Her bra and underwear were a white, silky fabric. We kissed, open-mouthed and eyes closed, as I moved my hands all over her bare torso. She reached hers inside my shirt, feeling my chest and back. I began to play with her small, firm breasts and then squeezed her butt and rubbed her pussy through the lingerie. Then I moved down and took her nipple and bra in my mouth and sucked. She shuddered. I lay her back on the bed and, now kneeling, moved my tongue to her pussy. I could feel the smooth and cool skin of her thighs against my face and shoulders and the wetness that now marked her underwear. My saliva mingled with it as I played with her clit through the panties and then moved them aside to directly taste her pungent juices. She began to moan in hushed tones and then to pant as I thrust a finger into her canal while I steadily continued to lick her clit. With an arched back, clasping my head with her thighs, she came.

I leaned over her to kiss again. Then she sat forward, put her hands on my hips, and told me, "Take off your shirt."

163

I obeyed.

She unbuttoned my blue jeans and, with some help, pulled them to the floor. She looked me in the eyes as she reached out and rubbed my erect cock through my boxers. She grasped it and felt the pre-cum that had leaked out most recently. Her expression turned to mock concern.

"Don't worry," I said, "there's more."

She lowered my underwear onto the floor and took my dick into her mouth. She sucked for several minutes and then, still rubbing me slowly with her hand, asked whether I wanted to make love with her.

The Truth is, I wanted to make love with Blanca. With Xóchitl, I wanted to screw. But I said yes. Excusing myself, I went quickly to the small, wooden bedside table and withdrew a condom.

And then we copulated ferociously—not like beasts but like people engaged in the mortal struggle, thrashing together like wrestlers, rolling each other in our arms, our tongues constantly engaging the other's mouth or skin, our legs flailing and pushing and sliding. My cock bulged like never before; the veins strained against the condom. She came again—and yet again when I did, gasping and exclaiming, "Yes yes yes."

I moved my hips back a little to withdraw and, with the condom slowly slipping off, lay atop her, slightly to the right, my chin aligned with the top of her head. Xóchitl grabbed me more tightly and curled into me. And I felt her whole body begin to shudder. She was crying.

Had I hurt her? Did she feel guilty about her boyfriend? Paralyzed by these thoughts, I simply caressed her for a moment, then asked, "Are you okay?"

She laughed softly amid her sobs. "Oh, Nat, don't worry. This happens every time. I don't know why." She paused, and I continued to hold her, wondering how to react. "It's why I can't go to True Bonobo. I went one time, and—imagine how it was—it scared the guy I was doing it with. It was too strange for everyone." Convulsing, she laughed again and cried more and burrowed further into me.

And I let her. Feeling massive, I wrapped myself around her more, her hair pressed to the skin of my beating chest. She depended on me and trusted me to shelter her in this momentary vale of tears, and I was equal to the task.

This was new. I had always reflexively avoided entanglements that penetrated too deeply, whether with my adoptive family or their dog or my girlfriends or their dogs and, I realized now, with my own deepest hopes and fears. Problem-solving rationality, irony, abstract analysis, and humor—these were my defenses against the flood. As Xóchitl sobbed within the refuge I provided, my heart, Grinch-like, expanded beyond its frame, and melted.

I began to weep, too, overwhelmed with tenderness for humanity and the beauty of feeling it. I was worthy!

Xóchitl lifted her head a little to look at me. "Oh, Nat, look how we are," she sniffled. How do you see it?"

I saw that now I could make love.

And then, slowly, we did.

I slept like a fetus.

I woke up not knowing where, when, or even who I was.

I became aware of a tender and amused voice cooing in my ear and saw Xóchitl leaning over me. She was standing by the bed, dressed. Her hand had shaken my shoulder and now stroked my face. "Nat, I'm going to Anaís' house before my parents find out." It was dawn.

"Huh?" I struggled both to awaken and to return to sleep. "Okay."

"I got the key. I'll lock the door from outside and throw it back through the window, okay?"

"Okay." I propped myself up on an elbow. "Hey, Xóchitl."

"Yes?"

"I enjoyed it."

"I enjoyed it, too."

"Do you need money for a taxi?"

"Thanks, Nat, but no. I'll walk. It's close."

"Okay, be careful. Wait—should I take you?"

"It's okay. Maybe I'll see you at Carnival tonight."

"Yeah, I hope so."

"Me too."

Did she? The next time I saw her was well after Carnival, with her boyfriend.

A SURPRISE VISIT

A few weeks later, Carnival was long gone. The weather was dry. Young Americans on spring break came each week to yell "woo" and hold fake-orgasm contests. Minor beauty pageants took place here and there. And the Chupacabras hadn't killed a dog or cow for more than a year. Remembering this time, I think of heat, blazing sunlight, and flies buzzing. For most Playatlecos, it was flatline time.

My research proceeded apace. The problem with studying mundane aspects of life, such as listening to music, was that they had become mundane to study. Sex with the prostitutes, once so novel and transgressive, had become routine. I asked a wide variety of people for clues regarding the vandalism at ¡Bonobo! but made no progress. A minority resented the resort, but not any more than they resented the rest of the imperialistic, exclusionary, and hedonistic tourist enterprise; a few were up for vandalism for its own sake but were hardly ready for repeated attacks against an island; some fantasized of a day when they might visit; and most just didn't care. Blah blah blah. My meetings with Ron and Dale were genial but becoming formulaic. So I, too, was tending toward the flatline; the explosions in my soul were more like carbonated bubbles than fireworks.

My most common method of generating thrills, however small, was to tune into the universal love and acceptance (with a tinge of beneficent condescension, I now see) that had over-

167

whelmed me between having sex with Xóchitl and making love to all of humanity, albeit with protection, in the form of Xóchitl. This beatific perspective was easy to mistake for the way a participant-observer was supposed to employ cultural relativism. So it fed my pride and increased my delight manifold to walk along what used to seem like the same tired streets lined with dingy buildings in which Playatlecos sleepwalked through the usual tired activities. Now, in contrast, I saw a familiar and welcoming landscape, where neighbors pursued activities that gave them comfort, where they based their pride on human relations more than on a clean house, where the low-level drug dealer on the corner was a local institution, where the near-comatose look on the face of a housewife signaled a rich inward journey.

By this time, I had developed a circuit of food stands and semi-formal eateries among which I alternated: the pancake cart at the corner, the hotdog vendor across from it, the taco stand a couple of blocks farther inland, the Pollo Loco across from the beach, the restaurant where I always ordered quesadillas mixtas, and so forth. On a fateful Tuesday afternoon, I decided that I wanted to eat marlin tacos at one of these favorites, a well-attended, open-air café a few blocks north of my apartment, where three streets met at an odd angle. I donned my baseball cap and rubbed in some sunscreen because the white plastic tables, spread out illegally across the wide sidewalk and into the street, lay exposed to the midday sun.

This restaurant served only lunch, which seemed to work as a marketing strategy, given that only a couple of tables remained available when I arrived. As was the custom, I walked directly to the counter, which sat on the sidewalk next to a building that housed the kitchen, and ordered the tacos. The clerk, with his dismissive air, tested my attitude of delight in all experience, but I reminded myself that such surliness was characteristic and a clear sign that Playatlecos weren't slaves to the consumer. I turned around to identify the best location for people-watching and noticed an open table close to where I was standing. I also saw, across the array of diners, Beto and Jorge, guys from my neighborhood whom I had interviewed several weeks before. Back then they had been sitting along the seawall, pisteando and listening to narcocorridos blasting from a boombox. We had enjoyed a good conversation, sticking to the music and avoiding any possible connection to their liveli-hoods. Since that afternoon, they nodded to me whenever we saw each other.

And so they raised their bottles to signal a greeting. I saw that two seats at their table were empty. Sensing a rare oppor-tunity to deepen my relationship with productive informants, I squeezed around the chairs of the relaxed, chatty crowd to talk with them. The guys greeted me jovially. We made small talk about the weather, and they recommended a new album by an artist they liked. Unfortunately, they were awaiting the arrival of a couple of associates, so the seats were not available. May-be next Tuesday.

I told them there was no problem, and I wended my way back toward the unoccupied table. I felt concerned and, de-spite myself, a little annoyed because it looked like a couple of other customers might beat me to it. Still, the world was good and things would work out—maybe we could share the space, allowing me to meet new informants.

Suddenly it happened. Working through the jumbled tables, I heard a loud engine approach along the street behind me, then people back there shouting for an instant, and, as the people before me looked up quickly, several booms like bal-loons exploding. I spun around, and the diners near me, their eyes wide, shouted to God in confusion and stumbled out of their chairs. The engine revved and tires squealed, and I saw, while turning, a black pickup speeding away with two men settling into the back. Hyper-alert and confused, I scanned the rest of the tables. The inert bodies of Jorge and Beto lay contorted in their seats, thick chunks of blood and internal goo polluting their faces and shirts and table. A middle-aged woman seated nearby was screaming and her sleeve was red with blood, while the man across from her bled into his guayabera and was trying to stand but couldn't.

I ran.

I didn't think. I pushed away chairs and tables and people and sprinted home. I passed others running away, too; some dodged behind cars parked along the street.

But other people ran in the opposite direction, to see the killing. With the same wide-eyed excitement and fear that we all had during the knife fight at Carnival, they left their shops and homes and hustled to witness the carnage. Fireworks!

I locked myself inside my apartment. I was shaking and hyped up and had no plan. What if this was part of a war between drug gangs, and more of my neighbors were targets? What if they wanted to get rid of any witnesses? What if the mere chance I was a DEA agent was enough to kill me now? Would Blanca's uncle take this chance to get me? I had to lie low, to play it safe.

My thoughts continued obsessively along these lines for hours. I closed the curtains and sat where bullets fired through the windows couldn't hit me directly. I turned on my boombox and switched it to the radio. I searched for news reports but found only the usual music, religious, and public affairs programs. I kept the volume low to hide my presence and to allow me to hear any other gunshots. Eventually, I found news reports, which told me less than I already knew. This probably meant that no other attacks had occurred, but I remained huddled against the wall in a corner of the middle room for a couple of hours, just to be prudent.

As I sat there, thoughts of the victims increasingly entered the stream of my consciousness, especially the couple at the table near Jorge and Beto. News reports eventually said the man had died on the scene and the woman had been taken to the hospital. That could have been me! If I had chatted with the guys for a minute longer; if I had arrived a minute later; if they had let me sit with them until their 'associates' arrived; if the table near them had been open ... I cried, rocking and sobbing with unspeakable emotion.

Then it occurred to me that Jorge and Beto looked and acted like a lot of guys in Playatlán. If they were narcos worthy of rubbing out in broad daylight, then I must be surrounded by such people. This could happen anywhere, at any time. What if a gangland war erupted?

You can see that I didn't handle my near-slaughter with aplomb. It wasn't gritty fun like watching *Reservoir Dogs*. I *knew* the targets; I was the last person they spoke with; maybe I heard their last, mundane words—"Órale," I think. My mind repeatedly played, unbidden, various possible movies in which I got gunned down with them, for nothing. Worst of all, everywhere I saw reminders of the innocent, dying man struggling to rise from his chair while his secretary (it turned out) screamed in terror. His ordinary, lovable life had been snuffed out, like an ant under the foot of some passing dog. These thoughts and emotions tore at me over the subsequent weeks, receding very slowly. Indeed, in some ways they continue to hobble me.

But back then, on the afternoon of the shooting, I eventually had to use the toilet and get some food from the kitchen, before returning to my safe spot.

The next morning, reassured by the news reports, I left my apartment to stock up on groceries so that I could avoid restaurants for a while. I went first to the neighborhood market, which was much more lively than usual. Vendors and customers chatted with animation about the attack—what happened, who saw it, who knew the victims, who the shooters might be, why it happened, how it was like previous murders, the innocent victims' reason for being there ... To all appearances, they felt happier that the shooting had occurred.

Their enthusiasm sickened me. It angered me.

As was my habit, I visited Carlos the Explosion Addict at his dairy stand, and he asked, with some avidity, whether I had heard about the shooting. When I answered that I had witnessed it, his eyes widened a little, and he pumped me for details. I felt dirty but obligated to give a basic account of what I had seen. Carlos told me that he and the other people in the market could hear the pops but didn't think much of them. "Maybe it was a truck." But, as soon as he heard sirens from the police and ambulance, he got someone to watch his stall and ran to see the aftermath. "There was blood everywhere! They must have put a lot of holes in them."

"I guess that was a big emotional explosion for you—and free of charge. Congratulations."

He finally noticed my agitation but retained his smile. "Nat, if you don't understand Mexicans and death, how can you understand those corridos? I once read a book that said we have three basic relations—family, friends, and La Muerte. And, yes, sometimes we get excited when Death pays a surprise visit."

A LEARNING EXPERIENCE

Carlos' cogent analysis did nothing to diminish the obsessive fear that wormed its way into all of my perception. To overcome feeling so frantic, I sought ... Actually, I didn't know what I sought, whether it was comfort, understanding, or a better perspective.

Not that this was my first knowledge of death. My parents had died together when I was quite young, so the capricious timing and consequences of death intrinsically defined my relationship to others. But seeing someone expire in the midst of a sunny, happy lunch, watching him struggle and fail to rise, missing being that person by a minute—or less! It overwhelmed me.

It was worst at night, as I lay utterly alone in the quietude and darkness, without even a full cover to embrace me, thanks to the heat. For the first time in a long while, I ached to feel my imagined parents' arms around me, their hands stroking my hair, their soft voices cherishing and soothing me. I lay curled in a fetal position, shaking, and indulged in bouts of crying. I feared death like a motherfucker, and I hated murderers and careless drivers and negligent doctors and armies and a long litany of shits who wantonly and selfishly took life and love away. I scrawled free-form cries of agony, anger, and impotence in my personal journal.

After my ordeal in the market and conversation with Carlos, I didn't expect to find relief from other Mexicans, especially not men. My interactions with friends, as I emerged gradually into society, reinforced this prejudice. They knew that I lived near the crime scene and pumped me for news and, to forestall flatlining, re-pumped me for more details. The shooting wasn't as productive for them as the mysterious murder a few years earlier of the ruling party's presidential candidate, Colosio—which had kept their mental sparklers going off for years—but it beat thinking about nothing new. Unfortunately for all concerned, I didn't want to be a living tabloid.

Yet I felt the need to truly connect with someone in order to get past this period of paranoia and existential terror. Of course, Xóchitl came to mind, but she had a boyfriend, and, anyway, she reflexively wanted sheltering too. I didn't need to wallow in co-dependence with another weakling. Blanca probably would have acted safely sympathetic if we still were dating, but it's doubtful that she would have sought a deeper understanding. I imagined that Sherry, my last partner at True Bonobo, might intuitively know the magic formula for soothing me, but in practice she no longer existed outside of my mind.

So my thoughts turned even more pathetic. I started to question why I was struggling to identify even a single emotional rescuer when any person should be able to rely on several obvious ones. Where was my group hug? With Xóchitl I had learned to tap into an appreciation of Humanity. But I still didn't feel right calling on humans I had known for years: my ex-girlfriends in the U.S., my classmates in graduate school, or, tellingly, my adoptive parents. I just didn't feel that kind of deep connection to anyone. Ordinarily I didn't miss it, and, in fact, I had found my girlfriends before Blanca to be a bit clingy, intrusive, and tiresome. It took a shooting for me to look my freedom in the face and yearn for a deeper bond.

So I reached out to Doris. I bought a phone card to call from a payphone in the main plaza downtown. Over my months in Playatlán, I occasionally had seen individual gunmen (of the sort that Blanca's uncle supposedly transcended) walking along nearby streets, pistol butts sticking conspicuously out of their pants. But they never approached the main plaza, which was an exposed location bordered by city hall and the cathedral, with numerous police milling about. Nonetheless, as I spoke with Doris I continuously pivoted to scan in all directions.

In response to my uncharacteristic outpouring of fear, she made no effort to soothe me. "I'm sorry, Nat." Her tone, while sympathetic, suggested neither remorse nor apology, "But that's not something I do well."

In my weakness and desperation, I tried again to provoke a verbal caress. This apparently made her uncomfortable. "Nat, please, I'm not your mother." But then she remembered and truly felt remorseful. "Oh, God. I'm sorry. I'm sorry sorry sorry. Nat? I mean that I'm nobody's mother. I just don't have it in me."

Now, oddly, I reassured *her* that she hadn't acted offensively—although obviously she had.

To return to more advantageous terrain, she suggested that I focus on using the shooting "to complicate your interrogation of the narcocorridos' discursive field." She dressed it up in academic finery, but this was tantamount to urging me to exploit the spectacle for my own gain, much like Carlos. I had sought comfort, but Doris could supply only advice. The idea of turning this tragedy to my advantage appalled me. I responded coldly, but she insisted: I hadn't sought to experience the shooting, and I was suffering from it—why shouldn't I get some benefit from it? It's not as though, by isolating and fixing its meaning as pain, I could change what had happened. Anyway, this was how participant-observation worked.

I was not ready to hear this, and I somewhat curtly ended the call. "Well, thanks. I gotta go. There are lots of people waiting for the phone," which was a lie.

Much later, when my anxiety had subsided a bit more, I began to see utility in strategically adopting the attitude that Doris had advocated. This led to an apparently dispassionate analysis in my other dissertation in which I contrasted the messy and mundane shooting that I had witnessed to the romantic portrayals of death in the songs with which Jorge and Beto identified. I have yet to discover a metric by which to judge whether this refined treatment was superior to my friends' excited gawking.

Finally, a couple of days after calling Doris, I accidentally found someone who knew how to soothe me, probably better than any psychiatrist could. At four o'clock on a blazing afternoon, I lay in a small, stale-smelling room with my collapsing penis and fresh semen still in a condom. I was curled inward and crying in the arms of "María," a prostitute. She patted my back and stroked my head and made soft, motherly tutting noises. She didn't ask or comment: she saw pain, she sympathized, and she expressed care. To call her a sex worker would severely underreport her duties.

Sure, she might have secretly checked the clock or used the moment to think about a soap opera or who shot Colosio or how she might find a better line of work. Or maybe she wondered why I was crying on her. If so, she hid her disinterest much better than she had during sex.

I guessed her age to be around mine or perhaps into her lower thirties. Nonetheless, when the paroxysms finally quieted to minor whelps, she called me, "Mijo" ('my son'), and I accepted it. Perhaps the Cesarean scar on her midriff made this easier for both of us.

Later, after I had regained my composure and paid her extra (the only thing worse would be not paying her more), I apologized. She replied that there was no need. "It happens all the time—especially with the narcos."

"I'm not a narco."

"No kidding." She laughed and escorted me out.

My capstone experience related to the shooting came while meeting Dale and Ron, as I did from time to time. The official reason was to discuss my investigation of the vandalism at ¡Bonobo! But we always ended up chatting about other topics: my research, their work, happenings in the region, tales from graduate school and the early days of Bonobo, and remarkable events in our lives. Their seniority over me in various ways—though not academically—remained implicit, as camaraderie dominated our interactions. A good-humored tone of distanced irony generally prevailed. They always acted pleased or at least satisfied with my reports regarding the investigation. Given the lack of results, it increasingly appeared that this job was simply a pretext to pay for my dissertation fieldwork, about which they expressed greater enthusiasm.

They had announced that this time we would meet at a popular taquería in my neighborhood. This taquería, like many, was completely open in front, with no wall, and a few tables were set up on the wide sidewalk, too. I couldn't stomach three gringos sitting exposed in an area I knew to be dangerous. So I rushed to the eatery a few minutes early, hoping to deflect them to a less conspicuous venue. Alas, they already were sitting, beer bottles before them, at a sidewalk table: a perfect place to get gunned down.

The restaurant's exposure was more pronounced in my mind because I knew that gunmen occasionally frequented a small grocery store nearby. A couple of weeks before the shooting, I had ventured inside to buy a Snickers when a man dressed like a Teflon cowboy briskly strode inside and down an aisle as if he were the only customer. He had a pistol sticking out of his waistband, and this was enough for everyone to clear out of his way. I looked out the front window and saw that he had double-parked his Corvette, which had a fake California license plate that read, "DEA." After he found his drink in the cooler, he walked straight past the line of four shoppers to pay for his purchase, saying nothing and looking at no one. What would have happened if some revolutionaries had pressed their right to shop in equality? Or had simply failed to see the gun?

"Hi, guys."

"Nat! Pull up a chair. We took the liberty." Ron indicated a bottle of Océano beer for me.

"Hey, it must be crowded inside," I said, still standing. The interior was empty, except for a couple of workers.

"Yeah," Dale replied, "we're missing all the action."

"But, really," Ron said, "we miss the action in town on most days. While we're here, it's good to get out in the thick of things." He meant the empty sidewalk.

"Well, if that's what you want, maybe we should go to a restaurant downtown. It's pretty dead around here in the afternoon."

I still hadn't sat down. But they insisted, joking that they would hate to miss out on the world-famous cuisine of Taquería La Negra Picante III. Actually, soon after I had arrived in Playatlán, the owner had bragged to me about his food's reputation among foreign tourists, but I found the occasion inopportune to mention this. Instead, I suggested that a nearby restaurant—which coincidentally had all its tables indoors—might have more customers.

"What's the matter? Do you owe this guy money? Did you date his daughter?" Smiling, Ron wrinkled his eyebrows in mock concern.

"His wife?" Dale piled on.

"We know better than to mention his mother. And, anyway, we heard about this place from a guy who leads tours around town, and we thought we'd check it out. We're thinking about bringing our guests here—on kind of a secure outing. You know: a quiet area where they won't get harassed and can't wander off to get in trouble—i.e. someone's pants."

Now I sat down. "It's not as quiet as you might think." And I let it all out. I told them about the shooting, how it happened just a few blocks away. How no place and time could be safe here. How life meant too little, and death was a form of entertainment. How, in fact, I had almost been killed and had seen an innocent man go in an instant from enjoying lunch to dying. How he tried to get up from his chair, like these chairs right here, but couldn't, forever.

I thought I just wanted to warn them, but it turned into my emotional history. They could sense the change in me, from open and free to full of fear. I tried to maintain control, but I felt my voice beginning to shake and my intensity increasing. I had started to ramble farther and farther off-message, mentioning the altercation with Benito at the cantina just down the street and even the gangbangers' duel at Carnival.

I looked down at the table as I told my tale of mortal woe, occasionally glancing from Dale to Ron to gauge their reactions. Ron mostly looked me in the eye with his brows pressed together and his head tilted a little in concern. Sometimes I found him looking at the table, too. Dale started out leaning toward me but eventually sat back, regarding me with a mixture of perfunctory concern and unsettling irony, as if he were judging me.

I tried to wrap up by turning my tragic monologue into something less, for the sake of decorum and easy conversation. "Anyway, maybe it was just bad luck, and I'm a sensitive lad. My neighbors don't seem fazed."

I looked up at them. Ron looked down, seemingly in concentration. Dale still had his eyebrows in and up, sporting a bemused but thoughtful expression. He sat forward. "Well, that sounds straight out of a narcocorrido." His tone was light. "I guess it's good we're safe on an island. The only thing we have to worry about is vandalism. Which hasn't stopped."

At this, Ron looked up and regarded Dale for a second. Then he turned to me and said how horrible the experience must have been and how isolated I must feel doing fieldwork alone, especially after such trauma. If I needed someone to talk with, I could count on them when they were in town. Would it help to spend a night or two away from the neighborhood, maybe in a tourist hotel, just to take a break? His voice strained to express tenderness, but there it was. I felt a tenuous echo of María consoling me, of my imagined parents soothing me.

Dale, more serious now, seconded Ron.

Embarrassed and depleted, I suggested that we order food and move on to other topics, which we did.

I'm happy to say that neither of the two asked me to show them the scene of the shooting, which I still took great pains to avoid. Toward the end of lunch, Ron asked whether I would like to share a taxi with them to my house, which they had never seen. They were a little curious about a real ethnographer's digs. At this, Dale indicated his watch, which irritated me even as I demurred: I planned to go from there to do some observations and, anyway, my apartment was too close to justify a ride.

As we stood, Dale shook my hand and turned to the curb to flag down a cab. Ron moved around the table a little laboriously, scooting a couple of chairs to the side, and, ignoring the hand I was raising to shake his, reached up and around to give me a full hug. He patted my back a couple of times, like fathers and coaches do to young men in the movies, and, disengaging, looked me in the eye. "Take care, Nat. We're here for you." Again, I felt calmed.

And surprised. My male friends in Mexico often gave me perfunctory hugs but nothing like that, and usually Ron seemed utterly businesslike. But, as it later occurred to me, his business was enabling, applying, and enforcing the Golden Rule. I think that, while I was letting loose, he simply asked himself what would make me feel better, and then he tried his best to deliver it: Bonobo beyond the bedding.

Dale glanced back at us but focused mostly on the sparse traffic, peering across distant intersections in the hope of spotting a taxi and magically hailing its driver. Ron went to pay and then joined him, as I trooped off into the city.

I learned a lot from almost getting shot. Love is a wondrous thing.

CATCH AND RELEASE

In outline, the next few months might look like the best of times. Indeed, I enjoyed the sort of life that I had daydreamt about before moving to Playatlán. That is, I started screwing tourists more often. And for that I'd like to plead guilty by reason of existential crisis.

I know my fellow feminists will hate this, but, in hindsight, I find these encounters less justifiable than those with prostitutes. The main problem at the time was that visiting the bordello had become routine. I knew the workers; they knew me; we might share a little love or a laugh, but we certainly weren't in love. And I cried only the one time. So, while I certainly didn't forswear the brothel, now I saw it as the all-night drive-through at Jack in the Box, rather than a culinary food festival. I sensed that the workers, although they appreciated the income, had started to harbor similar feelings about me. The thrill was long gone—or, as Dale might say, it was all porn and no drama.

The most obvious alternative, True Bonobo, presented different drawbacks. The biggest issue was logistical: getting there was too risky, time-consuming, and physically demanding. Maybe if I were closer friends with Líssy and the gang I could ride along, but I wasn't. In addition, I had no excuse for being there. I couldn't lie to myself about furthering my academic research or my investigation for Ron and Dale. And returning regularly would imply that I bought into Holly's religion—

which maybe I had, but on my own terms, and with my own agenda. Finally, and it hurts to admit that this mattered, because I know that probably it shouldn't—and I realize that I, too, might suffer in comparison—but ... tourists looked hotter.

Or at least the hottest ones were hotter than most of the women at the bordello and most of the people at True Bonobo. And of course I wanted to maximize the hotness of my fuck friends. Xóchitl was meat-thermometer hot but unavailable, and Blanca could light a cigar with the mere brush of her skin, but she wouldn't smoke it. I wanted sex with the closest physical equivalent, and, if further companionship were necessary, I preferred that it be stringless.

Unfortunately, with tourists strings were unavoidable and hidden in plain sight. Destinations like Playatlán owe their success to the illusion that Person A can show up on the beach, at a disco, or by the side of a hotel's pool and, simply by the force of shared circumstance, meet a Person B who is fun, drunk, and attractive for sexing—even if Person A isn't. It was the proverbial bill of goods, and I certainly had bought it. Sadly, obtaining a sex partner is often much more difficult, even among young Americans enjoying a Spring Break package replete with fake-orgasm contests.

Through trial and error and conversations with Mexican guys on the make I found that the sine qua non (my term) of sex with tourists was a display of cheerfulness. A willingness to yell, "Woo!" was even better. By and large, tourist women weren't looking for a radical intellectual who brooded about mortality. A friendly disco-dancer with an interesting backstory had a much better chance of getting laid. It came down to marketing.

Still, there was more to master. Watching Mexican beach vendors hit on American women, I developed the sense that I needed a few pickup lines and tremendous perseverance. Operating in English restricted the vendors' crude imaginations even further, leading to such wonders as, "You are so pretty. What's your name?" and "I love you. Do you remember me? I talked to you yesterday." Those guys were jackhammers of romance, and, to my amazement, it worked for some, sometimes. But adopting this approach not only degraded me in my own eyes; it led my female targets to humiliate me further. "Chaise-lounge lizard" was one memorable put-down. The implication was that Mexican guys were supposed to be cheesy, but I, an American (cue the fanfare), should pursue mutual sexual exploitation in a more dignified manner. The key was to appear as though I had no predefined goal in relating to bikini-clad women—as though I had determined that interacting with this otherwise randomly chosen, unknown Person B would be preferable to talking and carousing with my friends or, for that matter, anyone else at all.

I did enjoy some success. I fucked eighteen-year-olds and thirty-five-year-olds, skinny ones and chubby ones, drunk ones and almost sober ones. We did it in my room or her room or under a blanket at night on the beach or in a stairwell at someone else's hotel. I left soon thereafter or stayed the rest of the night. I met them the next day or got stood up or stood them up or wished them well on their flight home.

More often, I struck out on the first approach or wasted an evening doing inane crap without getting laid or got too drunk to stay hard with a condom on or had to endure my beloved's vomit or her passing out or her friends' intervention or her standing me up.

And then sometimes I just ended up hating the person I was trying to bed. But was that enough to stop me?

Here's a case study: a dalliance with Luz. She was visiting from El Paso with her two friends, Elsa and Elena. I first noticed them on a drowsy late afternoon at a thatch-roofed beachside bar called Shrimpy Jim's. Well, it seemed drowsy to me—the lull between prime beach-time and prime dinner-and-disco time. Nonetheless, diehards and new arrivals were partying hardy under Jim's shade and away from the zombie-like persistence of the beach vendors. Undoubtedly, "Margaritaville" was playing.

I had come for the bathroom. As a gringo I had ex officio access to Jim's toilet, but I occasionally ordered a beer as a token of my appreciation. Earlier in the day I had perambulated the main tourist area, in which Shrimpy Jim's sat, on the pretext of documenting coexisting regimes of popular culture—it was a pretext because I had already done this several times, finding leakages and covert similarities between cosmopolitan, national, and narco-focused (re)productions, blah blah blah: read my other dissertation. Anyway, Playatlecos could tell you that usually it's just more interesting to be in the tourist zone, and sometimes I wanted a jolt, too. Plus, I already had more than enough information for my dissertation.

So there I was, burnt out and cynical, exiting the bathroom and heading on autopilot toward the bar, when I found myself in the path of a diminutive, comfortable-looking woman with dark-brown hair and eyes and light-brown skin, wearing white shorts and a light-blue tank-top with a swimsuit underneath. Sunglasses on her forehead. Plastic sandals. Smiling pleasantly. Margaritaville. In my path.

We did that uncomfortable dance, blocking each other a couple of times. Then I stood rigidly still. "It's a pleasure dancing with you, but now I must get a beer," I witticized gallantly.

She smiled a little more deeply and put her hand on my upper arm as she strode to the toilet. I got my bottle of Océano and found a seat by the railing overlooking the beach. The sea was always so beautiful, mesmerizing, yet I spent such a small time in it. I noted a corner of ¡Bonobo!, sticking out of it. I tried to assess my research and plan the next steps, but my mind felt lazy. Thoughts flowed on their own, ever farther away.

Then a hand grabbed my arm. "Hey, Lonely, you want to come join us?" It was the smiling, dancing obstacle—Luz, eventually—and she gestured to her two friends at a table a few yards away.

I acquiesced.

They had been friends since high school, although now they were in their thirties. Luz was a school psychologist, and Elsa and Elena were office workers at UTEP. Each was single, or at least not married, or at least not truly married. Luz' companions had witnessed and laughed at our contretemps and, seeing an opportunity, urged her to retrieve me. Subsequent lines of conversation suggested that the reason for this forward reversal of expected gender norms, aside from my intrinsic allure and evident charm, was that Elsa and Elena had dates for that evening but Luz didn't. (So maybe it was my desperation that attracted them.) This surprised me, given that Luz was nice looking, even attractive, whereas the others, while friendlier, were a bit more porcine.

Luz enlightened me: "I don't like Mexican men." And the others' dates for that evening were beach vendors. So Elsa and Elena needed to find her a gringo plausibly in her age range. Bingo! We were made for each other: a racist and a penis on autopilot.

Technically, we could debate whether Luz was racist. From her perspective, the problem with all Mexican (and Mexican American) men was their Mexican (American) mothers, who spoiled them so thoroughly that they were useless romantic partners for anyone but a Mexican (American) woman who had learned from her parents to continue the spoilage. She called this the "Mijo Complex"—'mijo' meaning 'my son.' She bandied problematic terms like "culture" and "all" with such wantonness that I didn't take her argument seriously. (Now

I'm a bit more curious.) Tellingly, she didn't ask about my up-bringing.

Anyway, after about two-thirds of a beer, the two Els and maybe Luz encouraged me to join them and their paramours for dinner that evening. Despite some misgivings, I acquiesced again. Maybe the experience would have ethnographic interest.

A nice thing about American tourists was that, by local standards, they dressed like slobs. So I went home, took a shower, and put on some of my cleanest, most formal shorts and a short-sleeved shirt—with buttons and a collar! I rode the bus back to the tourist zone feeling like I was adorned to pre-side at a wedding or portray a vampire. I arrived late at the sea-side restaurant, where I instantly espied the three women and their two gigolos. Seeing these young guys—Héctor and Mar-cos—filled me with bemused disdain, and jealousy. They had Hershey-bar tans and long, sun-bleached hair, which was new-ly-kempt—both had used gel, and Héctor had also pulled his mane into a ponytail. They wore white jeans (borrowed from friends, I suspected) and billowy cotton shirts—one white, one blue—with a few buttons open to expose their modest golden chains. To me, they looked like disco-matador lifeguards. To Elsa and Elena, I think they looked like the Delightfully Ste-reotypical Fling Brothers. To most Playatlecos, they looked like uncouth bums who were inexplicably about to get fed and laid for free.

They weren't the only ones. Here and there around the res-taurant other guys, dressed to similar effect, came in and nod-ded to my companions with a reserve that contrasted with the boisterous and profane commentary that they flung about on the beach. In a way, the gigolos' conversation with Elsa and Elena matched their clothes—it was a boldfaced attempt to seduce: the women were so pretty and so smart; the Latin lo-tharios could arrange excellent excursions for them at a good price.

I didn't figure much in those conversations. Aside from a grudging acknowledgment of my fellow-traveling on the Pussy Pilgrimage, Héctor and Marcos had little use for me. The grammatical forms they used left it unclear whether they thought I would be joining them on the various romantic and remunerative rendezvous they proposed; more likely, they had a friend in mind. At one point, they seemed to suggest that even Luz might not need to participate in any future activities, but the two Els assured them in a firm yet friendly manner that we all formed part of a single group.

Luz had similar ideas regarding these guys: get rid of them after that night and, if necessary, substitute better partners. She was a little more definite in her verbiage, which was pointedly in English and directed to anyone but Héctor and Marcos. The two Els, for their part, just wanted to have fun together in a way that followed the script in their imaginations. The identities of their male companions mattered even less than they did to Luz, who at least cared about their ethnicity.

It seemed like everyone but me was lobbying for what they wanted, regardless of the others' agendas. I saw plenty of gold-plated jewelry around that table, but no Golden Rule.

At some point, as Luz yammered on about the problem with contemporary children's psychological development and I wondered who would pay for dinner, Elsa tried to build a Friendship Bridge across the conversational chasm dividing our table. "Nat, you live here, right? Do live near Héctor and Marcos?"

"I don't know—maybe." I acted curious and addressed the guys. "I live in La Colonia No Reelección."

They just looked blankly into space.

Maybe I wanted to figure more fully to the women, or perhaps I hoped to pimp my pain for sympathy. In any case, I added, "I'm considering moving." This was a lie. "I almost got killed there in a narco shooting a few weeks ago."

Initial indications were that I had made a successful gambit, as Elsa and Elena, wide-eyed, wanted to know details. Luz, though, rolled her eyes. Rather than motivating her to comfort me, this revelation confirmed her resolve to avoid entanglements with Mexican men. Her knowing, dismissive look suggested that somehow the 'mijo complex' was implicated. Her attitude provoked Héctor into saying that focusing on such isolated acts of violence bolstered gringos' prejudice against Mexicans. His grammar placed this observation in the abstract, but it was clear that he was trying to turn the tables on me. And, indeed, the appeal to ethnic solidarity led the two Els away from my story and, instead, to dwell on how they, their people, and El Paso in general had faced similar stereotypes.

Ugh. Fine. I pulled back into my shell and rode out the dinner and their scintillating conversation as blandly as possible. Was I there at all? Sometimes it was hard to tell. Nonetheless, decorum required that I physically remain, as did the sense that, having already invested considerable time and ego into getting laid, I deserved to receive my payout.

Eventually, Luz paid for my meal, thus confirming that I, too, was a local gigolo. Then we went dancing at a seaside disco. If the women wanted to dance in a group, we danced in a group. If they wanted to dance on a table, we danced on a table. If one wanted to sit, her partner sat. Mostly, though, the women danced with each other, and we fellers moved around them like desultory satellites.

Then Luz saw horses being led along the beach. So we rushed out of the bar to ride them under the puffy clouds and stars and moon, following a line between the surf and the couples engaging in sandy, chafing sex under blankets. Quiet, humble young men led the horses so slowly that even drunk, giddy tourists, sharing a mount with drunk, all-enduring ethnographers (who had no equestrian experience) wouldn't fall off. Luz yelled, "Woo!" and Elsa and Elena corresponded. Like me, Héctor and Marcos kept their own counsel. All along, from the minute she saw the incontinent beasts, Luz told me about her tremendous experience with horses: about her uncles' horses, about how she loved riding horses and brushing them and reading novels about them, about how these horses compared to particular horses she had known, about how she had drawn horses in her notebooks as a child and wanted to be a veterinarian specializing in … horses. She also had the courtesy to ask me about my experience, with such probing inquiries as, "Don't you just love it?"

It was a little reminiscent of Blanca with the Baby Jesus, but only a little. I would have sat it out gladly, but I sensed that mounting the horse was a prerequisite for mounting Luz.

Sadly, it was not a prelude. For next we had to eat tacos at a late-night stand. And then we returned to the disco, where some Mexican Mengele had once again put on "La Macarena," to which we performed the dance with great enthusiasm, again. Throughout, the women yelled, "Woo!" when appropriate. Eventually, though, their batteries wound down, one by one, and we lurched our way in the late, late night to a tall, clean hotel by the sea. Marcos had his arm around Elsa's shoulder, Héctor had his around Elena's waist, and Luz had hooked her arm into mine. Research has shown that the mere act of smiling makes people feel a little happier.

Alas, bad salsa doesn't. Some of the add-ons at the taco stand had been sitting out too long. Marcos had warned us against it, but the women thought that he meant that it was too spicy. They, Tejanas above all else, couldn't brook a challenge to their state's manhood. So now, as we stumbled along the uneven sidewalk in the quiet ebb of the night, past closed curio shops and restaurant workers turning off the last lights, Elsa abruptly felt ill. First her stomach ached, and then she needed to reach a bathroom—stat.

My initial thought—aside from any concern I might have felt (or empathy, given my own digestive history)—was that this could ruin everyone's chance to have sex, after so many sacrifices. Elena and Luz seemed almost panicked about Elsa's food poisoning, animatedly discussing whether they should find a doctor. I thought, Aren't they from the border? Marcos, though he must have known that he now had no chance of sex with Elsa (but perhaps a threesome with Elena, if he played his cards right?), kept his arm clutched around her and boosted her along. Maybe he still had hope for the subsequent nights, or for a longer-term relationship as sometimes developed. (It didn't occur to me, such was my decline, that he might be acting in solidarity.) Anyway, I then began to consider my own digestive progress—not that I felt sick, but my back teeth were floating, and Elsa likely would hog the hotel room's only toilet.

Finally, some luck: they were staying on the ground floor. Their room's sliding glass door opened onto a patio that subsequently gave onto a large deck with a darkened bar and pool. The guard quietly directed me to the men's room, and I let go my copious urine into the toilet. Happily, my sandals protected me from whatever liquid graced the floor.

My inebriated dick-brain worried that the others might leave me for a hospital or pharmacy, or that Luz—now sporting beer goggles—might suddenly find Marcos attractive, or that she might simply pass out. Upon returning to the room, these fears vanished, and a new concern arose: two beds for three couples. With a college girl, this would be the time to fuck on the beach or in a stairwell. But Luz was a full woman whose dignity probably wouldn't permit anything less than a bed as the platform on which she would drunkenly screw a stranger. Happily, the Three Amigas had worked out the logistics beforehand. Luz had her own complete bed by the sliding-glass door, Elena would take the mattress off the other bed and screw on it in front of the hallway door, and Elsa got the box springs.

As it turned out, Elsa got the box springs and the bathroom. Marcos, still solicitous and promising to check on her the next day, bid her adieu with a hug around her shoulder. He shared a soul shake with Héctor and nodded to the rest of us. Then he trod alone into the hallway and the oblivion beyond. Elsa promptly returned to the bathroom for another round. Héctor and Elena lay facing each other under a sheet, their legs entwined, their lips slurping, their hips humping.

Luz lay curled on her side under the covers of her bed and smiled droopily up at me. She raised her eyebrows, reached back and patted the mattress behind her. I could tell that she wore only a bra on top. "There's just enough room for you," she said, "but not for your clothes."

"I see: a tight fit," James Bond replied coolly, unfastening his bow tie and cummerbund. Out of the eyeshot of the others, I dropped my clothes on the floor and snuggled in behind Luz, who pressed her warm, pantied ass against my crotch.

Most of the details of our copulation were unremarkable, but two stand out. First, after we had humped my erection against her butt, back, thigh, and still-pantied pussy, which I could tell had gotten wet, I began to remove the final obstacle to my penis' happiness, for which the rest of me had martyred itself so thoroughly.

Luz slurred, "Wait."

"Huh?"

"Wait. We need protection."

"Totally. I have a rubber in my pants." I started to pick them up from the floor.

"Ew, not good. I have one in this drawer." She stretched over to open the nightstand and pulled out a variety that I hadn't tried.

I had my concerns about thickness and lubrication (too much and too little, respectively), so I offered again, but she insisted. As this transpired, Elsa returned from the bathroom and curled up on the box springs again. I thought, I've effaced myself up to this point, why jeopardize victory at the final challenge? My penis was counting on me. So, with a little fumbling, on went Luz' condom, and off came her panties.

Now, I imagine that you're thinking that I must have excellent blood-flow to maintain an erection while drunk, distracted, and contesting over condoms. And it's true that I'm a ready lover. But my secret that night was that I needed to pee again, while Elsa owned the bathroom. I don't know how it works, because I'm certain that the urine doesn't fill the penis, but a full bladder often leads to awe-inspiring hard-ons that provoke ecstasy in my partners and increase my own sensitivity, all while prolonging the time to orgasm.

So here's the second noteworthy aspect of our sexing: It felt good, physically. In fact, I noted how a thrill suffused my being each time I slid inside Luz' pussy. I registered how each extraction brought an intensifying charge of anticipation for the next thrust. It hardly mattered that Luz, though panting and whimpering in hushed tones, didn't turn to kiss me or reach back to grab my arm or stroke my hair. Nor did I flick my tongue in her ear or lift her hair to passionately kiss her neck. From what I could hear, Héctor and Elena had conjured the glory, but I mostly pumped away while holding various parts of Luz for my own personal pleasure: grabbing her small-ish, slightly doughy breasts, her smooth thighs, and her arms, and bracing myself to pump away much as I would with a sex doll. For her part, Luz ended up rubbing her own clit and nipples more than she stroked me. Nonetheless, it felt good, presumably for both of us, given the number of her orgasms.

I thought of all this as we humped in the same, adequate position. And I watched Elsa get up to go to the bathroom yet again and wondered how her illness would affect their plans for the next day. Would she see Marcos again? I also heard Elena give Héctor a blowjob and wondered whether it actually felt better than her vagina. Maybe she used her tongue. And I considered how much my pleasure had cost me; at some point, the line is too long to justify riding the roller coaster.

Well, time passed, and I started to feel guilty about not coming. It seemed as though Elsa was sleeping, but little signs suggested that Elena and Héctor had some other plan that depended on Luz and me finishing. Luz hadn't had an orgasm in a while and might have been chafing. So I considered faking one. Instead, in the nick of time, my imagination came to the rescue. Now Luz was really Blanca, and this was our honeymoon. I pressed my chest against her back and my cheek against her downy neck, clenched my arm across her torso, and came within a minute or two. So sweet.

Luz pulled her hips away to ensure my timely withdrawal. Then she slipped out from under the cover and tromped drowsily across to the bathroom. Once they heard the door click shut, Héctor and Elena giggled and walked past our bed and out the sliding-glass door.

I really needed to pee. Elsa had awoken and started toward the bathroom in crisis mode. "Luz is in there," I called. Elsa turned sleepily and looked at me as if she didn't quite remember who I was. "There's another bathroom outside, by the bar," I said, and I started to pull my clothes off the floor to dress clumsily under the sheets. Elsa plopped back onto the box springs and faced the bathroom door.

I could see that the wait for that toilet would be lengthy. In the meantime, a small, leather-bound book that Luz had left on the nightstand sought my attention. I reached over, opened it with a couple of fingers, and verified that it was a much-annotated address book. Sometimes those could say a lot about their owner. But I wasn't sure I wanted to know any more about Luz, and I really needed to pee. So I left the room again via the patio.

The aurora had begun, and in the grayness I again found the bathroom by the bar. After peeing, I came out and saw golden light beginning to bathe the deck, as the sun's first rays cut through the lobby from the east. I stared at it dumbly for a moment. My mind turned toward the hotel room, but my feet did not. A vision came to me of Luz politely but firmly dismissing me. I was such a nonentity at that point that no one— not even I—would miss me if I released myself. So I crossed the deck and descended the stairs onto the beach. Luz and Héctor were well out in the water, playing with each other. I removed my sandals, turned left, and started to walk home along the edge of the surf. The water refreshed me, like nothing else had for a long time. Fuck it, I thought, and waded straight out into the surf. I sat in the sand and let the small, rushing waves bash against my back.

The circumstances reminded me of that morning at True Bonobo, with Sherry. Since then I had gone from giving and receiving to giving and taking, or giving to take, or something like that. Using and being used. It wasn't violent, it wasn't asymmetrically exploitative, and it wasn't worthy of an academic critique. In fact, it wasn't so bad: now Luz and I each had our story to tell, and the sex, as usual, had felt good. I would hate to go without sex. But why did I have to endure this debasing and de-individuating rigamarole to experience something so fundamental? Why couldn't sex be easy, without the bad drama?

I turned and looked out at the wide ocean. There again sat ¡Bonobo! This explains that, I thought. I sardonically imagined swimming to the resort, flopping over its walls, and begging for asylum. Why wouldn't Dale and Ron invite me over, just once? What difference would that make anyway? What frustrated Playatleco—or ethnographer—wouldn't want to vandalize that impenetrable piñata?

I dipped my head underwater a few times and felt its cool refreshment wash over my skin. Then I trod back to the shore, took off my shirt, and strolled homeward in my dripping shorts, past the fishermen with their desperate hand-lines, past the lifeguards in training, and past the early risers on their power walks. I used the time to think systematically about my experience, to develop findings:

Surprise! I enjoyed unattached sex and even uninvolved sex. Romantic or transgressive sex felt better, usually, but that was like sprinkles on a cupcake. Perversely, though, my time with tourists showed the pervasiveness of bourgeois eroticism, even as we supposedly were violating it. We had to have full-fledged relations—conversation, eating, horse-riding—before we were qualified to have sex. Why was this? I had friends whose company I enjoyed for all sorts of reasons; some of them I liked for multiple activities, such as academic exchanges, tossing frisbee, and attending concerts. But I didn't expect to have sex with them. Why did I have to enjoy a woman's dinner conversation to enter her vagina? Of course, if I liked an erotic partner in other ways—à la Líssy or Doris—so much the better, but why not à la carte, too?

I started to re-evaluate traditional Mexican marriages, like the one Blanca's parents had. Many Mexicans accepted the idea that men would spend a lot of leisure time with their friends while women would do the same with theirs, or at least with their family members. Then, presumably, they'd get together at night for dinner, business, and sex. Heretofore, I had admired the minority of Mexican couples who spent almost all of their free time together because it was "modern." Now, unless they truly had a great, all-in-one relationship, they seemed like dupes.

Of course, sexism and patriarchy tainted the Mexican case. Women shouldn't automatically get stuck with caring for the house and kids, or be valued less if they did. But the principle of limited-purpose relations didn't require exploitation, and women shouldn't automatically get stuck with constantly enduring their husbands either.

À LA CARTE

The funny thing was, my encounter with Luz was hardly the worst. But after that night I was done with tourists and returned to my weekly brothel fix: easy in, easy out. Yes, I ended up taking a couple of trips to the STD clinic, but these presented less difficulty—and held more ethnographic interest—than a rendezvous with a tourist. Of course, sex with prostitutes was de-individuating as well, but I found it less irksome because the fast-food format made it obvious.

In addition, to my surprise and delight, I suddenly started to get propositioned by Mexican women for stringless sex. One woman approached me as I sat along the seawall, reading; another immensely enjoyed being interviewed one morning in her shuttered hair salon; others felt horny after a party or during a bus ride or while swimming or walking home along the beach or at a hot-dog stand outside a disco. A gay man wanted to be my "friend"—how could I say no? It was good drama—starbursts of adventure added to my satisfactory routine.

So, in the final couple of months of my time in Playatlán, I felt complete. I not only had learned to apply an à la carte approach to my particular situation, but I had learned to value it. Activities that previously had seemed incomplete—such as eating alone—now seemed progressive. No longer seeking the all-in-one answer, I leaned on more people and institutions for emotional support. Specialization increased the division of labor, which, as Durkheim argued, led to greater organic solidarity, and this was a superior organizing principle.

Yes, I saw the greater efficiency of combinatory relationships—dinner and good conversation, for example—and I accepted Society's claim that the sum of such combo deals could be greater than the parts: We're a team, we're working through this together, la dee da. But I avoided a lot of interpersonal difficulty by seeing every relationship as having a limited purpose. Thus I greatly reduced the frequency of complex discussions with someone inane, dinners featuring food I disliked, and partying with aficionados of Jimmy Buffett and the Macarena. I had achieved balance.

Would I be able to impose this slice-and-dice approach to life once I was back in Gainesville? Or would I have no choice but to party with my coworkers and help them move? These were questions I hardly asked myself. Instead, I daydreamed of how my days as a student and then professor would follow this exciting new logic. Sometimes, my heart actually raced as I considered how I would exemplify a better way to live to those around me. Maybe I should write a book about it. Boom! The fireworks filled my days.

I encountered endless prompts to consider how my newfound, à la carte approach fit with ¡Bonobo! I saw the island just offshore several times each day, Playatlecos talked—mostly joked—about it with me, and I still engaged in my fruitless investigations for Ron and Dale, meeting with them every week or two.

Speaking of whom—Talk about your fixed menu! Despite their obvious differences in temperament, those two guys had done almost everything together for several years, basically like a bourgeois married couple. They reminded me of Rock Gods of Yesteryear—Lennon-McCartney, Henley-Frey, maybe Strummer-Jones or Jagger-Richards: even though they were heterosexual, they were free to be intimate partners, soulmates, etc., because they had the sex angle covered in other ways.

Moreover, the comprehensive relationships extended beyond Dale and Ron. All the ¡Bonobo! staff lived sequestered—really quarantined—together on the island to prevent the acquisition and spread of disease. For *years*. And every relationship was multi-purpose: including at least sex, work, and neighborliness. Holly's True Bonobo was different only because the Revolution hadn't taken hold; one fine day, we'd all add erotic relations to our connections with everyone else, or at least adults would. Both versions of Bonobo contrasted with my ideas of limited-use, open-door relations.

Yet I loved Bonobo. I dreamed of its achievement. I masturbated to its image. My pants got a little tighter every time I thought of my night at Doris' house—a wonderful marriage (if you will) of intellectual exchange, mentoring, and pile-driving/soul-sharing. Moreover, despite hints of longstanding differences, Ron and Dale seemed generally as content as I then felt, and Líssy's gang acted exuberant whenever I espied them along the shore or at some concert. These thoughts provided an undercurrent of dissent, of counterhegemonic turmoil in my psyche, in opposition to my growing enthusiasm for slice-and-dice relationships. In any case I felt fireworks at the envisioning of new possibilities.

INTERVIEW WITH THE VAMPIRE

To illustrate my turn toward limited-use relationships, I could run through another sex scene, but the à la carte principle encompassed the full matrix of social relations. This realization struck with practical force when a complex fiend took me out for tacos.

Enrique directed the Social Sciences Department at the Autonomous University of Conaloa and served as my research sponsor. I had to maintain good relations with him because he vouchsafed for me to the Mexican government. Officially, he did so out of a keen interest in the important academic work that I undertook; however, I noticed over time that he never delved into it beyond greeting me with, "How's the research going?"—much as he asked Mexican acquaintances about their families. Before I realized that he had no real interest in my methods or findings, I would tell him about my most recent activities and working hypotheses. He would wait it out, let a moment of segue hang in the air, and then ask me for a favor. These almost always consisted of lightening his workload by delivering a lecture to a class. "I think the students will find your research very interesting. And it's valuable for them to learn another perspective, from over there," meaning the United States. Then he would effect a thin, unctuous smile.

I hungered to share my knowledge, which I considered to be great and ever-growing, so I never hesitated to say yes. It's also true that he never quite completed the paperwork for my research visa, blaming it vaguely on opposition from national-ists in some unspecified bureaucratic loop. Since this problem always arose in the same conversation as his request for free labor, I think it's fair to say that he was holding the visa over my head.

His approach reminded me of the busking cliff divers downtown. Sporting red speedos (only), these thoroughly tanned men ranged from twenty to forty-five years old and, along the same axis, from slim to robust. But, hey, cliff-diving is a gutsy business. One of the group would perch at the edge of a diving platform that towered over a break in a rocky stretch of coast, timing his imminent plunge to coincide with the onrush of surf. The other ten or so would fan out along the esplanade, pressuring any tourist, Mexican or American, watch-ing or not, to pay for the privilege of witnessing such a death-defying spectacle. After a while, the guy on the platform would climb down, and another would take his place, and the money collecting would go on. Thus, it was a promising business.

What separated the cliff divers from Enrique, I thought, was that eventually one of them would take the plunge.

Enrique's corrupt and authoritarian administrative method strengthened my suspicion that he was jerking me around. He had been appointed department head by the university rector, who had been elected in a scorched-earth campaign. Enrique had strong-armed and bribed students and faculty by promis-ing them better opportunities in exchange for the right vote and by threatening them with the loss of their positions or the alteration of their grades for the wrong one. Once Enrique's candidate won, he rewarded Enrique's ruthless loyalty with control of the Social Sciences Department. Enrique quickly cleared out his detractors and surrounded himself with syco-phants who—regardless of their official duties—laughed at his jokes, ran his errands, and applauded his academic initiatives. For pretty female students, he initiated a hostess service, through which they could gain income by serving at public functions; presumably he took a cut.

Given this history, few on campus dared cross him. Indeed, simply abstaining from campus politics had acquired the sheen of protest. My evolving analysis was that Enrique, by combining things that should remain separate, represented holism at its worst; his rise showed the superiority of specialized, à la carte relations.

As mentioned above, Enrique had caught me in his net of fear and enticement. However, by the post-Luz period I had given up on getting the visa from him and thus had stopped visiting his office. Nonetheless we saw each other one night, along with a large chunk of the local intelligentsia, at a book presentation in a historic building downtown. While scanning the rows for a seat, I nodded to him and to Lázaro—the museum director I had tried to not snub when meeting Ron and Dale for the first time. For the rest of the evening, I fitfully wondered whether Lázaro had badmouthed me to Enrique, leading Enrique to let me dangle.

Anyway, two of Enrique's student-hostesses, pointlessly flanking the dais in flight-attendant uniforms, attracted my attention much more successfully than did the panelists' florid discussion of Playatlán's educational history. One in particular made eyes with me throughout the learned exchange. Afterward, as the audience members milled about, greeting or ignoring each other, I made my way to her to chat wryly about the event. She saw nothing to be wry about, but still found grounds for light flirting. I couldn't tell whether she actually felt interest, so I didn't press for her address.

A little later, my friend the journalist Susana came up to me and did find humor in the setup—and in my horndoggery. She suggested, as was customary, that I would end up marrying a Playatleca.

"A spider had her chance at the Little Fly; now I avoid webs altogether," I responded cryptically.

"So now you just fly from crumb to crumb?" She laughed. "Males here have a saying, Nat: 'In times of war, any opening is a foxhole.'"

Much like Dale, I enjoyed Susana's good-humored critiques. But I rejected the premise: these were times of peace and love. I struggled to say: "In my eyes, every pot holds a flower—but the Little Fly has thousands of eyes."

Before I had to explain what I meant, Enrique came up and addressed me, but not Susana, in a friendly fashion. Susana took her leave in the same way. Then Enrique looked around the room. "What did you think of the presentation?"

I gave him my most polite analysis.

After a pause, he stated, "Look, Nat, I have an opportunity I want to ask you about. Can you come to my office tomorrow?" He continued to shift his vision around.

I wondered why he couldn't discuss it with me there. In fact, I had fully adjustable plans for the next day, but visiting campus could suck away half of it as I greeted friends and acquaintances, waited in offices for administrators who would never arrive, and discussed colleagues' proposals that would never come to fruition.

"I can visit your office if it's necessary, but is it possible to discuss it now instead?"

He acted as though only one ear had heard me. "There's something there I want to show you."

I accepted defeat.

When I appeared at his drab, concrete office the next day at the agreed-upon time, Enrique of course was not there. His receptionist informed me, as though she actually knew his whereabouts, that Enrique would be back "soon."

Ha! I had expected as much and came provisioned with reading material. After an hour, I had finished taking notes on the article, so I left, walking stoically across the denuded campus, whose buildings looked like so many cheap motels, toward the nearest bus stop. I tried to not look side-to-side, for fear of seeing acquaintances who might want to talk with me just to add minor fireworks to their morning. Fatefully, my path took me past the main office of Languages, out of which voices hailed me. Sure enough, Enrique had been chatting—probably plotting—with the equally corrupt head of that department, when they saw me passing. Now he insisted that the two of us go back to Social Sciences to discuss the weighty matter that required his office.

Once back in his lair, Enrique sank into a padded, swiveling chair behind his desk, I perched on a good quality metal-and-plastic chair, and two hangers-on lounged against the wall in cheaper plastic seats. He asked the receptionist to close his door. "Nat, have you seen this?"

Here, at last, was the object that required my presence: a small, bluish poster announcing Research Week. "No, but I do now."

He ignored my rudeness, as he did so many other things. In short, he wanted me, their special foreign visitor, to give a one-hour public lecture on my research, to take place on the coming Wednesday. This was a big deal. They would take my picture and put up posters around campus to publicize it. Flattered, I of course agreed.

In my enthusiasm, I sought out Raúl to tell him about this great opportunity. He was chatting with two other instructors I knew at a small, outdoor eatery on campus. Once I finished greeting everyone, I revealed my coup. My friends smiled slightly, raised their eyebrows, and glanced at each other, as if they knew something that I didn't. Raúl soon intimated, in his wry, sarcastic, and maddeningly indirect fashion, that some other departments had invited more-noteworthy researchers and paid them honoraria. He insinuated that Enrique had invited me as a last-minute, face-saving, and money-grabbing measure. "But you couldn't know, Little Fly," he soothed. "We from the Third World are grateful for your donation."

On the day of the presentation, I arrived a little before sunset, my shirt tucked in and a tie around my neck. It quickly became clear that no posters had been made. Instead, Enrique sent out emissaries at that moment, instructing all of the professors hosting classes then to herd their students into the courtyard for my talk. He also asked me to hold forth for two hours instead of one, which would somehow justify canceling classes later in the evening. The faculty members fully endorsed that idea. Anyway, the talk was well-attended, probably because so many people wanted Enrique to see their support.

Afterward, as the maintenance crew cleared away the white, plastic chairs, I stood by the punch bowl and chatted with a small group of students. The last was a woman who waited so that she could invite me to a party without openly excluding the others. As I tried to clarify the location, Enrique walked up and waited at a respectful distance. Once she walked off, he approached and offered to drive me home. This gesture—so common among my friends yet so unexpected from Enrique—made me uncomfortable, and my reflexive reaction was to decline. Surely it would be awkward. But I remembered to not refuse favors in Mexico and, in the name of science, 'to boldly go where no Nat has gone before.' So, after waiting longer for Enrique than it would have taken me to crawl home backwards, I strolled with him in the darkness to his sedan.

As we got going, he joked that I must be famished: the students had eaten all the canapés while I was talking. He invited me to tacos. I felt so keyed up from delivering the presentation that I had barely begun to register hunger, but he was right. And he probably planned to pay for dinner with my stolen honorarium. So again I yielded.

He suggested that we eat at El Vagón, a neon-lit spot down the block from my apartment. I told him that I preferred La Negra Picante III, farther along the street, because El Vagón served only beef-tongue tacos, even though its chalkboard menu listed several other options. He doubted that this could be true, so I regaled him with tales of my repeated attempts to either get a different type of taco or persuade the waiters to erase the longstanding falsehoods. Now he really wanted to eat there, just to experience this outrage firsthand. Nonetheless, to my surprise, he acquiesced to my stated preference.

After we had ordered and while we waited for the tacos, Enrique smiled, "Nat, whenever I try to speak with you, you're talking with a woman. I think maybe you're looking for a Playatleca to marry."

"I found one of those already. Now I just want to further explore the gendered aspects of Mexican society."

"And maybe establish a ¡Bonobo! annex? I hear you have friends over there."

"Uh, I think you already have ten discos and a red-light district."

"Oh, do we?"

This glib, egalitarian Enrique had appeared out of nowhere and took some getting used to. All of a sudden he was less like the neighborhood mob boss and more like Raúl (who loathed and supported him). Maybe it was the tacos. Anyway, his relaxed manner seduced me into confiding that I didn't get the same level of erotic attention in the United States. I worried that Mexican men would resent my success with Playatlecas.

Enrique seemed to find this preposterous—not the umbrage but my preoccupation. "Nat, this is your time. Make the most of it. Any of us would do the same. Of course, never fuck a friend's wife (or sister, for that matter)—

"Or mother … or daughter …"

"Or mother or daughter, if you can stop yourself. Fuck, Nat," he suggested merrily, "if you feel bad about the imperialism, you can tell us about your adventures so we can relive the days of our youthful independence. But nobody really wants the rich to keep their money in the bank. Look at the soap operas. If I win the lottery—which is unlikely since I never enter—I'm going to enjoy my luck, and everyone will understand. Maybe they'll envy me and even gossip about me, but they'd do the same thing, and they know it." He paused. "I read about this American billionaire, Sam Walton—you know about him?"

The founder of Walmart had garnered admiration among Americans, including me, for his frugal lifestyle. Now Enrique had me wondering why we thought that a billionaire driving an old truck trumped one driving a new Lamborghini—isn't it also insulting to keep what others desire but not enjoy it? It reminded me of a power display I had seen among gorillas: the bigger one commandeered the smaller one's favorite stick and then just threw it away. My case was even clearer, as I couldn't turn Cyrano and give away my erotic opportunities to someone else. Plus, unless I were gunning for sainthood, I couldn't continually forgo enticements in order to leave paths open for others; I deserved fulfillment, too.

Conversely, to take Enrique's dicta completely to heart would result in the sort of Machiavellian and megalomaniacal practices common among local drug lords and college administrators. I needed to strike a balance, even if its character were up to my judgment and the contingencies of circumstance.

Well, as you probably can tell, I enjoyed my one-on-one conversation with Enrique away from his courtiers. It would have been nice to share such times with him more regularly, if I could know him simply as a friend, à la carte. But he rarely operated that way, and, in fact, I never had the pleasure again. I didn't mourn this absence, however, as I regularly engaged in similar exchanges with other people, with whom I had voluntary relations. In one such conversation with Raúl, I described taco night with Enrique, which he dubbed, "Interview with the Vampire."

Ultimately Enrique symbolized, to me, not only the perverse combination of relationships that should remain separate but the over-emphasis on a single animating principle, in this case self-interest.

A TEMPTING OFFER

There's more to the episode with Enrique.

Later that night, after walking home from the taquería, I lay in bed alone, still feeling the ferment of the day's events. Obviously Enrique had made no appeal to the better angels of my nature—only the fallen ones. But his exhortations did harmonize with a guilty, suppressed strain of my mental babble: I deserved to win life's lottery as much as anyone else. This sort of thinking—extracting individuals from the unique sociohistorical contexts of their development in order to compare them as abstract equals—cut against my analytical beliefs. But as a simplification I accepted it: I had suffered crappy luck in losing my parents and thereby losing my chances at a rich family life and the sort of secure emotional development that it would foster, so perhaps I deserved to enjoy some good luck in compensation. Almost everyone I knew, outside of academia, would expect me to have this mindset; moreover, I felt certain that most of my hypercritical peers within the ivory tower would find sophisticated reasons to enjoy their own unearned winnings, as well. So I resolved to enjoy "my time."

But to what extent?

Obviously, extreme me-firsters such as Enrique, not to mention drug lords, had taken this principle too far. Or was this truly obvious? Once I admitted that it might be morally acceptable for me to benefit more than others, what nonarbitrary, 'universal' principle checked a person's greed? Was it simply social convention? Could I screw *anybody*? This question had haunted the dark corners of my mind for years.

Two mornings later, I returned to Enrique's office at his request. I hoped—fantasized, really—that he had a check for me for the Science Week presentation. Having internalized previous lessons, I arrived fifteen minutes late, only to find Enrique already waiting for me with Rosalva, a faculty member who was famed for both her productivity in research and her high-minded abstention from campus politics. I knew her slightly from parties, book presentations, and the like.

Enrique cheerfully related that he had just told Rosalva about my complaint regarding El Vagón. He actually had taken his family there the next night, just to see for himself. And I was right!

Rosalva smiled politely and told me that she had found my presentation interesting. I didn't remember seeing her in the audience, but I thanked her anyway.

It soon became clear that there would be no check. Instead, without explicitly making an offer that I might insultingly re-fuse, Enrique noted the benefits of serving as a faculty member in his department. He described Rosalva's impressive work, apparently to imply that, like her, I would not have to engage in politicking to win his favor. In short, Enrique finally took the plunge.

Wow! A full-fledged academic job in the place where I had developed a balanced life, where I would always be a little spe-cial simply by nationality, and at a university where the stand-ards for superstardom were quite low—and all of this by the beach. Plus, when I was homesick, I could hang out with Ron and Dale when they came to town. I felt flattered and flabber-gasted. I obliquely indicated that I would think about it.

This was Friday, and I gave myself a deadline of Monday to render a response. I spent long, pleasant hours that weekend, imagining how my life would unfold were I to stay in Playatlán and guessing (poorly) at my alternative future in the United States. I walked for miles along the coast, my head down, pondering. I sat on the seawall and stared without focus at the ocean. I lounged in the main plaza downtown and watched older men shine shoes and children play and teens loaf and country people try to sell herbs. One mother threatened to give her toddler to me if he didn't behave; the kid wailed in fear.

I loved Playatlán. I even loved the parts I hated. This was my time. I finally lived a charmed life.

Still: could I screw anybody? Drug traffickers could; certain noblemen of yore could; Chinese warlords of the early twentieth century, mean girls in middle school, and unregulated corporations could.

But I couldn't. The answer was no. I could be naughty—a vicarious thief of others' experience—but I couldn't do whatever I could get away with.

Who knows why? If it were simply a question of human nature, then there wouldn't be this difference between the Chinese warlords and me. However it happened, somewhere along the way Freud's superego had wormed its way into my brain. Maybe it snuck in while I watched *Happy Days* and endless reruns of *The Andy Griffith Show*. This moral sense, melded with some analytical sophistication, persuaded my consciousness that I had used my privileged sociohistorical position—my ability to do fieldwork as a representative of the First World—to create "my time" in Playatlán. No Mexican equivalent of me could go to the U.S. to enjoy complementary favors. Therefore, this unaccountable sense of fairness argued, my opportunities shouldn't come at the expense of Playatlecos' chances for fulfillment. To wit, any job I took at the university represented one less comfy position for a Mexican. Thus spake the angel on my shoulder.

But the ego-demon on the other side noted that the hypothetical unemployed Mexican whose job I might take probably had a rich and comforting family life. Almost every Mexican openly pitied or disdained Americans for their laughable cuisine and miniaturized familial love. Maybe, from that perspective, taking a mere job wouldn't balance out the loss of my parents.

Which side was right? This called for some research. I knew that Enrique's teenage daughter—a beauty contestant, of course—worked at an ice cream stand in the tourist district. Early in the evening on Saturday I decided to get a treat from her. She recognized me, and we exchanged pleasantries. As I licked my cone, she leaned forward on the counter to talk through the walk-up service window. I couldn't tell whether she was simply being nice or flirting, but I felt pretty sure that she was off-limits. I asked whether she worked on Sunday, too, and she said that she couldn't: the whole family gathered for dinner.

"At your house?"

"This week, yes—and sometimes at one of my uncles' or aunts' houses."

"Don't you get tired of it? Lots of Americans don't want to live too close to their parents."

"How sad. But no, we're not like that." She meant Mexicans. "I love my family. I love being with them!" The thought sent her into raptures. "You should come one Sunday to see how it is. You'll want to marry a Playatleca." She smiled slyly.

Somehow Enrique the Monstrous had helped to produce this wonderful girl—maybe that's how he justified his misdeeds. But if I stayed in Playatlán I might end up marrying into a family with monsters.

In any case, it was increasingly clear that, until I got married, people wouldn't know what to do with me. But, once I did, my wife and her relatives inevitably would want to have kids. So my à la carte lifestyle and my special, free-agent status in Playatlecan society would shrivel, and the life I loved would change.

Still, I thought, look how happy Mexicans are with their families. Haven't I hungered for this sort of comfort throughout my life? Maybe settling down would be an improvement.

Back and forth the debate seesawed. Late Sunday night I took my journal and sat on the seawall of a resort and tried to crystallize this ferment in writing. The waves crashed and frothed in the light from the hotel. I couldn't know with certainty which choice would make me happiest.

I appreciated the irony that pursuing a piecemeal approach to relations involved decisions with so many diverse and weighty ramifications. Thanks to reading Levi-Strauss, I knew that a logically consistent approach was impossible; no organizing principle could be absolute. So there I was, making a judgment call.

Finally, as I gazed without focus on the tiny lights of ¡Bonobo! across the bay, it dawned on me that I was selling myself short. I didn't want to merely not-hurt people; I actually dreamed of helping them. Was there not some way to 'get mine' and to help others get theirs—the proverbial win-win? Why not transfer the Bonobo Way from the orifice to the office?

Finally, peace suffused me. I returned to my apartment believing that I couldn't bring myself to colonize a position that otherwise would go to a reasonably qualified Mexican. I spent the entirety of that night at my little round table, drafting a gracious and indirect letter of nonacceptance. (Why call it a rejection letter, when the offer had truly enticed me?) As I crafted the text, I felt the warmth of universal affection envelop me like a sweater on an autumn evening.

At dawn the next morning, I slipped the handwritten pages under the ill-fitted door of the Social Sciences office. I felt the dirt on the tiles grate against my fingers when I gave them a push. A little hunched over, I scurried away, exiting campus by the shortest possible path to avoid detection by some early bird. I had considered commemorating this momentous decision at the beach but now thought better of it; the rising, un-clouded sun already made me feel a bit overheated. Instead, I caught a taxi back to my apartment and slept the day away in its cool, confidential shade.

The time to return home was drawing nigh.

¡BONOBO!

"Finally," I thought, as the small boat bumped lightly against the dock and tottered up and down. It was ¡Bonobo! time. After years of fantasizing, after a year of considering the resort from across the bay—even tooling around it with friends on an excursion to another island—I now would set foot on the land of my fantasies. How would it look up close? Would I get to tour the whole thing? Would I need to do the Bonobo handshake? Would I get laid? Was I sweating too much? Would Dale and Ron see through my suave façade and read these questions scrolling through my mind? Did any of these thoughts matter, or had I already ceded control of my fate?

It was easier to think the latter. So, clumsily clambering across the boat, I tried to go with the flow while counterbalancing the waves. Captain Steve boosted me a little by pushing against my backpack. "I hope I didn't turn your camera on. You'd better check." He referred to a small video camera that I had brought aboard to take panoramic shots of Playatlán from the bay. I knew that ¡Bonobo! outlawed photos or videos of people, so I already had removed the battery to prevent accidental discharges.

Ron reached out a firm, friendly hand to pull me onto the brilliant, whitewashed planks. Ta da! I had arrived.

In their own domain, he and Dale dressed more casually than in Playatlán, each wearing khaki shorts, staff T-shirts (Ron's was yellow, Dale's was powder blue), sandals, and sunglasses. Ron smiled broadly as he shook my hand (only) and welcomed me to their "penile colony." Dale's smile tightened briefly at the jest, but he quickly relaxed to shake my hand and make his own remark about me being an anthropologist there to observe their troop of Bonobos.

We proceeded up a few steps and through the gate in the four-foot-high wall that surrounded the resort. This barrier blocked most people in Playatlán from ogling the sex fiends on the island, whether by telescope or from boats. To stymie the wealthy few who lived on the two tall hills that had workable views of the island, along with the many tourists staying in high-rise hotels or condos, the backs of many of the resort's buildings faced the shore.

Captain Steve, who had walked that far with us, shook my hand and said he hoped to talk more with me later. Then he exchanged perfunctory Bonobo handshakes with Dale and Ron and returned to perform a little maintenance on the boat's motor.

I already knew a little about Captain Steve. Months before, while listing suspected vandals, Dale had explained that they originally had hired a boat owner from Playatlán to ferry people and supplies. Their goal was to foster local employment. But, despite repeated admonitions, this original captain "took liberties" with the guests—who certainly shared culpability—and also with his access to ¡Bonobo! So they replaced him with a permanent resident/worker of ¡Bonobo!, Steve. The other boat owners took offense at Captain Steve's presence. Perhaps they would have attacked him or blocked his path, as rival taxi associations did to each other on land, but for fear of the repercussions of harming a gringo—especially one with a narco landlord. (Nonetheless, to reduce Steve's vulnerability to attack and temptation to wander, other staff members took turns accompanying him on all but the quickest and simplest trips, such as mine.) So a little vandalism against ¡Bonobo! might have tempted local boat owners, and they obviously had the means to get to the island.

In my investigation, they mostly treated me with hostile suspicion or bemused contempt, and this made my inquiries comically unproductive. At least it was comical to them, as they tended to laugh to their friends once I impotently thanked them and turned to leave. Still, I found nothing to implicate any of them.

Anyway, off the three of us went on a grand tour of the entire facility. The pretext was to show me the various sites of vandalism, about which I had only heard. I enjoyed the tour, but it seemed a little perverse, given that I had visited the island to commemorate the end of my investigations. Plus, they had fixed all the damage. So, yes, there was the immaculate, seaward wall of the small, white warehouse. It once had been splashed with green and red paint, "presumably evoking the Italian flag," Dale had deadpanned months earlier.

Feeling festive, I now attempted a pun conflating 'ravioli' with 'revolution.' We ended up agreeing to move on.

So it went. I now think that what they, or at least Dale, actually wanted was to show off or perhaps justify their work to someone they could have been. I found it all fascinating, both from the sophisticated analytical perspective that saw Disneyland as an exemplar of social control and from the vantage of someone who had read and fantasized so much about the place. Magazine articles have reported much of what I saw, so please bear with me if what follows is old news.

First, thanks to Johnny Fish, the buildings were compromised variations on Earthships. ("We went Apeship," Ron explained; "Habitat for Onanity?" I ventured, second-best again.) The enclosed structures had thick exterior walls made from tires and dirt and interior walls consisting of recycled cans and cement, all plastered over and whitewashed. The roofs sported solar panels and rainwater catchment, which fed into a larger system of water harvesting.

The rest was much like numerous resorts along the Mexican coast. The doors consisted of thick, weathered wood. Any open structure, including the "Sin-a-Bon" bar and Pile gazebo, had exposed, unpainted beams supporting a thatch roof. Saltillo tile and concrete served as flooring.

The provisioning of sexification materials set Bonobo apart. Visitors didn't have to hope that the bathroom would contain a functional condom-vending machine that matched their pocket change. Instead, the resort had bought an untold number of curios from stores in Playatlán and used them to make supplies readily accessible: baskets, ceramic cars with open tops, painted seashells—anything that could hold a few lady's-choice ribbons, condom packages, or tubes of lube. I made a mental note that ceramic soap-dispensers filled with lube looked both attractive and handy. Each sported a large 'L,' to distinguish it from a sunscreen dispenser, marked with an 'S.' EZ-Kleen mats lay within close reach, whether already positioned for use, stacked in corners, or propped against walls.

Yes, I did write "Sin-a-Bon" up there. Tacky, kitschy, obvious touches were mixed with more-thoughtful ones, such that I swerved between dismissal and surprised appreciation. And, yes, in addition to their khaki shorts, sandals, and sunglasses, the staff wore the now-ubiquitous T-shirts, in different colors. At that point, the tees were only starting to provide a 'hip' alternative to the Hard Rock Café shirts worldwide. I noticed that the uniforms of the actual staff had one small difference. The back still said "STAFF," and the front sported the same line-drawing of a bonobo staring thoughtfully at the observer; however, it lacked the word "¡Bonobo!" in the resort's proprietary, Wild Sophisticate font.

The T-shirt logo was tasteful, even 'cool,' I suppose, but what did it mean? How did it relate to the activities or ideology of the Bonobo movement? It struck me as the equivalent of large abstract sculptures in front of corporate offices. The design provoked viewers into asking only what *its* significance was, rather than getting them to question their own place in the world and course through life. (This was before they added "We come in peace" to the front.)

Providing contrast were some of the drawings and paintings that lined walls throughout the resort. I had never read about these and found them intriguing. ¡Bonobo! offered free art classes for a couple of reasons: 1) the visitors needed something to do when not screwing, given the restrictions on their movement, and 2) Dale's original idea—much debated even among Bonobans—was to help people get beyond sex by guaranteeing them frequent sex, so the resort needed to provide the non-erotic activities to which the visitors could now get. The classes' popularity probably sprang more from the former reason than from the latter. Thus, only a small percentage of the thousands of productions had made it onto the walls, and some of these were simply seascapes or abstract doodlings. But several caught my eye. I particularly enjoyed a series—by different artists, often crudely created—that depicted bonobos and humans in different relations. Bonobos sitting in trees watched human villagers fornicate and fight, bonobos in lab coats observed humans playing soccer, humans disembarking at the resort's dock passed bonobos embarking to return to the mainland, a human and a bonobo rubbed genitals, a man choked a bonobo who gave him a hand job, and so forth. Compared to the T-shirt, these images had a much better chance of turning "What does it mean?" into "What do I mean?"

One feminist had cheekily depicted a bonobo spray-painting breasts and a vagina on portraits of Dale and Ron. We stopped to look at it. "Lord, how many times have I wished for that?" Ron's wistfulness was a joke.

But Dale sighed a little. "No, really, it could've solved some problems."

Of course, people were at the resort, too. ¡Bonobo! served lunch on the American schedule (noon). This meant that I had had to eat a full two hours earlier than anyone else in Playatlán in order to meet Captain Steve at a mainland resort's marina "after lunch, at one." Thus, Dale and Ron were escorting me around the resort at siesta time, when some of the visitors, looking worse for wear, were cuddling on a super-wide chaise longue; others sat reading or showily meditating; yet others painted depictions of the ocean, their abandoned dog, or their vulva, according to their inspiration; one was scribbling furiously and importantly in a notebook; and three others, not having received the memo from Dale, were fucking, at which I tried to not gawk.

"You get used to it," Dale half-gestured and shrugged.

I can confirm the rumors, subject to so much critique: every body looked physically fit, and no body appeared to be over forty years old. This corroborated the widespread suspicion that ¡Bonobo! filtered its guests.

The men and women on staff were yet more attractive, and they exuded a level of satisfaction, energy, and friendliness—to summarize: security—that only intensified their aura as exemplars of What Could Be. Apparently they understood from experience that they were not to diddle a visitor in Dale or Ron's custody, as none touched my crotch. A worker cleaning the pool, Luis, did squeeze my arm and ask, "So, will we be seeing more of you later? I think there's an opening you can fill."

As I stumbled over a response, Dale joked that they should establish a retirement age for some of those old lines.

I noted that he didn't say no—or yes.

Guests exhibited less respect for my personal autonomy, and a couple of them shook me à la Bonobo. For example, a woman in a yellow string bikini and the sort of loose skin that I associated, rightly or not, with recent weight loss came up to complain about the multitudinous, blue jellyfish that had washed up on the resort's tiny, gated beach. To start, she fully took and massaged my crotch and those of Dale and Ron. Each of them went for her left boob, but I saw my chance to try a pussy rub—I got harder upon feeling the softness of her vulva faintly through the stretchy fabric.

Had I been in charge, I would have acceded to her demand to remove the beached jellies and immediately create a permanent barrier against their future incursions, if that would get me inside her right then. Dale and Ron, in contrast, were more level-headed (soft-headed?), and promised only to have the thin blue line of dead jellyfish removed from the shore and to "look into" her "good suggestion" of creating some sort of barrier.

Eventually the tour led to Real Bonobo. This, in prosaic terms, was the staff quarters and administrative area, but believers revered it as the original, permanent Bonobo colony. My heartbeat quickened a little. I felt like I was about to spend time in the studio with the Beatles. Our route led us out the back of the bar, through a storeroom, and into the inner sanctum. Where buildings didn't create the boundary between ¡Bonobo! and Real Bonobo, a tall, red picket fence did.

Here things were more of a jumble, analytically. The quarters looked much the same as the tourists' lodgings on the other side, and, overall, the architectural stylings were consistent. The main difference in this domain was that all the buildings were fully enclosed and some looked more utilitarian. Condom-dispensers, lube-pumps, and mats lay about, but less commonly; however, they exhibited more variety, as if some residents wanted to personalize their paraphernalia. Also, artworks again adorned some of the walls, but so did hortatory posters, reminders of rules, and postcards from former Bono-bans.

I stopped to admire a full-sized poster, a bit faded from sitting in the sun, that showed two angry women, one of whom I recognized from the cleaning crew in the resort. They stood face-to-face, yelling, "Screw you!" at each other. Perhaps the shared speech bubble symbolized their intrinsic intersubjectivity, because the message printed below stated, "Fuck it out. It's the Bonobo Way." And between those two sentences lay a small photo of the same two women engaged in the G-G rubbing that made bonobos so memorable in primatology classes.

Dale and Ron explained that they held seasonal contests to design posters like this. The entire staff voted to decide the winner. In fact, "the staff—the permanent residents, from our perspective—vote on most of the policies on this side of the fence."

"And some on the other," Ron added.

Dale indicated the smaller print in the lower left corner, which I leaned in to see and read out loud: "The Hive has spoken." The right corner stated, "Long live the Hive."

Dale looked ready to sigh. "Someone's sarcastic complaint—now it's a slogan."

"So what does 'someone' think of that?" Ron inquired.

"I see the humor, but it strikes me as mean-spirited," Dale said, as if with forbearance. Addressing me, he said, "We're not as 'in charge' as it might seem."

"But we're not not, either," Ron clarified.

I thought, These guys have been together a long time.

TWO TAKES

Have I mentioned that this is a dissertation? It's reasonable for you to expect a summary judgment regarding ¡Bonobo!, and I fear that you might otherwise accept the facile analyses in journalistic portrayals and comedy sketches. So here are two brief, and optional, takes on Bonobo. Don't worry: the story is just one short chapter away.

I hope that you'll accept this analysis at face value, rather than see it as an attempt to expiate my later acts of betrayal.

Take I
Before I ever set foot on the island, I had enough information to form a durable opinion about Dale and Ron's version of the Bonobo movement. Unfortunately, fully elucidating this perspective would require yet another book. Here I would say merely that walling themselves off, albeit incompletely, from the rest of the humanity made their efforts to change humanity unlikely to succeed through direct influence. They might someday establish a chain of ¡Bonobo! resorts, like Club Med or Disney, but to most people these would always seem like a temporary alternative rather than a serious model for managing everyday relations.

As a social-science experiment, ¡Bonobo! had similar shortcomings. It's impossible to abstract a group of people from the flow of history and restart them with a blank slate. Even the core Bonobans had been formed in "chimpish" (non-

Bonoban) society, and the resort/colony depended on chimpish society for its protection, its access to land, its sustenance via tourism, and more. Indeed, their rules prohibited producing or raised children in an environment that would surely provoke arrests for child abuse, so by design ¡Bonobo! couldn't sustain itself. Thus, refugees reared in sick society—and perhaps permanently infected by it—would always be the ones to fill its ranks.

The resort's most significant promise as a catalyst for widespread change lay in its enduring notoriety. As you probably know, in diverse parts of the world Bonobo clubs and houses had sprung up. More widely, people held one-off Bonobo parties, strip clubs perverted the basic concept to cash in on the craze, and, through myriad websites, many individuals and groups advocated a Bonoban lifestyle. All of this resulted from the publicity that ¡Bonobo! had garnered. Each T-shirt and branded condom increased the aura of normality of ¡Bonobo!'s radical proposition. Could these diffuse activities snowball into a broader social transformation, as had happened with the increasing acceptance of homosexual rights or vegetarianism? It seemed unlikely, but I do believe that social changes sometimes occur like that. Thus it seemed possible that ¡Bonobo! wasn't the laughable, hapless sellout that, taken in isolation, it appeared to be. Anyway, the most consequential action now was in the rest of the world, away from the island that inspired it, in the lives of people like Holly, Líssy, Doris, and me. So describing and judging the movement based on the resort would constitute misplaced focus. That is, ¡Bonobo!'s importance was symbolic; the real action in the Bonobo movement was on the mainland, and that's what this book emphasizes.

But what was the change that Bonobo promised? It was fascinating that such a recent movement could have so many different versions. Dale (officially) saw sex as an obstacle, Holly saw it as giving, Doris as knowing, and others cast it as a sacrament, an aerobic exercise, a certain pleasure, a pacifier, and who knows what else. Somehow they all believed that frequent, guaranteed sex and eroticized contact throughout one's social relations would make society better. (The small scale and underground status of their movement allowed them to avoid the thorny questions of incest and child-rearing.) Nonetheless, their differing beliefs about the nature or mechanism of this improvement led to differences in the way that they implemented a Bonoban lifestyle. So ¡Bonobo! might someday inspire a widespread revolution in people's practices, but the character of this revolution—or of diverse, coinciding revolutions taking the same name—remained unsettled.

If Bonobo never conquered the world—would that constitute failure? Dale (and Holly) reflexively accepted the generally unquestioned belief that there's some identifiable unit called 'society' and that they should influence this unit to adopt a better way. In contrast, I had learned to see any so-called society (and, for what it's worth, family) as an ideological construct, an "imagined community." Revolutionaries too often gauged their success by whether they had supplanted an existing orthodoxy with a new one across this imagined 'society.'

If Bonobans aimed beyond a single society and strove to convert all of humanity, they employed a similarly faulty set of assumptions, just on a larger scale. The idea that we're all in this together—Team Humanity—is hardly self-evident. In fact, it's of relatively recent vintage and is belied by the death penalty, drug-gang rubouts, war, genocide, and pet ownership.

For me, success wasn't a yes/no question. Maybe it could be measured along a scale or a matrix, counting the number of people affected and evaluating the degree to which their lives improved. Of course, measuring an improved life would depend on the observer.

So, after all that, it seemed to me that Dale, Ron, and the other central figures in the Bonoban movement should celebrate their achievements. They had directly and profoundly improved scores of lives (in the eyes of those living them) through the Bonobo House and especially the resort. And they had indirectly done so among thousands of people—including me. In addition, they had sparked much more interest in research on and conservation of actual bonobos, some of which they funded. In all likelihood, these successes would continue to grow. It's doubtful that Dale and Ron would have had the same effect had they become college professors.

Take II

Without rejecting any of the previous analysis, I eventually came to regard the Bonobo movement from another angle, as well. This one starts with my reaction to Enrique's advice: if I followed the chain of deconstruction (questioning assumptions) to its logical conclusion, then I'd end up a purely self-seeking hedonist. Instead, for unknown reasons, I deeply wanted to not hurt and, really, to help other people. And that *feeling* was as real as the logic of deconstruction. What I mean is: both were in my brain, not in some ideal realm of Abstract Truth. Internal contradiction was inevitable, and it seemed to be part of the human condition.

Most of my Mexican friends experienced no cognitive dissonance in managing such contradictions. Blanca was a virginal sexpot; Enrique was an egoist and a devoted father, a corrupt supporter of incorruptibles like Rosalva; Xóchitl was a faithful cheater; the sex workers (well, some of them) switched between indifference and sincere sympathy at the drop of a coin; and music fans abhorred drug violence while choosing songs that exalted it.

Thus, if Dale and Ron were to succeed in a world of inevitable contradictions (humble popes? arrogant vicars of

Christ?), they would have to make moral compromises. At the time of my visit to ¡Bonobo!, being less wise, I judged them to have sold out the revolution. These days I wouldn't expect them to achieve purity. Of course, we should evaluate the way that they balanced different pressures, but our judgments will inherently flow from our own contradictory influences.

No doubt, you'll judge my impending actions in the same way.

AN EARLY NAVIDAD

The tour of ¡Bonobo! wound down, and, under the puffy clouds and blue sky of a blazing summer afternoon, we wound back to the main administrative building. The bland, one-storey edifice sat between the resort and Real Bonobo, with doors that opened from each into the reception area. This was not the resort's reception counter, which didn't exist, but a large, open clerical space. A broad desk made from untreated wood sat in front of Dale and Ron's offices. Another couple of rustic desks helped to fill out the space, along with a long, thin table that held office machines on top and paper and toner underneath. Behind the main desk and between the two offices arched a wooden banner.

"Thanks for the Fish," I demonstrated my literacy out loud.

"Nat, you can read!" Ron exclaimed in astonishment.

"It's another old joke," Dale said and tapped the banner, perhaps for good luck.

Most of the other items on the walls consisted of calendars of events and work schedules, copies of official documents with key phrases highlighted, postcards from former residents and visitors, party photos, and old posters from the Hive. In short, it looked suspiciously like a normal office—except for the small stack of mats, the condom container, and the lube pump.

A man wearing the requisite staff regalia sat at the desk against the right wall. He pointedly didn't look up, perhaps to maintain his concentration on financial calculations or whatever he was doing—or perhaps to avoid the rigamarole of greeting everyone. The other desks were empty. As Dale explained, anyone could use the main desk, but no one ever *had* to sit there, thus avoiding the appearance that other staff somehow served him and Ron.

Ron opened the door to his office and went in while we continued to banter. As he pulled open a file drawer, they joked about how they would have occupied the same windowless holes had they gone into academia. Dale and I followed him in so that I could judge for myself. Indeed, abstracted from its surroundings, Ron's office did look pretty similar to many offices I'd visited in my career as a student, although I noticed that his had a closet, which Doris probably fantasized about.

Soon he had extracted three folders. One was stuffed with papers. It contained printouts of the reports that I had given them on floppy disks. Ron showed that they had highlighted some sections and written notes in the margin, as an indication that they took my work seriously. "And anyway it's helped us get to know the neighborhood," he said. "Even though we've been here for, what, five years, we just can't get around like you."

"Of course, we have some contacts there that you don't," Dale added. This obviously was true. It would have been less so had I accepted their early offers to introduce me to, for example, the drug-money launderer who illegally 'owned' their island.

"The point is," Ron said, "even if this information doesn't help us stop the vandalism"—notice he didn't say, "catch the vandals"—"it might help us improve our relations with Playatlán, or to target our donations there."

"Corporate social responsibility if ever I saw it," Dale waved a finger.

Ron put an arm around my shoulder for a second. "Nat here was living in Playatlán and spending money in Playatlán. Ipso facto, the benefit went to Playatlán—and probably more efficiently than some of the other crap we've paid for. Not to mention his dissertation."

"Polyvalent pesos," Dale deadpanned.

"Multitasking money, to the layperson, which—being in ¡Bonobo! …"

"Please, not again." Dale rolled his eyes.

Fuck their banter. I felt stunned and sickened. Were they really saying that they had paid me with CSR cash, which could have gone to, for example, the poorly funded (and, yes, poorly run) orphanage? I was too confused and afraid to ask directly. That would have forced me to take a clear moral stance, which I couldn't afford financially and which would jeopardize my friendship with these great guys. Unless, of course, we fucked it out, which would work miracles for those orphans.

These moral concerns pulsed and swirled in my mind as Ron moved on to a thinner folder. It held the receipts that I had signed for my wages as an ineffectual sleuth. Ron withdrew a final slip, already filled in with my usual payment. Then, opening the top-right drawer of his desk, he pulled out an envelope like all the others I had received. "Thank you for your services—today is included, just in case." He extended the money toward me.

Conflicted and confused, feeling polluted and a bit panicked, I accepted the pay and quickly dropped it in my backpack, where it joined the sunscreen, snacks, and forbidden video camera. It wasn't out-of-sight, out-of-mind, but the deal was done, and now I could take some time to think about what really had happened and how I should react. It had gone down so quickly.

Plus, Ron had moved on to the third folder. Someone had doodled an awkward-looking bow on the outside. "It's an early Feliz Navidad for one lucky boy!" he beamed.

"Or a late one, if you were expecting a present last year," Dale said.

"Regardless: the Bonobo Way includes the Golden Rule. And what we would have you do unto us, if you were us, even though we actually are us—"

"You can use the information you gathered for us in your dissertation," Dale cut in, "if you think that's ethical, of course."

Ron pushed the folder across the desk to me, and I opened it.

"A contract! Worst Navidad ever, I bet," Dale said, as I bent over to read the brief agreement.

"I got the idea from watching *A People's Court Navidad*," Ron explained. "Little Judge Wapner dreamed of getting one of these."

Distracted by the string of dramatic surprises and inane witticisms, I struggled to comprehend the wording. Eventually, I grasped that the contract allowed me to use the information that I had obtained through my employment by ¡Bonobo! in my "dissertation, educational books and articles, professional presentations, and teaching." Other venues were off-limits unless I obtained permission in writing from ¡Bonobo!

Wow. This actually constituted a gift of amazing value to me as a budding academic. My mind quickly suppressed the moral quandary regarding the source of my funding, and my heart filled with universal human love. Tears started to form, and I choked out, "Thanks, guys—this is great," before a drop or two sullied the paper and I needed to wipe my eyes with my T-shirt. People could be so good.

"It's a gift to the person we didn't get to be," Dale said, kindly.

"Or at least didn't choose to be—and to everyone's big sister," Ron said, meaning Doris (and, hopefully, ignoring the incestuous implications). He took a pen out of the middle drawer and signed the receipt and the contract. Dale followed suit, and, just like that, so did I.

Oh, the ramifications!

"Let's go make a copy, and then we have one more surprise." Ron took the two documents and led us out of his office, over to the small photocopier on the long, thin table by the wall. Placing the sheets in the feeder, he pressed the button, to no effect.

"Doesn't work," intoned the guy who I thought might be a devoted accountant. He still didn't look up. Nonetheless, Dale and Ron coaxed him into revealing that Captain Steve should have obtained toner in Playatlán after delivering me. But he hadn't brought it from the dock yet.

"We'd call him on the walkie-talkie," a vexed Dale explained to me, "but the Hive doesn't like them." Among other shortcomings, they interfered in multiple ways with sex.

Ron assured me that they would get me my copies before I left the island.

This led them to the final surprise that they had planned. Adopting a childish air of conspiracy, they winked at each other grandly and signaled with a multitude of comically minimal gestures that I should follow them into Dale's office. Dale shut the door and searched for spies and bugs.

Ron looked at Dale. "Should I tell him, or do you want to?"

"Are we going to make him wait through these shenanigans again?" Dale rolled his eyes.

"So you think we should tell him straight away?"

"Obviously. It would be counter to the character of giving a treat if we were to induce or prolong the recipient's discomfort by delaying the delivery of the aforementioned treat."

"Point well made—and well taken, sir."

"Thank you, my fine fellow."

"So, now that that's settled ... should I tell him, or do you want to?"

Clearly, through the years, they had practically perfected this sort of repartee and enjoyed feeling their prowess through its exercise. I tried to look as blank as possible. I had learned from several Mexicans that 'he who gets angry loses,' so I just rode out the provocation.

"Well, if he's not even going to get mad, *you* can tell him," Dale said and then turned to me, putting his hand on my shoulder and looking me in the eye, "Nat, we're a man down tonight, so we're hoping you can man up, as it were, and join the Pile."

Best Navidad ever! My heart bounced up and down like a superball. "Sure—that sounds cool," I tried to sound cool.

They explained that they needed "to finesse" my participation, so they didn't want to discuss the issue in front of Garth, the barely communicative possible accountant in the outer office. He was more sullen than usual because, at the behest of the Hive, he would have to fuck out his long-running dispute with another Bonoban that evening. Anyway, another guy had fallen ill, so I would keep the genders balanced.

Neither they (as far as I could tell) nor I stopped to consider whether treating one-time access to an orgy as a great gift jibed with the ideology animating Bonobo. What did this say about the effects of ubiquitous, daily sex on their attitudes? At that moment, I didn't ask. I now suspect that Dale must have questioned himself later.

"We're assuming you don't have any creepy-crawlies that would disqualify you, do you?" Ron asked, a bit late.

I told them the truth, that I always wore condoms, so, no, I didn't have any STDs. I omitted those few trips to the local clinic, to spare them needless concern.

I felt really, very happy—big, multicolored rockets exploded in my chest. What a great, dramatic way to begin drawing
my time in Playatlán to a close. My dick was hard. Although I
was too cool to express my happiness explicitly, Dale and Ron
seemed to sense it and revel in the effect of their largesse. We
now regarded and bantered with each other as if we had taken
happy pills. I doubt that they could have made love to me
more thoroughly than they did that afternoon.

Why was I so lucky? What could I do to be worthy of this
kindness, to return the love or pay it forward? Enrique would
have said that this was unnecessary, that I simply should enjoy
my good fortune, especially since nobody more worthy could
replace me.

Yet, amid my joy, gratitude, and anticipation, a niggling
voice in my mental symposium asked, ever more insistently,
whether I had fully earned or repaid any significant kindness,
ever—whether from my foster family, my girlfriends and their
parents, my teachers, or Ron and Dale. Had I—trained by my
early victimhood, forever telling myself that my tragedy outweighed all possible gifts—only received? Had I only *thanked?*
Yes. I had allowed myself to count courtesy as a significant
beneficence and gone no further. Look how content Ron and
Dale felt in giving: couldn't I feel the same? Did Bonobo make
them more generous? Part of me wanted to hug everyone and
dance and fuck and sing and joke. Another part wanted to
drown my loathsome, irredeemable self in the ocean lapping
against the rocks a few yards away. Yet another part wanted,
like Scrooge, to make up for lost time. But in these short moments I could only form vague, sentimental images because I
lacked any obvious means—such as riches or a sex pile—to
overwhelm others with generosity.

Then it got worse. Rather, *I* got worse.

AN INTRUSION

Through Dale's office door, I heard someone suddenly talk loudly and urgently with Garth. Then Garth banged on the door and shouted, "Intruders! We have intruders!"

Dale and Ron rushed out. Wide-eyed, Garth repeated the little information he had heard: infiltrators were running around the resort area. He, Dale, and Ron started toward the door to the resort; Ron briefly turned back to me and pressed his hands down to indicate that I should stay put. "Sometimes these things happen. It shouldn't take long." As they hurried out, Ron locked the door to the building behind them.

Left alone, agitated and curious but afraid to open the door, I wandered around the office, glancing distractedly at the various papers on the walls and desks. Among the folders scattered on a desk, I noticed one labeled "reported security incidents." Stuffed inside were numerous forms documenting incursions by horny drunks, landings by cross-bay swimmers, disruptive chants from a circling boat of Protestant protesters, and, of course, occasional evidence of vandalism.

My thoughts had always emphasized ¡Bonobo!'s distance from Playatlán; now I began to see its exposure to all sorts of dangers, without easy recourse to police or neighbors. I suspected that the island's much-rumored association with a powerful criminal provided it with a protective veneer. But Bonobans were lovers, not fighters, and dropped trou too often to carry weapons. (Pretty obviously they didn't simply 'fuck it out' with all of their opponents, either.) The forms asked whether the "security procedure manual" had been followed and needed amending, but I didn't see the manual at hand—not among the scattered materials on that desk, on Garth's, or on the big one.

Maybe it was in a drawer. Outside I could hear distant, muffled shouts, doors slamming and the scraping sound of furniture being pushed. I glanced up at the exterior doors. The one to ¡Bonobo! was locked, probably the one to Real Bonobo was, too. Plus, anyone would come from the resort, where the intruders had entered. I pulled open the drawers and rifled through the files, but I didn't find the manual: just bills, receipts, administrative forms, manuals for machines—a typical office miscellany.

Maybe it was on Ron or Dale's desk. No, it couldn't be on Ron's; I would have noticed it before. Did they really divert charitable funds to pay for my investigation? That would be a dick move—and then to tell me, just to make me feel guilty after the fact. Dale—what was his problem? Maybe the manual was in Dale's office. We barely had spent any time in there, and I hadn't looked around at all. The door stood open. So I went in.

He had decorated it a bit like a faculty member's office. Two diplomas hung on the wall, as did postcards and photos of his parents and friends from graduate school—yes, including Doris. This reminded me that I needed to call her about my assistantship in the Fall. A built-in bookshelf shared the wall with the closet. It held a few volumes on business and tourism and some on Mexico and Latin America, but the preponderance were academic: introductory textbooks, graduate-level monographs, a student journal from his days at Arizona, some works of primatology, and multiple editions of a few professional journals, right up to the most recent ones—a sure sign that he still paid dues to the American Anthropological Association.

His closet sported the monogram D.B. The carved, wooden letters were sculpted to look like monkeys (not apes) linked together. These, of course, were Dale's initials, but I wondered whether they referred also to the legendary "Deep Bonobo," which some far-out sources on the movement described as the realm where Bonobo existed in its full and pure manifestation.

I extracted and opened a recent journal as an alibi and then began perusing the papers and folders strewn about his desktop, searching for the security manual or perhaps some other interesting tidbit.

Clack. Someone unlocked the exterior door, and I quickly grabbed the open journal—right-side up!—and leaned back against the desk as though reading.

Ron appeared in the office doorway. He looked intense and hurried. "Good, you stayed put. Has anyone else been in here?" His voice sounded louder and faster than usual.

I said no.

"It's going to take longer than we thought. We've had a TB infection." That is, he explained quickly, Holly and an unknown number of her disciples from True Bonobo had invaded the island using at least two boats that unloaded at different points. Naked, they were running around rubbing their unfiltered and unshielded genitalia on the furniture and architecture; on the condom, lube, and sunscreen dispensers; on the cups, dishes, and silverware; on the towels and, in unlocked rooms, bedding; and even on the mats. (Later, Susana revealed that at least some of them chanted, "No Bonobo is an island.")

"Nat, I have to ask," Ron looked me in the eye. "You didn't know anything about this, did you?"

"No!" That really offended me. They didn't trust me? "I didn't even know what was going on until you just explained it."

"Okay. Sorry. But we knew you'd met Holly." Then, as if he could delete the previous exchange, he explained briefly that ¡Bonobo! had a few handcuffs and a small detention room, but they lacked the staff to round up all of the True Bonobans quickly. Some of the intruders had begun hiding themselves, so the staff were proceeding building-by-building and room-by-room to check and secure each space. They had called for help using a marine radio, and Captain Steve also had sped to shore to alert the police directly. The staff had gathered the guests into a couple of locked hotel rooms; some seemed frantic, but, as long as the condoms lasted, they had a way to comfort each other.

I thought (okay, hoped) that Ron was about to tell me that, to simplify operations, I would need to join the guests. If so, I would get to witness the protest before comforting distressed visitors in the Bonoban way. But Ron had other ideas. "I see you're in your element here. That's good." He twisted the door handle to the closet to verify that it was locked. "I'm just going to check in my office and the bathroom, and then I'll secure both entrances to the building and you'll be safe here."

Everybody was "safe" from Holly. She obviously was making a point about inclusiveness in a dramatic but nonviolent fashion. Maybe she had given up on her colony and decided to go down swinging, as it were. On reflection, I thought she might want to strangle *me* if she saw me there with Dale and Ron.

Soon Ron had checked the building, locked the door to Real Bonobo, and headed back into ¡Bonobo! I pressed the button-lock on the exterior door, got a cup of water, and peed. I had lost interest in searching for the missing manual. Why was I snooping around anyway? What kind of person was I—didn't I have any gratitude? Maybe I should use the time productively and read some anthropology. I returned to Dale's office, urging good intentions on myself.

I had noticed a small collection of theses and dissertations on Dale's bookshelf. They were so unattractive, in their sturdy, generic, Soviet-style bindings, that only a deep interest in the topic or, more likely, a personal connection to the author would induce anyone to read them. And the texts, by and large, were even less appealing. They included Dale's and Ron's MA theses, Doris' dissertation, and other unintentionally arcane works by early Bonobans.

I untombed Doris' volume, which I had already read, to see whether Dale had written any notes in the margins. Scattered crumbs and food stains revealed that he had actually worked through it. But the only handwriting appeared just inside the cover, where Doris had written a brief dedication. The same was true of Ron's. I had saved opening Dale's for last, to actually read it, both as a courtesy and because I thought he might have interesting things to say.

Who knows? Maybe he did. But, when I flipped through the work to familiarize myself with it, I spotted a key inserted between a couple of pages. Intrigued, I took the key in my fingers, looked at its markings, and peered at the place in the text where it had appeared. These days I imagine that the page contained a discussion of Rodasky's work, but back then I saw no meaningful connection.

It didn't make sense that he'd hide the key to his office inside the room, and the desk's keys would have to be quite small. I became very still and listened for the voices of approaching people. None. I walked to the exterior doors and verified that they were locked. I strode back to Dale's office and, after listening for voices one more time, tried the key in the closet door. What was so precious, or horrible, that Dale would keep it locked in his office with the key hidden like that? Click! The lock resounded in the empty office, startling me. I checked the reception area yet again, then went back and swung Dale's office door until it was ajar. I returned to the closet, turned the knob, and opened the door.

It was dark inside, so I groped to find the light switch on the wall to the right, and … voilà, I was in a closet. It had enough room to stand comfortably, and shelves lined the three walls. They held, essentially, the same treasures my storage space in Gainesville contained: notebooks and boxes of files. This obviously was a collection from Dale's days as a student. I had seen similar archives in classmates' apartments and professors' offices. So, were it not for the disturbed atmosphere that the strange events of the day had created, plus the finding of the key, which conjured childhood fantasies stoked by the Hardy Boys and Scooby Doo, I probably would have closed the door and returned to my reading.

At least, that's what I argue to myself.

Instead, I wondered why Dale kept this door locked and hid the key so thoroughly. Did his notes from an old class conceal another surprise? Was "Rosebud" etched on a syllabus from "ANTH 310, Culture and the Individual"?

Now my heart's patter had upped its tempo, as fast little fireworks of exhilarating fear popped inside. I quickly and uselessly moved back into the reception area and listened. Nothing reached me except a couple of far-off shouts and slamming doors. I looked around for credible, noisy barriers that I could place between the exterior doors and Dale's office, to give me more chance to recover once someone came back. Seeing none, I instead timed how long it took me to walk the route, added a couple of seconds for closing the exterior door and probably re-locking it, and figured that I had that much time to remove the traces of my intrusion.

I walked back to Dale's office and reset the door ajar. I returned the key to its hiding place in his thesis and placed this back on the shelf. I picked out a recent journal, opened it to an article I plausibly would read, and placed this on Dale's desk to grab when someone returned. I felt impatient to start exploring the contents of the closet, but such protective measures were necessary. I tried to convince myself that searching the closet was an unwarranted thrill anyway, so I should appreciate any time I had.

Now I felt ready to delve in. I quickly took a survey of the items in the closet, lifting the lids off boxes and rifling through the files and withdrawing and flipping through notebooks. Most of it was too mundane to excite more than frustration: old tests, study guides, class notes, bibliographic annotations for his preliminary exams, notecards for his thesis and other projects, fliers announcing meetings of the Anthropology Club, student newsletters … on and on. I could get that sort of thing at home. Disappointingly, no other magic key to Deep Bonobo wondrously appeared.

By now, you might be wondering how I could be such a shit. This snooping breached common expectations of privacy that I shared, at least regarding my own life. Moreover, Dale and Ron, just moments before, had bestowed such gifts upon me that I had turned sentimental and wanted to emulate their generosity, so my actions constituted a personal betrayal, too. As I explored the closet, I intermittently interrogated my decency in these terms. But I felt as though this honorable part of me was chasing the madly curious part around my mind. Ethical Me occasionally buttonholed Compulsive Me as the latter pursued his plans with frenetic determination; Compulsive Me never paused more than a femtosecond before returning to his work.

Eventually, I came to a long line of plain, bound, black notebooks—the sort that are marketed as journals but, I assumed, Dale had once used for his classes or research. I opened the first one.

Jackpot. The bound notebooks really were Dale's journals—twenty-one volumes. Quickly I determined that they stood in order, from his undergraduate days to the present. They contained relatively free-form entries interspersed with more-structured notes, including, for example, financial calculations. Many contained ethnographic observations, all of which were of Bonobo.

What a goldmine! I took the first one out of the closet and sat to read his notes. A crunch between the chair and my body reminded me that I was carrying my backpack. I wore it so regularly that I often forgot until it got in the way. And now the thought popped up—courtesy of my fiendish unconscious mind—that I had a video camera in there, a small camcorder that I had used for my research in the municipal archives, at research informants' houses, and at concerts. I had recorded different texts, such as newspaper articles and song lists on mixtapes, that I could analyze later. Sometimes the results were too fuzzy to read, but the alternative was to copy everything by hand or to take photos, which would cost a fortune to develop.

Did I dare? Compulsive Me had already answered that question. Standing up, I moved to Dale's desk, cleared some space by putting the open academic journal in the chair, removed the backpack, and quickly and methodically retrieved the camera and a battery, leaving the spare tape and battery inside. Luckily, Dale had worked the journals hard, so they readily stood open on the desk. Holding the viewfinder to my eye with my right hand, I used my left hand to press the book open and then flip pages as I recorded the text. Page after page, journal after journal—I barely noticed what any entry contained. My mission now was documentation; in Boasian fashion, analysis would come later.

Suddenly, above the quiet whirring of the camera, a doorknob rattled. Someone was trying to open one of the doors to the building. As they continued trying it, I hurriedly returned the volume to its shelf, pushed the closet door ajar (to be shut quietly if someone actually entered the building), threw the camera in the backpack, and stood behind the door to Dale's office, listening intently. Now I heard them pound and kick against the door a couple of times—and then nothing. I crept, as silently as I could, across the concrete floor to each exterior door. My breathing sounded inordinately loud. Putting my ear to each door in turn, I listened: nothing nearby. I returned to Dale's office and restarted recording.

Later—the rush of adrenaline made time elastic—I heard voices semi-shouting outside.

"Maybe we could go through that office," a man called.

Probably a staff member was speaking, so I again decamped. He might have keys.

"We could, but it's locked," a woman replied. "Ron checked it."

"Good going, Ron—now we'll have to take the longcut."

"Yeah, what's he got against us?" The voices faded off.

Back I went to record more of the journals. The tape mechanism whirred, and I, too, had developed into a smooth-running machine, scanning and then flipping page after page, returning one volume and removing another, knocking them down until only a few remained.

Click.

Oh, shit—someone had just unlocked one of the exterior doors. As I heard it open and shut, and the pressing of the button lock, and footsteps covering the floor, and the sound of water pouring into a cup, I rushed silently to return the journal to its shelf and exit from the closet. I shut the door gently— oh, crap, I forgot that I had locked the handle.

Click! It slid into place like a gunshot.

The person sighed—it sounded like Ron—and I heard him toss a plastic cup into an open wastebasket. I stuffed the video camera in my bag. I heard his footfalls slowly approach the office door. I grabbed the academic journal and a retractable pen, leaned my butt against the desk, and feigned reading. To mimic the sound of the lock, I occasionally clicked the end of the pen against the desktop. As Ron pushed open the office door, my heart and mind were drag racing, but I looked up as if he had spoiled my concentration.

"What are you up to?" He leaned in the doorway, his face flushed and his eyes a bit tired. I thought he seemed suspicious.

"I found some things I hadn't read." I held up the publication. "I don't get these in Playatlán." All this was true.

Ron looked around, so reflexively I did too.

And I saw it. Oh, shit shit shit shit shit. The light in the closet was still on, and a thin, guilty line of Truth shone along the bottom edge of the door. I looked at Ron. Did he do a tiny double-take there? Did his eyes pause and narrow? Could he know whether Dale had left the light on?

Why had I committed such an indefensible act—especially one so risky? Ron would know what I had done and tell Doris, destroying my academic career. And I deserved it. Fear and self-loathing in ¡Bonobo!: I had ruined such a good thing, perverted it. Please let me escape. Please please please please.

Who knows what Ron thought? Maybe Dale's profligacy with electricity always gave him pause. Maybe he suspected me of somehow snooping in the closet, despite it always being locked, but couldn't imagine that I had found anything of value. Or maybe—and this is my guess—he just felt too tired and exasperated to deal with another fucked up situation.

Fear and guilt colored my perception, but Ron, my benefactor and friend (still?), looked at me, sighed, and spoke with an irritated and emotionally divorced tone, laced with a trace of disgust. "Nat, you're out of here." They were still dealing with Holly's gang of True Bonobans; thus there wouldn't be any Pile that night. In fact, they had offered to lodge their guests at a hotel in Playatlán if they so desired, and two had accepted. He had come to get me so that I could leave on the same boat.

Thus—without saying goodbye to Dale; without ever having sex in the place of my fantasies, where sex was obligatory; and after needlessly jeopardizing one of the best relationships I had ever had—I was escorted away from Bonobo, across the bay, and onto the mainland, where I belonged.

And that's the Truth.

PART III

HOW I CAME TO WRITE IT

JANET

Gainesville

Six months later, ushering in a new millennium, Janet moved herself in. Yes, it had taken me, the champion of the à la carte relationship, one semester to end up living with a girlfriend. How could such a reversal occur? For a long time I had turned up my nose at those bumper stickers that read, "Life is what happens to you while you're making other plans." (Death, too, I used to think.) Now that they seemed apt, I disliked them even more.

I met Janet at a Bonobo encounter in Gainesville. At the myriad parties thrown to open the new semester, I told everyone that I had just returned from performing research in Playatlán. Weakened by beer and a desire to shine, I also bragged that I had had some dealings with ¡Bonobo! and a rival Bonobo colony. Word spread through a very short grapevine, and soon I received an invitation to Gainesville's most prominent Bonobo event—a weekly orgy hosted by a "non-hierarchical collective" at the house of a perennial graduate student and her pony-tailed husband.

They wanted me to provide the non-erotic portion of the gathering (my reputation precedes me, I joked to myself) by making a presentation about Bonobo in Playatlán. Of course I accepted the invitation, but with significant qualms. I felt deep and lasting shame at having recorded Dale's journals; it was the opposite of Bonobo—no Golden Rule, no mutual exposure. So I had resolved to honor only the initial agreement that I had signed with him and Ron, ensuring the confidentiality of whatever I had learned in their employ. That included my time at True Bonobo with Holly, Líssy, and Sherry. Yes, on my last day with Dale and Ron I had signed another agreement that, arguably, would allow me to give an educational talk at a Bonoban event, but I had never received my copy—even after I wrote them a bland letter expressing gratitude. Taking this as a clearer sign that they now hated me for entering Dale's closet and rummaging around (they couldn't possibly know the extent of my malfeasance), I felt an irrational desire to punish myself by adhering to the original, stricter standard. Surely, had they known me then as they did now, they would never have bestowed this gift on me.

Ultimately, I devised a talk that contained information that anyone in Playatlán who followed the news would know, ending with an account of Holly's self-destructing raid on the island. Afterward, she and a couple of Americans were deported back to the United States (Wisconsin, in her case) with the proviso that they never return to Mexico. Dale and Ron wisely showed no interest in having her Mexican followers prosecuted. Their families paid 'fines' to the police, who promptly released the intruders, much as happened to youths caught battling with eggs on Student Day.

The Bonobo gathering took place a few weeks after I had returned. It was in an old, lopsided wooden house downtown where the couple lived. The group's composition discomfited me. Unlike at True Bonobo, I already knew a few of the twenty or so people involved: there was the guy who had endured the same linguistics class, a woman who worked at the computer lab, and, I think, possibly a person or two whose papers I had graded in past semesters. I had been gone for a year, so I felt a little abstracted from everything; nonetheless, I had lived in Gainesville for five years before that, and now, for reasons of mental colonialism, everything I did seemed more consequential than anything I had done in Playatlán. In short, I felt shy and weirded out.

The program took place in the living ('loving') room. A small, unbalanced table by the front door held a stack of rules sheets for newcomers to sign and optional ("bow/no-bow") breast-or-pussy ribbons for the women. The beaten up, splintery, and uneven wooden floor lay bare, except for two couches that had been pushed against the walls, alongside stacks of inflatable mattresses, plastic sheeting, and exercise mats. Gator-shaped plastic containers filled with condoms and lube also lined the walls, beneath the drawn shades. The adjacent kitchen held a pony keg and big bottles of soft drinks. I imagined that the early Bonoban gatherings in Tucson must have looked quite similar.

The main effect of my talk appeared to be tantric. Serious groping had already begun when I started, and quite a few attendees faced me but had pleased, distracted expressions, as if the hand caressing behind their ears or between their legs had stolen their interest. As I spoke, some people asked their neighbors if they wanted a drink, passed into the kitchen, and exchanged small comments when they returned. Nonetheless, a few listened with obvious attention, and among these was a cute, smiling woman, perhaps a few years younger than I, who nodded a lot, as if confirming my statements.

When I finished, the host thanked me for the presentation and everyone else for attending, emphasized a few rules, and reminded us of the schedule. At the end, she intoned, "We come in peace," and we repeated it with solemnity, as if it were the Bonoban amen and not a marketing slogan. Then she had us gather in the center of the room, put an arm around each neighbor, hunch over slightly, and sort of jump up and down while making hooting noises, presumably like bonobos. This quickly crescendoed into a unified shout of release into action, much like a football team before a game. We separated and got out the pads and accoutrements, and everyone got down to fucking.

Actually, I didn't do any of that, because I had to use the bathroom while I was speaking. Once my spiel ended, I hustled a short way down the hall to the john and, when I came out, the smiling, nodding woman was standing there. She reintroduced herself as Janet and praised my presentation. I enjoyed sharing another bonobo handshake with her, and I felt pleased when she followed me to the kitchen, where I hoped to get a quick beer while they did their ridiculous bonobo chant. We could see this from the kitchen, and Janet happily hooted along and half-jumped, while shifting her glance between me and the troop. Once able to speak human language again, she looked up into my eyes with enthusiasm and divulged that she had found my talk so fascinating because, during her freshman year, she had traveled to Playatlán on a Spring Break package deal.

One of *those*, I thought. She undoubtedly had yelled, "Woo!" with all the others while cruising the bay on the Party Yacht. The only mystery was whether she had entered the fake-orgasm contest or the wet T-shirt competition.

Janet said that while she was there she had met an American ethnographer like me at a disco and had vowed to him that she would return someday to study Playatlán. But suddenly, she said, "I had to barf my guts out" over the seawall, and she never got to talk with him again. Since that trip she had found Playatlán and ¡Bonobo! fascinating.

I told her the anthropologist's name was Tracy and said that I'd love to talk with her about his research, or even mine, but (and by now we were stroking each other's genitalia) perhaps we should join the others first. As we returned to the living room, a man and woman across the way smiled to Janet and beckoned her to join them. I saw that I was about to be left alone to scavenge some affection among strangers, all of whom already had at least one partner, when Janet told them, "Later," and turned to focus entirely on me.

In that initial encounter she wanted to be on her back and me to be on my knees—Bonobo style—seemingly so that we could lock our eyes throughout. This technique reminded me of Doris' desire to create an intersubjective bond with her partner at the point of orgasm. However, Janet had eyes only for me, even afterward. Following the first go-round we parted and screwed with others, but many times I scanned the room, only to find her regarding me from a distance. When she caught my eye, she would complement her moaning or panting with a chummy smile for me, which I found utterly seductive.

A few days later we met for lunch at a Cuban sandwich shop near campus to discuss all things Playatlán. I found myself again succumbing to her enthusiasm for my work, especially since, as I'll discuss later, this wasn't universal.

We also talked about Bonobo. Janet had attended only one previous party hosted by the Gainesville group, although she had had other experiences at one-off Bonobo-inspired events, including a small, orgy-like encounter in a hotel room in Playatlán, which she described as a "teenage version of playing doctor." She regarded all such transgressions as youthful activities that she would leave behind but cherish as she grew more mature. Already her interest in Bonobo—never commitment—was waning, and her excitement to do relatively grownup things, like finishing her Education degree and touring museums in Paris, was increasing.

In this she reminded me of many women in Mexico, who tended to conceive of each person's life in numerous sequential phases, to which they frequently referred in conversation. Mexican men were more likely to see themselves as existing in a vast, undifferentiated period of active adulthood, in which any man from about twenty to sixty was relatively equivalent.

My take on Gainesville's Bonobo scene was different from Janet's. While I had spent only one night at True Bonobo, a fairly chaste afternoon at ¡Bonobo! (although I frequently pictured the Pile I had missed), and a few hours at the Gainesville gathering, I presumed to judge: the latter was just an orgy, a party thinly disguised as part of a movement. Weekly encounters were too infrequent to change people's daily lives, and the event wasn't structured to provoke participants into considering its lessons and extending these into other realms of their lives.

Janet suggested that maybe I should attend one of their business meetings, which her friends had mentioned. The collective might benefit from hearing what I had to say. She had a point, and, more importantly, she took me seriously.

I liked talking with her, and I had no ~~better~~ other options, so we started seeing each other.

I'm sure you can see the slippery slope down which I had begun to slide. The à la carte principle did not preclude combining functions in a single person, in this case both conversation and sex. But the dominant expectation in our environment was for more: any couple who enjoyed these two activities was pushed into an all-in-one relationship that superseded all others. That is, everyone expected us to become a steady couple.

I felt gravity's pull and fought the slide. While Janet and I did go on dates that included sex, I tried to delimit these as much as possible without insulting her romantic sensibilities. For example, we might watch a rented movie and have sex, rather than go canoeing, cook dinner, watch a movie, and then have sex. Spending the night together followed only occasionally; neither of us had planted the toothbrush flag in the other's bathroom. I also dated other women—rather, I tried to date other women, but apparently I had left my charms at the border. Still, I made no commitment to Janet other than what she might infer from our continued, and increasingly frequent, dates.

Even though I had difficulty getting past lunch with other candidates, I did have sex (outside of the Bonobo party) with one other woman. Doris invited me to her bungalow for a dinner to celebrate my return from fieldwork. This time I found her come-ons less shocking. We engaged in a fluid give-and-take about issues surrounding my research and other weighty academic matters, and now I felt a little closer to being her peer. Our continuing and deepening intellectual comradeship confirmed my choice of her as my adviser. Nonetheless, I stuck to little-t truths when speaking of Ron and Dale, and I certainly didn't mention visiting prostitutes fifty times.

We shared several sweet things together, and, at the climax of each, Doris and I focused our eyes on each other. I knew that this was vital to her, and I enjoyed exploring different attitudes toward such moments. Thus did we talk about the still-distant day when I, her first advisee, would graduate. We raised our glasses to my projected success, fed each other a gooey brownie dessert, and made love.

Yes: we made *love*; I'm sure of it. But neither of us was in love (if I were, it would still be with Blanca). Moreover, this time I held a larger part of my psyche in reserve and cared only slightly whether she noticed a gauzy curtain waving across the windows to my soul. Maybe this change resulted from maturation or worldliness, or shame—or from practice with prostitutes. Anyway, it was nice to feel comfortable enough to modulate my self-exposure according to my own preference, rather than striving to meet my partner's expectations, whether for catharsis or control. Afterward, when I retrieved my bike from her garage, Doris rubbed my shoulder, among other parts, and remarked, "You seem more confident now."

Pedaling home, I turned this over in my mind. Could she see something that I didn't feel? As far as I was concerned, over the past year I had become less cocksure and more aware of my weaknesses. And perhaps a little numb.

Aside from that one time with Doris—I expected the next tryst with her when I graduated—the only opportunities for sex that I could arrange were the Bonobo party and dates with Janet. Presumably there were prostitutes in Gainesville, but I had no idea where they were, how much they cost, whether the police would arrest and ruin me, and, above all, why I needed to visit one if I had a ~~girlfriend~~ steady partner. And no one— not a single person outside of Playatlán—initiated sex with me out of the blue.

So, yes, I'm now confessing that, aside from enjoying her company, I dated Janet because I wanted to have a sexual partner. After all, I liked conversing with many people more than I liked talking with her. This isn't a criticism or insult: other graduate students and faculty members in Anthropology shared my background, interests, assumptions, experience, and outward sensibility much more than almost anyone else could. I had a great time at brown-bag presentations, in the vast TA office, and at departmental or grad-student parties. My heart popped like little daisies blooming when I saw friends outside the library, joked around while playing frisbee golf, enjoyed happy hours with the gang on Fridays, or shot the shit into the wee hours with a friend or two at one of our crappy abodes. So why would I spend time with Janet instead of them if sex weren't at stake?

From a bourgeois perspective, the nadir of my treatment of Janet probably occurred on those late nights when, after hanging out with my friends and possibly flirting with other women, I called to see whether she wanted to spend the night together. Most times, she said yes.

What about the local Bonobo group? If I subsisted on prearranged, weekly sex in Playatlán, couldn't I do the same in Gainesville? I soon found out that the Bonoban parties, for a multitude of reasons, required an invitation. A core group took rotations and reserved a few spaces each week for outsiders such as Janet and me to experience the revolution and, essentially, audition for full membership. Thus, more than a month passed before I received word of another opening. By that time, I was having comfortable sex with Janet several times a week, and I chose instead to attend a party to celebrate the completion of a friend's dissertation. Bonking with Janet afterward, I imagined the variety that I might have encountered at the Bonobo party, and I felt a twinge of regret.

Alas, some of my friends started mentioning my "girlfriend." They wanted to know her name, her major or job, her age. They asked why I didn't bring her along wherever I went. Didn't she like them? Some of these friends were women I wanted to date, or at least to have sex with, which was part of why I didn't want Janet with me. Sometimes friends would explicitly suggest that I bring her to a party or outing, but, presuming them to be unprepared, I never responded by explaining limited-purpose relationships.

Finally, tragedy struck when one of these women, Carmela, saw me with Janet at the video-rental store and invited us both, together, as a couple, to a dinner party that she and her boyfriend were hosting. Janet played it cool, but I think she felt a little starburst of joy. At the get-together she of course fit in nicely—remember, she fantasized about achieving the next level of maturity—and exchanged numbers and email addresses with Carmela and another of my female friends. I'll admit that I felt some pride at her success—Janet was smart, enthusiastic, and fun. The next day, Carmela actually called just to tell me how much she liked her. I didn't need Paul Simon to read the writing on the wall: in my friends' minds, we now were a couple.

Yet I continued to fight the good fight. I had broken Blanca's heart (I think) and didn't want to repeat that plot line with Janet. If she didn't receive her own invitation to an event, I still sometimes went without her. I knew that I wouldn't find another lover, given that the grad-school gossip had defined our relationship according to conventional expectations, but I thereby reinforced my commitment to build a different kind of life.

Despite all that, I sometimes felt the same future-flowing sense of unity with Janet that I occasionally had felt with Blanca. Unfortunately, ruts were developing, too. Only the casual nature of our relationship allowed us to avoid confronting issues that would have gnawed at us if we were progressing toward something like marriage.

SONGS OF THE HOLOCAUST

Thus, my commitment to limiting relationships to their beneficial functions was in peril. So what about my resolution to be helpful rather than merely grateful? Just before I left Playatlán, I gave all of my usable goods to the orphanage—take that, Baby Jesus!—but of course I wanted to do more.

This endeavor involved narcotics. I had grown to hate the drug trade. Living in Mexico made stark the damage that American consumers had indirectly wreaked on Mexican society, especially in Conaloa. Criminal gangs murdered each other in great numbers, killed uninvolved bystanders, and threatened everyone from beauty-contest judges to, of course, cops and actual judges. And their money suborned all of these people, plus priests and politicians. The rule of law, basic fairness, a sense of security—they all went a little farther up in smoke with each purchase of drugs in the United States.

My research, you'll remember, centered on popular expressions related to narcotrafficking—making me, by default, one of the world's foremost experts—so I felt a responsibility to apply this expertise to make the world ~~better~~ less bad. If I did nothing, it would be like visiting Nazi Germany to write a treatise on songs of the Holocaust.

Following the default route among academics would entail developing journal articles, conference presentations, and possibly even a book that expressed my analysis as accurately and precisely as possible. The people directly involved in lessening the scourge of illegal drug-trafficking wouldn't read my work, or, if they did, they wouldn't know how to apply my conclusions to their efforts. For me, this would not suffice.

An 'engaged' academic would do the same things but would also write simplified opinion pieces for newspapers; offer his or her services as a guest lecturer in a criminology class; and give talks to the Rotary Club. The history of the world, briefly surveyed, suggested that such efforts—sincerely motivated and beyond the call of professional duty—rarely changed much, although they sometimes planted a seed that later blossomed into someone else's greater movement. Doris encouraged me to take this route. She pointed, as an example, to the op-ed piece that she and other linguistic specialists had signed regarding the brouhaha over Ebonics in Oakland. The Gainesville *Sun* had published an edited version. A more inspirational example would have been Deborah Tannen, who had published a bestseller about gendered differences in communication; sadly, anthropology generated only one Tannen per decade.

A third, 'applied' route entailed working directly with government agencies or NGOs to improve their programs. Unfortunately, the resulting research usually stunk. In fact, applied anthropologists had to compromise so fully to get these institutions to heed them that academics debated whether their work fit within anthropology at all. Nonetheless, they did have more influence.

Thus I had to decide how committed I was to this cause and to what extent I would corrupt my analyses to be heard. Should I start my own NGO? Should I search for a job with one? Should I stick to discussing my own research or devote time to learning about related issues? I mulled such questions as I walked across campus or pedaled across town.

My friends had no useful guidance. If one of them lit up a joint at a party and passed it around a small circle, I would genially note that I had stopped toking because of the cost to Latin

Americans. "In fact, I personally saw an innocent dude shot dead by drug traffickers, just sitting there at lunch."

Someone inevitably would say, "Yeah, they should legalize it," and offer me the joint. Yes, "they" should legalize pot, but cocaine? Heroin? And, in the meantime, shouldn't we consider drugs the same way we thought about T-shirts and coffee? People who boycotted Nike and prided themselves on ethical shopping didn't seem to care that blood saturated their hash brownies.

In more-earnest conversations, downing wine late at night in someone's apartment, friends suggested that I perform the engaged-academic routine and then declare my duty done. But I wanted to pay back for more than I had smoked. I felt the weight of ¡Bonobo!'s CSR funds, of the generosity of the Playatlecos who had helped me, of the taxpayers' subsidies of my education, of of of … And, yes, if I earned "the Nobel Prize for Anthropology" (to steal a joke from Dale), then so much the better.

Alas, I faced a basic problem in using my research to change the drug trade. I placed the primary cause in the United States, yet my expertise related to Mexico. I could help explain the allure of drug trafficking and Mexicans' facilitating attitudes, but in no way did I support a foreign war on drugs.

Ultimately, after much reflection and trial-and-error in conversation, I determined that my comparative advantage, my ecological niche, was giving people guilt trips. After all, this was what had led me to stop smoking pot. Sadly, guilt trips weren't my forte. Of course, I had exploited my status as an orphan or a shooting near-victim, but in those cases I sought sympathy and generosity for myself. Trying to get a drug user to feel responsible for some far-off people's pain was altogether different.

Nonetheless, I held my nose and contacted the police program—D.A.R.E.—that sent cops into schools to scare kids

away from using drugs. The coordinator, Officer Morris, invited me to police headquarters to make my case. Sitting in her
small, institutional office, holding a coffee that she had insisted
I accept, I tactfully opened by noting that several studies had
shown D.A.R.E. to be ineffective. Perhaps, through graphic
details from Playatlán, I could strengthen the program's message by driving home to students the damage that drugs did to
others, thereby defeating the common argument that it was a
victimless crime.

Morris nodded thoughtfully as I spoke, with a friendly smile
on her lips. When I took a breath for air and sipped a little coffee, she said, "Wow, I can tell you really want to make a difference. That's great. You must have seen some interesting things
down in Mexico. I've never been there, but I've met some
DEA guys." I tried to not smirk. "Let me ask you, since you've
studied their culture: why do you think they're so corrupt down
there?"

Aaaaaaaaarrrgghh.

A dissertation should be an unflinching, unvarnished display of Truths. So here's one: I've never narced on anyone. In
the United States I met dealers and knew heavy users. I saw
cocaine sales completed on street corners. I smelled pot over
fences. I even met a cop or two who partook of the ganja in
my presence. But I never reported any of them. Wasn't I at
least as corrupt as Mexicans who said nothing? After all, they
~~could~~ would be killed for speaking up, but I just feared being a
dick. So how much did I care, really? And you? Blaming Mexicans was a convenient distraction from a self-examination that
would end in self-loathing. (Blaming Americans had the same
effect among many Mexicans, by the way).

Trying to stay calm, I launched into a diatribe along these
lines. To her credit, Morris maintained her composure and finished out our discussion as if she might integrate my suggestions into her program. "Let me talk it over with our advisers

at the state level. I have your number and email, and I'll definitely contact you if it seems appropriate." She handed me her card, and off I went, feeling innovative and useful.

Clueless, I left a message the next day, thanking Morris for meeting with me and expressing enthusiasm for working with the program.

A couple of weeks passed before I sent Morris another email to remind her of my proposition to improve D.A.R.E. She replied by thanking me for my offer but added, "Our curriculum is set for the current school year. I will keep you in mind next summer, which is when we will plan the next year's program." A classic blow-off.

Stymied, I settled for the 'engaged academic' route, giving guest lectures in college courses so that the regular instructors could loaf.

Looking back, I doubt that working within D.A.R.E. to make teenagers feel guilty would have affected drug-use to a significant extent. At the time, though, frustration, rage, and resentment commandeered me when I thought about this rejection. More than that, I felt embarrassed to have achieved so little, regardless of how sincerely I desired to help and how hard I had tried to do so.

The academic environment softened the pain of impotence. Having the wrong theoretical orientation provoked more derision than having helped no one. Plus, I found my dissertation research to be intrinsically interesting and felt pride in it as a work of academic art. Nonetheless, my heart knew that, beyond the Ivory Tower, my practical legacy would be "Songs of the Holocaust."

NOT JUST THAT BUT MORE

Janet, though, valued my work. When I confessed, without revealing my great embarrassment or the full extent of my cholera, that neither D.A.R.E. nor anyone else appeared interested in taking advantage of my expertise, she didn't simply pout in empathy, rub my shoulder, or emit some pacifying pablum about finding my niche. No, Janet got angry—and not on my behalf but on humanity's. How could they waste such a great opportunity? she asked rhetorically. This was why everything was so fucked up: nobody wanted to try something new, even when it served itself up on a silver platter.

Clearly she was in my corner.

And so was her father. He drove up from Winter Haven one weeknight, on his way to Tallahassee for some sort of certification. Janet seduced me into joining the two of them for dinner by predicting that her father would find my work fascinating. To reduce his detour, we ate at the Red Lobster by I-75.

Maybe he wanted to size me up, or butter me up, as a potential son-in-law. In any case, he acted fascinated whenever I started a comment with "in Playatlán" and proceeded to point out some surprising contrast or conformity with commonly expected behavior in the U.S. Most of these observations dealt with the practical application of topics tangential to my research—life lessons, in the popular parlance. So I took it with a grain of salt when her father averred, a little indulgently, a bit naïvely, that he'd buy a book like the one I was writing.

Janet tried to clarify, in my stead, that my dissertation dealt with a different issue, but he had declared his enthusiasm as a way of concluding our confab. She told me later, driving back to her place, that it was a shame I couldn't write two dissertations, because I had learned about so much more than "drug-trafficking culture."

Others had written that second dissertation already—even on Playatlán. In fact, I learned most of what I've reported to you about Mexico before I ever did my fieldwork. But I didn't know how it would feel to live there or how to apply this other research to my own decisions because these potentially practical observations were embedded within theoretical arguments. This analytical denaturing of experience has value, but so does building practical, everyday philosophies—that is, developing wisdom.

Ironically, my conversations with other students back from fieldwork focused more on these life lessons than on our theoretical revelations. For example, we commonly discussed how young people in other countries seemed to like their parents more than "we" liked ours, perhaps because they spent so much more of their time together. Or we'd note how people in some societies did or didn't associate holidays with drunkenness. And we'd marvel at the way people in other countries actually made space for social scientists to pontificate in newspaper columns.

Then we'd return to our computers to continue writing our dissertations, relating observation to theory in ways that only other illuminati might comprehend. The results were often fascinating, and I see no need to apologize for that. Plus, producing a standard academic dissertation was the only path to the life I craved as a university professor, like my friend and mentor Doris.

Still, the encouraging comments from Janet and her father reminded me that I wanted not just that but more. ('Everything in moderation,' perhaps, but *everything*.) Their faith nurtured the Me who had sheltered Xóchitl, who wanted to replicate Ron and Dale's beneficence and Ron and María's tenderness—that dormant, endangered Me who, without reason, loved and wanted to aid all of humanity.

THE WEB

From there to Janet moving in required only a few small steps.

Two weeks after I had passed up my chance to attend another Bonobo party, Janet received an invitation. She called me. "Did you get one?" she asked innocently. "We could go together, for old times' sake, I guess."

I suspected that she was testing me, but I hadn't received an invitation that week. Trying to not betray my envy—both of her good luck and of whoever would bang her while I spent the night celibate—I urged her to attend. Thus did I signal that we still weren't monogamous. This exchange occurred on Monday, and the party would take place on Friday.

Two days passed, and I increasingly recognized that I dreaded her going. Jealous thoughts of her meeting a better sex partner, for whom she would dump me, competed with the knowledge that being dumped would allow me to reboot my quest for limited-use relationships. Obviously, I couldn't lose.

Nonetheless, I could feel my blood rising as I obsessively pictured her looking at some other lover the way that she looked at me or hiding her disappointment the next time we had sex. Yes, I felt jealousy, and I knew that I could stop my pain and make her ecstatic simply by asking her to not go, to spend the evening with me instead.

But I did not. To do so would be either a capitulation to conformity or a misrepresentation of my commitment.

By Thursday, I could barely grade true-false questions; I could think only about Janet relishing sex with someone else and leaving me. I looked around the TA office and tried to identify who might be my fuck friend once Janet left.

Nobody, that's who.

Still I didn't bend.

In the afternoon, she called. As my stomach churned, we exchanged the usual pleasantries, both of us acting as though nothing momentous was afoot. Eventually she asked, "Hey, what are your plans for Friday night?"

I will sit at home, overwrought and aching, scrawling my fears into a journal. "Oh, pfffz, I hadn't really made any plans," I replied. "I guess I'll go to happy hour with the gang and see what happens."

"Oh, well, if you don't come up with anything better by then, would you like to go to a party with me? A friend of mine is having a birthday. It'll mostly be undergraduates."

Yes yes yes yes yes yes yes! "What about the Bonobo thing?" I asked. "You're not going to go?"

"Oh, no—I'd rather hang with my friends. I'm just not that into it, anyway," she kept her voice even. "I mean, you can go if you want to, whenever they invite you again; it's not that."

At that moment, I didn't care what it was. I gladly went to the birthday party with Janet, I stood by her side and didn't try to seed new relationships with other women, and I made sweet and passionate love with her when we got back to her place. The next morning I woke up with her head on my chest and an arm and a leg draped across me. I could feel her torso expand slowly with each breath; she let out a soft snore and dribbled a cute little cascade of drool near my collarbone.

She had me trapped. If she had been playing a game of chicken, then she had lost. Yet, somehow, there I was.

Please don't think that I capitulated and became the happiest man in seven counties. I continued to fight a principled campaign against an all-purpose, all-the-time relationship with Janet. As I wrote my dissertation, I deeply considered my time in Playatlán and the role of an academic researcher, and thus I became ever more committed to Truth. In the same vein I strove to not mislead Janet about my intentions.

Still, I have to admit that I didn't directly tell her about my commitment to limited-purpose relationships or my consequent unwillingness to devote myself to her. Probably I feared losing her support and her sexual availability. (That's right: more than one benefit.) So once again I hedged between Truth and truth.

Anyway, as the fall progressed, we spent more time together, including mornings, and we began to leave very basic toiletries, starting with her sanitary pads, at each other's place. In addition, I sometimes told her she could join me at events to which only I had been invited—a film or a grad-student happy hour.

Then, past midnight in early November, we were strolling through the tranquil, suburban neighborhood where she occupied the house of a professor on sabbatical. A light mist hung in the stillness. With a sudden, sharp swing of my hand, Janet said, "I love being with you." Lifting my hand high, she twirled herself around goofily. Her face shone like the moon as she looked into my eyes—not as a question but as a declaration of joy.

Obviously this was the chapter in the Book of Love just before the one in which she would announce directly, "I love you," which I dreaded. Not that I didn't love her. But she had said this while we were chatting about an idea from one of her classes, and just a moment earlier I had thought how much more interesting it would have been to discuss advanced social theory with my friends. I had less time to do this now that I devoted more of each week to Janet. She was as smart as any of us, but she lacked the specialized experience.

Probably my slight, involuntary hesitation communicated in a crude and inaccurate fashion that I didn't love her. This was a useful fiction. "Me too," I said and swung her hand and smiled. Even if she didn't know whether to believe it, this statement was true, just not all the time.

Janet apparently didn't need me to reciprocate fully. She seemed to have faith that everything would work out between two good people who appreciated each other's company. Unlike me, she intrinsically enjoyed expressing her love as she felt it, rather than calculating the progression of moves and countermoves that would lead to checkmate. Maybe she didn't need to participate in Bonobo to release herself into others.

I still did, and when the organizers asked whether I wanted to "come again" (har har) I said yes. I didn't inform Janet until two days before the orgy, when she asked what plans I had for that Friday. I broke the news to her in the same tone as if a friend wanted me to play a new video game at his house. Then I asked what she might do, and she said, "work on a project."

Was I hypocritical? You'll remember that, despite my jealousy, I never discouraged Janet from exploiting her opportunity to attend Bonobo. She had made her own choice. By choosing to participate, I wanted to make clear to her that she couldn't count on an inevitable progression to bourgeois coupledom. I also felt that, given the innumerable influences pushing regular sexual partners into all-in-one relationships, the Bonobo movement represented a rare chance for a 'free radical' like me to have frequent sex without breaking anyone's heart. I needed to give it a chance. Finally, it's true that Janet and I had a pleasing erotic relationship, yet I desired more variety. This already was on the decline between us, so why not try to maximize my pleasure?

Of course, it must have hurt and even frightened her, but she acted blasé, trusting in love, I suppose. I never had to fire off the phrase, "We met at a Bonobo party. What did you expect?" Indeed, in some perverse way my return to the orgy appeared to increase her determination to settle down with me, her bono-beau.

As for the sex at the party, it was like eating a delicious meal on the toilet. Fearing that this might be my last fling, I felt a little frantic to have the most cathartic sex possible, while striving to commit each moment to memory. It felt good, even great, as I pulsed inside my partners and caressed the men and women around me and came with force. Plus, it was refreshing to meet new people and have freewheeling discussions between the bouts of sex.

I slept alone that night. When I met Janet the next afternoon for lunch at the burrito shop, I felt awkward and shy, but quietly defiant, too. We sat down with our orange plastic trays.

Smiling candidly, she asked, "So, did you have fun?" as though she wanted to hear all about it.

Finally, on paper, Janet won. The professor whose house she was minding would return in December, between semesters. As final exams loomed ever closer, Janet still didn't have an apartment arranged for the Spring semester. She occasionally reported on her haphazard effort to find one, but I interpreted these comments as prompts to invite her to live with me. Instead, I expressed sympathy and suggested other search strategies.

Then, one day in early December, Carmela found me in the TA office and suggested that, since it was warm, we get lunch from the Krishnas' operation on campus. Sitting on the lawn, we performed the usual chat about writing our dissertations.

Then Carmela said, with a little sharpness to her voice, "You know, I had lunch with Janet yesterday."

Preemptively mortified, I wondered whether Carmela was about to lecture me regarding the Bonobo party. I began rehearsing a response.

"You know, she's embarrassed to ask you, but it's ridiculous—she shouldn't have to—so I told her I would." She looked me in the eye, a little challenging. "Why don't you ask her to move in? You know she needs a place, and, from what I hear, you guys sleep together all the time, anyway."

Blindsided, my mind flashed like a pinball machine. I hadn't prepared an answer. Besides, what business did Carmela have asking me this? If she's mad, can't we just fuck it out? Did Janet put her up to this? What about my solitude? This is so grade-school. Is this the end? And so forth. I stiffened slightly. Picking apart a blade of grass, I spoke slowly. "Why doesn't Janet ask me herself?"

"She didn't ask me to ask you, if that's what you think."

"But does she know you're asking?" Ironically, now I was acting like Holly, probing for the Truth—although mostly I was stalling.

"Of course. I told her I was going to talk with you. It's stupid."

I pictured Janet working anxiously at her clerical job on campus, nervously awaiting Carmela's report, fearing rejection yet anticipating deliverance into the next big step in our relationship. I realized at that moment that Janet had asked almost nothing of me, that she wanted me to freely desire each new step, including this one.

And I couldn't do it. No no no no no no no no. It was impossible. Even without family members to appease, even living among other anthropologists—all hyper-questioning social critics who were aware of the vastness of human diversity—I couldn't escape the pressure to conform to this domestic/romantic ideal. To do so would be to disappoint my friends and break the heart of a woman I loved. I had fought and struggled and resisted, but now I succumbed to the sociohistorical context in which I existed.

Nonetheless, this conversation was absurd. "Because I'm not thirteen, I'll talk with Janet myself. Indubitably you'll be the first to hear what happens." I sighed with mild disgust.

We chatted a while longer about grad-school politics, and then, just like Richard Gere at the end of *An Officer and a Gentleman*, I strode across campus to find Janet in the History Department office. She looked fresh yet professional at her desk, typing a professor's hand-written manuscript into a PC. Seeing me, she brightened like a maxed-out daisy and asked her supervisor whether she could escape for just a minute. This middle-aged lady smiled at us with restrained indulgence and said of course. We sat on a concrete bench under a tree by the building. Holding Janet's hand, I told her that I had just talked with Carmela.

Lowering her head slightly, she looked up at me with shame. "I didn't want her to."

"Do you want to move in with me?" Notice how I didn't quite phrase this as an invitation.

"If you want me to. God, I'm so embarrassed."

"We could do that."

Thus, with epic romance, we became a cohabiting couple.

Perhaps, though, I had merely postponed and deepened the inevitable heartache.

THE TRUTH

Aside from trying to 'pay it forward' and to live according to my predilection, the third major strand of my life was professional. In this I met with greater success.

Writing a book-length research report—in other words, a dissertation—occupied my thoughts and time more than any other aspect of my life, including Janet. Despite kvetching with other grad students, I mostly enjoyed the process. While living in Playatlán I had produced scads of notes and recordings for analysis, and now I embraced the challenge of making sense of it: applying the interpretive perspectives that I had learned in class to explain the social processes that I had experienced and observed. It was worrisome that I didn't generate the creative leaps in theory that could make me an academic superstar. But I did have a talent for applying others' insights, tinkering with them, or explaining how they didn't apply as universally as their creators contended. Doris convinced me that this talent, plus a sexy topic, would propel me into a successful academic career, which gave me the confidence and desire to plow through untold hours of transcription and analysis.

Other faculty members filled out my committee—one officially co-supervised me, since Doris was still striving for tenure—but they already had busy lives, which perhaps explained their benign neglect. They burdened me with relatively few revisions, and these tended to be straightforward.

One, Dr. Hoff, imparted some simple advice that had a profound impact. Being older than Doris and less newfangled in her analytical approach, she perhaps suspected that my heartfelt and brainthought perspectives resulted from fashion-following. Conversely, I regarded her more lightly than the more up-to-date professors, although she struck me as kindly.

When I visited her office to get comments on a draft of an early chapter, she leaned forward at her desk to ask whether I intended to pursue an academic career.

I said I did.

"I think you'll be successful."

"Thanks! I hope so."

"I'll tell you what my adviser told me as I was writing my dissertation, several decades ago." She smiled as old ladies do when they obliquely reference their age. "I tell this to all my students. He said our role in society, as academics, is to tell the Truth—capital T," she slid into a professorial tone. "We're supposed to be insulated from the pressures that might corrupt us, but you'll see it's harder than it seems. But if *we're* not Truthful, who will be? This is our role." She adopted a self-pleased expression. "So when you choose to apply a particular method or to foreground one observation over another, make sure that it's the one which makes your story as close as possible to the Truth—as you see it, of course."

My immediate thought was, The Truth? You can't handle the Truth. However, after she had planted this seed, which jibed with my mindset after betraying Dale and Ron, I increasingly saw barriers to telling the Truth, some of which I had skirted rather than removed. For example, admitting the real weaknesses of my research proved quite difficult. And I literally winced at my computer as I contemplated deleting the analysis of an amazing corrido because it was exceptional rather than representative. Perhaps *I* was the one who couldn't handle the Truth. Over time, though, I developed a habit of greater honesty (in my research) that I found more liberating than limiting.

But complete honesty? Have you ever told the Truth on a consistent basis—no white lies, no shading, no withholding of inconvenient information, no waiting to be asked directly for information that you know someone else expects? I bet not, because then you'd be exposed, the equivalent of walking around naked, and everyone would know what your mental and emotional private parts looked like. That's something we usually save for intimate companions, in a time of crisis. But that was how a Truthful dissertation would read. Anyone would be able to see and judge the author's mistakes and triumphs, his or her original insights and idiocies, and the interests that truly drove the work.

Instead, most reports presented the varnished truth in a form that merely simulated the Truth. For example, a friend wrote in his dissertation that he had chosen the topic because of its unique importance to the field of criminology; however, he complained to everyone at happy hour that his adviser had forced him to 'choose' it. And the statistical measures that he described as being essential to test his hypothesis had actually been forced on him by the same adviser over his objections. Then, this mentor demanded that he "massage the data" until they supported his foregone conclusion. None of this history made it into his dissertation. Less egregiously, another anthropologist chose his field site in northern Mexico so that he could visit his family more easily—information left out of the report. Or sometimes researchers had original ideas that, unbeknownst to them, someone else had developed decades earlier; the researchers had to cite those earlier works as if their own ideas followed from them, even though they hadn't. And so on. In fact, much of any research report served as hands strategically placed over the author's mental genitalia, as a way of meeting a formal requirement, rather than as a baring of the real process, without airbrushing.

If, on the contrary, every researcher were to tell the Truth, then it would be like an intellectual Bonobo. We would share a bond of intimate knowledge about each other and the knowledge we had produced. Perhaps this would allow us to improve our research as a collectivity of Truth-producers, much as Bonobo was intended to enhance interpersonal relations. What was good for the 'body' would be good for the 'mind.' This quickly became my dream.

These were suicidal thoughts for a budding academic. Clueless, I thought they might be my One Great Idea. So I rewrote my methods chapter with great honesty. Here's a sample: "While some questions addressed in this research might lend themselves to statistical interpretation, my difficulty with mathematics prevented me from considering this option."

After reading the revisions, Doris called me to her office. "Nat, I read your chapter. Is everything all right?"

I told her about Dr. Hoff's lecture on Truth.

Aborting an eye-roll, Doris said that Hoff had told her the same thing soon after she was hired. Doris' advice: "Pick your moments, Nat, and this isn't one of them. This isn't close. Maybe once you get tenure—maybe."

Even so, after that I did pick occasional moments of Truth as I wrote, balancing between Hoff's idealistic (and hypocritical) advice and Doris' desire to see me successful in conventional terms. You can read the result in my other dissertation, if you're interested.

This dissertation, though, is my full moment.

GUILTY PLEASURE

That story about Dr. Hoff actually happened, and it's the one I told Doris—and Janet, for that matter. But really I had in mind another model of Truth-telling: the private diary of Bronislaw Malinowski, one of the long-dead founders of modern anthropology. Published posthumously, the diary revealed how messy Malinowski's psyche was while he conducted fieldwork, and thus it shone Truth from a different perspective onto his elegant and orderly analyses. Following that example, an honest account of any research would integrate the person with the interpretation.

Doesn't that sound professional? It's in my other dissertation. Ironically, it's just another smokescreen to protect my image. Really, I had come to appreciate Truth-power from my most guilty pleasure—reading Dale's journal, which I did almost daily.

To handle the images of newspapers, cassette labels, and other texts from my legitimate research, I had bought a gizmo that allowed me to convert the picture on a video screen to a computer file that I could view on my monitor. So I also used it to convert the surreptitious recording I had made while visiting ¡Bonobo! Parts of many pages were fuzzy, but I could make out the vast majority. Despite feeling self-disgust, I developed an obsession with reading the entries. This mania distracted me at times from focusing on my dissertation, yet in some ways it inspired me in my work. To a greater extent than

I had ever experienced, it was clear that other people had complex personalities, circumstances, and intellectual lives, just like I did. It served as a great reminder of how cartoonish most descriptions of anthropological subjects tended to be: 'young rural proletarian'; 'married, middle-aged, actively Catholic homemaker'; 'flamboyant drug lord'; etc.

No one else knew about my voyeurism. The ethical crime was too heinous to admit, and, until Janet moved in on me, we didn't hang out at my place to study. After she got her key, even though she maintained a respectful distance while I worked, I hid my delvings into Dale's diary.

By now you know much of what I learned. Dale included a wealth of vignettes, dry observations, and reflections scholarly and otherwise regarding Bonobo's development. The pages also contained entries not germane to the present book: poetry and the like, which I read with perverse curiosity despite empathetic embarrassment. Perhaps fortunately, Ron had interrupted me before I finished recording entries from the second year of ¡Bonobo!'s operation, which was more than a year before I arrived in Playatlán. So I didn't discover Dale's opinion of me.

Here are four things that I did find:

Dale was the vandal! Of course, you've known it all along, but this revelation floored me. After the attack on the resort, I'd have bet on Holly and/or her sympathizers as the culprits. Knowing that Dale had duped me, I felt myself blush painfully at being exposed to him, and myself, as a fool. Anyway, given the amount of time and effort I had spent on identifying the perpetrator, and perhaps as analytical revenge, my thoughts now turned to explaining him. A bit whimsically, I tried out a range of anthropological approaches. My favorite involved a study of how nursing mothers' reactions to nipple-biting by infants affected the children's development. I imagined a twisted psychodrama as Little Dale tried to secretly attack the teat that fed him.

On a related note, I wondered whether Ron knew or suspected who the vandal really was. Dale did too, scribbling, "Does R know?" at the end of an entry documenting one of his attacks. But maybe this was just Dale's fantasy. After all, on a later date he wrote, "If I get caught?"

And, yes, I could see that his vandalism and my pilferage had some similarities, but I chose to not work out the details. After all, I was a voyeur, not a narcissist.

Second, Dale continued to dream of academic success. He wrote reviews of the journal articles and ethnographic tomes that he had read, made conjectures of varying completeness and rigor about social theory, listed courses he'd like to teach and the qualities of a university at which he'd like to work, thought through ways of integrating Bonobo with an academic career, and wondered, "How to get there from here?"

Third, Dale's diary revealed that, from the start, he had made ethnographic observations and taken research notes on Bonoban activities as if he were conducting research. He did so despite having drafted and signed a series of agreements against this from the very start. In fact, a couple of other Bonobans and then many outsiders had sought permission to take notes, but the group in Tucson and then the Hive in Playatlán consistently maintained the no-research rule.

Not surprisingly, Dale questioned his own transgression. He scrawled in the margin by one early entry, "Why do I do this?" On another day, he crossed out his observations with two thin lines forming an X across the page; however, the notes remain completely legible. Over the first year or so, these signs of self-loathing fade away.

Dale's interests and therefore analyses were academic rather than managerial. Given the Hive's dominance over policy, this makes sense. Nonetheless, he did have the power to make some adjustments, which he used to observe how Bonoban relations would change under different conditions. Overall,

Dale's attitude toward Bonobo struck me as more distanced than Holly's or even Ron's. Although to others he personified the movement, he never stopped testing its character and promise.

Fourth, Dale generated fascinating ideas. He proposed novel theoretical concepts and unconventional interpretations of phenomena at a rate that I envied. It was tempting to lay claim to them in my dissertation, but my growing commitment to Truth stopped me—along with Doris' assurance that a conventional approach was valuable in job-seeking. If she was right, then Dale might not have had the qualities to develop the academic career that he dreamed of.

An example of Dale's inventiveness was his contrast of porn versus drama, which captivated me. He saw that his existence at ¡Bonobo! had become highly pornographic, and not because of acrobatic sex. Instead it was because, on an island with a routine designed to meet tourists' expectations, his life was formulaic and provided daily satisfactions. He manufactured some drama (and expressed a deep-rooted mania) by committing the occasional, minor works of vandalism, and he fantasized about a dramatic escape to academia.

Let me give you a sense of how it played out in the journal. In one entry, Dale reported on a routine but fruitful meeting of the Hive, which he swayed to his viewpoint on scheduling; his final comment was, "And I saw that it was good (porn)." In the entry describing the resort's first security alert, he led with, "Drama on the high seas!" Overall, it was clear that Dale still yearned for more drama, yet ¡Bonobo!, and the prestige of leading it, worked well enough that he couldn't leave its comforts for the big, scary world across the bay.

As for me, I yearned to compare Dale's porn/drama heuristic and Carlos' metaphor of explosions in my dissertation. For example, boredom didn't menace Dale; he felt explosions all the time, and their differing character was his focus. I saw how exploring this distinction could enrich my analysis, especially in the contrast between musical portrayals of drug violence and the actuality of Jorge and Beto's murder. Alas, doing so would entail either committing plagiarism or admitting that I had broken into Dale's closet and read his diaries. So, instead, I fashioned an interpretation less true to my thoughts but more true to my ideals, and safety.

Also, away from research I often found myself making mental references to porn and drama as I considered the life I was constructing, especially since so many aspects had to remain unsettled until I graduated.

GOOSE AND GANDER

"Hop in," Doris said, and I obeyed. "Now tell me where we're going."

"Our first destination," significance hung from my words like Spanish moss from a live oak, "is Micanopy—where, among other delights, we'll say Micanopy many more times."

"All right!" She pulled out and began driving south. It was just after lunch on a cool Saturday in late January. A thin, ribbed layer of high clouds filtered the sun as we headed out of Gainesville in Doris' silver, four-door Civic, which was neat enough in front, apparently because she had chucked everything into the back. I slung my backpack onto the midden of loose papers, publications, cups, and food wrappers. We had the windows cracked and the sunroof open. "You know," she said, "I've spent so much time slaving for tenure that I've only been there once, and that was a few years ago. I barely remember it."

"They say you'll always remember your second time the best …"

"Already! I guess this isn't going to be *My Dinner with Andre*."

Ultimately, it turned out to be much closer than she anticipated, but that wasn't my fault.

For Doris, the new millennium was off to a roaring start. She had just learned that Cornell University Press would print her book—an easier version of her impenetrable dissertation on Indonesian language ideologies—and that the *Journal of Linguistic Anthropology* would publish her article on an aspect of the same topic. Adding these lines to her c.v. was tantamount to gaining tenure, although the formalities of investiture would not take place for a couple of years.

Recognizing that, as a single academic far from home, she was a bit of an orphan as well, I had invited her to a day and evening of celebration. I saw myself as emulating Dale and Ron's largesse, not to mention her own. Bonobo had reinforced a version of the Golden Rule within me, and this was my attempt to do unto Doris not as I would have her do unto me but as I imagined she would most enjoy.

Three obstacles faced me in this project. First, there was Janet. We couldn't celebrate at my house because ... well, I suspect you know why not. However, I did tell Janet that I would spend the day with Doris. At first she reacted with disappointment, but soon she cheerily wished me a happy time and, kissing me, said that she "loved" my generosity. She felt sure that Doris would appreciate a fun day with me. Who knows what Janet really thought, or feared? Anyway, despite my openness and my girlfriend's nonchalance, I met Doris a couple of blocks from my house. She didn't ask why.

Transportation constituted the second obstacle. I had access to a bicycle and to Janet's car. I couldn't bring myself to use the latter, so I pathetically had to ask Doris to chauffeur her own limousine.

Finally, I possessed limited funds. Sharing rent and other expenses with my new roommate had freed up a little cash, but the excursion had to be cheap for me to avoid using the almost maxed-out credit card that I recently had forsworn for all time. Indeed, the only available balance on it was the pittance I had paid down since returning from Playatlán.

Despite those problems, I popped a little with pride. This would be the first time that I had gone beyond the basic set of expectations to treat someone grandly, as others had so often treated me. To you, this might seem like a modest beginning. For me, any beginning was a dramatic step across the threshold of responsibility.

We cruised down the highway and across a vast marsh south of town. We stopped at an observation deck and leaned on the railing to look out at the sea of grass and water. "When I interviewed here," Doris sounded happy but a little wistful, "someone brought me down to a spot like this. It was so beautiful, with the tall grass waving in the wind and the puffy clouds casting shadows. I thought I'd take my portable down here every day and be a real Florida gator."

"Hey, that was a thousand years ago. It's a new millennium."

"Yeah, you'd love to ride your bike down here for my office hours." She bumped me with her shoulder. We started to look at each other directly, like when we made love, but turned back to the car instead. I thought, once again, how odd it was that the university was about as far from the sea as you could get in Florida. In Playatlán, the ocean haunted my every step. Here, you had to find something else that would serve.

We drove the few miles to the small town of Micanopy, which possessed the giant oaks, Spanish moss, and clapboard bungalows that you'd expect. As homage to Doris' success in publishing, our main event was to shop at a fantastic used-book store, filled with old volumes of research and travel. Sometimes the pages included the handwritten notes of well-known academics who once had owned them.

Not long after we entered, I turned a corner and happened upon her as she stood reading an old volume of Southeast Asian adventure. She looked up and said, "What a great surprise," and smiled to me before returning the volume and picking further along the row. Seeing her eagerly explore the stacks of treasures, I felt not an explosion but a melting, warm ooze in my chest.

We spent a long time there. I bought her two books, and, over my objections, she gave me an old tome of Mexican history that one of my professors had owned. We also browsed a couple of antique stores and then bought cookies to eat on a bench. "Nat, you're a bad influence on me. Where am I going to put two more books?"

"There might still be some room in the backseat."

She laughed outright for maybe the first time since I'd met her. "Touché. I guess I should contact Honda to see whether they sell dividers." Again, we glanced directly into each other's eyes, this time holding it a split-second before returning to our cookies.

Our next stop, at which we arrived as the sun was setting, was an Italian restaurant on the outskirts of Gainesville. A friend had recommended it as good and inexpensive. I told Doris it was in honor of her heritage.

"But I'm not Italian."

"Who said you were Italian?" I'd rehearsed this in my mind.

"Oh, God, your poor girlfriend."

"They give our Gators statues or rings or banners in honor of their championships—none of which, I feel certain, was in, e.g., ring-making or even ring-using."

Doris regarded me with mirthful, appreciative indulgence.

"At least this restaurant is heritage-centric," I persevered, implacable.

"So bringing me here to celebrate my 'heritage,'" her fingers made quotation marks, "is like giving the football team a basketball instead of a trophy."

"Yes—exactly!" We laughed together. Humor, intellect, and sex: we matched each other so well in several different ways.

Not far into dinner, I raised my beer and proposed a toast: "To another thousand years of academic excellence." Doris clinked her mug to mine and drank, but her expression turned a little serious, especially around the eyes, which beaded and regarded something indefinite inside her beer. Then she snapped out of it and proposed a toast to my budding career. Being trained (by her) in linguistic analysis, I noticed that we repeated this pattern throughout dinner: I'd ask her about her plans for research and teaching, and, after a light reply, she'd try to redirect the conversation to my academic future. I didn't want her celebration to focus on me, and she apparently didn't want to talk about herself, so I tried to steer the discussion onto more-general topics, such as politics, design, and, alas, the weather. We did all right, but here Doris held no advantage over most of my friends, or Janet.

After dinner, it was dark but not late, so for dessert I directed the driver to take us along a rural highway to a Dairy Queen farther outside of town. I feared that our destination was too crummy for Doris' refined sensibilities, but she giggled and acted happy to relive her high school days. It had turned a bit chilly, so we returned to the car with her Peanut Buster Parfait and my Mint Oreo Blizzard and sat inside with the windows up and the sunroof closed. Doris spooned the cherry off the top and raised it for my consideration. "I fear you want this."

My jeans felt uncomfortable. "What's good for the gander … It's the Bonobo Way. Plus, it's less creepy if I'm the instigator. Get it? 'Insti-gator.'"

Doris objected that she probably was starting her period, and I assured her that I had no qualms about that.

She sighed, but not unhappily. "In that case," she said resolutely and took the cherry between her lips. She leaned over, and I leaned toward her with my mouth open, and she pushed that cherry into it, along with her tongue.

We rented a twenty-dollar room at one of the old motor inns along the highway. The walls and carpet were dingy, especially in the weak overhead light; a bullet hole lent character to the bathroom window; and a gentle aroma of mildew suffused the entirety. While Doris used the bathroom, I tested the bed, which was loud, lumpy, and concave. The cover had a couple of cigarette burns and scattered, unidentifiable stains, so I threw it into the chair, moved the desk and bed around, and slid the mattress onto the floor (a useful lesson from Playatlán). I quickly lay down and fished through my backpack for supplies. When Doris emerged, she saw me lying there, posed seductively. A homemade greeting card lay on her pillow.

"Nat."

I patted the Nattress. My heart pattered: ~~I was growing up~~ I had learned techniques of caring and developed the confidence to use them. Doris came over, and we sat cross-legged as she read the card. She looked me in the eye and said, "Thank you," holding that look for an instant before leaning over to kiss me.

For the third time we made love. Now I took control and held little back. I licked her clit (no blood yet) until she came, and I didn't ask her to suck me. Straight away I put on the condom and entered her, bonobo-style. On my knees, one hand on her breast, I regarded her expression as I drove back and forth. Several times she opened her eyes and looked into mine, only to close them again. Soon she reached up to pull me against her, and she wrapped her legs around me as we ground and thrust, her face touching mine, her whimpering in my ear, my tongue in hers. When she felt me thickening and hardening, moving faster, and starting to moan, and when to please her I started to pull back and look into her eyes, Doris wrapped herself around me more tightly. So, my face buried in her neck, I came.

I eased my dick out of her. She continued to grip me, as I felt her jerk with little spasms. Then I felt her tears slide onto my cheek, and I held her. I embraced her much as I had cradled Xóchitl before, although Doris didn't seem to seek shelter, just comfort. And this time I soothed my mentor and friend, rather than all of humanity. And I felt no need to cry.

Soon Doris stopped herself, let me go, and, wiping her eyes, confessed. We lay on our sides, facing one another. Sniffling, sometimes placing her hand on my chest, she explained that she didn't know what she was doing there. I thought she regretted our sexual celebrations, but she had greater concerns. She had devoted herself single-mindedly to her career for well more than a decade—since she was an undergraduate!—and now she had, barring disaster, achieved her dream (singular). But at what price? Was tenure better, more valuable, than feeling free to sit and gaze at a marshy meadow, to spend the afternoon guilt-free in a bookstore—*on a weekend*? And she didn't even look at novels, which she wouldn't allow herself to read unless they somehow contributed to her research. And it wasn't going to get better: next she needed to earn a promotion or she'd be stuck forever as an "associate" professor: a labeled mediocrity, unfulfilled promise personified. With tenure she'd have more departmental responsibilities, more students to supervise, more more more more more more more more. That's how the other faculty spent their lives. And it's not like she was saving anybody's life. She was just cranking out more anthropologists, or mildly affecting her other students' lives. But even the undergraduates who got A's would greet her on campus and say how they had thought recently about something she'd taught them, and then they'd mischaracterize it. No, mainly she was doing "all this, this shit," for her own gratification—or at least she should be. So this beautiful day had driven home to her how maybe another path would have gratified her more. "And I thank you for that. I know it's not what you had in mind."

She was right about that. As she got ever more bitter, I juggled the desire to comfort her and my shock at her words. My role model regretted following the path that she was helping me go down and that was my dream (singular), as well.

I knew enough to not mention that maybe her period was exacerbating her justifiable emotions. I suggested that she was feeling—I wanted to say 'post-partum depression' but thought better of it—a normal let-down after achieving something so impressive.

This statement already rang a little hollow, even before she said, "Thanks, Nat, I know you're being nice. But look at me— I live alone, I shop alone, I work alone most of the time. I have a lot of time to think." She meant that, from her perspective, this lengthy lament hadn't erupted without warning.

Suddenly, though, she adopted a can-do expression and thumped my chest lightly. "Okay, I'm done crying. Let's get out of here." She scampered to the bathroom but looked back from the doorway. "What time do you turn into a pumpkin?"

I told her my fairy godmother worked on Hawaiian time, so we had hours left. Plus, the pumpkin would be her car, not me.

I don't know which Metallic Rule has Doris and Nat doing unto Doris as she would have Doris and Nat do unto herself, but I was happy to go along for the ride. We got into the car and drove along the ever more lonesome highway. The night was cold, a big moon was still rising among the pines, and I saw a few puffs of cloud and several bright stars through the transparent sunroof. Together we enjoyed the solitude of moving across the landscape at night. Whenever we passed water, I looked for the red reflection of alligators' eyes, but I found none.

Doris took us back to the vast sea of grass where we had started the afternoon. She found a place to park from which we could look out across the marsh under the emerging moon. We sat there for a few minutes in the darkness, pointing out features of the landscape, and then Doris asked whether I still had some condoms in my backpack.

We climbed into the backseat amid the papers and publications and plastic lids and, giggling and gasping, slipping and grappling, made good-natured love, honest and True. After we had tried several positions, she ended up with her back on the seat. "I see stars," she exclaimed, looking past me through the sunroof.

"It must be your reflection in my eyes."

"Oh, God, they turned you into a Latin Lover."

"Pedicabo ergo sum." High school Latin was practical, after all.

"Ergo cum," she replied.

This might be the most embarrassing stretch of dialogue in the book, but, our eyes now locked, we started fucking harder and, yes, therefore came.

Afterward, we sat in the backseat with our clothes on again, half immersed in printouts, journals, and coffee stirrers. We conversed in low tones about her crisis. Far from disclaiming her earlier outcry, she said that she sometimes wondered whether having sex with me sprang from an unconscious desire to vandalize her career.

On hearing that, I yearned to tell her how Dale had semi-vandalized both his academic career and his position at ¡Bonobo!, but this revelation would have ruined the mood and possibly *my* career. So I didn't, just as I didn't suggest that our trysts spiced her overly pornographic life with some drama.

Instead, I broached my conviction that, in a world of contradictory influences, people had to find a satisfactory balance among their conflicting desires, even though the result might not make strictly rational sense. This was hardly a revelatory idea, but it was easy to lose sight of the lesson, especially in pursuit of a dream (singular). With a little trepidation, I added that I had learned in Playatlán to value limited-purpose relationships. Maybe she had invested too heavily in the professorial role as a holistic, all-in-one approach to happiness.

This was the first time that I'd exposed my own practical philosophy to anyone. To my surprise and gratification, Doris reacted with interest. She didn't reflexively reject it as neoliberal or ethnocentric, as I had feared. We discussed the idea broadly and with specific application to our lives, until finally a cop pulled up and ordered us to move.

Probably it relieved Doris that I didn't want more from our relationship. Forty-five minutes later, when I saw the lights on at home and knew that Janet was still awake, I doubted that she felt the same.

UNANSWERED QUESTIONS

Doris and I sat in a dingy café along a dusty, desolate, and depressed boulevard in the empire of sand that was Tucson. It was April, and we were visiting "the Baked Apple" to participate in an academic conference—a low-level affair focused on the linguistics of sex. This wasn't my forte, but I had cooked up a title and abstract at Doris' suggestion. She assured me that either she or, as it turned out, the Anthropology Department would cover the cost of my flight. Sweetening the deal, one of her friends who had remained in Tucson (Rudy) would let me sleep on his futon couch. She wanted to do this as my mentor and friend and because she thought I might enjoy meeting some other Bonobans "from back in the day." For her part, she would get to see her old haunts, friends, and professors while showing off her first Ph.D. student. We'd both get drama, positive fireworks, da da da.

Tucson was all beach and no ocean. It was interesting to see the mountains and cactus and the Mexican and Native American stuff and to hear coyotes yipping at night, but everything was so dry that you'd need lube to shake someone's hand, wink an eye, or even breathe. Dale's diary revealed that he initially felt ecstatic to move to the ocean, and I now could see why.

Speaking of Dale: the graduate-student 'organizers' of the conference took a long time to release a schedule. So I found out only a week in advance, to my shock, that he would participate, too. Likewise, when he agreed to come, he had no way of knowing that Doris and I would be there.

His official role was to serve as the discussant on a panel of graduate students who had analyzed media representations of ¡Bonobo! or the Bonobo movement in general. Everyone knew that it all had started in Tucson. Dale and Ron had sustained the connection by donating massive supplies of ¡Bonobo!-brand condoms to the student health center. So students lacking imagination often chose this as a research topic. Anyway, even though they all undoubtedly considered Dale and Ron to be (cool, enviable) sellouts, the organizers invited them to return to the scene of the crime. Given their duties, only one could leave for an extended period. Dale told us, "I won the coin toss," but I doubted that he had left the opportunity to chance.

The modest conference lasted only Thursday and Friday, and a pall of anxiety hung over me the entire time. Doris and I flew in on Wednesday afternoon and were to leave on Saturday. She presented her research on Thursday morning. It was almost exactly the same presentation she had made at a more prestigious conference earlier in the year, but I attended anyway. A couple of her former professors showed up, and it was fun to see her change from senior colleague with me to junior colleague with them. Someday that would be me, I hoped. Most of the presenters—obviously nervous but happy to get a line on their c.v.'s— were students who just spewed self-important, underdeveloped, post-everything critiques of whatever, which I generally enjoyed considering. Tomorrow that *would* be me. Doris was more masterly, and once again I saw how, despite some give and take, despite her co-opting some of my insights, she really was my senior. When she went for lunch with a couple of former professors and then dinner with a couple of old friends, she generously made sure that I tagged along, seen but not heard.

My presentation took place on Friday morning, and Dale's was that afternoon. He apparently had business to conduct much of the time he was in Tucson—with the Anthropology Department? the local Bonobans? suppliers? university administrators seeking donations?—but he had emailed Doris beforehand, asking for the pleasure of our company at lunch. They had decided to meet at one of their favorite old haunts. My preference (a Mexican hot dog stand in a vacant lot) was not canvassed.

Thus, after my session, Doris drove me in her rental car to a run-down café. It looked like the kind of joint where desperate deals went down in Hollywood films, but really it was just another hipster dive. We went inside. My stomach was churning: I had spent the entire morning nervous about my presentation, and now I feared what Dale might say about my breaking into his closet. I hated having no control over things. I hated it. But here I was, and I couldn't run away; coyotes might rip my flesh to shreds. I urged myself to be zen.

"God, I love this place," Doris enthused, looking around. Dale wasn't there, just a couple of dudes with striped shirts and truckers' caps and a pale woman with a black dress and tattoos. Piercings all around. Probably a tarantula behind the counter, a rattlesnake in the toilet. Maybe Dale wouldn't show; maybe he'd be so late that we'd barely have time to talk. I just wanted out.

Doris and I sat across from each other at a formica-top table by the large plate-glass window. I had planned secretly to make the magnanimous gesture of paying the entire check. Looking at the menu, I joked that the café should have been called, "Everything's a dollar ... more expensive." Doris laughed perfunctorily and then abruptly said, "There he is!"

The bell on the door jangled as Dale breezed in. With his dark slacks, his white button-down with rolled-up sleeves, his outrageous tan, just-cut hair, sunglasses perched on his forehead, and resort-living demeanor, he looked more out of place in hipsterville than he did in Playatlán. He came up to us, smiling at Doris, and they hugged happily—no bonobo handshake. He turned to me and shook my hand. "Nat." It came out as a formality.

"Hey, Dale."

He took the third seat, which was between Doris and me, facing the window. For the next forty-seven minutes, they caught up, reminisced, and remarked. I half-listened, watched out the window for tumbleweeds, and constantly checked the clock above the counter. It moved at a geologic pace. Dale remained oriented to Doris and barely turned my way, even when she mentioned me or, rarely, tried to involve me. That was fine; I just wanted out. My mind kept rehearsing responses to possible attacks. Doris must have suspected that something was awry—after all, she taught conversation analysis—but she feigned ignorance.

Finally, Dale looked at his watch and announced, with businesslike regret, that he needed to go. I had worked myself into a state of such apprehension that I feared to say anything that would require his attention. Nonetheless, the words came out: "I'll pay."

Doris smiled to me and said, "Thanks, Nat." Dale simply raised his eyebrows and leaned back.

I went to the counter and paid with my accursed credit card. When I returned to the table, they were still sitting there, quietly. So I sat down again.

Dale finally addressed me. "Before we go—Nat, we were unhappy with the way things worked out the day you came to ¡Bonobo!"

Oh, crap, I thought, he's about to expose me as a burglar, snoop, and ingrate in front of Doris. He must have seen that I put the key back incorrectly, that I entered his closet to turn on the light, that the dust on the volumes showed that I had opened them. My heart raced, and sank. "I'm sorry about that, too," I tried to speak with an even voice. And I truly felt sorry, but I couldn't change the past. I felt Doris' eyes on me.

"Anyway, a deal's a deal." With an inaudible sigh, he handed me an unsealed manila envelope.

Huh? "Thanks." I opened the flap and withdrew a document far enough to see what it was. Surprise—it was a photocopy of the agreement allowing me to use the information that I had gained through my employment by ¡Bonobo! He and Ron couldn't stop themselves from being generous, even to a traitor. "Oh, yeah," I said. "This is great. Thanks again." I didn't know how to react, so I kept it cool. To my profound regret.

"That nut Holly mentioned you, by the way," Dale's voice hardened further. Doris must have been wondering what was going on. "She said you told her we were after her." Now he added a tinge of menace to his words: "You really shouldn't look for work as a spy."

I got the message. He knew. But why not just expose me outright? Was he too nice to embarrass me in front of Doris— was he employing the Golden Rule? Or maybe he feared that I knew he was the vandal—or that he'd taken notes on the orgies—and that I'd spill those beans in retaliation. Had he declared a stalemate, then? If so, that was a relief. I just wanted it all to end.

We would see each other again at the conference, so our goodbyes were easy. Dale added one last thing, as if it were an afterthought, "Anyway, the vandalism stopped, so I guess we got our man." I had no idea how to interpret that claim and, now that our lunch had ended at last, didn't want to. I settled into Doris' car feeling like I had dodged a train.

But I had not. As soon as she pulled onto the street, Doris asked, a bit sharply, "Nat, what was that all about? It looked like Dale hates you. What did you do? What's that paper?"

I hadn't rehearsed for this, and I couldn't take it. Doris would hate me, and my world would flush down the toilet. Doris would hate me. Doris would hate me. Other words refused to appear in my mind or mouth. Tears started, and sobs, and my terror of losing everything, of losing her respect and support, of losing my academic career, of losing my future … it all overwhelmed me. Doris would hate me.

"God, Nat, what's wrong?" She put her hand on my shoulder.

I couldn't look at her, and I couldn't stop sobbing. "I don't want you to hate me. Oh, please please please please please."

Doris didn't answer. She continued to caress my shoulder and neck as she drove back to campus. Eventually, she said, "Okay, I told you I don't do this very well. We can talk about it, whatever *it* is, next week. But I'll never hate you, Nat, so please don't worry about that."

She didn't know.

By the time Doris parked the car, I had cried myself out, and we pretended that nothing untoward had occurred. But a subtle stiffness and distance now marked our interactions and reminded us that an unanswered question dangled between us.

Back at the conference, not long after the first panel of the afternoon got underway, Dale entered the venue (a classroom) from the back and took a seat. He obviously was striving to look at home, but what once was natural had evolved as strange. Amid our radical-academic poses, he looked like a time-share vendor, like someone we categorically loathed, at least officially. Yet he showed more attentiveness than any of the dozen or so students and professors sitting there. He distinguished himself simply by gazing at each speaker rather than at the printed program. Going for sainthood, he even furrowed his brow to think about provocative claims, nodded in agreement at times, and chuckled along with poorly delivered humor. Attending this trainer conference—a dramatic return to the path he semi-regretted abandoning—must have thrilled him.

Finally, Dale's panel began. Doris and I sat near each other, and I noticed, among several other attendees, an older woman who Doris informed me was Dr. Rodasky. I felt happy for Dale. I recognized that he had more reason to feel angry at me than he knew, so I couldn't blame him for my crisis, which was entirely my doing. He, too, had done some crappy things, but to me he had shown only generosity—even at lunch that day. I expected this to be the last time I would see him in person, so I framed the occasion as an upbeat and hopeful final scene in the film of his life as I had witnessed it.

Before the panelists spoke, the moderator briefly introduced each and then Dale. It probably dismayed him that she barely mentioned his graduate training and instead cast him as a research subject responding to academics' analyses. She thanked him for performing this favor, but I knew that the satisfaction was mutual. Anyway, as the graduate students droned on, sometimes woodenly reading inflammatory challenges to the Bonoban project, Dale maintained a distanced and thoughtful expression. When it came time for his remarks, he didn't retaliate. He not only remained above the fray; he spoke as though he weren't personally implicated at all. There was no, "I'll have to consider these valuable critiques as we continue to improve ¡Bonobo!" Instead, he produced a well-reasoned and polished discussion of each talk's strong points and provided suggestions for further research. Watching, I again forgot that I outranked him in academia. It was such a shame that I had fucked up our friendship.

Afterward, a clump of idolaters gathered around him to engage him in conversation—after all, he was rich, famous, and interesting. He looked happy to entertain their desires. Best Navidad ever for Little Dale, I thought.

Doris finally had her turn in line and prevailed on him to join a few original Bonobans later at a hipster club downtown. I told her that I had made plans with other students, which was fairly true. Someone had announced happy hour at a nearby bar, and I planned to join this valuable networking opportunity. I'm sure she heard this with relief.

All that night I feared that she would pump Dale to explain the tension between us. In fact, I barely slept, as worries about my future overwhelmed any attempt to relax. The next morning, with brutal butterflies still roiling my guts, I rode with Doris to the airport and boarded the flight home. We spoke very little, and then we merely exchanged light observations. Eventually I calmed down and tried to put off thoughts of the fateful confession that I soon would have to make.

I longed to be with Janet, who knew nothing of this and felt proud of me. At the airport I had bought her a little ironwood carving from Mexico, and I fantasized about the happiness it would bring her.

BREACH OF TRUST

I had resolved to not cry this time.

I trudged with dread through a light rain toward Doris' office, on the second floor of a standard-issue academic building. Every Tuesday afternoon she reserved an hour to meet with me. Mostly we discussed my dissertation, on which I had made rapid progress. Indeed, here toward the end of my second semester back in Gainesville, I had written a draft of every chapter except the introduction and conclusion. Now I feared that all this, all seven years of grad school, were about to be invalidated. But there was no escape; the show must go on, at least one more time.

I knocked.

"It's open." Doris sat behind her desk, smiling in a businesslike manner. We said hi, and I hung up my rain jacket and sat down in the chair across from her desk. "Did your girlfriend like the figurine?"

I said yes. Janet had made room for it on a shelf with other doodads from her parents and her own adventures.

We paused, both knowing that there was only one item on the agenda. My heart pattered like a spastic rabbit, but, at the same time, inevitability gave me calm resolve. I plunged ahead.

As I talked, Doris sat at her desk, sometimes flicking a pen, and listened. She constantly watched me, a serious expression of concentration on her face. I glanced at her only occasionally, and mostly looked blankly at the side of her desk or off into the rain streaking across her window.

I told her everything, as you've read it here. I recounted how Ron and Dale had helped me, how I had stolen into Dale's closet and found his diaries, how ashamed I felt, how Dale wouldn't know that I'd made recordings of several volumes, and how I couldn't stop myself from reading them.

Here Doris finally spoke. "What do they say?"

"That's why I keep reading them. They go all over the place, but it's really fascinating. Dale's kind of brilliant." I wasn't sure that was the right word, but he deserved any extra appreciation I could give him. "He's kind of fucked up, too."

"What do you mean?"

I told her about Dale's creative ideas, especially porn vs. drama, and she seemed intrigued. I recounted his acts of vandalism, and she giggled and said, "Oh, God." And then I mentioned that she was in the diary, to which she replied, "I should hope so. But don't tell me what it says. I can't handle it." Finally, I explained how happy I was for Dale at the conference because it was clear that he longed for an academic career. Doris snorted, in reference to her own ongoing crisis. I said how frustrating it had been for me, because I would have loved to use Dale's insights in my dissertation but couldn't possibly cite his diary. In fact, I couldn't cite any of the things they had paid me to learn until Dale gave me the signed agreement in Tucson. But Dale had even done his own research on Bonobo.

"What?"

As I surveyed Dale's observations and interventions, from the first party to the last volume, Doris entered a slow burn. I finished up candidly with, "The rest is just so personal that it's embarrassing to read," which shows how low my standards really were.

"What the fuck, Nat." Doris stared at me, incensed.

I braced myself for her to lower the boom. Then I would beg.

"What. The. *Fuck*." She looked ready to damage some furniture, if only we weren't flanked by other offices. "Holy crap."

"I'm sorry. I knew you'd hate me for this." I tried to suggest a way out. "I can understand if you want me to find another adviser."

She focused on me fully and said, "Relax, Nat. What you did was wrong. It was bad. Shitty. I certainly won't trust you around my silverware anymore. But I'm pissed off at that fucking liar Dale much more than at you." She pointed out that she had stolen her cousin's diary when they were kids and blabbed about it; the family still teased her victim. Indeed, other kids—and adults—had betrayed her confidences all the way through graduate school. Hell, maybe they still gossiped about her when they got together; she certainly did, about them. It was all reprehensible and unethical, like my actions, but hardly a capital offense. Moreover, I hadn't even told anyone, and I didn't have an ongoing relationship with Dale, so, until now, the tree had fallen in the forest without anyone really hearing it. Despite her anger at Dale, she acted a little bemused at my fears.

On the other hand, doing research when you've signed and enforced an agreement forbidding it—that was beyond the pale. Doris wanted Dale's blood. She cast the affront in universal terms, but it was obvious that her own victimization made his crime much more grievous. Maybe hoping to win back some karma points, I played devil's advocate by pointing out that Dale hadn't disseminated anything, and I asked whether doing so would be horribly unethical. After all, Dr. Rodasky had urged him to use Bonobo in his research. (I didn't mention that Dale had rejected her suggestion as improper.)

This information didn't help. Doris' mind was looking for problems, and now she saw that Rodasky's presence at Dale's panel might signal that he would somehow use his observations and manipulations of Bonobo to write a dissertation under her guidance. He had to be stopped. Doris wanted to inform everyone on whom Dale had taken research notes about this breach of trust and contract, starting with her old friends from Tucson, including Ron.

I can't enunciate exactly why, but I recoiled from this plan. Maybe it was because Dale had been so good to me. His generosity far outweighed my qualms about the possible use of CSR funds for my work. Or my resentment that he had played me for a fool with the vandalism investigation. Plus, reading his diary had made me more sympathetic and empathetic to him than to anyone else, ever. As Doris was sounding off, I felt a generally oppositional sentiment but said only vague things like, "I don't know …" and "I can see your point but …"

Then it got worse. Doris suddenly had a sharp gleam in her eyes and said, "You know what would fix him? We should publish the diary, just put it online—but only the embarrassing stuff, like poetry to old girlfriends or rants about his parents."

"So much for the Golden Rule," I said.

"It's the Golden Rule, all right. If I'd betrayed *his* trust like that, I'd expect him to come after me. Look at you: you stole a diary—big whoop—and you thought you deserved to be ostracized."

"But Dale didn't do that. He actually gave me that agreement allowing me to publish stuff."

"You said yourself that he might have been protecting himself."

So it went, back and forth, over several days. Doris realized that the signed agreement might give me permission, legally at least, to publish the diary. However, I wanted to do generous things, to help others, as Dale and Ron had done with me, and this just seemed ugly. Yet I knew that doing nothing was not an option, because Doris would expose Dale one way or another.

Eventually, though, we produced a plan. It took an exhilarating week of debate, brainstorms, and epiphanies to achieve a workable agreement. It was a heady, dramatic time, filled with emails, impromptu phone calls, discussions in cafés, and unannounced visits to each other's office.

At my insistence, we made a vow of secrecy. Unfortunately, Janet could see that something was afoot, and being excluded clearly perturbed her. I longed to tell her about my previous fear for my career and how it had suddenly turned into this exciting project. I hoped she wasn't jealous, because my partnership with Doris was a separate issue from my love with her. My impression now is that, instead, Janet felt envy: she wanted to participate in all the important aspects of my life, especially the dramatic ones.

A SECOND DISSERTATION

Doris and I agreed that, since the contract gave me permission to write a "dissertation" with information for which ¡Bonobo! had paid, I would write a second one. This additional dissertation would redress the many peeves about academic writing that I've described already. Thus, it had to include original insights; retain analytical sophistication; be interesting, valuable, and comprehensible to a general reader (which meant reconstructing some scenes); and be Truthful about the genesis and development of the work.

Moreover, the farther I got into my academic dissertation, the more I felt that another great lie was embedded in its various abstractions, including my narrative persona. My research—on which I'd worked so long and so obsessively—was as at least as intrinsic to me as anything I shared during sex. So why did I have to write as if my analyses were outside me, like clothes, instead of being part of me, like my skin—or heart? Thus, the reader (you) should know: *This matters like love.*

For Doris, the second dissertation needed to preempt any effort by Dale to use, or continue, his covert observations and, preferably, to punish him for them.

She and I both loved academic research, but here was a chance to try something unique. I was the author and Doris the editor. She let me write my Truth and didn't even try to censor my description of her "decent breasts" (although she did underline it on the first draft and write "Really?" in the margin). Her hands-off attitude flowed from an anthropological commitment to 'let our subjects speak for themselves.' However, it was rare that the native—or 'Nat-ive,' in my case—was an anthropologist himself.

While we retained our vow of secrecy regarding Dale's diaries, Doris did put me in touch with some early Bonobans to interview, and I found other figures on my own. I already had met Rudy and some others during the trip to Tucson. A few members of the original band had long resented the media's focus on Ron and Dale as the sole originators and representatives of Bonobo, and they especially disliked the ¡Bonobo! resort's prominence in the movement. The still-anonymous coiner of "We come in peace," while acknowledging the inevitability of the phrase, resented their trademarking it for commercial use and wanted revenge. All of the old-timers had some juicy story they now felt ready to share.

Issues of privacy were a concern. In the 1990s some anthropologists had hit upon a 'tell-all' mode that gave license to write almost anything about anyone. One award-winner published criticisms of her supportive parents, her supportive husband, and her dutiful professor—all readily identifiable—without giving them warning, much less a chance to respond. While Doris found this to be an attractive model for attacking Dale, I felt that, for purposes both karmic and Bonoban, I had to balance any revelations about him with confessions of my own.

Some figures seemed more innocent—in this story, at least—than others. Nonetheless, a review of biographies, memoirs, and feature stories led me to think that people connected to public figures often have their stories told whether they like it or not. This attention is what happened to them while they were making other plans.

The stringent rules regarding privacy in academic research didn't really hold in other realms. And they certainly didn't prevail among my neighbors in Playatlán. Everyone living nearby in Colonia No Reelección could hear me take a dump or shower or, for all I knew, screw Xóchitl, and I heard their arguments and birthday parties and saw them cooking meals. Thus, many of the 'private' things that I report here would have been public knowledge there. And Playatlecos just lived with it, knowing that everybody else knew and gossiped about their embarrassment. Photos of Blanca and me were in the newspaper, and her mother bragged about me to the neighbors: undoubtedly she later had to face their barely concealed schadenfreude. She knew the risks because she, too, had gossiped about neighbors who had moved to a ritzy subdivision only to return to their dusty street when the father was busted for drug trafficking or lost his job because the opposition party finally took power. Everyone knew plenty about everyone else, and they got on with their lives. That standard of privacy seemed as legitimate as choosing any other. Nonetheless, you might be surprised at how much I've left out—and how many names I've changed—purely to follow the Golden Rule.

My biggest qualms regarded Dale and Doris. In Dale's case: how personal was too personal? We agreed to strike anything that didn't develop central themes. I also wanted to demonstrate that Ron and Dale's works and ideas deserved attention beyond the sexual jokes that have cast them as young Hugh Hefners.

Doris allayed my fears for her career. I argued that, since she didn't officially have tenure yet, reporting on our sexual celebrations might put her in jeopardy. She again laughed at my concern. "You should go to one of the faculty parties, Nat. My first year here, I'd meet someone's spouse and ask, 'Oh, how did you two meet?' 'She was my professor.' 'He was my professor.' They might deny me tenure for *not* screwing students."

The rest of the spouses, she claimed, were from the faculty members' field sites (akin to my marrying Blanca). I thought she must be exaggerating and pressed her on this issue, especially given her previous remark about sabotaging her career by boinking me, but she seemed convinced of the principle. "Anyway, Nat, we just have to try it—go for the gusto, swing for the fences. Let the chips fall where they may. Have you read *The Remains of the Day*?" It was her decision.

So what made this project worth the danger to our careers and the embarrassment to Dale? I could go the chicken-shit route and point out that this text has served the public interest, first, by revealing that Dale committed crimes against property that actually belonged to Johnny Fish and, second, by exacting retribution for Dale's repeated abrogation of written commitments to not do research on his friends and comrades. Plus, he and Ron paid me to spy on Playatlecos, possibly with money that they listed as charitable donations. Okay, I guess I just went the chicken-shit route.

Still, I've tried to apply the Golden Rule to two sides of Dale: not just the one who hid his malfeasance but also the one who helped to create something great. Indeed, more important to me was this positive goal: the Truth might free Dale—my lost friend, trapped in a cage of his own making—kind of like a long-distance intervention for his addiction to porn, or whatever ¡Bonobo! is for him. For some kinds of love there is no condom. And, who knows, his example might help others.

When I was young, kids teased me only a few times about being an orphan. For example, in fourth grade, a young wit raised his hand in Art class and asked the teacher what I would do while the other kids made potholders for Mother's Day. On a much greater number of occasions, people reminded me through their *kindness* that I wasn't like them and they knew it.

Other boys never wanted to tell me that my mama was so fat, when she went to the zoo people threw peanuts at her. So in a basic way I've known for a long time that my path through life must be different from the expected one. This Truth, painfully communicated, has instilled a sense of freedom in me to find, within the constraints of my sociohistorical context, my own way to satisfaction. (Of course, other orphans respond in their own ways.) People constantly reminded me that the default script didn't fit me, so, over time—and not always consistently—I've tried to write my own. I don't have complete freedom, but I feel I have fewer people to answer to than you might.

Then again, you're probably a weirdo in your own way. All sorts of people get myriad mundane reminders that they're not typical. Black kids get followed by mall cops, left-handers can't use ladles or butter knives, blondes are subjected to insulting jokes, and colorblind guys have trouble with stoplights. Some man is named Evelyn. Someone's favorite Beatle was Pete. In all sorts of ways, big or small, everyone deviates from the expected norm—anyone who didn't would truly be the freak. And not just here: an anthropologist lived in a small village in Papua New Guinea among men who all seemed to think and behave very similarly. When he interviewed them confidentially, he found that they differed greatly in their actual adherence to the ideal that they universally espoused in public.

You, they, we—anyone might find reasons in their own life to question the dominant expectations that channel their aspirations. And they then might try to devise altered expectations that fit them better. In a way, I was fortunate: other people planted my freak flag for me. I'm trying to do the same favor for Dale … and you. Not living in a coercive context like those villagers in New Guinea, Dale has the chance to take the Truth and forge his own path in a more satisfying fashion. Perhaps you, too, might find a tale Truly told as a starting point to assess and reorient your life, to add some fireworks, to shift the balance toward drama or porn.

Taking that a bit further: if Bonobo portends great things for all humanity, then obviously its development deserves to be known intimately, sans condom.

QUALMS?

I sense that you still have qualms. Any 'violence' done to Dale in the name of knowledge is minor. Think of all the money that goes into astronomy or the opera—when those same funds could revolutionize the lives of multitudinous poor, hungry, and sick people. In short, government agencies and 'philanthropists' indirectly commit mass violence by deviating vast resources from people who desperately need help, all in the name of esoteric knowledge or Culture. So, once you're done picketing NASA, feel free to attack me regarding Dale's embarrassment, which I've caused in the hope of directly improving human relations and experience.

AND FINALLY

Wait just one second before you award me that Nobel Prize: I also wrote this book because it seemed like a cool idea, an interesting challenge, and, at the very least, a good story to tell at parties. Moreover, given the sick reward-system in today's world, it provided a possible path to fame, fortune, or guruhood.

Of course, that's what Dale wanted, too.

JIM WEIGHS IN

Blah blah blah. I did what I did.

Before I did it, Doris had the great idea that maybe we would get sued and lose all of our fabulous wealth. So she contacted the university attorney's office for an assessment. She forwarded a memo that I had written explaining the project, the use of Dale's diary, and the contract granting me permission to employ the info for which ¡Bonobo! had paid.

(In case you're wondering: I also worked a mutually pleasing deal with the Gainesville Bonobos to write about my time with them.)

One of the attorneys, Jim, contacted Doris, and they set up an appointment at her office to discuss the matter. I was allowed to attend, too. I expected to see a drab loser wearing Sansabelt slacks and a polyester tie, overwhelmed by all but pro forma intellectual challenges, but Jim turned out to favor khakis, a button-down, and no tie, and he exuded a businesslike self-confidence. Probably he was a few years older than Doris. That, plus their permanent positions at the university, made me the kid.

I had rehearsed any number of scenarios in which I would make an impassioned or highly reasoned argument to save the day. But such was not necessary. Instead, Jim told Doris right away, "Leaving aside questions of ethics, you're almost certainly safe as long as he"—and here he fully acknowledged my personhood with a slight nod of the head in my direction—

"writes the work and does so separately from his degree requirements or employment." In addition, Doris should eschew any recompense for her involvement and avoid using university resources, including her office or computer. "Call it your hobby."

That was a relief. Now Jim would take his satchel and head back across campus.

Instead, he added, "What I mean is, the university's safe, which is my mandated concern. Unofficially, I doubt that any case would be brought against you as private individuals, and I doubt further that it would be successful, but I didn't perform research on that question."

I butted in to ask whether he would feel the same doubt if I'd recorded the information somewhere in the U.S.

He turned to me more fully, and, to my surprise, answered my question as if Doris or some other adult had asked it. He said that, of course, the location of the misdeed mattered. But what, really, had I done? By questioning me about the details, he confirmed his assumption that I had been invited onto the property and had not engaged in any activity that the proprietors had forbidden expressly. (You'll remember that initially I had turned off my camera because photos of *people* were verboten.) Nor had I removed any object. Finally, ¡Bonobo! had employed me through that fateful day, transported me to the island as part of my employment, and signed an incautiously broad agreement giving me permission to use any information I found, which should protect me against allegations of stealing intellectual property. "Again, this case has a lot of unusual aspects that I didn't research fully—at all, actually—but my off-the-record guess is that you're safe. Still, you might want to open a bank account in the Bahamas, just in case."

Doris laughed and assured him that I hadn't followed standard anthropological practice.

Jim remarked to her, "You know, each field has its own ethical issues." The university library's special collection harbored documents from government archives in Latin America that had been stolen years ago by private individuals—was that acceptable? Heck, some Native American activists considered any information about Indians that the Spanish had obtained illegitimately—that is, all of it—to be stolen. Ethically, he saw their points, even if legally they didn't score any.

Smiling, Doris found all of this "fascinating," and pretty quickly I felt like a third wheel again. No doubt, his ringless fingers would soon be knocking on her bungalow door. That was fine, but I didn't want to know about it—not because I was jealous but because it was creepy to see my adviser flirting. Doris and I simply didn't discuss our romantic lives. Here before me was another reminder of the benefit of limited-purpose relationships.

Finally Jim finally checked his watch and saw that he had to make another meeting. As he was buckling his case, he said generally (maybe more for Doris' benefit) that the project sounded quite interesting; he looked forward to reading the book. Then he addressed me in an avuncular tone: "If it were me, after dealing with so many different ethical standards on campus and, okay, after reading a tiny book on Buddhism several years ago"—he held his thumb and forefinger close to each other and smiled at his own good-humored modesty—"I would want to make sure that the benefits to *others* outweighed the damage."

What an insight, Jim! "Okay, thanks. That'll be my goal." Following his algorithm, I didn't reveal that it was Doris who hoped to inflict pain.

TELLING JANET

At this point I had a partner, a plan, and something like per-mission. All that remained was telling Janet the Truth—the way Dale should reveal himself to Ron. Of course, I didn't have to come clean right away. I could have strung her along until either we broke up or the book came out, detailing my actual thoughts and feelings for all to read. But I wanted to avoid being a total shit, and I felt eager to start living ever more honestly.

Here's something I've never told anyone before: I've often imagined my birth parents giving me general advice on how to live—kind of like Obi-Wan, Yoda, and Luke's dad at the end of *Return of the Jedi*, but talking. Or maybe more like Obi-wan at the end of *Star Wars*. (But definitely not like Darth Vader at the end of *The Empire Strikes Back*.) Anyway, I actually can't re-member my parents at all, and what's True is that nobody is going to tell a kid what his dead mother and father were really like—plus, they would have changed over the decades if they hadn't died. So it was really just me talking to myself from the perspective that life could end at any minute. In short, my re-animated parents never told me, "Nat, try to fit your life to others' ideals; settle for 'good enough' if you otherwise might fail." Instead, holding my head against their collective chest, they would stroke my hair and tell me that I was a good boy, they were proud of the man I was becoming, and I deserved happiness as much as anyone else. "We know it's hard," they soothed me, "but living someone else's dream is worse."

Thus, I needed to explain myself to Janet. But how? Even a cockroach learns from experience, and this time I strove to avoid the big mistake I had made in breaking up with Blanca. Janet wouldn't suspect that I bore good news.

The summer term had just started, as had my first stint teaching my own class, "Peoples of Latin America." After a Tuesday session, I strode professorially across the sweltering campus to my spot in the TA office. Sitting at my old wooden desk, with his feet propped on its much-scuffed surface, was my friend Terence. Using his keen analytical skills, he had deduced that few people of balanced mind wanted to be outside, especially to exercise, so it would be a perfect time for us to play frisbee golf (which he pretentiously called disc golf, "because, dude, 'Frisbee' is just a brand name, and we don't use Frisbees anyway"). Actually, he proposed once again to "teach" me the game, which was a jocular euphemism for beating me at it, as he usually did. In contrast, I felt that my example "taught" him better sportsmanship and a relativistic attitude toward competition. Aside from these didactic pursuits, we drank beer from opaque plastic bottles and chuckled a lot.

Perhaps his proposal was a message from the cosmos, telling me to wait before talking with Janet. After all, what difference would a day make? Maybe Janet wouldn't even come home at the usual time—a coworker might have a baby shower. Or she might go shopping at the craft store, now that she was into making stained glass. Or maybe she'd come home feeling so upset about a political issue or event at work or news from one of her parents that I couldn't possibly drop my own bomb on her.

Then again, what difference would a day make with Terence? "Sorry, güey, suncheck. How about tomorrow? I need to work through some heavy shit that can't wait."

"Well, if it's *heavy* shit ..." He didn't pry, which I appreciated, and we joked around and chatted for a few minutes while setting a date for the next afternoon. (It rained, but our friendship survived.)

After he left, I biked down to a tiny lake on campus where alligators and humans would sun themselves on the banks. It was the closest equivalent to the ocean and jellyfish that I could find within easy pedaling distance, so I occasionally went there to work through issues or simply be. I sat by my bike on the lawn. My sunglasses filtered out the glare from the lake, allowing me to keep one eye on the gators. Idly picking blades of grass and tearing them, I rehearsed what I would tell Janet and my responses to her potential reactions. The certainty of intent and the control over my immediate fate calmed me. I just didn't want to lose sight of my main purpose.

After a quarter hour, I rode home, took a cold shower (as I'd grown used to in Mexico) so that I wouldn't sweat, and made adjustments to the next day's lecture. When Janet arrived from her job on campus, we kissed hello and exchanged little pleasantries and notices about our days. (It strikes me now that we never greeted each other with Bonobo handshakes.) It was my turn to make dinner, so, while she luxuriated in her summer break by reading the latest *Utne Reader* on the couch, I toiled in the kitchen for several minutes with the radio on. Once the food was ready, we ate my classic spaghetti-and-salad combo and chatted. My heart pounded but my mind remained clear. I asked whether she had read anything interesting in the magazine, and she said there was a short notice about drug trafficking and the Mexican presidential election, which reminded her of my research. (Why do people get more attractive at the exact moment you plan to lower the boom?) We talked about the article and a couple of other tidbits that she had found provocative. And then it was time.

She was using her index finger to wipe remnants of the spaghetti sauce from her plate, when I said, "I wanted to tell you something important about, about me." Her finger in her mouth, she raised her eyebrows in interest. "You know I've been working on something extra with Doris. I feel bad that I haven't been able to talk with you about it, and I still can't tell you a lot of it, but it's a book. And the book says a lot of things publicly that I should have told you already, but I just haven't found the right—the guts." We sat there across from each other at the dinner table as I continued. Janet at first stopped fiddling with her plate and gazed at me. After a while, she began to look down occasionally at her dish and swipe a finger along absentmindedly, apparently lost in thought. Eventually, she started to make a sort of intermittent humming sound, of which she seemed completely unaware, and which always drove me to distraction. It must have irritated the crap out of her classmates when they were taking tests.

Except for Dale's diary, I told her everything: about taking her and her father's suggestion and writing a history of Bonobo and my time in Mexico, a second dissertation about mutual, intimate exposure, about living more Truly, about balancing contradictory desires, like porn and drama. I told her (again) how seeing people get shot and almost getting shot myself had sharpened my desire to live happily and to help others. And I told her generally about Ron and Dale's generosity and my worthlessness in that regard.

At this point, Janet seemed to want to take my hand as I held forth, but how could I remain strong under that pressure? I ignored the bid.

I told her that I didn't want to live 'happily enough': I wanted to live as happily as possible. From observing Playatlecos and thinking about things, I had realized that, for me, this meant having different kinds of relationships with different people, not expecting anyone to fill every role but appreciating each person for what we did well together and not seeking more from them—because a friend who's good for soul confessions might not be good for discussing professional aspirations. And I thought that lots of those things could be very intimate, and possibly more intimate than sex, depending on the particular situation. In fact, I had sex with prostitutes in Mexico, and often that wasn't very intimate.

Now I told Janet that I loved her in several ways, but I didn't want to share every experience. I loved living with her and making love with her and sharing emotional comfort with her. I loved going to loud parties with her and exploring new places around Gainesville. I loved seeing her happy and thinking that I had contributed to that. But I loved doing things with other people too. For example, I loved discussing fieldwork and our careers with Carmen, goofing around with Terence, and having sex as part of Bonobo. And I loved working with Doris. I had made love with Doris three times, including once while living with Janet—here her humming and finger-swirling stopped—and I probably would again when there was some occasion to celebrate. I also loved falling in love and hated to think that I never would again, although I saw that as separate from our relationship. Finally, sometimes I just loved being in a situation as myself, not as a semi-autonomous half of a dyad. I didn't know whether she wanted me to share every part of life with her, but I couldn't be her "Swiss army knife of love."

"That's the Truth about me," I concluded. "I love you, and I don't want—I want to stay with you, really, but I want you to know the kind of life I want to lead. I want you to want me as I am. Someday this all could change, you know, but you shouldn't count on it." With those uplifting words, I finished.

For the last bit Janet had remained a little slumped, gazing at her dishes. Now, as she looked up to reply, I could see that her eyes were red and moist. "You think about yourself a lot." This statement, spoken more as a realization than as a reproach, was obviously true, and it verified that I had followed the anthropological maxim of being self-reflexive. So I didn't know why it stung. After a pause, she said, "I guess … I guess I want to think about me for a while before answering."

Even though it was her turn, I collected and washed the dishes. She remained slumped at the table, so then I moved out onto the screened porch.

JANET REPLIES

The next evening, after twenty-three hours of near silence, we sat awkwardly together to eat the burritos she had prepared. I thanked her for cooking and told her that the food tasted delicious, which was an overstatement. Then we had it out.

Janet said, first, that my words the previous night had hurt her because sometimes it sounded like I thought she wasn't smart enough to understand me. (I interrupted to object, but she made it clear that that would be worse.) Nonetheless, one of the things she loved about me was my ideas, including some of the things I'd said last night. She just wanted to be sure that I didn't have some permanent rule against sharing more types of experience with her.

I shook my head no and said quickly that I thought she was smart, just with a different specialty.

More importantly, she didn't have a clear image of how she wanted our relationship to go. Of course, she wasn't stupid—she'd thought about our staying together indefinitely. But she wasn't campaigning to get married, as some of her friends were. "I was reading these articles about marriage in the *Utne Reader* and then your speech last night made me think, Why would I want that? I mean a traditional marriage. Fifty percent of them get divorced! And a lot of the rest probably should, too."

I tried, perhaps a little too hard, to show my sincere appreciation of this truly insightful comment.

The main things she wanted were my respect and to stay with me, sharing ideas and experiences. She was "happy enough" the way things were, at least until last night, so, if that's basically what I had in mind, then she was willing to continue working on our relationship—with some changes. First, she deserved to know when I did something "intimate" with another person. If I thought that playing backgammon could be as intimate as sex, then she deserved to know whether she was getting sloppy seconds. But clearly her main concern was sex. She didn't want me to come home after sex with Doris (I speedily interjected, "It's not like that") and then she would try to start something with me. And I had to use a condom (Janet and I had stopped). And was I seeing prostitutes in Gainesville? Because she wasn't sure that she could deal with that.

I always did. I wasn't. And, I added, "I really love making love with you."

Imperceptibly to me at the time, her tone started to change. She still wanted to work out some ground rules with me, but she also enjoyed exploring these ideas that, until then, I thought I had mastered. She felt that it would be disrespectful to her if I made a move on someone else while she was at the same party or—now entering the realm of fantasy—had sex in another room.

"What about a heart-to-heart conversation?" I asked. "I've heard women say that's more intimate than sex. Or what about sharing food? Or watching a sunset together?"

"So you're saying," she adopted a feisty little smile, "if you're having a deep conversation with one of my friends, I could blow one of yours in the bathroom, and it'd be the same to you?"

Then she wanted to know what would happen if she preferred to do something with another person that I wanted to do with her—say, share dinner most days, or talk about her day. Did she get her way just because she *didn't* want to do something? Did no automatically outweigh yes?

So it went.

And it kept going that way. It was a work in progress, and sometimes regress. At times it was unbearable to discuss these matters instead of just letting them slide. After talking that night, we made love, and Janet wanted to know whether that was porn or drama for me. It was drama, and I said so. But most times our fucks—in, out, in, out; start here, end there— slid down the scale much closer to porn. Unfortunately, she asked on some of those nights, too.

"They're both good; I just want balance. And they're just imperfect heuristic concepts."

"So mostly it's porn with me? You get your drama from … from others." She paused. "I noticed you didn't say you loved taking care of me when I'm sick."

These conversations added some drama to our relationship, but often it was painful and increasingly tedious. Such was the consequence of blazing a new trail. I couldn't go wandering off on my own through the woods. I needed other people, like Janet, who had their own preferred path and, of course, had only one life to walk it. So I knew what I wanted, but I also was learning that I had to make arrangements with the world as it was.

BACK TO BONOBO

A couple of days after I had revealed myself, Janet came home and asked, "I guess you want to keep going to those Bonobo things?"

"Yeah, I do. I like the drama." I also enjoyed the fireworks with different sexual partners, the continuance of my idiosyncratic involvement with the movement, and the reminder that my relationship with Janet no longer depended on sex. On the other hand, the Gainesville group hardly fit with Dale's original vision, or Holly's for that matter. They met too infrequently to eroticize daily relations to the point of making sex mundane (if that was even possible). And, lacking the ritualistic setting and tone of True Bonobo, it was too much of a weekly orgy to reorient participants' daily lives to the Golden Rule. At least that was my assumption. Still, participating in their parties expanded the matrix of people to whom I had exposed myself and whom I'd seen exposed, all in a safe and loving fashion.

"Then maybe we should go together. Almost everyone's out of town over the summer, so my friends said we could arrange it."

Argh. Fucking with others was one of the things I preferred to do alone. Janet's presence might inhibit me, and I didn't want to see her having orgasms with someone else. But, of course, she had as much claim to the scene as I did. Plus, I needed to get over my double standard regarding sex with others, and now my chance had arrived.

Still, I wondered what Janet's game was. Did she want to show me that sharing the orgy would be better than going it alone, or to keep an eye on me? Or perhaps to teach me a lesson? Maybe it was a sentimental return to the scene where we met. Or maybe she just wanted to screw someone else for a change.

Maybe we hadn't fully mastered Truth yet.

She offered to drive to the party separately, but I saw no sense in it. However, I didn't object when she said, "Don't worry: I know we need to split up once we get inside." And that's what we did. We moved to different parts of the living room, gave the Bonobo handshake to people in a different order, and stood in different sectors to observe the presentation (a performance-art piece on the plight of the manatee from someone's MFA thesis).

I felt Janet watching me constantly—even when she wasn't. As we did the ridiculous Bonobo chant, I looked across at her, expecting her to smile at me as she did when we met. But she was looking at the leader in the center and only turned my way when she sensed my gaze upon her. Later, I was thrusting into Shauna from behind, cupping her breasts. We both were on our knees as she propped her elbows on a chair. Then D'Andre, who was getting blown, reached over and massaged my balls and prostate. That felt goooood. Who knows why, but I turned my head to see whether Janet could see this. She certainly could have, if she had decided to open her eyes. But she kept them closed, and not in ecstasy, while some guy went at her from the side. I felt jealousy rising, but I told myself to imagine them having an intimate conversation instead. That had a slight effect, but D'Andre's hand and Shauna's pussy had a stronger one. I turned back to my main task, moving my fingers to caress Shauna's neck and shoulders, sliding them along her fleshy yet muscular back, tracing the furrow of her spine and licking the sweat from my finger. I really hoped that Janet still had her eyes closed, because that was something I did with her, too.

I realized then that Bonobo didn't expose its participants only to their partners, as Doris thought of it. I lay open to the consideration of anyone else present—including my girl-friend—as my actions disclosed things that I usually considered to be secret, known only by my lover. Here was more Truth-telling; the alternative, to don a mask, would thwart the point of it all.

Later, while I was on my second round, I noticed that Janet—still not following my every move—hadn't formed another coupling and instead moved around, lending a hand (mostly) here and there. Nearby men and women pumping away would have a go at her—fondling one of her breasts or buttocks, attempting to insert a finger or put a mouth on something. Her non-rejection/non-acceptance reminded me of tourists I'd failed to seduce in Playatlán. Eventually she jerked off a guy against her torso and breasts for a few minutes until he came. Once again, in my jealousy, I had to picture her in conversation with each of these people, and again it worked only a little. Luckily, I had my own concerns on which to focus. I had happened upon, and within, a chunky monkey who actually preferred anal sex; by happy coincidence, I did too.

Finally, after exchanging parting gropes with the others on our way to the door, Janet and I walked out into the hot, still night.

I took stock. I had enjoyed two fantasy-level episodes of sex, met several new people, and improved my chances of becoming a regular member. Conversely, I had felt guilty about taking Janet and uncomfortable about her monitoring me—neither of which had actually occurred. As for my struggle with jealousy, the pros and cons ended up a tie, as I knew I needed practice handling it.

We walked down the block in silence. Once in the car, Janet started the engine and pulled out into the dark street. "So, was it good?" she asked.

"Yeah, pretty much. You?"

"Eh. I just wasn't into it this time."

This time. She switched on the classical radio station, and we rode home quietly.

SO MANY LOVES

That's no way to end a tale of hope. Let's go back to the night I told Janet the Truth ...

From the rocker on the porch, I could hear her inside, weeping. Eventually she slammed the bathroom door. After a short while, I heard her come out and blow her nose. The floor shook a little as she trudged around, looking for the phone. It beeped when she turned it on and punched someone's number. Was she calling a friend? Her father? It occurred to me that I no longer had the right to know.

I rocked back and forth under the light of a half moon. I felt oddly at peace, absorbing the sound of frogs and crickets, the occasional car on a nearby road, the neighbor's TV. But I also heard—although I could barely discern any particular words—a woman I loved, crying from the pain I had caused her. Alongside my oneness with existence, I struggled, despite myself, to contain a barrage of regret and guilt, detonating and reverberating throughout my torso.

I heard Janet say "stupid," and I wondered whether I were getting a fair hearing. I really did love her. Then she exclaimed, a bit hysterically, "fucking Swiss Army knife," and I knew she needed more space.

I walked across the porch, unlocked my bike from the railing, and started pedaling through the dark and still neighborhood. I rode all over town. The same duality of experience persisted, but the percussion in my chest shifted, bit by bit, to a volley of starting pistols. I glided past my friends' quiet houses, past parties I was missing, past the frisbee golf course, the Bonobo place, and the library, past the Krishnas' lunch spot, several much-loved bars, and the campus alligators. I rode past a man singing an infant to sleep. It takes a village to raise a child, so why not an adult?

And, yes, I went to Doris' house and stopped for a moment outside. It sounds creepy, especially at midnight, but I wasn't looking for her. No, that was the place where I came into the story of Bonobo, and now, I felt, I was coming into my own.

Could I have fuck love and make love and know-you love and be-yourself love and puppy-dog-eyes love and found-interesting love and you-need-help love and do-it-together love and everyone-is-beautiful love and trust-you love and self love and there-there love and let's-play love and Merry Christmas love and love-the-one-you're-with love and you-can-do-great-things love and hang-out love and proud-of-you love and for-give-you love and Golden Rule love and so many other loves? Could I return the favor, somehow?

Who knows? But I had to try.

AFTERWORD

I've been asked to address the attacks on September 11, 2001, which occurred not long after I submitted the manuscript for *Bonobo!*

Aside from sharing others' shock upon witnessing the destruction, and feeling the same confusion regarding how the attacks fit into any larger project, I felt sadness—and, yes, some reflexive anger—at seeing so many people around the world celebrate. The cheering crowds could have led 'us' to question our relations with these multitudes who wished us ill: Did they really know us? Did we know them? Did we know ourselves, truly? That Americans might engage in such an inquiry was my hope, which fizzled out two days later. At the university where I now work I heard a senior anthropologist, of all people, comment angrily that "Arabs better not bitch if they can't get on planes anymore."

I believe firmly that these attacks and the tenor of our march to war show that the world needs more Bonobo—Holly's and Doris' versions, at least—and more anthropology, which should be the same thing. To know others and be known intimately, and to know ourselves Truly: this would ramify throughout our relations in ways that would make war less romantic and the Golden Rule more likely.

TRACY DUVALL

CPSIA information can be obtained at www.ICGtesting.com
Printed in the USA
BVOW02s2324270916

463481BV00018B/151/P